THE
OPERATIVE

THE
OPERATIVE

ANDREW
BRITTON

PINNACLE BOOKS
Kensington Publishing Corp.
www.kensingtonbooks.com

PINNACLE BOOKS are published by

Kensington Publishing Corp.
119 West 40th Street
New York, NY 10018

All Kensington titles, imprints and distributed lines are available at special quantity discounts for bulk purchases for sales promotion, premiums, fund-raising, educational or institutional use. Special book excerpts or customized printings can also be created to fit specific needs. For details, write or phone the office of the Kensington Special Sales Manager: Kensington Publishing Corp., 119 West 40th Street, New York, NY, 10018. Attn. Special Sales Department. Phone: 1-800-221-2647.

This book is a work of fiction. Names, characters, businesses, organizations, places, events, and incidents either are the product of the author's imagination or are used fictitiously. Any resemblance to actual persons, living or dead, events, or locales is entirely coincidental.

PINNACLE BOOKS and the Pinnacle logo are Reg. U.S. Pat. & TM Off.

ISBN-13: 978-0-7860-2623-4
ISBN-10: 0-7860-2623-5

First printing: December 2012

10 9 8 7 6 5 4 3 2 1

Printed in the United States of America

PROLOGUE
ISLAMABAD, PAKISTAN
2010

Asif Kardar crushed the brake when he heard the hiss of the tire through the open window of the bread truck. The pads were old, and they squealed as the squat white vehicle lurched to a halt. The hard stop caused the peppermint air freshener to swing in long arcs from the rearview mirror and a marble in the ashtray to smack violently front to back.

The young man sighed as he looked out the mud-splashed windshield, stared at the wide dirt street awash with the red of the rising sun. He had only a half dozen or so blocks to go before he reached the market. Why now?

Because Allah willed it, thought the devout Sunni. *Why else does anything happen?*

A boy on a badly dented bicycle passed him. Then another. And a third. They waved as they passed. Asif knew them. They shared breakfast at the coffeehouse some mornings—though they didn't today.

Why?

He couldn't remember. It didn't matter.

The young men were workers who lived near Asif, in cinder-block shacks in the *katchi abadi,* the slum off Service Road West 110. They were commuting along Seventh Avenue, past the doctors' offices, banks, and parcel companies, and then on to Kashmir Highway, near the universities, post offices, and the always popular Sunday market, on their way to the richer sections of the capital, where they were employed as street cleaners. All of them saw the irony in that, yet all of them were happy to have jobs. It was either this or the military.

Asif found himself grinning. In the year he had been driving this route, he had never suffered a blowout. He supposed he was due. And it was no one's fault, he knew. Metal shards were everywhere in the streets of the slum: pieces of discarded appliances, rusted tools, even belt buckles and pocket watches.

And the remnants of car bombs. There had been three in the last year, all of them accidents. They were meant to blow up *after* leaving here and arriving at their destinations—some government building or military installation. Except for the loud bangs, the children liked it when vehicles blew up. They quickly came and collected the fenders and fan blades to dig in the rubble for treasure. To a child, anything free was a treasure.

Asif's smile drooped as he considered his situation. He looked at his watch.

Drive on, he thought. He could probably make it, even with a rim that was clanking and sparking.

The morning sun was rising higher, clearing the clay

tile roofs of the structures that lay ahead. This was the "better" section of the slum. Where he lived, the roofs were all corrugated metal. The daily sun-scorched metal created such intense heat within the homes that being outside in direct sunlight was preferable to being slow cooked alive inside. And while the temperature on the roof of the buildings was occasionally more comfortable for sleeping, the distorted, grooved surface was no place to remain grilling for too long. He peered at the buildings. There was something he was supposed to do. . . .

He shifted gears, started the truck ahead slowly. What was it?

Clanking and growling, the truck rounded a sharp curve. Two hundred or so meters to the east he noticed soldiers standing watch outside a Humvee. It was the end of the slum. They were parked in front of a one-story building that was used by South Korean Christians to feed hungry children. At one time it was a police recruiting station. It was firebombed, but the missionaries had plastered it over. That was what outsiders did. They covered things with paint and activity and believed that they had begun to heal what was wrong underneath. The soldiers were looking at him.

Asif stared back. He had a spare tire. He should stop and replace the blown-out one. If he continued driving, the men would wonder why he was willing to do permanent damage to his truck. Spare parts were not plentiful, unless one were willing to hammer out the bent and broken pieces found in scrap yards, and what he was doing was not just odd. It was *suspicious*.

So why are you doing it?

He had no good answer to that.

He slowed, but he did not stop. Something told him to drive on.

The early morning air was already warm, and the driver was perspiring. He was wearing a white silk kurta, a hand-me-down from his elder brother who was in the army. He dragged a sleeve across his forehead and looked anxiously ahead. There was a Shiite mosque across the street. Men were beginning to arrive for prayer. Something about it seemed familiar—not just because he had seen it before as he drove by. It was something else.

The street was suddenly paved beneath him. The truck chugged over the lip, the naked rim cutting the asphalt, the glove compartment snapping open, the marble rolling, the air freshener smacking the windshield. Three of the eight soldiers started in his direction. The one in front had his arms raised, motioning for him to stop.

You mustn't, Asif told himself.

If he stopped, they would examine his truck. That was what the soldiers did at checkpoints. The sweat was no longer only on Asif's brow; it was everywhere. They would surely see that; the sun had just cleared the low rooftops and, shining redly, was striking him directly. He felt as though he were naked, exposed, and starting to melt. One of the soldiers talked into a radio. Asif couldn't make out what he was saying, but he knew that tone, flat and low. They were assuming that his intentions were hostile.

They weren't, were they?

He was confused.

Asif reached for the bottle of water that lay on the

seat beside him. He saw a few young families coming down the street, toward the Christian building. The doors would not open for another hour, but for many of these impoverished souls—many Afghan orphans who had been taken in by relatives, families who had come to Islamabad to escape the Taliban or the war—this would be the only meal of the day, the only food they had enjoyed since the previous morning's charity.

Asif looked ahead, past the soldiers and toward the mosque. The Shiites were gathering in larger numbers.

The murderous fools, he thought. They believed that only the heirs of 'Alī, the fourth caliph, were the true successors of Muhammad the Prophet. Their idiocy had bred a thousand years of bloodshed. *You hate them, don't you?*

Do you? he wondered.

"Rokna!" the soldier in front shouted in Urdu. "Stop!" He had already unshouldered the G3A3 assault rifle and was aiming it at the truck.

Yes, Asif decided. He hated the Shias. And the military.

The young Pakistani put the water bottle down and pressed hard on the gas. He reached toward the sun-faded brown dashboard as gunfire shattered the window. Bullets punched through Asif's shoulders and chest, and he was knocked back hard against the seat as he pressed the cigarette lighter. Bloody and no longer in control of his dying body, he was unable to reach the marble. . . .

Thirty pounds of plasticized pentaerythritol tetranitrate explosives wired to the underside of the dashboard exploded. The truck literally expanded as the concussive force of the PETN hit the inside walls, splitting them. The vehicle vomited engine parts to the front and sacks full of nails, bolts, and glass to the rear. It pushed a wall of sound in all directions. The soldiers were simultaneously knocked back and torn open, rusted chrome, burning canvas, and grotesque body parts flung in all directions, as the blast rolled toward an empty lot to the south and the mosque to the north. The twisted chassis of the old truck tumbled toward the ancient structure, stamped forcefully across the door and lower façade before falling back onto the street. Several men, just arriving, were crushed by the initial strike, while several inside were injured by falling lanterns and flying pieces of broken stone. But the structure itself held.

The remaining soldiers and the missionary building were peppered with shrapnel, none very seriously, save for a young Christian volunteer who had just come to the window to pull open the shade. Shattered glass razored her face and chest, and she stumbled backward, slipping on a quick-made slick of her own blood. Rats ran quickly from behind the shattered foundation, waves of them pouring through the rubble like water. From above, a flaming kestrel dropped to the ground, its wings slapping furiously and then not at all.

The sound of the explosion faded quickly, the rain of debris stopped, and soon all that remained were sirens from a few late-model vehicles, the moans of the wounded, and the smoke that obscured the sun with an ugly charcoal film. Shopkeepers and pedestrians who ran toward the scene were silent, their ears filled with their own racing blood.

Dr. Ayesha Gillani was sitting at an open-air café near the market when she heard—and felt—the powerful explosion. It echoed through the crooked streets like faraway thunder. In the square, people on bicycles stopped, turned, and looked down the street as smoke followed the sounds, curling lazily from between the low buildings. Vendors ran in fright from their stands and sought cover in alleys, in shops, behind trees, anything that was far from parked vehicles. These things often happened in twos and threes.

Not this time, Dr. Gillani thought.

Though she knew that, there were things that had surprised her. The location of the blast, for one. She looked at her watch. The timing of the blast was off, as well.

It was early, too, she thought. Six thirteen. It wasn't supposed to happen for another two minutes.

The changes were unexpected but not unwelcome. There were always variables in even the best-planned scenario. A rotating checkpoint. A mechanical malfunction. An accident. A distraction.

The important thing is he pulled the trigger, she told herself. That was the most difficult and time-consuming part of the process.

She took out her cell phone, sent a one-letter text message—S, for *success*—and resumed eating her *nāshtā,* a traditional Pakistani breakfast of *paratha,* a flatbread, as well as mangoes and Earl Grey. The tea felt much cooler than it had moments before. Or maybe it was her. The anticipation had passed. The event was history. And her confidence—of which she was the harshest critic—had been validated.

She watched as people slowly, cautiously returned to their stands. *The poor, poor mice,* she thought. Sunni, Shiite, Kurd, Christian, Jew—the religion or sect of the victims did not matter to her. The tribe or nationality was of absolutely no importance. All that mattered to the forty-two-year-old was that the trials were completed and the real mission could begin. The task for which she had been training herself for over twenty years. The only possible response to what she had endured.

She was about to bring lasting, eternal peace to the world.

CHAPTER 1
QUEBEC, CANADA
PRESENT DAY

The silver-white Gulfstream IV charter jet was idling outside its hangar at Jean Lesage International Airport. It was nearly 11:00 a.m., and the sounds of commercial jetliners coming and going rumbled toward the cavernous building every two minutes or so.

Reed Bishop took comfort in the sound. Being in a strange airport was like going to church or McDonald's in a foreign land: you always knew just what you were going to find. For an FBI agent, predictability of any kind was a godsend. Sights, ambient sounds, traffic patterns, personal habits. It was all part of the baseline. It helped you realize when something was off, either because it stood out or it caused a ripple effect.

So far, everything was normal. But then, there were a lot of moving parts in this operation. There was still enough time for something to go wrong.

Bishop spotted the black Mercedes as it pulled around a slow-moving catering truck and sped along the service road. He squinted his forty-three-year-old eyes to check the tag irregularity that he'd been told about before he took off. The macron, the accent over the *E,* ran the entire length of the letter, instead of partway. That meant the car was bona fide Canadian Security Intelligence Service. If there'd been a hijack, a substitution along the way, there was a sure way to tell. It was one less thing to worry about. The car flashed its brights. That was the second way to tell. A hijacker wouldn't have known to do that.

The sun was hidden behind thickening gray clouds, making the sedan's dark windows seem even more opaque, more forbidding. A chill crept along Bishop's arms. The FBI agent spit his chewing gum to the tarmac and reached into his Windbreaker for his cigarettes, feeling a pinch of guilt. He'd promised his ten-year-old daughter he would quit by her eleventh birthday. That left him two weeks to make good on his pledge. But he'd barely managed to cut down from his usual two packs a day, and the nicotine gum only made him want it more. He'd have to SARR the habit—follow the Self-Administered Recovery Regimen, as they called outpatient work in Allison Dearborn's deprogramming division.

He remembered when they called it "cold turkey." It was difficult then, and it would be just as difficult however it was dressed.

Cold turkey or aversion training or hypnotherapy or whatever the hell, he would deal with it after this business was done, he promised himself. When the prisoner was airborne, he could relax a little. It had been two weeks since her capture. He'd practically lived in his small office on Pennsylvania Avenue since then. There had been arrangements to make; egos to deal with; rules to bend, rewrite, or ignore. And he still had his regular work to do, tracking the internal flow of information on top secret operations and counterespionage activities so that none of the intel went from the inside out.

He lit up, aware of others on the tarmac looking at him. Smokers had become like FBI agents, acutely aware of their surroundings and who was glaring at them. He ignored them. The SOBs were breathing jet fumes, for God's sake. And they were Pakistani. Surely they were around smokers enough to not give a damn.

Bishop did not know the three men standing beside the jet, nor had he seen the faces hidden by their bala-clavas. The Pakistanis had worn the masks since he arrived at the airfield an hour ago. Dressed in black suits, like corporate ninjas, they had gathered silently outside the hangar to await their prisoner's arrival. Bishop was here as a representative of FBI internal affairs. He was present in case human rights watchdogs heard about what was going on. He was supposed to give the transfer a veneer of international legality.

It was all a public show, of course. He was partnered with Jessica Muloni of the CIA's Rendition Group One—"the waterboarding people," as they laughingly called themselves. *She* wasn't here to make sure the prisoner's rights were protected. And he wasn't here to make sure she was held accountable. Though he was technically in charge of this operation—another of Homeland Security's increasingly less uncommon joint, cross-jurisdictional operations—professionally and ethically he felt their captive deserved whatever Muloni and the Pakistanis had planned.

He took a deep pull of smoke, held it in his lungs

for a glorious moment, then let it swirl from his nose into the morning breeze. He should have worn his leather flight jacket. It was chilly even for Canada, the sky low and overcast. The damp gusts carried the smell of pines and imminent rain from the Gulf of Saint Lawrence.

They could have told me the weather before I left, he thought. He and Muloni had left Washington on a 7:00 a.m. flight. Before he headed to Dulles, the Canadians had given him details about the Mercedes, photos of the agents, satellite images of the terminal. Everything but the goddamn weather report.

Maybe it was a sign from God. The weather was ugly to suit the job he and Muloni had arrived to manage.

He drew hard on the cigarette as he watched the progress of the charcoal Mercedes. He was glad, at least, that the CSIS was the one who had made the nab. So far, the Canadians were proving more cooperative than some of Washington's other "allies," who insisted on follow-through and quid pro quo and complicated every mission threefold. It was tough to be clandestine when you had a half dozen agents trying to be inconspicuous, instead of one who actually was.

A woman came up behind him.

"How's the room?" he asked without turning.

"Fine. Clean." There was something in the clipped tone of her voice he didn't like. Perhaps he'd thanked God too soon. "What's wrong, Agent Muloni?"

"Your question."

"You lost me."

"The question should be, 'What's right?' The answer—nothing. I just got word that our plans have been modified."

Bishop slowly turned to face the African American woman, saw the cell phone in her hand. "Got word from whom?"

"Someone we can't just ignore, like we'd usually do," she said. She wobbled the phone. "Our consul general here called me directly. Seems that two high-level CSIS officials paid him a visit in the middle of the night."

"Official, or did they creep through a window?"

"All on the up-and-up," she said. "They insisted that the Mounties accompany Veil to her destination."

"You're not serious."

"I am *so* serious."

The Royal Canadian Mounted Police and the CSIS were one unit until 1984. Since then, there had been very few jurisdictional battles because the responsibilities were clearly defined: the CSIS collected intelligence, while the RCMP acted on it. This job was what Bishop's people called a fence straddler.

Bishop snapped his cigarette butt to the ground. *Why give up smoking at all?* He'd only have to start again when crap like this came down the chute. "He told them it would compromise security, having extra targets?"

"Yes," the woman replied. "He said that the Canadians were intransigent. They told him that if we wanted *their* prisoner, we'd have to trust *their* guys."

"It's not about trust, for Christ's sake. It's about numbers."

"Don't tell me," she said.

Bishop shook his head. "Not a good precedent."

"I'm not happy, and word is the prime minister isn't thrilled, either," she said. "If something goes wrong, he doesn't want to catch any blowback."

"But the Mounties want to share the glory if everything goes right—"

"When," she said firmly.

It took a moment for him to understand. "*When* everything goes right," he corrected himself.

Jessica Muloni smiled. He regarded the woman's big brown eyes. There was nothing about them to suggest that her calm had been ruffled by the unexpected turn of events. She did not in any way fit the stereotypical mold of a cold CIA field operative. She was warm and easygoing. There was something about her that made you trust her, not just personally but professionally, a combination of her relaxed confidence and poise. Plain, thin, her natural brown hair cut functionally short, she wore almost no makeup and shapeless clothes, giving her a subdued, relaxed appearance. In her case, looks were somewhat deceptive, however. According to her file, she *was* easygoing until someone displayed the kind of dangerous incompetence that frontline personnel could not afford. Whether Jessica's takedown was a physical assault, a psychological strike, or any combination thereof, witnesses reported it was a frightening thing to behold.

"Listen," she said. "Let's give them some leeway here. The CSIS found her, the Mounties snatched her from the school, and the Canadians are letting us circumvent their deportation laws without squawking."

"Without squawking *too* much," Bishop corrected her.

"Fine," she agreed. "Look, there are legitimate concerns, and the brain trust here feels they need to have hands-on, so it's not technically a turnover. Seems they read File four-oh-four-one-one in the ASD."

The ASD—the Archive Sharing Database—employed by the FBI, the CSIS, Britain's MI5, Interpol, and twenty-four other agencies, had a different name in Washington: Ass So Demolished, from the number of times the United States got screwed in that exchange program. Not that he didn't see the Canadians' point. Bishop had been part of that operation in 2001, at Bromma Airport in Stockholm, when Egyptian asylum seekers Ahmed Agiza and Muhammad al-Zery were turned back by Sweden at the request of the FBI, which had Middle Eastern resources to protect. The file contained a detailed explanation of the diplomatic maneuvering that took place to make it seem like a Swedish decision in response to concerns voiced by Cairo, and not a decision cooked up in Washington. Even so, Sweden took a lot of heat for having failed to let the United Nations Human Rights Council study the case before taking unilateral action. It wasn't just Swedish neutrality that took a hit, but the country's reputation for independent action. Canadian authorities would accept the first, not the second.

"Are we expected to fly all three to Pakistan?" Bishop asked.

"No. Just two of them," she said.

"Well, there's a blessing," Bishop said cynically. Two sets of regionally trained eyes on the worldly Pakistani operatives, a gaggle of suspicious Pakistani eyes on the territorial Canadians, fewer eyes on the package. "You cleared them?"

She wriggled the phone again. "They're clean. Uninspiring but stainless."

He produced a weary, resigned sigh and shifted his attention back to the vehicle. There was no point arguing over the stipulation if the diplomats had consented to it. No point, and no time. It was times like this that made him want to become a green badger—the nickname for former Bureau personnel who joined private industry to handle security in global hot spots. The stress was high, but the bureaucracies were thinner and the pay was better. And frankly, it was easier to protect a region or a city or just a business with international outlets, instead of the whole damn world.

Bishop watched as the Mercedes eased to a halt and the stocky driver exited. A moment later a second man in civilian clothes slid from the backseat, followed by a blond woman in a leather jacket and jeans who emerged from the opposite side and then turned to lean back in, reaching to unclip the prisoner's seat belt.

Muloni took pictures of each individual with her cell phone. She tapped a six-digit code on the keypad. Facial recognition software from the Company's sophisticated XApps database compared the images with the JPEGs she'd been sent. The password she'd used was phone specific; without it, the app would not function.

She showed the results to Bishop. The images all matched. They had no reason to prevent the Canadians from sticking around.

Bishop and Muloni had already been ID'd at the outside gate. Still, he thought, the first Mountie to emerge from the car should have done a backup check.

All it would have taken for ringers to get through and cut them down was one bribed guard.

Bishop's eyes narrowed as a fourth party, the notorious killer Veil, emerged from the vehicle. She had been named in at least a dozen attacks, from pinpoint assassinations to RPG attacks. Her hands were cuffed behind her back; her ankles shackled; the second plainclothesman helped to steady her on her feet. She wore a short black skirt over a wine-colored blouse that drew Bishop's attention to her figure for longer than he hoped anyone had noticed. Her beige slip-on sneakers didn't match the rest of her clothes: the Mounties had removed whatever shoes or boots she was wearing when she was bagged to make it easier for her to walk in restraints.

"Dressed to kill," Muloni remarked.

"Cute."

"No, really," the woman replied. "You wouldn't have been watching her hands, would you?"

"Damn it." She was right. And he was busted.

"My great-grandmother was a painter in Uganda," the woman said. "Made her own pigments, stretched animal skins for canvas. She painted village life. There were a lot of bare-chested women, and do you know why?"

"It was a hundred and ten in the shade?"

"That, plus it inured men to the sight of barely clad women so they wouldn't be distracted in tribal wars or in trading," she told him.

"I wonder what those women thought when they encountered European women," Bishop said.

"The Zulus thought they were comical," Muloni told him. "Not the kind of high ground the British missionaries wanted."

Bishop didn't want to tell her that overexposure wouldn't have worked with most of the men he knew. Then again, some of them—like himself—might actually have been studying the woman's face instead. Veil's expression was nondescript. No anger, no frustration, no fear. Just neutral. It wasn't even a kind of practiced blankness that made you think something might be working inside her skull, like a plan of escape. She was simply a woman who was going along with whatever came from moment to moment. Undistracted, if an opportunity presented itself, she'd be ready. That was how assassins worked. But all that aside, there was something riveting about a woman who seemed to have no opinion in her expression.

Bishop reached for a cigarette, thought of his promise, then let it go. He chewed his cheek and watched as the woman shuffled ahead amid her captors, her shoulders squared, her head high and defiant.

The woman the Bureau had code-named Veil—she called herself Yasmin Rassin, though that was believed to be an alias—was responsible for the deaths of at least fourteen individuals around the world. She was wanted in the United States for trying to kill the deputy director of the CIA, Jon Harper, outside his home in Washington, a hit paid for by Tehran, according to a mole in the *Majles-e Khobregan,* Iran's ruling council of clerics. The trail that led to her capture had been long and convoluted. Photographed by a street-corner security camera, she had vanished for almost a year after the attempted hit. Eight months ago, a pair of MI5 antiterror agents on another assignment had made a chance ID at Heathrow and taken her into custody. On the way to Thames House in London, their car disappeared. It was later found burning in a field northwest of the city. A month later, the body of one of the agents was recovered from the water under the Westminster Bridge. His throat had been cut with a razor. Pink cotton fibers found in the wound suggested the razor had been tucked into the sweater she was wearing, probably the sleeve. Though her hands had been zip-tied behind her, shavings suggested that the restraints had been slashed, apparently by another razor blade. Rassin had undoubtedly made a lengthwise slit in the back of her leather belt and tucked the razor inside so its edge was even with the top of the belt.

The other driver remained missing.

Despite a hunt involving the cooperation of multiple international security and intelligence groups, Rassin had again gone to ground until last May, when the CSIS got a tip about an Egyptian boy who kept to himself at school, never took gym class due to vague religious restrictions, and—what had surprised fellow students—remembered his locker combination the very first day. Simultaneously, the Mounties turned up an inconsistency in his passport that had been recorded at customs and eventually passed along: the customs agent had clandestinely noted the young man's travel history—routine with young men coming from the Middle East—but there was no record of his having gone to the places stamped on the document. The Mounties tracked Rassin's movements, compared photographs of the "boy" with the computer-enhanced security camera image of her, and finally made the arrest.

According to Bishop's hurried briefing, Rassin did not resist the takedown. With the headmaster of the school present to lend an air of invisibility to the arrest—he was always talking with education officials—Rassin was taken away at gunpoint, outside, during lunch. And that was that.

Bishop watched as she was brought toward him. She certainly looked different from the security camera image he'd seen. She no longer had wavy raven-black hair tumbling to her shoulders. She was a redhead, her hair clipped short, boyish. Her features were more strongly defined, probably the result of Botox and malar or submalar implants. The eyes were slightly more rounded at the corners, and she was no longer wearing blue contacts. Her eyes were dark and piercing. Finally, Bishop noticed that while her skin was still olive smooth, her Mediterranean complexion was lighter, possibly due to topical melanin inhibitors, like hydroquinone or glucocorticoids.

She was slight, no more than a few inches over five feet, and with the proper clothes, he saw how she could pass as a teenage boy. The CSIS had subsequently learned from school officials that her "widower father" was an oil company geologist who was always up north, looking for untapped deposits. Presumably, visitors to her rented home, like her handler, would have come at night, wearing "dad" clothes and carrying luggage. E-mail would be checked only on school computers, which, as a rule, were off provincial law-enforcement radar absent specific tips about violence—which were virtually nonexistent in Canada. With hacking codes provided by her allies, she could even track CIA or FBI pursuers.

It was a brilliant disguise, one she'd maintained for seven months. Unfortunately for Veil, the RCMP was off *her* radar. It was like the traffic stops that turned into big drug busts: the law usually came at you by accident, from a blind spot.

Leading her across the tarmac, one of the Mounties stopped in front of Bishop and inclined his head formally. "Good morning. I am Inspector Javert."

Bishop grinned. "Really?"

"Indeed."

Bishop nodded toward the driver. "Valjean?"

"Yes," the inspector replied humorlessly, then indicated to the female plainclothes officer. "This is Cosette. She and I will be traveling with the prisoner to her end point."

Bishop had expected the Canadians to use aliases around their prisoner. It gave them added deniability and would protect their families from retribution if she ever passed them on to her associates. Still, he was used to traditional military-style assignations with Greek letters attached, like Tango-Alpha or Foxtrot-Beta. The *Les Misérables* references gave this a kind of amateur, community theater feel.

Javert looked at the men in black on the runway. "You are ready for us to bring the detainee aboard?"

"Not quite, Inspector. We have to make some preparations before takeoff."

"Of what sort?"

"They won't take long," Bishop insisted. "In the meantime, you can wait comfortably aboard the—"

"Please answer my question," Javert said, his face tightening. "What type of preparations?"

Bishop hesitated. There were no written-in-stone guidelines for what he was compelled to share with local authorities. Still, he preferred not to lie to them.

That could lead to mistrust at best, complications at worst. Cooperation did not, however, mean he was inclined to share everything.

Bishop let the pause stretch out, still weighing how much to reveal. Muloni spared him the decision.

"We're going to conduct a body-cavity search on the prisoner," she said. "We also have different clothes for her. There's a room in the terminal where she can change."

The inspector studied her flatly. "We searched her last night and found nothing," he said. "She has been under constant observation since then. You needn't be concerned."

"I'm not," she replied. "We have our own protocols and ways of doing things. This is going to happen."

"They'll be with us," Bishop said quickly, pointing toward the masked Pakistanis.

Javert's eyes remained on Muloni. "Is that supposed to put my mind at ease?"

"Not my problem," Muloni replied.

Alone time with the prisoner was vitally important, but the reasons were secret. Mulling how to break the impasse, Bishop let his gaze drift toward Veil. He discovered she was staring back at him, her gaze hot and penetrating. He made himself wait an uncomfortable moment to see if she looked away—she didn't—before turning to Javert.

"Inspector, no one disputes that it's *your* prisoner being transferred to the custody of Pakistan," Bishop said. "We have simply come to assist—"

"As needed," Javert pointed out. "That was the agreement."

"It was," Bishop agreed. "But the rules of extradition in Canada are largely uncharted legal and political territory, while we have a great deal of precedent. To deviate from standard procedure without authorization . . . Well, it would take hours to contact the proper parties on both sides. Ten minutes," he said. "That's all we need."

The Canadian scowled with a mixture of reluctance and skepticism. But they both knew he would have to relent. He had carried out a kidnapping sanctioned by his country's top intelligence dog. The more talk that went back and forth, the more phone logs there were, the longer Veil remained on the ground in Quebec, the more someone might start to take a closer look at how all of this had been accomplished.

"Very well," Javert said. "We will escort the prisoner to the terminal and stay as observers until you are finished."

"Shouldn't you be checking the aircraft?" Muloni asked.

"Why? It got here, didn't it? The Pakistanis have been watching it, haven't they? What exactly would we be looking *for*?"

There was no arguing with his logic, however naive it was, and Bishop couldn't fault him for insisting on that condition—it might have been partly about alpha-dogging the operation, but it was more likely the inspector wanted to see that nothing too extreme happened on Canadian soil.

Muloni's eyes remained on Javert for several seconds. Then she glanced at Bishop, gave him a disengaged little shrug. Javert seemed to have become his problem exclusively.

"Observe all you want, Inspector," Bishop said at

length. "The only thing I ask, respectfully, is that your people don't get in our way."

"Why would we?" he asked. "It's just a search."

"Right," Bishop agreed. "But as with the airplane, we tend to check in places and with ways that might not be part of your tool kit."

The inspector eyed him suspiciously, then looked back at his Mounties and waved them forward. They all fell in more closely around the shackled Veil, the two men flanking her, the blond woman a step or two behind. Bishop and Muloni watched the service road and the tarmac, respectively, in case anyone made a rescue attempt. But there were no sounds of car engines, nothing to break the reassuring monotony of the roaring turbines.

When they reached the jet, Bishop noticed Veil's eyes shoot toward the masked men. It was the first time she was in a position to see them. The woman moved ahead without halting as they followed her into the charter terminal.

Bishop felt a chill. In his nineteen years with the Bureau, the former field operative had learned to respect his intuition almost to the point of obsession.

She knows who they are, who they were, he thought. She would not want to go back to Baghdad with them. Any prisoner would rather die. It was a dangerous game they were playing now, but if it worked, the payoff would be considerable.

The terminal was a barracks-style concrete structure with a small functional waiting area and a corridor running back along one side of the unattended reception desk. On her arrival at the terminal that morning, Muloni had picked a small boxy storage area at the end of the corridor for the holding room. She directed the others toward it. Javert entered the corridor first, followed by the other Mounties and Veil. The black-clad men from the Gulfstream came next, with Bishop and Muloni in the rear. She shut the door behind her and locked it.

"He's not going to like this," she warned as they lagged well behind.

"I know. But what's he going to do about it? Quote regulations at us? We'll be done before he can even start to explain this to his commander."

"Our boy here can still shut down the tower," Muloni said. "Veil's got to be airborne before it hits the fan."

"She will be," Bishop promised. "Remember what Harper's buddy Ryan Kealey did to that United Nations security guard in oh-seven?"

She grinned. "It's legend among those who knew what went down. Said he mistook a walkie-talkie for a gun. Threw the guard across the room. And he wasn't even the target—it was the diplomat who was crossing behind him. The guard got credit for the takedown."

"Classic," Bishop said. "I'll make sure only Javert comes in, and make it seem like it was *his* idea."

Muloni was still smiling. "Perfect. My move, if it comes to that."

Bishop nodded as the group clustered tightly around the door.

"You can stand by in the corridor," Bishop said, reaching for a doorknob. "We'll let you know when we're set to roll."

"No," the inspector said. "We will observe *all* of it."

"All right," Bishop said. He pretended to consider

his options. "But just you. Nobody else. And no talking. Take it or leave it."

Javert's jaw muscles were working. He nodded once, sharply.

"Who has the key to the prisoner's restraints?" Bishop asked.

Cosette came from behind Veil and flicked her right hand up from her side. The key hung from a steel-plated bracelet locked around her wrist.

Bishop extended his hand, but Javert inserted himself between them.

"I'll take it," the inspector said.

The woman unclasped the bracelet and gave it to Javert. Bishop nodded to Muloni. She entered the office first. Javert grabbed the prisoner's handcuffs and, walking behind Veil, guided her in. The Pakistanis went next, followed by Bishop. The American shut and locked the door behind him. It was a solid oak door with a shoulder-high dead bolt. While Javert watched Muloni, Bishop slid the bolt into place.

The room was empty except for a small card table against one white cinder-block wall. On the table were a folded tracksuit, a digital camera, and a scalpel. Surrounded by her captors, Veil took notice of the surgical implement for scarcely an instant before letting her eyes move on to study the rest of the room. Bishop felt an uncharacteristic edginess as her roving attention fell on him again. Muloni had examined the room personally, so he was confident no one had hidden a weapon where Veil could grab it. Perhaps it was because this was the first time a woman had been rendered with his direct involvement. If anything definable was bothering him, he supposed that explained it.

Bishop watched as one of the men in black coveralls took the scalpel from the tabletop. He was tall and square-shouldered, only his eyes visible through the balaclava that concealed his features. Bishop was assured that he had been cleared by voice recognition, as had all the others. The FBI phones had an XApp for that as well. The Pakistani looked at Bishop.

"Let's get it done," the American said.

The hooded man crossed the room to the prisoner with two large strides, raising the scalpel and then sweeping it down the front of her skirt. The skirt came apart with a whispery shredding of fabric and dropped over her ankles, revealing her bare thighs underneath as he brought the blade up again to slit open her blouse. For a moment she stood, shackled, in her bra, panties, and the plain low sneakers. Another swipe of the blade sliced the bra in half, leaving her nude from the waist up, the limp remnants of her blouse hanging from her arms and wrists above the cuffs.

Bishop wasn't sure who was more surprised by the act, the prisoner or a visibly horrified Javert.

The photos came next, a second man in black rapidly snapping pictures of the woman with the digital camera. Bishop caught himself looking at her tanned, nude flesh and guiltily lifted his gaze. When he did, she was staring back at him, her dark, bright eyes steady, burning into his own as they had on the tarmac. There was no trace of embarrassment or submission in her expression, nothing to indicate she was at all intimidated. Just her seething anger and steadfast eyes.

Bishop could tell she was thinking. Hard.

"What's the need for this?" Javert asked, frowning unhappily.

Bishop was glad for the distraction. "Remember our agreement, Inspector? No talking."

"Yes, but you go too far," Javert replied.

"You think so?" Muloni cut in. "How would *you* ID her if you found her dismembered body in a Pakistani street?"

Javert's mouth snapped shut, audibly.

"Okay, Inspector," Muloni went on. "We'll need her out of those arm and leg cuffs."

Javert stepped forward. The man with the scalpel backed off to make room for him. The inspector bent and opened the ankle restraints, then straightened, slipped the key into the handcuff lock, and gave it a three-quarter turn. The manacles clicked open and came loose in his hands. He took two steps back, holding them with both hands.

The man with the scalpel nodded to his teammates. "Check her. Everywhere inside," he said in Arabic.

Bishop recognized the words. He'd heard them in more rooms like this than he could remember. They were not really instructions, since his companions knew the drill. They were meant for Veil, designed to cut away her dignity the way the surgeon's blade had slashed away her clothes. This repatriation unit of the Pakistani *Quêl Affada* intelligence division had been active for twenty-four months, its members handpicked from Saddam Hussein's disbanded *Mukhabarat*. Amnesty International and other human rights organizations insisted the infamous secret police were the wrong people to rehabilitate criminal Pakistanis operating abroad, but the FBI had gone ahead with the plan. Part of the QA charter was to prevent Baghdad from exporting terrorists and criminals. The threat of being turned over to a unit comprised of professional torturers was credited with helping to discourage black market operators and the export of terrorists.

For the masked men, the routine was familiar. For Bishop and Muloni, it was necessary. For Javert, it was a new experience, and as two of the masked men closed on her, he let his eyes drop.

That was when Veil struck. Her left hand shot out in a palm-heel strike. It connected with Javert's chin, causing his teeth to clap shut on his tongue. Blood oozed from the sides of his mouth as he stumbled back, dropping the shackles. Veil remained in motion. As the nearest of the Pakistanis moved forward, she side-stepped him and made for the man with the scalpel. Her right hand formed a tiger claw and raked laterally across his eyes. He screamed, temporarily blinded. As Muloni stepped toward her, Veil was already pivoting and struck her in the gut with a perfectly executed backward kick. She reached for the blade in the blinded man's hand.

Fists pounded on the door.

"Inspector? Is everything all right?"

Cosette's cry went unanswered as Bishop and the other masked men rushed to form a tight circle around the prisoner. She ignored them, fighting with the Pakistani for the scalpel. Veil grabbed his wrist in an effort to twist it from his hand. Before she could successfully apply the wrenching *kote gaeshi* maneuver, Bishop grabbed her from behind, pulled her back, twisted, and threw himself atop her body, both of them facedown. He easily outweighed the killer, but she hadn't relented and was thrashing wildly on the floor, arms and legs flailing, her gums peeled from her teeth, trying to turn and bite the hands pressing down on her shoulders.

"Somebody get the goddamn chains!" Bishop yelled.

Recovering from her blow, Muloni spotted the shackles on the floor. She grabbed the hand restraints. The key was still in the lock as she wrestled one of Veil's wrists into the iron band and snapped it shut. Bishop moved slightly so Muloni could get to her other arm. After some fierce wrestling, the woman's arms were once more immobilized. Breathing heavily, Bishop sat up, still on her back. Meanwhile, one of the Pakistanis had found the ankle restraints and was working to clamp them on while Muloni held down her legs.

Five of us, Bishop thought. *Five of us to bring her under control.*

Cosette was still pounding on the door. Muloni opened it, disdainfully pushed the bloodied Javert out, then closed and locked it behind him. He had wanted to see the examination, and he had. What he had missed, because he wasn't looking for it, was the start of the breaking of a high-value prisoner, one who had killed energy officials and politicians the world over but would soon be asked to kill Iranian politicians and the sons of oil sheikhs. The struggle proved that the FBI was right about her: she'd be a hell of an asset. Soon she'd be conveyed into a purgatory inhabited by other malign ghosts like herself. Confined, interrogated, if she refused to work for the good guys instead of the Iranians and oil sheikhs who had trained and paid her, she'd be eliminated.

But Bishop didn't think that would happen. No

human being who operated solely as a mercenary would endure what lay in store when the option was simply to shift their loyalties. And they still had one more card to play.

Bishop was still kneeling over Veil when Muloni crouched beside them. The agent leaned close to the Pakistani woman.

"I have some information for you," she said, snarling.

Veil tried to spit, and Muloni punched her in the nose. There was a loud, ugly crack.

"You'll want to listen," Muloni said.

"*Dozakh,*" she cried.

"*Jannat!*" Muloni hissed back with a wicked smile.

Addressing her in Urdu got Veil's attention. Bishop could see the assassin's shoulders relax slightly.

"You will want to hear the reason we brought you in here," Muloni continued in English. "It involves your daughter, Kamilah."

Veil's eyes instantly lost their fire. It was the first time Bishop had seen anything get to her.

"What about her?" the assassin demanded in thinly accented English. "What have you done?"

"What have you done, *ma'am?*" Muloni corrected her.

Veil stared at her. She didn't spit. She didn't struggle. She was already starting to understand. The American would tell her nothing and would hit her again, and again, until she did what she was told.

"What have you done, ma'am?" Veil asked.

"Nothing, yet," Muloni said. "But we know where she is. We're watching her."

"No one knew," Veil muttered.

"Akila did," Muloni said.

The name drained the color from Veil's face.

"If you want to keep her safe, you'll do everything you're told, starting now," Muloni said. "You're going back to Pakistan, where you'll tell these boys everything you know. Names, contacts, safe houses, everything. The interview will be taped, a copy given to us. If we like what we hear, Kamilah will be fine."

Veil did not move. Jessica Muloni rose slowly. She swiped a hand across the orange suit folded on the table. The outfit landed on the floor next to Veil.

"Help her up," she told the Pakistanis.

They did. She stood unsteadily, blood flowing from her nose.

"Forget the cavity search," Muloni said. "Help her get dressed ASAP."

The group leader, the one who had been holding the scalpel, translated for the others. Bishop rose, and they got to work. Muloni was obviously on the clock now, trying to get the jet off the ground before Cosette or Valjean got in the way.

"You got anything to add?" Muloni asked Bishop.

"I'm good," he said.

There was no point telling her that this was a shitty business. They knew it, the Pakistanis knew it, and now a small group of Mounties knew it.

The team escorted the prisoner back down the corridor. Javert, Cosette, and the Mercedes were gone by the time they reached the tarmac. Valjean looked shaken. He told Bishop they went to the hospital. There was a bloody handkerchief on the tarmac beside him.

"These individuals are free to depart without the

RCMP contingent," the Mountie said of the Pakistanis and their prisoner.

"Understood," Bishop said. His voice was matter-of-fact, as though it had been a tactical decision and not the result of the team leader nearly biting off his tongue.

"I'm to remain with you until you leave," Valjean added.

"Of course," Bishop replied. He looked at his watch. "Our flight home's not for another ninety minutes. Can we buy you coffee?"

"If we can find an open bar, I'd prefer a scotch," he answered.

"Sounds good," Bishop replied.

Within five minutes, Bishop was driving the three of them to the terminal building. The Gulfstream IV, with Veil and the Pakistanis on it, was just one more rolling boom in the succession of jets leaving the runway. Bishop relaxed a little. Muloni was calm.

"I didn't realize you knew Urdu," Bishop said.

"Women who work for the Company need an edge," Muloni told him. "Farsi and Urdu were mine."

"Impressive. What did you say to her?"

"She started to swear at me. She only got as far as 'hell.' Probably going to tell me to go there. I said, 'Heaven.' The inflection suggested that was the only place I'd be going—unlike her."

"Crap. You did all that with inflection?"

"That's a lot of what language is," she replied. "Language was my major. In the Semitic world especially, you find so much of language is just taunt and counter-taunt, with the ante constantly being upped.

'Your father picks lemons.' 'Your mother *sucks* lemons.' 'Your sister *is* a lemon.' That sort of thing."

"Only a little rougher, I'm guessing," Bishop said.

"Yes." She smiled. "My father's family had a Moroccan strain. They were Muslim traders. Very vocal."

"You get that in my Irish and Italian heritage, as well," Bishop told her.

"We're all more alike than we care to admit," Muloni said. "That's the damned thing about us killing each other."

Bishop shook his head. "That's what happens when you run out of insults, I guess."

"Screw you," she said with a little wink.

She was right. Inflection was everything.

The man removed his black mask several minutes after the Gulfstream had taken off. He swept a gloved hand through his damp blond hair. He was Caucasian, with the hulking build of an American football player.

He was clearly not Pakistani.

"Close one," he said, blinking sweat from his pale blue eyes. "I thought we were going to have to waste them."

The man sitting across the narrow aisle yanked off his own balaclava. He was an African American male in his thirties. He pulled off his gloves and tossed them, and the mask, on the table in front of him. This man was not Pakistani, either.

"I wouldn't've lost any sleep over it," he said. "Javert. Valjean. What are they? Freakin' librarians?"

There was general laughter among the men. Across the table were two other deep luxury seats. The third man sat in the one by the aisle. Their prisoner sat by the window, her olive complexion ruddy in the sunset, her eyes narrow as she watched the last man unmask himself. He had Asiatic features, possibly Hawaiian.

"All that matters is it worked out," the first man said. The blue eyes settled on Yasmin. "You don't look surprised, little lady."

Yasmin didn't bother explaining. She didn't want to provide information that might help these men or their handlers in the future. Their affected accents had been good, but she had doubted from the first that any of them were Pakistanis. Neither they nor the aircraft cabin smelled of cigarettes. She had never met a Pakistani agent who did not smoke. She had also noted the bulge of wallets in their pants. Pakistanis typically carried folded currency. They were not big on credit cards. These were mercenaries. Working for the highest bidder.

"She's got a good poker face, I'll give her that," the African American said.

"But a looker," said another.

"Yeah, well, that's all you're gonna do," the African American said.

"I know. I'm just saying."

Yasmin was instantly tired of their locker-room banter. She had heard it in the barracks as a young girl; a world and a decade away, there was nothing different in their looks and remarks. It was pathetic.

"What is going on?" she asked. She did not expect them to tell her much. But any information was more than she had now.

"It's a classic good news, bad news situation," the man beside her said. "Do you understand that expression?"

She nodded.

"The good news, as you've probably figured out, is that we're not taking you to Islamabad."

"Where, then?"

"That's a secret, I'm afraid. But that's also good news. You won't be cooped up here for the better part of a day. We'll have wheels down in—"

"Two hours or less," she said. "In New York, I think."

The men fell silent. The Asiatic man confirmed her guess with his look of open admiration.

"What makes you say that?" he asked.

"That's a secret, I'm afraid," she replied.

A jet such as this one had a ceiling of 13,000 meters. They were leveling off at around 2,000 meters. That suggested a very short flight. There would be nothing in a Canadian city that Quebec would not provide, so she guessed they were headed to America. Only New York made sense within a two-hour radius.

"Who are you people?" she asked.

"Sorry. That, too, is need to know only," the Asiatic man said.

"Do you, in fact, have my daughter?"

"We do," the Asiatic man went on. "We needed a way to get your attention."

"For what?"

"That's the bad news," he said, but he did not elaborate.

She wanted to ask about Kamilah, how she was, when she might see her or even talk to her, but she doubted they would tell her anything. Information was power, and their body language told her that her little display had set them on guard. That was exactly what she wanted. A man on defense was easier to provoke.

Yasmin regarded the African American. "What is your code name?" she asked.

He just smirked.

"Dr. Fed? FBI-Zee?"

The man's expression soured, and he moved forward suddenly, as though he intended to strike her. The Asiatic man held up a hand, palm out. The other man hesitated, then settled back into his seat.

The leader turned to her. "Don't talk."

"Why?" she asked.

"Because I'll have them cut off your daughter's finger and show it to you on a live feed," he said and held up a phone.

It was a Tac-Sat Elite. She was right. He was FBI.

"Let me talk to her," she said, pressing—not because she expected him to oblige, but because he would feel in control again if she asked.

"Maybe . . . when you show us you can behave," he said as he slipped the phone back inside his jacket.

Feigning obedience, the woman sat back. Her hands were still cuffed behind her, and she had to roll toward the window, keeping them as far to the right as she could, in order to sit comfortably. Even that was painful, however; they had not treated her gently back at the terminal, especially the two agents who had been unmasked. She had pulled every muscle in her back and shoulders trying to escape.

Yasmin contemplated what might lie in store. It was unlikely they wanted her to go back to Pakistan, blend in, and start killing radical elements. All that would have taken was the right price and the release of her daughter. That would hardly be "bad news" to a mercenary.

No. The scenario suggested a suicide mission, though even there she saw problems. Why go through the trouble of hijacking a skilled assassin, then waste her on a mission that anyone with a family could be forced to execute? Because she was a woman? That made no sense. Any whore could be paid to get close to someone in power. Any whore with a child could be coerced into killing him.

And what of the other two Americans at the airport? Yasmin didn't think they knew the identities of these three men. They had behaved as though the three were Pakistani security. The African American was right: the Canadians weren't sophisticated enough to have made that level of deception necessary. Her abduction was a covert operation within the FBI that the other agents had not known about.

All she knew for certain was that, before too much longer, she would have answers. And given that they still held her daughter, she probably wouldn't like them.

CHAPTER 2
BALTIMORE, MARYLAND

A llison Dearborn looked spellbound at the medusa as it parachuted through the large tank of the aquarium. She had just told Ryan Kealey she loved the colors of the jellyfish, and he said he understood. Then, suddenly, Kealey turned his back to the curved glass of the aquarium tank.

"You okay?" she asked, her blue eyes following him.

He nodded. She wasn't convinced.

"What are you thinking?" she asked.

"Just random—"

"Ryan? Don't try to smoke me."

He smirked. "It isn't that. . . . I don't know if I can explain," he told her. "It might sound a little crazy."

Allison shrugged. "I'm a psychotherapist. Without craziness, I'd be unemployed."

His smile broadened, but he remained silent.

"We've got nearly an hour before Julie's dinner at the convention center." She hooked her arm in his. "Come on. Give it a shot. I want to know."

Kealey patted her hand and glanced back at the tank. Allison took a moment to admire this man, who was not only a good friend but also an exemplary patient. Lean and of medium height, his dark hair nearly reaching his collar, Kealey had dressed for the banquet in a Caribbean-blue collared golf shirt, navy Dockers, and loafers. He looked good, and he looked healthy, relaxed. He was certainly in a much better place than when they had first met. There was a long way to go, but he was making progress.

The creature was hovering now, barely drifting, its bell expanding and contracting with slow, rhythmical pulsations.

"The medusa could be at rest right now or hunting its prey," Kealey said. "You can't tell the difference by looking at it."

"Fascinating and deflecting. What's that got to do with—"

"Bear with me," he said.

"Fine. How do you know this?"

He raised the brochure he'd picked up at the exhibit's Pier 4 entrance. "I read this while you were on the phone. It describes the creature's survival mechanisms, like those venomous tentacles. It doesn't wait for its enemies to mature. It eats their eggs. It's a perfect biological machine. Tell me, how would you go about injecting humanity into something like that?"

"I wouldn't try. It's not a human being."

"Exactly," he said. "It's the same with some people. People who watch other people and hover and kill for a living—they're not quite human beings, either. I was thinking, How do you instill that, or if lost, how do you get that back?"

"There are numerous approaches to rehabilitation—"

"On the surface," he said. "You acclimatize some-one. Do you really change them?"

"You mean brainwash?"

"That's a little harsher than I meant," Kealey said. "You scrub out so much in the process. I'm thinking more along the lines of, how do you integrate new ideas with old to make a better person?"

"That may be more a job for a priest than a shrink," she said.

"Maybe." He smiled. "I told you it was kind of nutty."

"Only the part about equating yourself to a jelly-fish," she said. "That *is* what you were doing."

"Maybe," he admitted.

"Do you know what *I* was thinking? How its beautiful orange and violet stripes match my bracelets."

"Perfectly understandable."

"Why? Because it's girl-brain stuff?"

"No," he replied. "Because you've never carried a gun."

His hand was still on hers. She gave it a loving squeeze. "Self-awareness is the cornerstone of psychological healing. I don't think that's crazy at all."

She looked back at the tank, caught a glimpse of herself in the glass. A tall, lithe blonde in her mid-thirties, she was dressed in her banquet attire, a brief, sleeveless black dress with box pleats, gold drop earrings, and the vintage Lucite bangles on her wrists. They looked good together, but that was as far as it went. She had met Kealey at a party thrown by Julie and her husband, Jon Harper, in D.C., and they'd gone on a long, rambling moonlit stroll that wound through

Georgetown's cobblestone streets to the Mall and, eventually, to his hotel. But their instant attraction had been counterbalanced by her strong professional ethic; Allison, a former CIA trauma counselor, had thought she was being introduced to a likely patient and had reluctantly stayed in the lobby while he went up. For his part, Kealey later admitted he hadn't been sure what to think when she left. He did say he was glad she took control. His romantic history was spotty at best, deadly at worst, and he might have scared her away before getting to know her as a dear and trusted friend.

Allison continued to watch the medusa in the cool radiance of the hall. "So," she said. "Flotation is groovy, huh?"

He gave her a questioning glance.

"A line from a Hendrix song," she said.

"I see. I was more of a Peter, Paul and Mary kind of guy."

"I didn't know that about you." She smiled. "Folk-singers, eh?"

"Apple pie and peace, that's me," Kealey said without a trace of irony. "I'm the product of their vision. Or, more accurately, trying to *protect* that vision."

Allison stared at him in silence. She recognized the monotone, the distant look. It was the hint of post-traumatic stress that many soldiers and virtually every field operative acquired at some point. Kealey was no exception. He had been relaxed, sociable since he returned from his last mission in Darfur and South Africa, which was anything but.

Sent in as part of a "peacekeeping" tactic, Kealey had been on the ground to assist in ending the ten-year rebellion between the Eritrean government and a group of former eastern Sudan rebels that had united as the Eastern Front. Kealey had convinced both divisions that a peace treaty between them was their only option. *Either that or get disintegrated, one way or another.* But unfortunately, the deal had kept the Federal Alliance of Eastern Sudan, a fragment of the former eastern Sudan rebels, out of the picture, and Kealey feared a possible merging of the Justice and Equality Movement and the FAES, which would only prolong the peoples' unremitting penury and extreme economic downturn due to an impossibly dense "national vision." Not to mention the illicit guidance of their capital city, Khartoum, whose feelings toward its bordering African Nuba people was holocaustic.

But America did it once, balanced peace, Kealey thought. *Why not Sudan? Was our revolution, our own civil war so different? Yes. Because our leaders weren't insane. America had erudite leaders then, on both sides of the battlefield. And this unmatchable lunacy is what's causing the political collapse. The inescapable massacres. The contagious spread of demise. But learning that human nature is the ultimate technology, that will be the key to releasing their ancient manacles, and the beginning of their modernized advancement.*

When the deployment of a thousand South African troops to the western front of Sudan had been delayed due to elaborate passport and visa oversights—allowing the Janjaweed militia to raid a dozen more villages, killing hundreds more residents—Kealey was redeployed to inspect, scrutinize, and inform Washington about the sufficiency of the refugee camp outside the North Darfur city of Al-Fashir, which housed more than fifty thousand expatriates. Reporting first to the South African National Defence Force, to comply with their awkwardly strict regulations, Kealey observed firsthand the SANDF's vast gaps of inexperience in dealing with the fallout of these radical wars, realizing further that foreign assistance was going to be insurmountably crucial to the survival of these people and their region. Being short on supplies and munitions notwithstanding, the numerous Islamic taboos and the South Africans' critical views toward refugee women only increased tensions among gathering allies, which split the allied tribes into even more jagged, irreparable shards.

But Kealey was not prepared to just sit on the bench and watch his side, the reasonable side, continually lose lives and ground. He had been trained to do far more than the SANDF even knew to ask for. In the mentally tormenting months he was out there, Kealey ran personally sanctioned special ops—planting perspicacious residents across enemy lines to filter critical intel back to the *good guys,* or *vriende,* as it had to be explained to the locals—and Kealey used the information to personally direct small bands of troops to several previously undisclosed mass graves containing nearly five thousand African corpses in various states of butchered decay.

Despite Janjaweed leader Musa Hilal's and President Omar al-Bashir's repeated admissions that death was merely the path that war took, *genocide* was still the only word for it. And even the windblown sands couldn't cover the killers' scent. Kealey only wished he

could follow the tracks all the way back to the mani-
acs' doorsteps, kick in the doors, and do the same to
their testicles. *If they even had any*.

Those intense desires to right terrible wrongs didn't
diminish easily, not without help. Giving it "time" didn't
relieve a warrior's hardened beliefs; it only made them
swell like a corpse left neglected. Some sights, some
smells, some instincts weren't meant to go away that
simply. If ever, at all.

After returning home and renting a small house in
Jesmond the previous winter, Kealey started to think
about teaching again, about taking a break from conflict. Certainly, there was something about conveying
critical information that was a passion of his. Besides
letting him ventilate some of his painfully accrued wisdom, he liked the way people, especially students, reacted when their minds opened in new directions. Like
the snaking vines that were steadily making their way
up the sides of his rented quarters, he enjoyed watching
them make progress, grow up, *grow stronger*.

And dealing with unfamiliar people was constantly
a challenge for Kealey. People always asked questions
and made him reassess his easily slung answers into
more exigent responses. In a classroom setting, despite
his deeply sympathetic almond-shaped eyes, he couldn't
get away with just surveillance; he had to inspire students, push them, make them understand ideas outside
their assorted upbringings. And students often required
from their teachers what they could not get from their
parents. They needed a scholar, someone who had all
the answers, or knew how and where to find them
quickly. Someone who could keep all the blank, staring

faces separate but could still get them to work together, no matter what the course, no matter what the assignment. *No matter what the mission.*

Unquestionably, there was concentrated pressure on being a teacher, and after considerable reflection, Kealey just wasn't sure he was ready for that sort of pressure test yet. He had put the world's humanity on the front line for years, and he didn't think he could manage to "phone it in" for another 180-day school year, at least not as capably as the students really needed. Instead he booked some guest lectures on global issues at the University of Virginia. That was where he'd met Allison's nineteen-year-old nephew Colin, who happened to attend school there.

Kealey was better adjusted than most special agents, but there were times when the deaths he'd caused and the risks he'd taken gripped his soul. He had said it himself once: "My life is like the old joke about the waiter who serves a matador burger at the restaurant in Vera Cruz one day apologizing to the patron, saying, 'Sometimes the bull wins.' "

Thinking of Colin became an act of synchronicity. Allison reached into the small leather purse under her arm and pulled out her cell phone.

"Hold on a sec," she said. "I want to see what's going on with Colin."

"Didn't you just talk to him a half hour ago?"

"Yes, but I want to check his posts."

"He's blogging?"

"Blogging? You're so twenty-ten," she said as she browsed down her queue of updates. "He's tweeting from the convention center for his student newspaper. It's called ambient journalism."

"I see. And how's that different from reporting?"

"Anyone can do it," she said.

"So the difference is it's for amateurs."

"That's harsh."

"Not at all," Kealey said. "Where's the editor, the veteran eyes?"

"It's the public, Ryan. The process has been democratized."

"Cheapened—no offense to Colin."

"You're wrong," she said confidently. "The good journalists get repeated hits. The bad ones are relegated to Facebook. The worst ones are left to *comment* on what's relegated to Facebook."

"No fair," Kealey said. "You lost me at 'repeated hits.' "

"It's no different than all the civilian eyes being used in the war on terror, watching for something unusual. Isn't that how we recruit in Afghanistan, Iraq? Find the people who have a knack for observing, blending in, collecting images on cell phones?"

"It's a good thing I'm retired," he said, shaking his head.

"Why? Technology doesn't scare you. You've used portable uplinks—"

"It's not the technology," he said. "It's the lack of privacy. The exponential noise. What spy would welcome that?"

Allison smiled at something she read on her display. She started pecking out words of her own. "Sorry. As much as I'm enjoying your 'poor us' monologue, I have to respond to Col's latest tweet."

"My point is made," he said confidently.

"Your point is beside the . . . ," she said, typing

slowly with the sides of her thumbs, pausing once or twice to check for misspellings before she returned the phone to her purse. "Done," she said.

"What's the word from the front?"

"The red carpet is lined with local paparazzi and ready for the glitterati to begin arriving."

Kealey glanced at his wristwatch. "It's a quarter to four," he said. "Why don't we take a leisurely walk back to the car, get my sports jacket and your high heels, and head over to the center?"

"Sounds good." She hooked her arm in Kealey's and gave the creature in the tank a final look as they strolled away. The medusa tumbled through the water on an internal current, bumped up randomly, briefly, against another jellyfish, then spiraled away. It was a beautiful, functional life.

But hollow, she thought. You could sum them up in a brochure. They weren't conflicted, the way Ryan Kealey was, yearning for peace but missing the thrill of the hunt, walking chastely beside her yet caring deeply and wanting more.

She hugged Kealey's arm a little tighter, cherishing the prolonged contact, and quietly thanked God for the good that came with the bad. It didn't make life easy, but they at least could actually *hold* each other.

And walk away from the fish tank.

The petite woman with short dark hair and Asian eyes approached room 306 of the Baltimore Hilton. There was a DO NOT DISTURB sign on the door handle. She ignored it and swiped her key card, entering the large, modern room with its panoramic view of the city's Inner Harbor.

The harbor had come a long way since its taxpayer-paid restoration in the early eighties. Much like Times Square, prostitutes and crackheads were "relocated" or arrested, and their tainted syringes and condoms, which clung to the grates of gutters, were finally cleaned out. Warehouses, crack dens, rotting fuel tankers, and out-of-favor dog tracks were replaced by new shopping malls, fine dining, a world-class aquarium, and a new convention center. These improvements helped draw other corporate entities back into the suddenly decorous setting, bringing tourists and families back into the historic marina and closer to its famous "star-spangled" Fort McHenry. And thanks in part to home-town hero Cal Ripken, Jr.—and his just over 2,000 consecutive played games record, which was quickly sneaking up on record holder Lou Gehrig's 2,130 games—the Baltimore Orioles got their new brick Camden Yards stadium in the early nineties, nearly completing the once-sagging city's late twentieth-century facelift.

But somehow, unlike Midtown Manhattan's redo, no matter how many distractions and special events tried to cover up Baltimore's seamy history, echoes still hummed from the still neglected canneries lining the shore, from years upon years of painfully obtained sugarcane and oysters-turned-mother-of-pearl that were toiled through and exported by gifted, poorly paid women who needed pennies for provisions and by skilled slaves who sorely needed their autonomy liberated, as is memorialized in the often sightseer-slighted Museum of Industry.

The woman put away her key card as the door clicked shut behind her, went to the dresser, and opened the second dresser drawer from the bottom. She withdrew a black, satchel-style photographer's bag, pulled it up by the strap, and hefted it over her shoulder. With its bulky contents, it weighed between 5 and 6 pounds, which was substantial but not heavy enough to make carrying it difficult.

She wore a sleeveless champagne-colored blouse and black Capri pants with a damask rose printed on the right outer thigh, and had a wireless mobile headset on her right ear. She also wore trendy sixteen-button gloves. In her line of work, she thought, women had two advantages: they could get close to men of influence, and it was easy not to leave fingerprints.

My line of work, twenty-one year-old Jasni Osman reflected bitterly.

Three years ago, the gifted gymnast was training for the Singapore Youth Olympics. All she had ever wanted was to express herself in movement, revel in the joy of being free. Then her eldest brother, Yusuf, a journalist, was arrested for what the ruling People's Action Party termed radical activities and sentenced to thirty years in prison. He suggested from his prison cell that she could help him by attending a meeting of *Jamaah Anshorut Tauhid* at a local mosque. Although she had to pray apart from the men, in keeping with strict tradition, the organization's religious instructors fully welcomed her as a daughter of Islam, instructing her on the lies and deceit of their government's rulers and the hateful imperialism of their masters, the United States.

Seven months later she was arrested in a raid on a

JAT camp at Aceh, Indonesia, accused of being a courier of illegal funds. Her captors were American agents, and she vividly recalled the terrible place to which she was brought in Jakarta, the suffocating torture by the CIA, the brutal sodomy committed by the *BIN,* the state's fearful *Badan Intelijen Negara.* Before her arrest, she had been interested only in bringing down the PAP and freeing her brother. Now she wanted jihad against all oppressors of the Muslim people.

Captivity and restraint were unthinkable to Jasni. It took repeated assaults from the *BIN,* in her cell, for Jasni to locate and steal the key to the restraints of the waterboard. After a near drowning the Americans left her—and she escaped, using her flexibility to hide and then to cling to the underside of the very nondescript scout vehicle they were using to hunt her. She returned to the mosque, committed to jihad, and was assigned by *JAT* leader Al Su'al to *Alef,* the group responsible for bringing bloodshed to the American homeland.

Today she would honor all those who had helped her on her journey—and her brother, who was still languishing in that filthy prison.

Before leaving the room, she slipped two fingers into the front change pocket of her Capris, extracted a red glass marble. She held it for a moment, enjoying its smooth, cool exterior and the strange heart that seemed to beat within. A sense of well-being permeated her, and she reluctantly put it in the drawer. Then she pushed the drawer shut, adjusted the satchel so it hung more comfortably on her shoulder, and bowed her head.

Oh, Allah, I will infiltrate the enemy and kill them without fear of death.

Jasni Osman left the room and went downstairs. Soon afterward a young male stepped from the elevator. Wearing a navy blue sports jacket and dark trousers, he used his key card to enter the room and took his specified package from the dresser.

It was shortly after 5:00 p.m. when he dropped his colored marble in the drawer and exited.

The order to strike would come over the headset exactly thirteen minutes later.

Colin Dearborn frowned as he got on the fast-food line at the rear of the convention center. Almost fifteen bucks for a chili dog, a side—chips or fries or a paper cup of slaw—and a Coke was nuts. The disorganized mass of customers, paying more attention to their cell phones than to the lines, and the glacially slow service didn't help.

Faced with the prospect of languishing there awhile, Colin slid his smartphone from his pants pocket to tweet his displeasure. As a contributing editor to the *Cavalier,* UVA's student newspaper, he'd been an enthusiastic champion of fully integrating the grid into its content delivery model. While he wasn't among the hard-core geeks who insisted print journalism was dead, it had clearly become the lowest-growth segment of a broader information market.

He opened his Twitter application and thought a moment, smoothing his chin beard between his thumb and forefinger. Getting his message across in 140 characters or less was an enjoyable challenge. In a sense it was like composing a haiku; you had to be super clear and tight with your writing.

His thumbs rapidly flurried over his touch pad as he typed: #Food vendors// This is a career fair. We r here looking 4 #JOBS//. #Affordable// hot dogs wanted. Lower prices, plz

Finishing the update, Colin scrolled down his timeline to check the responses to his earlier tweets and smiled to see one his aunt had pecked out minutes before: On way from aquarium w/RK. Bringing u jellyfish burger. Lettuce, tomato, fries. Pick tentacles w/stingers out b4 you eat.

Colin considered calling her the old-fashioned way so he could ask her to bring something to eat, but he figured he might miss her, anyway. He'd turned the volume down on his phone so it wouldn't sound in the middle of the interviews he had been conducting with company recruiters and potential employees, all of which would be used to write his story for the school paper.

Closing the app, he put the phone back into his pocket and realized the line in front of him had shortened while he'd stood there tweeting. It was still another ten minutes before he reached the cashier and five more before somebody gave him his order in one of those cardboard carrying trays that resembled egg crates.

Colin eased from the roiling mass of customers to look for a table, saw one on his left, and rushed over, holding his tray in front of him. A woman in a huggy tan-colored blouse and loose-fitting Capri pants with a big stuffed photographer's satchel on her shoulder stood directly between him and the table. He noticed her partly because she was very attractive, and also because she seemed strangely oblivious to the hustle and bustle around her—neither recruiter nor job seeker.

Reporter?

He was squeezing past the woman when she abruptly turned, banging her satchel into his elbow so hard that his soda cup tipped over sideways. Halting in his tracks, Colin tried to catch it with one hand but was too late. It had spilled over everything else on the tray, drenching his chili dog and fries in a foaming puddle of Coke.

Colin's angry eyes snapped up at the woman. She was oblivious to their collision, and it was then that he saw the earpiece of a Bluetooth headset on one side of her face and realized she must be listening to somebody over the phone.

"Pay attention, idiot!" he shouted after her.

People around him turned to see what was up as the woman made her way through the crowd as if he wasn't there.

Colin looked back down at his flooded tray. Frowning, he walked over to a row of trash bins on one side of the dining area. He shook off the soggy hot dog and gulped it down, then dumped his fries into the bin labeled FOOD and the tray into one that said RECYCLABLES. Turning, he saw that the table he'd been approaching was still unoccupied and headed for an empty seat. He needed a couple of minutes to chill—and post another status update. People: if you MUST carry a bag or backpack in crowded places, plz b aware of ur turn radius AND the people around you.

Colin put away the phone and looked around. Another thing about those bags, was anyone even scanning the oversize monstrosities? He'd seen guards in the center's Pratt Street lobby, but he was pretty sure they didn't have metal detectors at the door. Also, he hadn't noticed any security checks whatsoever over at the skyway entrance from the Hilton Hotel.

You can check on all that later, write it up as a sidebar, he thought as he eyed a bag of chips someone had left behind on another table. Scooting over and grabbing it, he felt slightly redeemed, as if the universe had regained a little bit of balance.

Tearing open the bag and snacking down happily, Colin left the food area, his eyes actively searching for the woman so he could return the nudge and even the scales a little more.

From the start, Julie Harper had realized that agreeing to cochair the planning committee *and* deliver the keynote speech for tonight's advanced nursing conference was a recipe for trouble. No one had forced her to micromanage the entire agenda. As her husband, Jon, had sweetly reminded her before they left the house, "Most of this is none of your goddamn business."

She didn't disagree. But in a town where image was everything and spies and saboteurs were everywhere, where a social disaster was also a political disaster, hands-on was the only way to be. Jon knew that, too. After three decades of marriage—most of that spent in Washington—he had come to rely on his wife to have his back like this.

What was it that the former first lady had told her? "You have to host to be seen. You have to host well to matter."

The Baltimore Convention Center contracted out to a professional catering service that set the course list and handled the food preparation for all its banquets. Even if you paid their fee and chose not to use the food, no one else got in the door. She was assured they knew their business and wouldn't need her input, but that would make this conference no different from every other conference.

That was not "hosting well."

So she fretted, even as H hour approached. Was the coquilles Saint-Jacques really the best choice for a seafood entrée? They had assured her it would be, but she'd insisted they use only a high-quality imported Gruyère in the recipe. She'd paid for the upgrade out of pocket. Or rather, her husband did. He hated to see her upset because of something that money could fix. And what about their wine pairing? Did they have a white varietal, something textured and flowery like Esprit de Beaucastel Blanc? As for the poultry offering, Julie had requested—and paid for—a substitution for the caterer's chicken Kiev. She wanted a lighter alternative. Lemon chicken, for example, was a reliable crowd pleaser. And what about the vegetarians or, God help her, the vegans? Asparagus with plum tomato casserole was the expensive solution.

Even now, as she greeted guests in the lobby outside the ballroom, standing near a table covered with name tags, Julie was mentally reviewing the seating chart, wondering if it was wise to segregate the Tea Party affiliates from the Democrats. It was a coin toss as to which was worse, a perceived snub or a political catfight.

". . . introduce you to Dr. José Colon."

Julie started slightly and glanced at Donna Palmer, the director of pediatric nursing at Sloan-Kettering in

New York and nominally her assistant coordinator for the event. Beside her, a young man stood in the hall, his hand extended.

"Good Lord!" Julie exclaimed. "Am I really looking at Helen Colon's little boy?"

"You are." He smiled. "Mom has spoken often of you over the years, Ms. Harper."

"What a dear she is! I haven't seen her since our Mayo Clinic days." Julie was suddenly choked up—pressure waiting for an emotional trigger like this. "How is your mother?"

"Very well," he said. "Mom does in-homes for an insurance company. She told me I have to take pictures of us together, but you're busy. I'll find you later?"

"Please do," she replied. She almost called him back to take the photo now—*Carpe diem,* she thought—but he had moved on.

Donna ushered over a man and a young girl. She turned to them and smiled. "Mr. Reed Bishop and his daughter Laura," Donna said.

Julie took their hands, one in each of her own. Her eyes were beginning to glisten. The whole thing was more emotional than she had expected.

"Your wife's trust fund," she said to Bishop, "your mother"—she smiled at Laura—"has been a lifesaver for our organization."

"Caregiving was her passion," Bishop said. "I couldn't think of a better way to honor her."

"Thank you," Julie said. She looked at the slender girl with strawberry blond hair. "Are you going to be a nurse?" she asked.

Laura Bishop nodded. "I'm getting my dad to stop smoking."

Reed Bishop smiled awkwardly under Julie's playful scowl. The words *secondhand smoke* all but floated above her head.

"That's a very noble goal," Julie said. "I'm sure your dad means to help."

"Every bloody inch of the way," he said.

Another round of thank-yous and the Bishops moved on. Julie looked past Donna at the next arrival. As she was shaking the hand of Connecticut senator Victoria Bundonis, she noticed a man standing just inside the door. He looked to be in his late twenties. He was wearing a navy blue sports jacket and dark trousers and carried an expensive-looking hard-shell briefcase. What caught her eye was his posture—slack and loose limbed, his eyes lowered. As she watched, he was visibly swaying on his feet.

As the senator moved on, Julie took Donna by her elbow and pointed from her waist. "Do you know him?"

Donna glanced briefly at the man. "No. It appears as if he spent too much time dodging the afternoon heat in the hotel's cocktail lounge."

"I don't know. Looks to me like he's dancing to his iPod. See the earbud?"

"I do now." Donna was reaching for her cell phone. "Should I call security?"

"No. They'll stick out."

"Aren't they supposed to?" Donna asked.

One of the things Julie insisted on was that her guests not be inconvenienced with security checks. Between herself and Donna, they knew almost every one of the 250 people who were attending. To search them would have been insulting. Still, this merited watching.

"Wait until everyone is inside and chatting," Julie said.

The women resumed welcoming new arrivals.

Glancing at his watch, the man with the briefcase finally came over. His blue wristband meant he'd paid over two thousand dollars to attend the dinner. Donna put out her hand as he approached.

"Good evening," she said. "I'm Donna Palmer, your cohost, and this is Ms. Julie Harper."

He bowed in a slightly courtly fashion but said nothing.

"The name tags are in alphabetical order," Donna went on. "If you'd like, you can check your briefcase at the counter behind the table."

"Thank you," he said as he scanned the table for the plastic tag.

Julie couldn't place the accent. It sounded Israeli, and he had what looked like a deep Mediterranean tan. As he reached for the tag, she noted that his name was Michael Lohani. It meant nothing. She exchanged looks with Donna, who shrugged. The name wasn't familiar to her, either. It was then that Julie saw the way he held his briefcase against his side, his fingers tightly clenched around its handle, his shoulder dropped low, as though it were quite heavy.

He moved ahead with a weak smile. Julie turned casually to watch. He didn't check his briefcase but went right to the ushers at the door.

"Okay, something's not right," Julie said to Donna. "Call security."

* * *

Zuhair Khan Afridi paused in the tiled, narrow court outside the Hilton's Eutaw Street entrance, his hand closing around the marble deep inside his trouser pocket, rolling the smooth glass ball between his fingertips. Silently, without moving his mouth, bowing only slightly, reverently at the knees, he repeated the affirmations he'd learned at the camp where his mind and body were healed and he received his instruction as a *mujahid*. The words had helped to dispel the painful recollections of his treatment by the American CIA: the blindfolded trips by plane, helicopter, and van; the interrogations and repeated water tortures; the rats in his tiny cell.

He had waited out these final hours at an afternoon baseball game, reviewing the plan in his head as he gathered himself for his task. Zuhair had paid no attention to the game until shortly before he left Camden Yards, when people suddenly began exiting the ballpark.

Had someone identified him and given an alert? Was the stadium being evacuated? That was when he realized the visiting Boston Red Sox had a large 10–0 lead in the eighth inning, and that people were leaving.

Zuhair wore an Orioles baseball cap and jersey outside his baggy chinos, aware he would be inconspicuous enough disguised as one of the many who had come to cheer the home team. He departed with the others, confident that his somber mood would be perceived as nothing more than the disappointment of a fan.

As the time approached, he vacated his seat in the right-field stands, exited the park through Gate A, and went to room 306 at the hotel. Zuhair closed the door behind him and briefly looked out at the busy piers, then glanced over at the wall-length furniture unit to his right. A combination dresser and desk, it had drawers at his end, a plasma television in the center, and an office chair pushed underneath it near the window.

Zuhair went directly to the dresser and produced the yellow marble from his pants pocket. Opening the bottom drawer, he found a plastic grocery bag with a bulky object folded inside. He removed the bag and dropped the marble into the drawer before shutting it, leaving it as confirmation that he, and no one else, had removed the bag and its contents.

Not that anyone would ever find them. These tokens were for the team only, to let one another know they had each made the pickup and no one else. Zuhair left his marble simply to complete the ritual.

They'd given him the belt, not one of the overstuffed backpacks or shoulder bags. He had no preference, as long as it got the job done.

Inside the grocery bag was a nylon weight belt of the sort designed for scuba divers. He momentarily set it down and reached behind his back to unclip a safety pin that had cinched the waistband of his oversize chinos so they would fit him, letting the pants fall almost to his knees. Then he opened his baseball jersey, put on the belt, and adjusted it using a Velcro closure strap. The waistband would now close snugly over his middle—and the scuba belt's explosive-filled pouches—without the safety pin.

After he'd rebuttoned the baseball jersey and carefully smoothed it over his chinos, Zuhair moved past the double beds to the desktop for his second piece of equipment. He slid the chair out, found the computer

carry bag that had been left there for him, and unzipped its outer compartment. He transferred the wireless detonators it contained to his pocket. The C4
charges and battery inside the belt accounted for two-
thirds of its 7-pound weight. The rest of the weight
consisted of nails and shards of glass. When triggered,
the explosive charge of the bomb and his two shrapnel
packages would kill anyone within 10 or 15 feet of the
blast.

He left the room and strode along Eutaw, the Baltimore Convention Center casting its expansive shadow
to his right, beyond the parking lots, train tracks, and
wide crosstown thoroughfare.

Now he stared up at the enclosed sky bridge that
spanned the court, connecting the Hilton's main building and business meeting facility and then leading on
across Howard Street into the convention center. Peering through its glass-paneled sides, he could see long
streams of people moving in both directions—the ball
game and other events had filled the center and caused
nearly every room in the hotel to be occupied.

*Oh, Allah, our caravan seeks your assistance inflict-
ing the maximum damage,* he prayed. *We are honored
to sacrifice our lives in your path.*

Zuhair lowered his gaze from the sky bridge, pressing the earbud of his Bluetooth headset more securely
into place with a fingertip, watching a pair of attractive
young women cross his path as they approached the
hotel entrance. One of them made chance eye contact
with him and pointed to the Red Sox emblem on her
T-shirt. She smiled a gloating smile and moved on with
her friend. He smiled back, feeling the confidence of
one who walked freely among his enemies, wrapped in

their very skin, unnoticed as he prepared to attack. Perhaps he would kill the woman and her friend.

Yes. That appealed to him.

Following the women, he made his way back into the hotel lobby. They sat, probably to wait for friends or plan what they were going to do for the rest of the day. Zuhair looked around the crowded space, at the support columns. He went there to wait for the call.

Allah, forgive his vanity, but he experienced something of what the Prophet himself must have felt when he sat in his cave, meditating, and the word of God was revealed to him. Zuhair could tell the women exactly what they were going to do today, just minutes from now.

They were going to die.

Julie Harper looked at the diamond-studded Cartier watch her husband had given her for their twenty-fifth anniversary. She touched it, treasuring it, treasuring him, and saw that she had just fifteen minutes before the doors closed and the event officially began.

Julie was backstage, reviewing her welcoming remarks, when her cell phone rang in her clutch bag. The tone, assigned to her husband's number, was a snippet of "My White Night" from *The Music Man,* the show they saw on their first date. It was a regional production, nothing spectacular, but they were sobbing and in love by the time Harold hugged Marian at the end of act 2. Julie smiled every time she heard it. Jon knew that, knew how tense she'd be.

"Thanks," she said, picking up. "I needed that."

"I figured you would," he said. "You'll be great."

"As long as I don't trip and the microphone works, I think I'm good."

"Big turnout?" he asked.

"Fabulous."

"I saw you had a security alert."

"Doesn't the CIA's deputy director have anything better to do?"

"Puckett received it, sent it on. What's up?"

"Guy came in with a briefcase, acting strange," she said. "He's at the bar, talking on his Bluetooth. Center security is watching him. I had Donna check. He's with Interglobal Pharmaceuticals, a sales rep."

"Must be some very special samples he's got."

"I guess." Julie was looking at the man. She saw the head of security, Bill Roche, standing at the other end of the bar, facing him.

"Well, I don't want to keep you," Jon said. "I just wanted to say I'm so proud."

"Thanks. And, Jon? Don't beat yourself up for being in Washington."

"Hon, I'm not—"

"I think you are," she interrupted. "I hear it in your voice."

He said nothing.

"I'm telling you it's okay."

"No, it isn't," he admitted. "Tonight's an important moment in your life. I should be sharing it with you."

"President Brenneman needed you," she said. "I don't—"

She froze as she noticed Michael Lohani's hand emerge from his pants pocket. He raised a cylindrical object that looked like a pen. And then she saw his eyes turn upward and his mouth form words and the security guard look over. . . .

In the final instant before the explosions, she became conscious of her husband repeating her name over the phone. "Julie? Julie?"

And then the roar swallowed everything.

CHAPTER 3

BALTIMORE, MARYLAND

Ryan Kealey and Allison Dearborn had walked along the brick pier where day-trippers were moving by in noisy clusters. Beyond them came the high, excited voices of children farther down the pier, where they were lined up with their parents for paddleboat rentals. A stranger meekly approached the pair and began hashing out a story about how he'd been separated from his friends the drunken night before and just needed a few more bucks to take the Greyhound back to his place in nearby Owings Mills. Apologizing to the stranger, more for their dismissal of him personally than of his far-fetched story, neither agent felt it necessary to flash their official credentials to further discourage the poorly rehearsed beggar, who was still wearing a noticeably fresh hospital bracelet.

They reached the indoor garage on the corner of Charles and Conway at 5:06, exactly nine minutes before the chain of explosions rocked the convention center.

The attendants had parked Kealey's Saab 9-3 Aero on the ground level, nosing it against the garage's outer wall, and he needed only to inform them he wanted something out of the backseat to be waved along.

"Think I'll freshen up my makeup while I have a chance," Allison said as they approached the silver convertible. "I want to be at my spiffiest for Julie."

Kealey got his remote key fob out of his pocket and pressed the button to unlock the doors. She sat in the passenger's seat and flipped down the visor to use the mirror. He got his jacket and her shoes from the backseat.

"Allison, I still haven't thanked you."

"For what?" she asked after applying lipstick. "Dragging you to see my former teacher's keynote speech at a nursing conference?"

"The Harpers are my friends, too," Kealey said. "No, what we were talking about earlier. I was in a bad place when we met. You pulled me out of it."

"A jellyfish isn't a man, and a man isn't a jellyfish. Anyway, you did most of the heavy lifting."

He laughed. "If by that you mean after a couple of weeks I did more than grunt one-word answers to your questions, okay."

She quickly brushed her hair, frowned, muttered, "Best I can do," then slipped on her heels.

"You look aces," he said.

"Yeah, thanks. Two minutes of humidity and I'm the Wicked Witch of the West." She faced him in the hot, stuffy garage. "That process, emerging from a depressive emotional shutdown and post-traumatic stress, is one of the toughest climbs a patient can face. Tougher than most suicide attempts, who have already accepted their situation and want help. You were in some pretty serious situations in South Africa, with the security of our nation squarely on your shoulders. That's what we euphemistically call 'Deep Rubble' in our business."

"We have another word for it," Kealey said.

"I know," she said, shutting the door. "Those of us in wood-paneled offices try to have a *little* more class."

"Whatever you call it, I've got a long way to go. But I couldn't have gotten where I am without you," he said. "I haven't *said* that before, and wanted to."

They looked at each other a little longer than client-patient propriety should allow. It was Kealey who turned, who locked the doors, who offered her his hand and started back toward the street.

They walked silently up the ramp toward sunlight.

"You're thinking again," she said.

"Tough habit to break," he replied. "It's all you do sometimes for hours on a stakeout. Look and think."

"You're not in Sarajevo or Cape Town. You're going to a nice, boring dinner," she reminded him.

"Right. Focus."

"Tell me, is it a good thought or bad?"

"Somewhere in the middle," he said. "I've told you about Maine, about the house where Katie Donovan and I lived in Cape Elizabeth."

"A little."

"There's an old suspension bridge that runs into the state on I-Ninety-five," Kealey said. "Katie's parents lived outside Boston, and one day we went across that bridge during winter, when there were no leaves on the trees. Off on a hill we saw this old house with a FOR SALE sign out front, so we decided to check it out. The place was a shambles, built around eighteen-forty, abandoned for over a decade, completely run-down. But there was something special about it, and we were able to buy it for pocket change. We went up whenever we could, a couple times a year. I did all the stonework, some carpentry, and was convinced it was where I'd settle for the rest of my life." He grew reflective. "I remember thinking at the time that it was probably tougher to restore a home than to build one. To look for all the leaks and cracks and rot and fix them without destroying the rest of the structure. But there was something rewarding about it, as well. I guess what I'm feeling now, my appreciation, is knowing that you're doing what I did, getting in there and making something whole—"

The rest of the sentence was lost as the first blast pounded the air, pushing a concussive wave through the concrete structure.

Kealey's first thought was that a cannon had been fired at historic Fort McHenry, which was situated nearby. But then there were two more blasts in rapid succession, each from very different places. He knew at once that it was not a celebration.

"My God, what's going on?" Allison asked.

"Stay here," Kealey snapped and ran.

Allison took off her heels and ran behind him. He didn't have time to argue.

He reached the Saab and popped the trunk. It was mostly bare: a tire jack, a plastic jerrican, a first-aid kit, a couple of neatly folded blankets . . . and a padded black pistol bag about the size of a typical carryall.

Moments after telling him that he was going to a dinner, that he was not in a war zone, Allison watched Kealey arm himself with movements so precise, they were almost mechanical. He pulled off his jacket, then opening the bag, he took out a right-handed shoulder harness and put it on over his shirt. Then he produced a pistol rug containing a Sig P229R chambered for .40 S&W rounds, a more powerful variant of the 9-millimeter variety that was standard issue for the U.S. Secret Service. Transferring the gun to his holster, he reached into the bag again for his backup—a Beretta 9mm. This one *was* a nine, lighter and with quicker action than the other.

"Did you ever learn to use one of these?" he asked Allison. "Take basic firearms training, anything like that while you were with the Bureau?"

She shook her head. "It was never intended that I shoot my patients." She watched with rising alarm. "We were just attacked. Hit again."

"Yeah."

Kealey set the gun down in the trunk and reached back into the bag for his concealment holster. Sliding the Beretta into it, he tucked the holster into his pants behind his right hip and clipped it to his belt. Then he opened one of the bag's side compartments and extracted a doubled-handled metal knife, a Filipino *balisong*. Kealey put the knife in his jacket pocket and reached into his bag one more time before finally dropping it back into the trunk. He removed a magazine pouch and nylon web harness, strapping it on so the magazine pouch rested snugly against his left side.

He shrugged into his jacket. "You really need to get out of here."

"No. I'm coming. Open the door. I want my other shoes."

"Listen, Allison," he said. "I don't know if this is over—"

"I don't care, Ryan. I have medical training. That may be more important than a gun."

He looked at her. He took a deep breath, exhaled, remotely popped the back-door lock, then slammed the lid of his trunk.

"All right," he said. "In that case, stay close."

They emerged in the humid air, made even stiller, more uncomfortable, by the dust that already hung in the air. Cars were screeching to a stop in the eastbound lanes approaching Charles Street or veering toward its central traffic island to avoid collisions. Kealey looked up, saw rolling clouds of dull white smoke, typical of urban demolition. Only this wasn't a controlled blast. The smoke was coming from the direction of the convention center. Out on the sidewalk pedestrians had reacted to the explosions with shock and confusion, many of them becoming rooted where they stood, others scattering wildly across the sidewalk and roadway or trampling the traffic island's manicured grass. Some were wriggling fingers in their ears, trying to clear hearing impacted by the blasts.

There was a crash on Charles, and Kealey whipped his head around as a semitrailer scissored across the intersection. The large semi partially overturned in the middle of the road, where its driver apparently attempted to make a hard stop to avoid the fender bender in front of him. Just as on Conway, the men and women in the crosswalk were either frozen with shock or scrambling around in a panic, some running away from the blast, a few toward it, a few others stopping to help the driver of the semi.

A few seconds later, Kealey heard a rumbling noise from somewhere behind him, the unmistakable groan of twisting, tortured metal and a monstrous *snap*. It was followed by a crash that shook everything around him, sending tremors through the street.

"Ryan, look!" Allison screamed from behind him. "God help us. Look over there!"

He turned back, following her eyes. The hotel sky bridge had come down, and a gray ram of smoke and dust was pushing up the block, whipping through the trees on the traffic island, rushing over the taxicabs at the stand across the street to coat their yellow bodies with cinders. Dashing blindly for cover, people had thrown their hands over their noses and mouths as the choking ash swept over them.

"The hotel is burning!" she said.

Kealey had already caught sight of orange licks through the cloud. His temples throbbed. He heard sirens and clattering fire bells, the sounds blaring up from every direction. Going to the hotel was not an option. They'd choke before they got there. The convention center was a better bet. It appeared to have taken two hits, judging from the three blasts they heard and the twin columns rising from the site, but the boxy structure covered a much larger area, with discrete support sections. There would be more ways to get in.

And then, suddenly, there was another noise, so ordinary against the dissonant clamor of the alarms that it drew his attention: the electronic chirp of a cell phone alert. He turned to Allison, who was digging at her purse with trembling fingers. She fumbled out her phone and thumbed the HOME button.

"Colin?" Kealey asked.

"I think so," she said, fighting tears. "I enabled Twitter pushes when we left the aquarium." She nervously scrolled down the timeline queue to read her updates. She stopped, her eyes on the display, her cheeks draining of color.

"What is it?" Kealey demanded.

She just stood there, gaping mutely at the phone, a numb expression on her face. Kealey stepped closer, took the cell from her cold, loose fingers, and scanned the messages on its screen. The last one was a post from Colin. It consisted of only two words: Help us.

"Jesus," she said.

"Do you know if he was near Julie's event?" Kealey asked. "I'm guessing that was at least one of the targets."

"The food vendors are usually set up nearby, so yes—"

"All right," he said. "Maybe we can get to him and to Julie. Do you have her number?"

Allison nodded and scrolled to it. She pressed the name, the phone rang, but the call went to voice mail. Allison put the phone away. Her dusty cheeks were tear-streaked.

Kealey cupped her face reassuringly, then turned toward Pratt Street to the north. Beyond about halfway up the block the downtown skyline looked blurry and indistinct, as if it had been partially erased. Aside from the smeary glow of emergency lights—the fact that they had come on meant the main power was gone—

and the scattered, ghostly forms of pedestrians, it was impossible to see anything clearly through the haze.

"We need to keep ourselves from breathing in the fumes and dust," he said.

Allison reached into her purse and produced a floral silk scarf, yellow and violet chrysanthemums against a green background.

"I've got this," she said, handing it to him.

Kealey took out his knife and cut the scarf up the center. He gave one half to Allison and wrapped his segment over his nose and mouth like a bandanna. He helped her do the same as people ran past them. He heard the sirens of emergency vehicles in the distance.

Her cell phone beeped again. She looked at it.

"Colin's checking to see if I got his last post. *Shit!* I didn't even think to answer him."

"It's all right," Kealey said. "Ask him where he is, any landmarks we should look for. Tell him to keep it up. We need his exact location."

She nodded, typed out her message, sent it. "Okay," she said. "Done."

He put a hand on her shoulder, kept it there, felt her relax a little. As a young lieutenant with the 3rd SFG in Bosnia, he'd learned to read his men's pressure gauges before leading them into peril. A certain amount of tension could keep you sharp, but too much and you became distracted. Allison seemed as steady as could be expected.

Kealey looked north toward Charles, swiveled around, and looked west. The smoke was lighter on Conway Street and thickest over the rooftops several blocks to the northwest, where it was brewing up in a massive rooster tail, its dark fan-shaped crest spreading out almost directly overhead.

"What do you know about the layout of the center?" he asked.

"Not much," she said, raising her voice to be heard through the scarf and the surrounding commotion. "It's really two different buildings. The one right here on Charles is the original center."

"Where is the job fair being held?"

"The newer one," she said. "The main entrance is on Howard Street. It's a busy part of town."

"Busy in what way?"

"The warehouse on Eutaw borders on the Orioles' ballpark," she said. "There are shops on the main floor, offices, just a lot of things like that."

Kealey continued looking east, lowering his gaze to the long, ruler-straight building that cut off Conroy about a quarter mile up.

"The sky bridge connected the Hilton Hotel to the convention center, right?"

She nodded. "Across Howard, where the entrance is."

"We'll never get in that way."

"There's another walkway between the old and new parts of the center on Sharp Street, a smaller version of the sky bridge. It crosses Conway a block or so up, right past Old Otterbein."

"Past what?"

"Otterbein's a landmark church," she said. "When you turn up Sharp, there are entrances to both buildings on either side of the street. The walkway runs above them."

Kealey tried to shut out the frenzied commotion

around them. Charles was impassable, with vehicular traffic at a standstill all the way from Pratt Street and people moving between it. The first responders would already be establishing control of the remaining access points to the area. There was a time when his CIA credentials would have gotten him past whatever barriers they raised—but it had been years since he'd had any official connection to the Company, and the expired ID he'd never quite managed to clean out of his card holder wouldn't bear scrutiny.

He gazed up Conroy. While traffic there was also at a crawl, it hadn't gotten nearly as bad as on Charles, probably because it wasn't a crosstown artery. Nor did he see any police cars or firefighting vehicles shooting along it yet—for the same reason, he suspected. They would have gone directly to the scene of the explosion on Howard, then cordoned off the roads and sidewalks there around the center's newer extension. The back and side approaches were the last that would be restricted—and therefore were his best shot at gaining entry.

"We'll take Conroy," he said. "I'm going to need you to guide us as we get closer." He gazed into her red, tearing eyes, then clutched her hand. "I'm glad you overruled me."

She offered the thinnest of smiles beneath the mask as they moved into the maelstrom.

CHAPTER 4
ATLANTA, GEORGIA

The red and orange dahlias already clipped and in water, Jacob Edward Trask lifted one of the galvanized-steel flower containers that Robinson had filled and set out for him. He carefully checked that the water level wasn't too high, then moved down the greenhouse aisle toward the gerberas. It would be another half hour or so before his visitor arrived from Atlanta's Hartsfield-Jackson, assuming light airport traffic on Interstate 20. That the roads would be clear seemed almost a given; everyone would be watching the news on whatever devices one watched the news these days. He was no longer sure.

That's part of the problem, the sixty-four-year-old man thought, his thin lips tightening. *News comes from networks, from cable, from newspaper Web sites, from amateurs on the scene, from bloggers who turn fact into opinion, and then from other bloggers who transmit that opinion as fact. It's the game of telephone with pathetic results.*

It was another component of the continuing fragmentation of America. Disinformation and misinformation were an extension of the misbegotten hyphenates—the African-Americans, the Muslim-Americans, the Gay-Americans, and the latest absurdity, the Single-Mom-Americans. Nearly one hundred years ago, Theodore Roosevelt had warned about the carving of the nation. "A hyphenated American is not an American at all," he'd said. "The one absolutely certain way of bringing this nation to ruin would be to permit it to become a tangle of squabbling nationalities."

Dressed in a gray sweat suit, the tall, lanky, still-athletic man continued to move down the line. Reaching the trays of potted daisies, Trask began clipping them with his floral shears, cutting the stems at an angle to give them more surface area for water absorption. He would place each flower in the container, one at a time, after pinching the dead cuttings off their stems. Then he would give them to the executive housekeeper to have them displayed around the mansion, where he could see them and be comforted by them. They were like children, except that they didn't fight over the estate.

Trask enjoyed his horticulture, particularly at dusk, when the wafting fragrance was at its peak. And especially now, when his mind was consumed with all that needed to be done. The physical activity and sensory input helped him to relax, to forget the awesome burden he had taken on.

He smiled inside when he thought back to all the times he had heard himself referred to as a dabbler, a dilettante. That had not happened so much in recent years. There was a benefit to seeing one's youth recede farther and farther. On the one hand there was wisdom accrued and insights formed. On the other, the insatiable paparazzi, who had once fixated on him, had long since moved on to newer, younger heirs, men and women who knew how to play the media rather than duck it. That was not a skill he had ever mastered. His methods had been pointlessly confrontational, since only that fed the beast.

Even his own child was largely immune. Industrialists' heirs were out of favor, along with the scions of tobacco, steel, and auto-industry families. They were toxic by association, too twentieth century, too American. While U.S. consumers were still passively fixated on young celebrities in rehab for drugs or drink or sex or food addictions, the international gossip trade wanted to know about the youthful tech titans, not from Silicon Valley, but from Japan's Fukuoka City and India's Bangalore. They wanted more about the "green teens," the youthful champions of clean energy in Birdsville, Queensland, and Jesmond, British Columbia. Outside of the United States, visionaries were the new idols. Other nations were producing the next generation of Fords and Carnegies, of Jobses and Gateses. Their lives were followed and actively emulated.

They were on track to shape the future.

While we are marginalized, he thought, *our carcass picked apart by speculators and gloaters, by the third-world mouths we continue to feed and protect to maturity so they can spit in our eye.*

The glass door opened silently behind him. Trask knew it from the faint whisper of cool air that brushed his neck. He also knew, without turning, the angel-light tread of his valet, Peter Robinson.

"Sir?" said Robinson.

"She's here?" Trask asked without turning.

"Yes, sir," the young man replied.

"Take her to the sunroom. I'll be there when I am ready."

"Yes, sir." There was a catch in his voice.

"Mr. Robinson, what's the latest on Baltimore?"

"The situation is still very chaotic," Robinson replied. He seemed pleased to have been asked, allowed to react. "No one seems to know whether this is an isolated incident or part of a larger-scale event. Homeland Security has promised a press conference at seven p.m."

"Thank you," Trask said. "It's horrible, but we will survive this, Mr. Robinson."

"Yes, sir," he replied.

The door shut, and Trask placed the daisy he'd just clipped into the container. He'd never thought he would treat such delicate things with care. As a boy, he would take pleasure in kicking up the moist soil in his mother's garden, unearthing the thin, spirally roots of the freshly planted flowers of the month. He'd hated how she bragged about them. Her hands never even touched the dirt. It was always the gardener. Never her. That was his small way of getting back, taking some of her unearned credit away. Too bad the dog had to take the fall.

Setting the shears on a towel-covered tray at the end

of the aisle, he walked to the small locker beside the door. He changed into a leisure suit, then paused to mop the perspiration from his face and brush back his full head of gray hair. He checked his appearance in the mirror before closing the locker and heading out.

You never cared how you looked until there was no one around to take pictures, he thought ironically. Yet it wasn't vanity that drove him. This was no different than the maestro who tugged the hem of his swallow-tail jacket before heading onstage or the on-deck batter checking his helmet. He was preparing to put something in motion. Every man in every field had a moment of reflection, of self-examination, before setting out. The physical manifestation of that was just an excuse to pause, to steel oneself.

He was ready. Great events were about to transpire. History was not just going to be made.

It was going to be directed.

It was with rage and a sickening sense of déjà vu that Jessica Muloni watched the events in Baltimore play out on the large flat-screen TV. It reminded her—as it would anyone of a certain age—of the attacks on September 11, 2001.

She had been newly arrived in Washington then, recently graduated with a master's degree from John Jay College of Criminal Justice, where she had been recruited to work at the CIA. She was outside at Langley, having arrived at the office later than usual, when she heard the distant explosion at the Pentagon, saw the black smoke curling upward.

Those attacks in New York and Washington were many things, but most of all they were a bookmark. Thereafter, like so many other people, whenever she heard a siren or smelled tart smoke that lodged in the throat—even at a barbecue or passing a car fire on the highway—the entire event came back.

As it did now.

No one knew yet whether these new attacks were homegrown or the efforts of a foreign network, whether they were an isolated occurrence or the first part of a wave. Just like on September 11, Langley and the White House and the Capitol and other buildings were evacuated, because no one was sure what was happening.

But there was one difference between 2001 and today. Now Muloni was an agent and she had a mission. And it was clear that her mission was suddenly more significant, more *urgent,* than it had been when she left D.C. ninety minutes before.

She turned from the TV at the gate and headed to the baggage claim area to rent a car. There must be no record of her destination; indeed, only her supervisor and Jacob Trask knew about it.

She had read numerous files on the reclusive billionaire. A profligate for the first decades of his life, spending exorbitant amounts on cars, boats, and turning his home into a fortress. The perfect place to stay out of the spotlight and the perfect excuse not to leave his home office. If there needed to be a gala or benefit, it could be hosted at his estate, where after an hour he could tuck himself safely away in one of his hiding rooms.

Trask was a master of hiding out, something he'd

perfected in his teen years. The day Trask got his driver's license in 1965, he uncharacteristically got the courage to ask his boarding school crush, Kathleen, to the drive-in to see *The Beach Girls and the Monster,* a beach murder mystery starring Jon Hall and Sue Casey. Halfway through the opening credits Kathleen noticed Christopher Andrews. The most athletic, the most likely to succeed and, apparently, the most likely to take whatever he wanted. Kathleen made up some excuse—Trask couldn't recall it, or maybe he pushed it out of his mind—as he watched her toss her thick golden hair over her shoulder and slide into the front seat of Christopher's '64 Morgan Plus Four Plus. Trask finished the movie solo. Seventeen years later he introduced the extremely rare '64 Morgan Plus Four Plus to his personal collection.

Things changed for Trask upon the unexpected death of his father, Clark Trask. According to the files on Trask, it was the discovery of a cache of letters written by his grandfather, Foster Trask, that had turned the young man around: his father was the beneficiary of shrewd, if contemptible, dealings his own father had enjoyed with the Nazis. Foster Trask was a junk man–turned–antique dealer who had buyers in Scandinavia, Switzerland, and Morocco. During the final days of the Third Reich, he had set up a small bank to channel mountains of cash from German institutions—concealed in Spanish chests, Louis XV dressers, and other pieces—to banks in South America . . . for a 10 percent fee, of course. The German expatriates benefited and the Trask family benefited, though young Clark was given all the credit.

Not only was Jacob Trask humiliated by his family's close association with Hitler's top advisors, but he was liberated by the revelation that his father was not the wunderkind investor he had pretended to be, but a front for the secret dealings of his own father. Since that discovery, Jacob Trask had used his resources to stand up for America, first against the Japanese takeover in the 1980s—when he bought an interest in every publicly traded company that mattered—then against the Saudi buying spree in the 1990s, during which he outbid the Saudis for property and corporations wherever possible, and now against the slow Chinese influx of capital. Muloni was particularly impressed as she considered what a remarkable mind Jacob Trask must possess to have foreseen that a mission like this would be necessary.

Muloni had been an active participant in the war on terror for her entire career, but now she would be on the front lines. She had a sense of being somewhat in control, which set her apart from other anxious passengers and airport workers who were looking into one another's eyes, searching for anything foreign or dangerous.

She stopped as she entered the main terminal, looked around for a driver with a card that had her host's name. She saw none.

After a moment of scanning the busy hall, Muloni noticed a liveried older woman approaching.

"I was afraid you had missed the flight," she said.

"Sorry. No . . . I was watching the news at the gate."

"Tragic. Just so tragic."

Muloni nodded.

"I'm Liz," the driver said.

"Happy to meet you."

"Do you have any luggage, ma'am?" the driver asked.

"I don't," she replied.

"Will you follow me, then?" She smiled.

Muloni nodded. It was a nice smile, woman to woman, probably warmer than most new arrivals got. It was probably more than most of her passengers would have noticed. It didn't unnerve Muloni, and it shouldn't have surprised her that her host would have given her driver a photograph to identify the pickup. A name scrawled on a piece of cardboard was not the style of Jacob Trask.

There was no small talk. The silver-haired driver moved purposefully through the crowd; she was only about five foot two, but she had a no-nonsense stride. There was a spotless white stretch limousine at the curb, with a uniformed officer with Airport Security Services standing beside it. He wasn't ticketing the vehicle or waiting for it to be towed. He was there so it wouldn't be.

When the driver came through the automatic doors, the big man tipped his cap and walked away.

Clout, Muloni thought. A barrage of synonyms followed involuntarily. *Influence, sway, wealth, control.*

Power.

The democrat in her recoiled slightly at the thought of one man getting special treatment. But the child of a lower-middle-class home enjoyed being around it. The higher she'd risen in the CIA, the more she'd been exposed to privilege and the more she liked it. Like the reason she was here. It wasn't just to give her a bit of control in a disordered world. It was to be part of something important, something special.

Muloni stepped into the car, filled with a feeling that was closer to resolve than to optimism.

But today that was enough.

CHAPTER 5
BALTIMORE, MARYLAND

Jostling through knots of confused, terrified pedestrians about a quarter mile west of the garage, Kealey and Allison saw the church a short distance ahead, its white-domed bell tower rising above Conway.

"That's it," Allison said, panting a little. "Sharp Street's on the other side."

They raced by an outdoor parking lot toward the churchyard, Kealey gripping her hand. Then he stopped abruptly a step or two past the lot's chain-link fence. In front of him was a curbless lane running off to the right.

"What's this road?" he asked.

"That's the back of the original center," Allison told him. "Events aren't held there anymore, so I'm guessing the road's used for deliveries."

Kealey looked up the strip of pavement for another ten seconds or so. He noticed a car pulled parallel to the building at the end—a small black sedan. There was another vehicle in front of it, possibly another sedan. With the church partially obstructing his view, Kealey could barely see the rear bumpers or tell if either car was occupied.

"Ryan, what's wrong?"

He didn't answer. He wasn't sure *wrong* was the word. He could not even explain what it was about those cars that had snagged his interest, other than that he couldn't think of a reason for them to be there. They certainly weren't delivery vehicles, and they seemed a little too sharp, too clean to belong to staffers or folks who had come over to look for work on their day off. Anyway, why would just two cars have parked *here?*

"It's nothing," he said, nodding up the block. "Come on—we'd better hustle."

They went on past the front churchyard, then jogged around the corner past the west gate. The smoke was thicker here, the noxious odor easily penetrating their improvised face masks. The moment they turned the corner, Kealey saw the roadway curve slightly to the left, to the mouth of what looked like a narrow ramp behind the original convention center. The second-story walkway between the old building and its extension was no more than 15 yards ahead, along with the doors Allison had told him about.

He quickened his pace, his hand firmly around Allison's. Ten yards to go now. There were flashing red, yellow, and blue lights ahead on Pratt Street, commands from loudspeakers—indecipherable here, but probably shouting instructions to survivors. The police and firefighters themselves would be using their radios.

If not for being focused on his goal, Kealey might have instantly seen the cars shoot toward him from his right. As it was, his reaction was quick enough to avoid getting run over. He sprang out of the way as the first one barreled down the ramp in the back of the center, pulling Allison along so forcefully that she almost tripped.

He steadied her against him. As the vehicles had come shooting onto Sharp Street, he'd noted that they were compact sedans similar to the cars he'd seen behind the building from Conroy. He'd also glimpsed the first vehicle's driver through his windshield and registered his clenched, fixated expression.

"Ryan?"

Kealey was quiet. That obsessive look on the driver's face. He'd seen similar ones before, and they had never signified anything good.

"Ryan?"

He shot her a glance. "I should have checked those sons of bitches out," he said.

"Who?"

He jerked his head back the way they'd come. "Those sedans. What the hell were they doing behind the building?"

She stared at him, frightened and confused.

"The cars, the driver, the lack of any stickers on the windows or license plates—they smelled of Feds," he said. "So why were they *leaving?*"

Allison's phone pinged.

"It's Colin," she said. "The dust is starting to settle. He says he's near the men's room just outside the food area."

Kealey stood there a heartbeat longer, his eyes disgusted and angry. Then, mindful of the nearby police sirens, he reached under his jacket for his Sig, thumbed its decock lever, and held the weapon down at the low ready.

"What is it?" Allison asked.

She took a step back, probably unaware that she had done so, Kealey thought. It was anxiety, her nerve gone, her mind unable to make sense of anything.

"I don't know," he admitted. "But whatever it is, I want to be ready."

Grabbing hold of her hand again, he started toward the ramp.

The entrances faced each other beneath the walkway. The letters above the automatic sliding doors to the left read OTTERBEIN LOBBY. Those above the opposite doors said SHARP STREET LOBBY—EXECUTIVE OFFICES.

Kealey turned to his right. The extension on his left was where the blasts had occurred, where Colin and Julie might be trapped, if they hadn't already escaped or been evaced. But he had to resist the temptation to head inside. The cars gunning out of the back ramp as if all hell was at their tails had convinced him there might be more trouble on the way—and that he might still have a chance to head it off.

Allison was pointing to the left. "Ryan, wait! We have to go—"

"That way, I know," he said. "But we need to get there through the back door. I'm not sure this is finished."

She did not protest any further but came along with

a rag-doll limpness. Kealey knew the feeling. She had shut down, her mind and body overwhelmed.

Entering, he heard the earsplitting racket of the convention center's internal fire alarms. He spotted a pair of uniformed guards inside the entrance, about six feet apart, their backs toward him. The rent-a-cops were no surprise: he'd assumed that there were security guards on premises, and that it would be standard operating procedure for them to remain at their posts until the police arrived to seal the exit. The real question for Kealey was how to get past them.

"Come on!" he said, walking forward cautiously, unclasping his hand from Allison's to reach into his pocket for his card holder.

One of the guards noticed him, shouted to the other, and they both turned, their eyes on his weapon as they drew their own sidearms from hip holsters.

"*Halt!*" one of them shouted from behind his Glock 9-millimeter semiautomatic. "Don't take another step!"

"CIA!" Kealey said, stopping and flashing his outdated credential. "We need to get through."

"We were told no one gets in—"

"We have people at the Harper event," Kealey said. "We need to get to them."

The rent-a-cops stood with the pistols extended in two-handed shooter's grips, their muzzles aimed straight at Kealey and Allison.

"Toss the ID over."

Kealey kept his gun lowered. He was trying to decide what to do next when he saw Allison bend and slide her own ID across the floor. Without lowering his gun or taking his eyes off Kealey, the guard squatted and picked it up.

"Drop the kerchief and come over here," he said, rising.

Kealey and Allison did as he asked. As they approached, he compared the photo to the woman standing before him. He seemed satisfied, and Kealey folded away his own ID. The guard didn't ask to examine it.

"Go ahead," the man told him.

"Thanks. You have any intel, Officer Goldstein?" Kealey asked, reading his name tag.

"Not much," the beefy man replied. "Three explosions—ballroom, food court, and hotel lobby. Emergency personnel having a tough time getting through traffic."

"Some son of a bitch did their homework," Kealey remarked.

The two moved on, leaving the scarves hanging around their necks.

"Nice move," Kealey said.

Allison didn't answer.

"Do you know how to get where we're going from here?" he asked.

"Upstairs. Then double back," she said.

Kealey grasped her hand again, saw a sign that said FIRE EXIT, and led her through the door. They hurried up the stairs, pausing behind the closed fire door. Kealey looked through its wired glass panel before he pushed into a wide public corridor. A misty film hung in the air, thicker at the bottom than at the top.

"Better put your mask back on," he said.

Glancing back and forth, he saw separate signs for the administrative offices and the walkway to the center's newer wing, the latter pointing around a bend in the corridor to his right. They moved in that direction at a full-tilt run.

No sooner had they rounded the corner than they saw the dead man. He was sprawled on the floor, faceup, wearing the same uniform as the guards downstairs in the lobby.

Allison stopped short an instant before she would have barreled over the corpse's legs, horror dawning over her features, her eyes jumping from his grotesquely mutilated face to the overturned electric scooter beside him. It was splashed all over with blood.

"My God," she said, gasping.

Even as Kealey moved between her and the dead man, his eyes snapped to where a second guard lay several feet to the right, also dead, his shirtfront soaked with blood. He'd fallen with his head propped against the wall, one knee upraised, the other leg extended, his arms spread loosely to either side. A long dripping red skid mark ran down on the wall where he must have fallen back against it before sliding to the floor.

Kealey studied the body near the scooter. The head was tilted sideways to the left, a large puddle of blood under the cheek and blown-out skull; the eye on that side rolled lazily up in its socket so only its white was visible. The right eye socket was a swamp of red.

"Shot at close range," he said, noticing that the dead guard's hand was wrapped around the butt of his half-drawn sidearm. "Executed."

"What do you mean?"

"He was beaten to the draw," Kealey said. "It doesn't look like they ordered him to surrender."

"They were probably making sure the offices were evacuated."

Kealey nodded. "And then someone came up the stairs, the same as we did." He shook his head, looked up toward the juncture of the wall and the ceiling. A camera was mounted there, but the red light was dark. It hadn't been shot out by the killers, because someone on their team was using it. Whoever it was, they were watching him now.

The long black box reminded him of a vulture on a tree branch, patiently waiting for him to die.

Allison was breathing rapidly. "Ryan, what kind of madness *is* this?"

"I don't know," Kealey told her. "Let's go."

Raising the barrel of his Sig, he grabbed her right hand with his left and continued toward the walkway.

The gunfire erupted as they reached its entrance—a staccato burst from the far end of the span, then another overlapping volley.

Kealey dropped to his belly, simultaneously pulling Allison down and gathering her against him with his left arm. He used his body to cushion her fall. The bullets rapped into the glass panels to their right and left, sending an explosion of jagged shards over their backs.

He pushed her head closer to the floor, growled through the mask, "Stay low!"

Kealey felt her stiffen against his side, heard her shallow, frightened breaths. The walkway represented the only access to the extension. It could also be a perfect place of ambush, closing them in, offering no cover from fire.

Keeping his hand protectively on her head, Kealey raised his eyes to look across the walkway. He saw two gunmen through the thin, hovering veil of smoke. They were just beyond the entry, one on each side, using the outer walls for partial cover. Kealey noticed that they were clad entirely in black, wearing black bandannas over their mouths and grasping semiautomatic weapons. The firearms looked like sound-suppressed MP5K variants. Whoever they were, they didn't want the authorities to hear them. Presumably, the dead bodies would be attributed to the bombers or accomplices.

Whatever this part of the operation was—and whoever was running it—the plan had been orchestrated according to classic guerrilla techniques. The main objective reached, a raid force had been inserted, a trap laid for whoever might try to follow them.

Kealey realized that he and Allison couldn't just stay out in the open. Even if they didn't reach Colin right away, they had to get out of here.

"Listen to me," he said, pressing his lips to Allison's ear. "Stay flat, and move to your left. We need to get closer to the wall."

She made a small sound of acknowledgment and wriggled toward the wall on her stomach. Kealey moved along with her, his gun fully extended in his right hand. Their movement prompted another barrage of fire from the other side of the walkway. More glass popped and sprayed around them. They slid a little farther and stopped, Allison having gone as far as she could, pressed between his body and the passage's wall.

Better, Kealey thought. Propping himself up slightly on his elbows, he pulled his left hand away from her, shifted it to his pistol grip so both hands were folded around the weapon. He was breathing heavily, and the smoke was pungent enough to sting his nostrils. But the haze itself wasn't too bad. He could see the shooters if they moved.

He stared over his sight, waiting. Then he glimpsed the snub-nosed barrel of an assault weapon poking from behind the wall to his right, fingers in cutoff gloves wrapped around its forestock. A poor target, but his goal was not necessarily to score a hit with his first shots.

Taking a steadying breath and exhaling quickly, Kealey squeezed off a round. He missed the gunman, as expected, but the killer went for the bait. He leaned around to return fire and this time exposed himself enough for Kealey to get a clear shot. He pulled the trigger, and the pistol discharged with two sharp cracks, his arm jolting with recoil. The masked man fell back silently, clutching his throat, the MP5K dropping from his grasp.

Kealey quickly rolled onto his left side, saw the second gunman lean through the entrance from the right, his weapon spurting. Bullets splattered where Kealey had been just moments before, pecking into the low walls and fallen glass to the left of Allison. Kealey took aim over the nub of his sight and fired three rounds in rapid succession. His shirt puffing at his chest, the shooter jerked violently and then sagged forward onto the floor of the walkway.

Kealey didn't waste an instant pushing to his feet. It bothered him for a moment that he might have just killed two Americans, possibly brothers in arms with the Company. For all he knew, the rent-a-cops had been part of an enemy plot and these guys were just cleaning up.

In which case they should have identified themselves, he told himself.

It was all that gray in a world that had once been black and white that had driven him to seek Allison's counsel in the first place. Espionage was not a business for anyone who craved clarity.

"Stay down until I call you," he said to Allison when the gunfire failed to draw reinforcements.

His pulse thudding in his ears, he ran across the walkway in a half crouch, stopping to check on the first man. He was completely motionless where he'd fallen, a fist-sized hole in his throat, blood pooling on the tile. Kealey whirled toward the second shooter, who was still alive and was struggling to get off his back by rolling onto his side. Seriously wounded, the front of his shirt soaked with blood, he had managed to hang on to his gun and was bringing it up into firing position.

Kealey took a lunging stride toward him, kicked the weapon from his grasp, and smashed his foot into the vicinity of his chest wound, at the same time driving him back against the side of the walkway. The gunman produced a low, froggy croak and went limp, sagging against the wall.

Moving swiftly to retrieve the shooter's weapon, Kealey slung its strap over his arm, knelt over his motionless form, and pressed the muzzle of his Sig into the man's temple. But he realized at once that additional force would not be necessary. The man was unconscious, a pinkish froth dripping from his wide-open mouth to his chin. If he'd coughed that up from his lungs—and Kealey had seen pulmonary bleeding often enough to recognize its signs—then it was a safe bet that he wouldn't last much longer.

Kealey lowered the Sig, pulled aside the bandanna, and studied his face. It had no distinctive characteristics. A light-skinned, brown-haired Caucasian, he could have come from anywhere on the planet. A Bluetooth headset on his right ear did, however, catch Kealey's attention. He removed the headset and, checking it for any obvious tracking signals, saw none and dropped it in his jacket pocket.

Searching him quickly, Kealey found a cheap prepaid cell phone in his trousers and pocketed it alongside the headset. Besides the weapon and a six-magazine ammunition pack over each shoulder, that was it, all he was carrying. The man had no wallet, no documents, no identification of any type.

Kealey slipped the 9mm packs over his shoulders and hurried back to the other shooter. He took the MP5K from his unresisting fingers, shucked the unfired round from its chamber, removed the partly spent magazine, and put it in a separate pocket from the headset and phone, tossing aside the gun. Then, curious, he pulled off the man's mask, tugging a little to get the edge of the fabric out of the wound. It came free with a spray of blood that splattered Kealey's shirt and jacket.

The dead man had black hair, olive skin, and a long, narrow face. His features might have been Middle Eastern, but they also could have been Spanish, Greek, Indian, southern Italian, or something else altogether. If the gunmen had the same ethnicity, or seemed to, it might be a clue to their origins and motives. As it was, Kealey could glean nothing from his appearance.

Tellingly, neither man carried hand or finger re-straints of any kind. That proved his earlier assumption, when he saw the dead rent-a-cops: these guys were here to kill people, not take prisoners.

The Bluetooth receiver was identical to the other man's. Kealey stashed the headset with the other one, then turned and gestured at Allison. Already on her feet, she ran and joined him in the entry to the walk-way. Her face pale and distraught, she was holding her phone in her hand.

Kealey looked at her. "What is it?"

"They have hostages," she said. "He's with them."

"Does he know what they're demanding?"

Allison stared at him, her lips working in mute silence, as if they could not quite fit around the words she wanted to speak.

Instead, she simply showed him the post.

We r on 3 flr. Many wounded in exhbt hall. Men w/guns killing ppl no reason, don't know when I can post agn, they say will kill all of us if—

CHAPTER 6
WASHINGTON, D.C.

"Jon, I'm so sorry," said President David Brenneman as he strode into the small breakout room off the Situation Room—officially, the Executive Conference Room—and shut the door. "I'm not sure if it's any comfort to you at all, but I have some idea what you're going through."

"Thank you, Mr. President."

"And we don't know anything yet," Brenneman added. "We've been there before."

Sadly, that was true. And anguished as he felt, Harper knew that the president was sincere. But it was still ironic hearing the president of the United States speak those words under these circumstances.

The ECR was part of the five-thousand-square-foot White House Situation Room complex occupying half the basement level of the West Wing. Set up by President John F. Kennedy following his dismal strategic attempt to overthrow Castro's Cuban government, the complex continued to function as a command center for the president and his council of advisors, and as of the 2007 revamp, it was operated by the National Security Council, whose nearly two dozen military and intelligence watch teams perpetually supervised and identified domestic and global emergencies. Each team varyingly consisted of several duty officers, an intel analyst, and a communication assistant, who compiled and submitted the Morning Book—which included the National Intelligence Daily, the State Department's Morning Summary, and any intelligence or diplomatic reports—to the active national security advisor. The NSA also received the hand-delivered President's Daily Brief from the Office of the Director of National Intelligence and personally updated the president at the beginning of each day and at the end with a Sit Room Note, summarizing reports, graphs, maps, and photos from other agencies and how they were publicly received.

Harper and the president had been waiting for the meeting's teleconference attendees to be brought online when Brenneman asked Harper to step inside, hitting a switch to opaque the window into the ECR so they could speak in absolute privacy. Now the men stood facing each other, bonded by grief. Two years earlier the second-term president had lost his niece, Lily Durant, to an insurgent group in Darfur. They had ruthlessly wiped out an entire refugee camp, but Lily, who had been doing volunteer relief work with UNICEF, had been their real target. Caught in a surprise raid on the camp, she was raped and murdered in their effort to mislead Brenneman into believing the Sudanese government was culpable.

The twist was that Harper had been among the core

advisors to have met with Brenneman at Camp David not long after the early evidence came in, as had his own boss, the director of the CIA, Robert Andrews. Andrews, along with a fellow intelligence advisor and two top members of the cabinet, was even now waiting at a conference table in the ECR, on the other side of the electronically fogged glass panel. Back then, Andrews and Harper had both smelled something amiss in the raw data coming from Africa and had advised Brenneman to be patient. No one wanted to launch a misplaced retaliatory strike. Waiting appealed not only to the commander in chief's moderate inclinations but also to his grasp on common sense, which was uncommon in Washington. Their instincts had proven correct, though they could not have known then that the architect of the Darfur incident was one of the president's handpicked confidants: the chief of the Defense Intelligence Agency, General Joel Stralen. He had been determined to set the nation on a course of war with Sudan, killing great numbers of people in the hope of disrupting a nexus of anti-American sentiment, a hatchery for the next generation of terrorists.

Success in that crisis had depended on Harper and Andrews probing beyond the obvious and being willing to gamble on a wild card named Ryan Kealey doing the job. Of course, that had been an overseas situation, a third-world battleground. It was not a major American city, with emotional resonance to the last attack on major American cities.

Now he stood looking at a changed Brenneman in the gloved silence of the room. A month shy of his fifty-eighth birthday, the president had thick gray hair, which had been almost completely brown before his niece's death had leeched it of color, even as his once youthful face had become permanently lined and careworn, almost seeming to age a full decade overnight. Even the lyrical tone of his once sanguine voice, the narrative tool that had propelled him through college debates at Georgetown, long campaign trails to Congress, and had ultimately carried him through the crowds and into the White House, was stained by years of distress. Harper couldn't help but notice the toll his friend had paid to pass through these gates, the hell that came with it. Nor would he wish to change places with the hard-lined leader. This time, he knew America had picked the right man for the job. And Harper was determined to give the guy the legroom with which to do it. Only one of them was faced with a personal loss, but both were processing the shock of another homeland assault.

"I appreciate your concern, sir," Harper said, with deeper gratitude than the president might have realized. "It's funny. I was talking to her when it happened, telling her I felt bad about missing her big dinner. She was telling me I shouldn't." He looked down. "What were we here to talk about, Mr. President? God, it seems so long ago."

"It was the CIA," the president said. "The Coyote. It was important."

Harper nodded, his mouth tense, despising his show of weakness.

"Jon, listen to me," Brenneman said, sensing Harper's anger and jumping into the pause. "You have every reason to be excused from the meeting—"

"That won't be necessary."

"No, but it may be advisable," Brenneman said.

"There are plenty of good heads here to keep mine straight. I promise you'll be fully briefed."

"Sir, I prefer to stay involved. It's really the best thing I can do in every respect. When the rescue workers have news . . ." His voice trailed off.

"Of course," the president replied.

What Harper told Brenneman was the truth. As he'd risen through the Company's organizational hierarchy, his functions had become increasingly administrative. But intel gathering was his area of special expertise, and it was hardwired so that he could process critical events quickly, accurately, and intuitively through the rapid assembly and cataloguing of information. Personal or professional crises, they were alike in how he dealt with them. In this case the two were sadly inseparable.

"Who's with us via video linkup?" he asked, wanting to shift the focus of their discussion from himself. The only way he could function was to actually start doing it. To turn his mind toward the tasks that lay right in front of him. "Sandy Mathis insisted he'd be glued to his desk at Quantico this weekend, so I'm assuming he was easy enough to find?"

Brenneman's twisted expression indicated that Harper's taut sarcasm had registered loud and clear.

"Sandy was coming online as we stepped in here. But I've left overall coordination of our remote participants up to SIOC," he said.

That was a good call. The president was referring to the FBI's Strategic Information and Operations Center at the bureau's Pennsylvania Avenue headquarters. There the data pouring in from the nation's one hundred independent Joint Terrorism Task Forces was merged into a single shared pool—a common watering hole that could be tapped by the FBI, the CIA, and other intelligence agencies. A spin-off, SIOC-I—from which particularly sensitive information was withheld—was for the country's international allies to draw on. SIOC-I also had access to similarly redacted documents from thirty-two other nations.

Brenneman had kept his eyes on Harper's face, reading the determination there.

"Okay," he said finally. "We'd better rejoin everyone before they feel neglected."

It was a joke, but just barely. People whose job it was to be paranoid found it difficult to keep that out of their own intra- and interdepartmental dealings.

The president went to the door and opened it, politely gesturing for Harper to precede him into the next room.

Its six large flat-panel wall displays situated around a rectangular conference table, the ECR had been designed to conform with other presidential chambers at sites inside and beyond the capital, including Camp David, Air Force One, and the top secret bunker installations in Mount Weather and elsewhere. The goal being to enhance the commander in chief's familiarity with and instant comfort in his surroundings at times of critical deliberation and national emergency.

The president's closest advisors on matters of security and intelligence sat in six big black leather chairs around the table. Among them were two members of his cabinet, Secretary of Homeland Security Max Carlson and the newly ratified secretary of state, Jeff Dryfoos, the latter taking the place of the vice president, who was in Asia. Dryfoos was a newbie, having as-

sumed the post after Brynn Fitzgerald's recent resignation and formal announcement of her presidential bid.
Her run had surprised no one less than Brenneman,
who'd encouraged her to enter the heated race as his
preferred successor.

Also, there in person as Harper entered were CIA
director Andrews and the director of National Intelligence, Shirley Choate. If the full fifteen-member
cabinet had convened, they and all other noncabinet officials except the chairman of the Joint Chiefs of Staff
would have sat in a row of chairs along the wall. With
only two executive departmental heads in attendance,
there was ample room for everyone at the table.

Harper took his place next to Andrews, saying nothing, having gotten his preliminaries out of the way before the president pulled him aside. That consisted
primarily of learning that no one knew very much
about the attack, and even less about the situation in
the ballroom.

There were laptops in front of each seat. As Harper
sat, Andrews turned his own monitor toward his colleague.

Harper recognized the familiar box in the center of
the screen. It was from TA, the Company's Tech Analysis division—findings from the Iridium 11 geosynchronous satellite that scanned the Baltimore to
Philadelphia corridor:

NUMBER: 202-Private
USER: Harper, Julie
STATUS: Blocked
BASELINE: Operational

Harper drew breath sharply. He had to struggle to keep from showing any emotion when he read the last line. It meant that while Julie's phone could not be accessed, the number was still online.

Her phone had not been destroyed. That was the first positive sign he'd had since they were cut off.

"Thanks," he whispered to Andrews.

The director nodded once and turned the monitor back.

Breathing steadily to calm himself, reminding himself that this was only the faintest positive sign, Harper turned his gaze to the wall monitor opposite him. He saw Mathis waiting quietly behind his desk 100 miles to the east. With his wire spectacles and horseshoe pattern baldness, he looked very much the part of the career administrator, which would accurately describe his résumé.

As the president took his seat, a voice came over the multidirectional PA in the center of the table. It was one of the watch officers in the next room.

"Mr. President, we have SIOC online. It will be up on screen four whenever you're ready."

"Thank you." Brenneman settled into his chair. "Let's roll."

The presidential-seal wallpaper on the indicated video panel vanished and was replaced by the image of a short-haired man in his forties with heavy features and a thick, fleshy neck that looked as if it had been uncomfortably mashed into the starched collar of his button-down shirt. His hands folded on a desktop, his sleeves rolled to just below his elbows, he sat amid computer banks, monitors, and circulating facility personnel. Save for the missing crawl and the time stamp in the lower right corner, it could have been a feed from Fox News.

"President Brenneman, introducing assistant director of the FBI Joseph Ferrara," said the watch officer.

Brenneman looked at the display. "Joe, let's get right to it. What's the latest?"

"Sir, in the last twenty minutes the Maryland state police have gotten an AW139 helicopter into the air over the center," Ferrara said in his thick voice. "It's streaming video, including thermal infrared imagery." The SIOC chief glanced at a laptop. "The feed is being sent to you, File Code CC-A."

That was the first feed from the convention center. The group all looked at their laptops. They clicked on the box in the center of the screen to access the image. It showed mostly smoke and chunks of concrete, moving from left to right, with batches of red and yellow shapes scattered throughout.

The shifting red shapes were people. The stationary yellow shapes were also people—those who were losing heat.

Dead bodies.

"Our field units from Baltimore have established a perimeter control and have agents outside the building—"

"What about the hostage situation?" Andrews asked. "Our I-eleven has intercepted tweets from several sources."

"I was getting to that," Ferrara said with a trace of annoyance. "We've seen those in the database, forwarded them to the agent in charge. She tells us that patterns of ongoing gunfire suggest people are being herded and executed."

"Jesus," Secretary Dryfoos said.

"They have six SWAT teams ready to go in, three from the FBI, two from the Baltimore PD, and one from the state police. They're organizing now so they don't shoot each other or innocents, with a T-minus of four minutes."

Andrews sighed and Harper knew why. A lot of people could die in that time period. But the team leaders also had to make sure that they had a single protocol for shoot-to-kill, surrender, explosive vests, wounded civilians, and anything else they might encounter.

Brenneman thanked Ferrara politely, though Harper knew him well enough to know that the president would have liked to hear that units were inside the convention center already and collecting data and video.

"Is there any surveillance footage?" Harper asked Ferrara.

"We've got a streaming video from emergency vehicles, and we're just starting to look at data from the convention center's computers," Ferrara said. "They have twenty-four discrete cameras, and we're running the footage backward."

That made sense. It would bring up the actionable images first and would leave the forensic images for later.

"Show us what we're dealing with," the president said. "Start with the ballroom and food area."

It was the logical choice, the place where a large percentage of high-value targets from D.C. had been gathered. It was also the place where a great deal of yellow had showed up on the thermal imaging.

"Yes, sir," Ferrara said and sent over CC-B and C. Each file had images from four separate cameras.

The president glanced at Harper. "Jon, you don't need to do this."

"It's okay, sir," he said. "I may see something."

Harper reached for a glass of water as he opened the files on his laptop, his eyes fixed on the carnage.

The video images were arrayed in two rows of four. Clicking on any panel would give the viewer a full-screen view of that particular video.

Seven of the videos were virtually static. Even the particulate matter hanging in the air barely moved. Because the cameras were all at an angle, they were looking through more of it than if they were at ground level and facing straight ahead.

Everyone seemed to react as something moved.

"Camera eight," Dryfoos said. "Did you all see that?"

Most of the others had already clicked and maximized the image. Harper set the water glass aside and leaned closer to the screen.

There were two people, a male and a female. There were occasional glints of light from the floor, like luminous algae in moving water.

"There's glass from the barricade beside them," Andrews said. "Three separate blast patterns."

"They were shot out, not blown out," Mathis added needlessly.

It was the first comment from the head of the FBI's Behavioral Analysis Bureau. The psychiatrist was a college friend of the Speaker of the House, an archrival of Brenneman's. Mathis's reliance on "cloud profiling"—identifying potential terrorists based on geographical and socioeconomic data rather than on actual affiliations—had taxed his allotment of FBI resources without providing any tangible results. While dismissing him would be easy, getting a replacement through the House would be impossible.

"Who is in charge of this footage?" Andrews asked.

"An outfit called Steel Guard Solutions provides building and event security to the center," Ferrara said. "A couple of rental cops reported a CIA presence in the Pratt Street lobby. These two fit the report."

"When was that?" Harper asked, squinting at the image. He was ignoring the backward motion, concentrating on the faces.

"About fifteen minutes ago—"

"It can't be," Harper said suddenly.

"What, Jon?" the president asked.

Harper froze the image, clicked on the drop-down menu, kicked the size up to 150 percent, and hit the auto-enhance button. Most of the smoke seemed to vanish as the contrast in the figures was pumped up.

He glanced at the time stamp. "Frame 5:28:02," he said. "Go fifty percent up and enhance."

Everyone did as he'd instructed. Dumbstruck, Harper sat hunched in front of the screen, just staring. There was no mistaking the identities of the two people on-screen. The man with the coal-black shock of hair, the tall blond woman with him. Harper knew them as well as anybody in the entire world.

"Good get, Jon," Andrews said.

"Thanks."

Neither Ferrara nor Mathis had any idea what they were talking about, but neither man would have admitted his ignorance. Fortunately, Secretary of State Dryfoos asked the question for them.

"Who are we looking at?"

"Incredibly," Harper said, "that's former Company man Ryan Kealey with CIA psychotherapist Allison Dearborn."

Harper clicked back to the backward feed. There were gun flashes from the couple's position.

"Yeah," Andrews said, sitting back. "That's definitely Ryan Kealey."

CHAPTER 7

BALTIMORE, MARYLAND

Crouched beside Allison Dearborn in the walkway, Kealey read her nephew's latest update off her phone:

Split into 2 grps. Conf. rms 224–256. Am in 224. 3 guards in rm w/us. Dn't know h/many in hall.

"Maybe we should phone for help," Allison suggested.

"I'd love to, but we don't know who's in on this or where the cavalry is," he said. "I'm sure there are also jurisdictional turf wars that have to be settled before any boots hit the ground."

Gunfire echoed through the main exhibition hall, a single burst of unusual duration. The sounds prickled the fine hairs at the back of Kealey's neck; Allison breathed through clenched teeth. There had been no return volleys. They were listening to a bloodbath being carried out.

"Why are they doing this?" she asked. "They have to know the police are coming."

"They may be counting on that," Kealey said.

"Murder-suicide?"

"Worse." He rose, bending low, the 9-millimeter held straight in front of him. "A dozen or more blue funerals buy a lot of airtime. Exposure advances terror."

Allison seemed to want to say something. She couldn't find the words, but the horror was there, in her eyes. Kealey didn't bother to remind her that an hour ago she had said craziness kept her in business. What she meant, of course, was the benign kinds of disorders that comprised the bulk of her practice and affected only the individual: PTSD, depression, schizophrenia. The rational evil they were facing here was a very different kind of animal. It did not believe it was sick.

"Let's go," he said, starting forward at a brisk walk.

"What's your plan?" she asked.

"We need to take out the guards," he said.

"That isn't a plan."

"It's all I've got right now," he said without apology.

They remained crouched, out of sight, moving forward until they were about 50 feet from the convention center's main exhibition hall, just outside the entrance to the mezzanine level.

"We could use a layout of this place," Kealey said. "See if you can pull one off its Web site."

She nodded and tapped the screen with her thumbs. Waiting, watching for anyone who might emerge—an escaped hostage was his main concern—Ryan heard screams below him and then the rattle of an automatic weapon. It was the third peal of gunfire since he'd taken out the two masked gunmen.

Any one of them could have involved Colin.

"Okay," Allison said now. Her voice was cracked,

her hand trembling as she passed him the phone. Kealey took a moment to hold her hand as he took the phone. She hadn't lived through Bosnia and other hotbeds of genocide. If he couldn't block out the violence, how could she be expected to handle it?

Kealey studied the display. There were separate diagrams for each level of the building, all viewable as PDF files and nearly as detailed as architectural blueprints. A glance at the third floor immediately showed where to find the food area and the block of conference rooms. Better yet, it gave the individual locations and door numbers.

"The room where they brought Colin is on the southeast side of the building," he said and touched a finger to the display. "Right across from that church we passed. What was the name of it?"

"Old Otterbein," Allison said.

For her own sake, he needed to keep her involved in this. He held the floor plan out to her now, pointing at the long block of conference rooms on the floor above them.

"Looks like there's a public space, then a hall running off it to the conference rooms," he said. "It's going to be guarded. The hostages, too, as Colin said."

"How do we get by them?"

"There are elevators running up there, but we have no way of knowing if they're working. That leaves the escalators and stairs about midway down the length of the mezzanine."

He pointed them out, and she nodded.

"We're going to need a distraction," Kealey said. "Something to draw their attention from us."

"I can—"

"Inside," Kealey said. "We need to draw the guards *in*."

She looked up at him. "No," she said as she realized what he was saying. "I won't ask my nephew to risk his life."

"It's already at risk. The hostages are going to be killed if nothing's done."

"Maybe not. They haven't, yet—"

"It's a tactic," Kealey said. "I've been timing the shots. They're killing people every three minutes. If I'm keeping track, the police are, too. The killers are trying to rush the rescue effort, give the police less time to get organized."

"Ryan, who . . . *what* kind of creature thinks like that?" She realized what she had said a moment later. "I'm sorry, Ryan. I didn't mean that you—"

"Not important," he said. "Twitter updates. Can any account holder read them?"

"Unless I block somebody, they're public."

"Is there a quick way to track updates on a particular subject?"

Allison nodded. "There are hashtags—number signs before a word that categorize the tweet."

"So if you tag the words 'Baltimore Convention Center,' then somebody looking for updates about it would see them?"

She nodded again.

Kealey paused thoughtfully. "I want you to send Colin a post. Tag it the way you described."

"But if someone hears—"

"I want them to," Kealey said. "Trust me, Allison."

They heard another spurt of gunfire down below. It dramatically underscored the need for haste.

"Okay," she said. "What's the message?"

After reviewing it in his mind—and aware of the trigger he was about to pull—he gave it to her.

Colin Dearborn was sitting against a wall, in a corner, surrounded by sobbing, dust-covered, terrified fellow hostages. The air was thick, and the mood was even heavier.

They had all heard the shots and the screams. They knew those weren't SWAT teams giving or receiving.

Colin's cell phone was on vibrate, hidden down the front of his boxers. When he felt the rhythmic buzz of a push notification, he knew there was only a small chance that it was something important. More than likely, it was one of his friends checking to see if he was all right.

But it could also be his aunt Allison with important information.

He passed his eyes around the room. The guard who'd entered with his group had turned almost entirely toward the open door to converse with another masked lunatic in the hallway. If he was quick, Colin believed he could reach for the phone without being seen. He'd done it once already, albeit when they were still standing.

There were walls behind him and to his right. To the left, no one was paying him any attention. The young man quickly unbuttoned his waistband and slipped his hand into his trousers.

Grabbing the cell, he worked it awkwardly from his undershorts and tucked it between his bent legs. He huddled down, as though he were resting his head on his knees. That would also help to conceal the glow of the screen. Then he focused his eyes on the display and scrolled down his timeline with his thumb. At the top of his feed, he read the words:

Leave yr phone somewhere w/vol LOUD. In 5 min. it will ring, DO NOT answer. #BaltimoreConventionCenter // Stand by.

Colin felt his stomach drop. He clutched the phone for several seconds more, rereading the message.

Pressure, he thought.

There was no way of knowing what their captors would do if they heard the cell.

Shoot into the group of twenty-odd souls? Take him out and execute him as an example to the others?

She wouldn't have sent that message without good reason, he reflected. And it wasn't a stretch to conclude that it had something—no, *everything*—to do with Ryan Kealey. It was no secret on the university campus that the visiting prof was former CIA, and even that didn't begin to define what set him apart from the other academicians there. Colin had read news articles about his role in preventing a terrorist incident near the United Nations a few years back. From the day they met, Colin had gotten the sense he had seen things most people hadn't, and was capable of doing things most others weren't.

But there was always a price for action.

Colin exhaled until his lungs felt entirely deflated. He estimated a full minute had passed since her tweet. Four minutes left to figure this out. Allie had hash-tagged the words *Baltimore Convention Center.* That told Colin she—or rather, Kealey—believed the tweets were being monitored. Obviously, Kealey had given this some thought. He had a plan. He knew what he was doing.

Or so Colin needed to believe, if he was going to disobey the commands of his seriously unbalanced keepers.

He looked around him. The spare décor didn't afford many places of concealment, even for a small object, but he thought he saw one that might do the trick.

Making certain the guard was still turned toward the door, Colin made his move.

CHAPTER 8

WASHINGTON, D.C.

Facing the Pentagon from the green, tree-clustered slopes above Bolling Air Force Base, the Department of Homeland Security's vast new 4,500,000-square-foot facility occupied federal land on the west campus of St. Elizabeth's Hospital in Washington, D.C. All bald concrete and glass, it housed more than sixty DHS offices, which had been previously scattered across Washington, Virginia, and Maryland, though the vast majority had been relocated from the department's original temporary headquarters at the historic Nebraska Avenue naval complex across town.

It was here that the National Operations Center, or the NOC, worked year-round, twenty-four hours a day, seven days a week, to monitor, protect against, and manage foreign and domestic threats to the United States under the umbrella of the DHS Office of Operations Coordination and Planning. While it shared some similarities with the FBI-SIOC synergy, the DHS-NOC relationship was a much more separate and different wheel on the massive wagon driving the nation's homeland security efforts. Thus, while SIOC served as an intelligence hub for law enforcement and investigative agencies, the NOC was the focal point for information flowing between state, regional, and tribal governments abroad, as well as private infrastructure elements—power and telecommunications grids, mass transit companies, airlines, school systems, hospitals, and other essential service providers. The idea was for these wheels to spin in smooth coordination and keep the wagon moving forward, rather than flying off its axles when things got bumpy.

Despite all the happy talk about cooperation, there were still rivalries between the subsystems in each of the branches. SIOC and the NOC competed for funds and thus competed with one another. Brenneman had learned that early on, which was why only SIOC had a voice in today's meeting. But that did not mean the NOC hadn't turned its considerable resources on the convention center attack.

The NOC's Social Network Monitoring Center, or SNMC, was located on the second floor of the building, in a large, nondescript room with rows of computer workstations along the aisles. Established in 2008, the unit monitored social media networks and other public Web sites for information related to terrorist activities. In accordance with Constitutional privacy guarantees, the NOC was barred from setting up fraudulent user accounts and was restricted to utilizing publicly available search engines and content browsers. But its Web-based platforms had been configured to skim through and pluck potentially valuable morsels of intelligence from Internet traffic.

Of the social networks, Facebook, Twitter and, to a lesser extent, Myspace—with their combined 800,000,000 unique monthly visitors—received the most attention, although there were scores of other personal and professional networking sites, from Plaxo to LinkedIn, which accounted for millions of additional users. Also identified, sorted, and analyzed were scraps of information collected from blogs, news sites, online forums, and message boards that might, in NOC parlance, contribute to "situational awareness and establish a common operating picture" of a particular threat or event.

On the day of the Baltimore Convention Center attack, DHS 10:00–5:30 action officers Dick Siegel and Clare Karl were preparing to carpool home to the Arlington County suburb where they both lived. Workers on the 5:30–1:00 shift were just beginning to arrive. They exchanged quick, impersonal hellos with their daytime counterparts. All the shifts shared desks, which limited the personalization and added to the sterility of a room that was already function oriented.

It was Siegel's turn to drive, and he'd been about to grab his cell phone from his desk when there was a three-tone computer ping alerting him to a "situation." He glanced at the leftmost of his three monitors, the one earmarked for general use, and saw the red-boxed "alert" prompt.

"Got something," he told Karl, who was already watching other officers checking the update. She stepped behind Siegel as he leaned over the keyboard.

"Hope it's not important," she said. "I have a T-ball game to get to."

"I think we're playing you," Siegel said.

Almost as soon as word of the attack reached the NOC, the first dribbles of intel began coming from the center. The SNMC's automated software applications, or web robots, generated hundreds of meta tags that enabled them to sniff around for suspicious or otherwise noteworthy keywords, and the ones that got the Twitter bots hopping at approximately 5:15 p.m. that Sunday evening were all of a kind: *explosion, blast, bomb.*

"What the hell is this?" Siegel wondered aloud as updates came up on the other two computer screens.

Karl had moved to her desk.

"You seeing these tweets?" Siegel asked.

Sitting at the workstation on Siegel's right, Karl was nodding slowly. "I think we should report this to—" She suddenly interrupted herself. "Holy Mother of God, Dick. Look at the TA board!"

Her eyes had snapped up to a sixty-five-inch flat-panel angled downward from the top of the wall in front of her, where the national threat assessment level was on constant display. It had jumped straight from "guarded" to "severe," bypassing the "high" alert advisory.

She looked at Siegel and he at her, but only for a moment. They had been here several years apiece and had never seen that kind of leap.

It took only seconds for reports of what was happening in Baltimore to flash across the lower third of their screens. These were identified by their sources: Fox News on top, CNN in the middle, MSNBC at the bottom. At the same time phones throughout the room started ringing, beeping, and singing, and there was a low hum of voices talking to sources, superiors, and one another. The room crackled with portent; this was why the unit had been formed, its reason for being, validation for all the stiff necks, sore backs, and strained eyes that went with monitoring Internet chatter day after day.

Siegel felt like he had as a boy of ten, a budding fisherman in a deep pool of water who'd suddenly, unexpectedly felt his boat rocked by something big and powerful. He knew, now as then, what he had to do, what his father had trained him for. But in an instant he was no longer navel-gazing in dreamy tranquility but was aware of the much bigger, much more active world around him.

For NOC cyber-snoops, the responsibilities and protocols of data collection during a crisis were well defined. Each action officer had a preassigned duty, and Siegel's was to trawl the Twitter feed, capturing and sorting meta-tagged updates of interest while scanning subjects trending within Twitter's own network. This was a simple matter, since trending topics were determined by commonly repeated terms that were either user hashtagged or detected by Twitter's internal search bots. Twitter then listed these on a home-page sidebar that could be set to view either worldwide or localized trends.

Siegel had picked up on the tweets from Colwriter123 early in his search. Showing up on the network as frequent re-tweets—when one user copied and posted another user's message to disseminate the information—they appeared to originate from the convention center. They had been floated to the top by the scan programs because there was an event taking place with a larger than normal number of dignitaries from the D.C. area. Now that he looked at the latest tweets, they seemed to give very precise information about what was going on inside the center, even indicating where a particular group of hostages had been segregated. *Appeared* and *seemed* being the operative words, because Siegel had to allow for the possibility that the tweets were part of a ghoulish hoax. His gut told him they weren't, though, because a number of the abbreviations Colwriter123 had used were not standard and they came at irregular times, as though the tweeter were trying to impart information in a hurry. Fully 80 percent of faux tweets could be ruled out by those two criteria.

Added digging reinforced Siegel's initial conviction. According to his user profile, Colwriter123's real name was Colin Dearborn and he was a journalism major at the University of Virginia, a self-described "new media evangelist." The profile page also bore a link to a column he wrote for the school newspaper, where a peek at his most recent piece revealed that he had been planning to tweet what he termed "live dispatches" from the career fair at the Baltimore Convention Center.

That essentially clinched the tweets' authenticity as far as Siegel was concerned, but to add further confirmation, he went back in Colwriter123's timeline to search through the updates he'd posted in the hour or so leading up to the attack. Colwriter123 had been a busy, prolific correspondent during that period, tweeting about everything from the degree of courtesy and helpfulness at individual booths to the high price of fast food at the concession stands. He had even included observations on security lapses, which Siegel himself found troubling, and had hashtagged his tweets with the term *#BaltimoreCareerFair* to make them easy to follow. From the event mark forward, Col-writer123 had been sending updates that read like combat reports from the front lines. The kid was impressive: not only did he have courage, but he was showing a composed, perceptive eye for what was important.

Running down Colwriter123's post-event timeline, Siegel examined the replies to his tweets from other users. Each of these showed the respondent's username after the @ symbol, enabling Siegel to click on his or her profile and see whether it offered anything of interest. Like criminals returning to the scene of a crime, terrorists were known to follow reactions to their sociopathic activities.

The tone of the responses ran the predictable gamut, ranging from deeply concerned to callously idiotic, but Siegel didn't immediately see anything useful in them. Then he noticed repeated tweets from someone with the username AlDearborn. A relative, possibly the young man's mother. The posts looked like direct communications with the kid from someone who was trying to help him, which was more than enough to grab Siegel's eye on its own. But the most recent post made him stare at the screen with acute fascination, a long, low whistle escaping his lips.

"You got something?" Karl asked.

"Maybe."

She was too involved in her own research to look over. Siegel read the tweet again. It had been sent just two minutes ago, according to the timeline, and it read:

Leave yr phone somewhere w/vol LOUD. In 5 min. it will ring, DO NOT answer. #BaltimoreConventionCenter // Stand by.

Siegel hastily clicked on the user's account profile. It belonged to Baltimore psychologist Allison Dearborn—and she was CIA. But what was the purpose of those instructions she gave him about his phone? The hashtagged term had popped out at him, too. *Baltimore Convention Center.* Ms. Dearborn had clearly wanted her tweet to attract the attention of someone other than Colwriter123. Someone a CIA employee must have hoped would be monitoring Internet traffic for messages from the center.

Someone like himself.

He was not about to sit around guessing, nor did he intend to just flag the tweets and kick them upstairs. These looked much too critical.

"Clare, hold the fort. I'll be back," Siegel said, springing from his seat.

Karl looked at him inquisitively. "What is it?"

Siegel didn't answer. He was already hustling up the aisle, feeling like a ticking clock thundercloud had just appeared over his little boat on the pond. . . .

Word reached Max Carlson in a circuitous fashion, which was unbecoming for the secretary of Homeland Security.

With his cell phone deposited in the small lead-lined cabinet outside the woodshed—which was what Carlson and other old-timers called the Situation Room—he'd been out of touch with the Office of Operations Coordination's acting director, Joseard Levy, who had oversight of the NOC and was responsible for keeping Carlson in the loop. Under most circumstances, Levy would have left Carlson a routine voice message. For a higher priority communication, Levy would have routed a call to the Situation Room, where a watch officer would have informed Carlson of its receipt; if the secretary felt the message warranted an immediate callback, he would excuse himself from the presidential huddle and return the call from one of the encrypted privacy phones that sat in soundproofed booths outside the conference room. But the information that had come out of the NOC was of such crucial importance that DHS protocol required it be conveyed directly to the president himself in the event that Carlson wasn't immediately available.

That was precisely what occurred, even though Levy was always kept informed of Carlson's whereabouts and had known he might be found not 10 feet apart from the president inside the Situation Room. So when a watch officer called to inform Brenneman that OOC director Levy was on the phone with urgent news, Carlson couldn't have realized it was coming from his own department, least of all Joseard Levy, his right-hand man.

The call lasted less than a half minute, during which time the president said nothing other than "Yes?" when he picked up and "Thank you" when he put down the receiver. Then he briefed the others. The Homeland Security chief hadn't viewed it as a personal slight; ego had nothing to do with this. It just felt odd to have the commander in chief tell him what his own people had learned: that within the last five minutes instructions were sent to one of the hostages, Colin Dearborn, a student at the University of Virginia, from an account belonging to his aunt Allison Dearborn.

To his credit, Brenneman turned first to Carlson to

ask his opinion. The Homeland Security chief quickly put his personal feelings aside to digest the latest development and advise the president.

"The five minutes would have just expired," Carlson said. He was already busy accessing the file with the tweets of Colwriter123. "Joe, any changes in the grid?"

The SIOC chief was looking off camera. "Checking," he said, drawing out the word. "Thermal imaging shows movement in one of the rooms. It's in two-twenty-four."

CIA director Andrews had brought up Kealey's RAP sheet—his Retirement Assessment Profile. Though Kealey's sessions with Allison Dearborn were confidential, psychotherapists were required to file a brief analysis on all retiring personnel with high-level security clearance or a history of "personal enforcement"—a polite way of saying they'd killed someone on the job. The RAP was a series of twenty-five questions with boxes marked VERY LIKELY, LIKELY, and NOT LIKELY. The RAP sheet was designed to flag agents who had a history of money problems or would miss the excitement of government-sanctioned murder. For these people, personal issues such as divorce, unemployment in the civilian sector, or dissatisfaction with political issues could drive them to sell information to foreign operatives or commit violent acts.

Kealey had scored extremely low on the "selling information" likelihood, just 2 percent, and very high on the "likelihood of violence". If he happened to come upon a situation like the current one, the formula said there was a 90 percent chance he would not only become involved but would find a way, in Dearborn's own words, to "finesse the scenario toward his strengths."

Finesse was not a word Andrews would apply to Kealey. He had once described the agent as the nuke they'd fire at an asteroid rushing toward earth. But Kealey also knew Julie Harper, knew where she was. Andrews had no doubt that her safety was in his mental heads-up display, and there was no one Andrews would rather have on-site than him.

"Mr. President," Andrews said, "Kealey would know we're monitoring chatter on the SocNets—"

"I think we all got that part," Shirley Choate interrupted. "He was *your* guy. What's his game?"

The National Intelligence head was the former Detroit chief of police. Her aggressive tactics had brought peace to the impoverished city and an impatient muscularity to the president's team. While they all respected her judgment and out-of-the-box thinking, her style did not make her any friends.

Jon Harper—who hadn't needed the RAP sheet to put him in the mind of Ryan Kealey—swiveled toward her.

"He was *my* guy, actually," Harper said. "And he doesn't play games."

Expecting the question from someone, Harper had pulled up Kealey's service record. He sent it to her. Had Choate done more than glance at it, she would have seen how Kealey was fast-tracked to U.S. Army major in eight years, made captain a chestful of medals later, led an A-team in Bosnia, and became a Company man at thirty years old. He spent the next three years with the Special Activities Division, putting out wildfires in places no one else could get to, in ways no one else had even considered.

"What he's going to *do*," Harper went on, "is draw

the hostage takers' attention to the phone—which is obviously taking place as we speak." He regarded the president. "Sir . . . whatever turf wars may be going on outside the center, and they surely are, we need to cut through that and get him support ASAP."

The president turned to the wall monitor. "Mr. Ferrara, where are your men?"

"Preparing to go in," the FBI officer replied.

"No, get them in that building *now*," he ordered.

"Yes, sir."

"Joe, Kealey is armed and he will probably be firing," Andrews added, his eyes on the 90 percent number. "Tell them not to shoot him."

CHAPTER 9

BALTIMORE, MARYLAND

Kealey glanced at his chronograph wristwatch.
It was nearly time. The five minutes were up.
Hopefully, Colin had done as his aunt had instructed.
Kealey had built in a minute after that to execute his
own section of the plan.

Down in the exhibition hall, guns had sporadically
resumed their raging outbursts amid the cries of the
wounded and panic-stricken.

He turned to Allison, who was still crouched with
him in the walkway. Her eyes looked glazed.

"You with me?" he asked.

She nodded.

"Okay. Once we're out of here, run straight across
the mezzanine to those conference rooms. It shouldn't
take us more than fifteen seconds—half a minute,
tops."

Allison looked at him. "That's going to leave me a
moving target, Ryan."

Kealey regarded her steadfastly. "No, it isn't." He

shrugged a shoulder, slipped off one of the MP5Ks he'd taken from a fallen gunman. He tugged open its folding stock. "You see how I'm holding this?"

She nodded slowly.

"Once the stock's extended, it locks into place. If you have to fire, brace it against yourself, like so." He demonstrated, pushing the stock against his upper arm. "Keep one hand around the grip, the other around the foregrip. Your fingers should be rigid, but don't squeeze. It'll help prevent the gun from jerking."

She nodded slowly as he gave the weapon to her. She held it as he'd shown. "Is this right?"

"Yeah," Kealey said, his eyes intent.

He was thinking that Allison appeared to be in good shape, certainly strong enough to handle the weapon. Other than with the M60 machine gun, he'd never found kickback to be a major consideration, and even that hadn't been too bad. She would have no chance to get used to the weapon's feel and was apt to miss a lot. The advantage of an assault weapon was that it would give her more opportunities of *not* missing than a pistol.

"You've got a full magazine," he went on. "That's thirty rounds. The selector's set for three-round bursts. If you have to fire, pull the trigger with your fingertip. Don't wrap your finger around it like you're scratching. You want to maintain a light touch, and you want to keep the weapon as steady as possible."

Allison nodded again. She had already slipped the MP5K's strap over her shoulder, in a practiced motion that made it seem like a handbag. Now she was looking over the gun with what appeared to be rapt revulsion. It was a strange expression.

"Guess I should have taken some firearms training," she said.

"You can start tomorrow," Kealey said. He was checking the dial of his watch again. The second hand had just crossed the one-minute mark. "Last thing, Allison. When we move, bend as low as you can. In any case, keep your head down. That's coming out of the walkway and on the mezzanine. Got it?"

Allison nodded. She looked down at the phone, which she held in her left hand. Even knowing that both the cell and his watch were set by radio transmitter, Kealey had made sure they were in time-standard sync. Every moment would be crucial.

He started counting down at a whisper. "Five, four, three, two . . ."

At the zero mark Allison touched her finger to Colin's one-touch call listing, raised the phone to her ear, and listened for the first ring. Then she dropped the phone into her purse, the connection with her nephew left open.

They sprang to their feet, Kealey sidling his MP5K with his right hand and gripping Allison's forearm with the other as they launched themselves onto the mezzanine and went racing over the wide-open hell of the exhibition hall.

Colin Dearborn had scuttled to his right, still crouching, and thrust his phone deep in the pot of an artificial silk Ruscus tree. It was the nearest of the four trees that lined the wall. Then he scuttled back, putting as much distance between himself and the ceramic container as possible. He froze as soon as the guard at the door turned back to look across the room. It was a routine pass, nothing suspicious in the set of the man's head, shoulders, or weapon.

No one had moved for as long as they had been here, not even when Colin made his little crab move. Most of the people were either sobbing or praying, aware of nothing but their own immediate space and the disposition of the guards at the door.

The first power chords of "London Calling" by the Clash chopped rhythmically from his cell phone, the bass line sliding into them as their volume swelled and the vocals broke through on a heavy, crashing downbeat:

> London calling to the faraway towns,
> Now that war is declared—and battle come
> down . . .

His assault weapon snapping upward in his hands, the guard inside the room vaulted from the door toward the mass of prisoners huddled toward the back of the room. There was a surprised, befuddled expression on his face. His gaze darted across the sea of mostly bowed heads, swept over them, settled on the tree even as the door flew wide open and a second masked killer came charging in from the hallway.

The music went on for thirty seconds before it cut off and his aunt's incoming call was transferred to voice mail. By then the masked guards had pushed through the group and were pulling up the fake Spanish moss in the pots, flinging it madly across the room. It took them just seconds to find the phone—not long, but long enough he hoped. Kealey certainly couldn't have expected more. He had to know Colin's options were limited.

Now that he thought of it, though, Colin realized it was more than just the few seconds he'd bought. It was the time it took for the guards to come through the crowd, find the phone, look at it, and start to try and figure out who it belonged to. During that entire time, he, Colin, had taken four eyeballs off the corridor to help enable whatever Kealey was planning.

His heart was pounding hard. Sweat rolled down his pants legs. Each instant seemed stretched—not taut but loose, drooping, like Silly Putty—as he wondered if this . . . no, this . . . no *this* was going to be the last second of his life.

The first guard whipped around and held the cell phone aloft to show it to the gathered hostages.

"To who this belong?" he shouted in broken English. "Who?"

His stomach a band of tension, Colin remained squatting in fearful silence. His brain ticked off the added seconds he was buying Kealey.

"*Who?*" repeated the masked man. Gripping the phone hard, waving it in the air, shaking it furiously in the air. *"Tell me!"*

If anyone had a suspicion, they were too afraid to voice it. Or maybe it was courage, a last act of defiance. Colin didn't know.

Jesus, he thought. *You're writing tweets in your head.*

With a gruff oath, the other guard said something to the man with the phone. It was in a language Colin did not understand. He didn't have to. He knew what they were doing. The men were to his right. Colin rolled his head slowly in that direction.

They were pressing buttons on the phone. The men might not be able to read the tweets or figure out real names from Twitter accounts, but there was one language he knew they would understand.

They were going through his photos. Colin estimated there were two dozen pictures of him stored in the album, shots in which he was posing with a smile, which might as well be a giant bull's-eye.

More seconds were passing. Each one was a small triumph for Colin, but he knew they were running out. He pulled in a breath, hoping it would settle him, but he was beyond any semblance of calm. His legs were shaking, barely able to support him. He shifted to his knees. The men were so intent on the phone, they didn't notice. He looked at the door, wondered what his chances were of getting there, over and around his fellow hostages, before the guards could fire. The likelihood was probably real small, but he knew he did not want to die here, doing nothing except perspiring into his Nikes.

He was wondering how much longer he could hold himself together when he heard the commotion, a sudden uproar in the corridor. The noise was like fresh air blowing into the room. He heard a radio crackle on one of the men, heard the masked men move, saw them step on hands and bags on their way to the door, bringing their guns around with them.

It was only as the shooting started that he realized he still hadn't exhaled.

* * *

Kealey saw the stairs leading to the third floor as they emerged from the walkway. They were straight ahead. He ran with his shoulders rolled forward, his chin tucked into his chest, and his legs working like pistons, the way he'd once run through simulated cross fire on the training courses at Fort Bragg; the way he'd run through the war-blasted streets of Kosovo, loaded down with weapons and 150 pounds of combat gear, dodging sniper rounds from windows, rooftops, and doorways as he moved from one position to another; the way he'd run to avoid getting cut to ribbons or blown out of existence in burning deserts, steamy jungles, and urban hellholes around the bloody, violent world.

His hand still clutching Allison's forearm, she kept her head low alongside him, a quick study, and it was a good thing, too. This was a natural kill zone, open, without concealment, but he'd had no time to spell out the risks, nor seen any upside to it. It was in or out, and she would not want to leave without trying to help her nephew.

Anyway, what would he have told her? Just keep *moving* so you weren't a large, exposed target—survival could be that basic in a fight no matter how alert you were, how effective your weapons, how thorough your training.

Incredibly, most of the interior systems seemed to be on in this section of the building, the air-conditioning cycling to make it breathable in here, the large metal halides overhead merging with the brightness from whatever late-day sunlight was still pouring through the glass walls and ceiling. That made sense: whatever backup electrical system the facility had, this would be an area from whence the most people were leaving or, in an emergency, where the most would naturally congregate.

Glancing neither left nor right, his eyes on the stairway a few yards in front of him, Kealey still managed to scan both sides of the mezzanine with his peripheral vision and caught glimpses of the horrible scene down in the exhibition hall: fallen debris, blasted plywood booths, toppled signs, broken glass, bodies everywhere. Those still alive and able to move appeared to have been herded toward separate ends of the hall; Kealey supposed their captors' next step would be to gather them into conference rooms with the other hostages or massacre them right there on the spot, an undeniable possibility.

It won't come to that, Kealey thought. He wouldn't *let* it.

They dashed across the last few feet to the stairs. Kealey figured they would need less than thirty seconds to make their way through the open mezzanine, and hoped the gunmen downstairs would be too preoccupied with the prisoner roundup and Colin's cell phone to spot them immediately.

Reaching the stairs, they bounded up them, taking them as quickly as possible. They had gotten to within four steps of the mid-floor landing when Allison produced a kind of clipped, horrified gasp. They both snatched hold of the handrail as their feet nearly slipped on the blood. Slick and dark, it was everywhere, reflecting the overhead lights and streaming down the risers to puddle on the flat marble treads.

She could not help but stare up at the body, even as Kealey pulled her around it. Riddled with bullets, one

leg dangling loosely over the edge of the landing, it belonged to a young man about Colin's age. Kealey had
noticed the momentary dread that passed over Allison's
face before she focused on the bloodied clothes plas-
tering him. They weren't Colin's. There would have
been no way to tell his identity from his features; the
shots that had torn into his skull had left the victim
badly disfigured.

Kealey squeezed her hand as they hurried up the remaining stairs to the third-floor hallway.

On the wall to Kealey's right were signs for the conference rooms, and past them the large glass door to
the corridor. He raised his weapon slightly as they
drew closer, and that was when he saw the masked man
in the slight recess leading toward the door, guarding it
there on the mezzanine. The man saw them, too, and his
submachine gun came up quickly.

Kealey caught him with a 3-round burst at close to
point-blank range, then instantly triggered a second
burst. The man dropped without firing a single round,
blood erupting from his chest, hitting the floor with a
soft smack as his weapon went twirling from his grasp
like a flung baton.

"Come on," Kealey grunted, leaping over the man's
body and pushing through the door into the corridor.
He immediately saw four black-clad men outside a
room up ahead to the left, maybe 20 feet up the corridor. They had started turning toward him, toward the
sound of the gunfire. Kealey cut them down as he simultaneously pulled Allison directly behind him. It
was an easy strike; the masked men were all in a row,
one behind the other, all but the first man blocked from

firing at him by the man in front of him. And that first man never got a chance to do anything but die.

The fact that the men were clustered around the door, not fully turned toward the corridor, showed that his plan had worked. They had been facing the room, waiting to see who had managed to get a cell phone inside. That had bought him the seconds he needed to cross the walkway after shooting the guard.

As soon as the four men went down, Kealey stiff-armed Allison across the chest, pushing her back toward the wall and following her up against it. He waited. He did not think that whoever was inside the room would strafe the corridor without first making sure the four guards were down.

A masked forehead poked out, one eye looking down the corridor. The side of the man's face evaporated in blood. The head dropped.

"*Down!*" Kealey hissed to Allison, simultaneously pulling her and dropping. He held his firearm in front of him, arms extended, hands cradling the weapon. He might have only a second to fire.

Someone else inside stuck his automatic out and fired chest high down the corridor—just as Kealey had expected. He saw the black glove and ignored the flashing gunfire, which chewed ceramic projectiles from the wall and painfully peppered his head and cheek. He found the hand with the nub on the barrel and destroyed it with a three-shot burst. The man yelped, dropped the gun, and withdrew his hand.

Though his ears were singing from the gunfire, Kealey had long ago trained himself to filter sounds through the hum. It was like listening underwater: the activity was there, but at a different pitch and volume. Fortunately, the enemy usually suffered from the same disability without Kealey's training.

There were no sounds from inside the room. The hostages hadn't been emboldened to take him out, which meant he had another weapon or there were still other gunmen inside. The fact that killers had not emerged from any other locations suggested they assumed this was just another mass murder of hostages. Still, it wouldn't be long before some centralized control checked in. There had to be a unit leader. The room had to be taken before then.

He turned to Allison. She was breathing like a rabbit.

"As soon as I take off, I want you to count to thirty Mississippi," Kealey said. "When you're done, call Colin's number."

"Why?"

"I haven't seen his cell phone anywhere," Kealey told her. "One or two thugs may still be among the hostages. I'll try and use my target as a shield, tag whoever's left. But if more of these guys come down the hall from ahead, get out the way we came. Fast."

She was processing the information, nodding numbly.

"Stay strong," he said. "I think reinforcements are on the way."

She shot him a questioning look, but he did not elaborate.

Kealey let his weapon hang from its strap. He got his feet under him, reached into his jacket, and withdrew his *balisong*. A flick of his wrist and the double-handled knife snapped open, its six-inch stainless-steel blade locking with a soft click, coldly mirroring Kealey's eyes as they stared ahead.

Taking a breath and exhaling, he took three charging steps forward. Kealey swung into the open door like a bull, low with his hands in front like horns. He saw the man with the wounded hand kneeling. He was snarling in the ear of a blond woman, his gun at her head. Her hands were raised, and she was sobbing, shaking her head, but she was rising just the same. The gunman was getting up with her. He obviously intended to use her as a human shield. The wounded man turned just in time to be hit, full on, by Kealey.

The American locked his left hand around the wrist with the gun, pointing the weapon up. With his right hand he sank the blade into the hollow of the man's throat, a quarter inch above the collarbone. The blonde shrieked and dropped and covered her head with her fingers, still screaming. The man gurgled and thrashed, hot blood brewing from the wound, his hands clutching at Kealey's, trying to pull it away from him, pull the knife from his throat. But Kealey thrust it in deeper, angling the blade up toward the subclavian and giving it a hard, sharp twist to completely sever the artery and finish him.

All the while Kealey held the man up by his forearm and the blade, keeping him between himself and the hostages—and any potential attacker.

His knuckles wet and slick around the knife, he felt the man go limp. Kealey was carrying his deadweight now and went to his knees. It was quiet enough for Kealey to hear the splash of the man's blood as it hit the floor around him.

No one fired at him, but that didn't mean anything. Kealey had a dead man for protection and an assault rifle on his shoulder. He was still a formidable enemy.

The phone sounded. Someone barked with surprise, threw it with a grunt. The phone cracked on the floor.

The voice had come from the corner ahead and to Kealey's left. Kealey glanced under the dead man's armpit. He saw a gunman rise from the back of the crowd, pulling Colin Dearborn with him. He had the young man by the collar, the bore of his assault rifle pushing into the soft flesh under his chin. Kealey guessed the man had heard him talking to Allison or had simply assumed there were others out there, possibly an entire unit. He couldn't know for sure, and there had been enough shooting to create that impression.

Which is probably the reason no one from the other rooms has attacked, Kealey thought. He had a good idea the bad guys hadn't been able to confirm anything with video surveillance. Someone on the outside had seen Allison's tweet. Somewhere, someone had either cut the trunk line that ran the system or had gotten into the security center. That could also have fueled the idea that they were under siege.

This ape was supposed to find that out. He had a Bluetooth in his ear, like the others. He was going to try to hostage his way into the corridor, see what was up, let the others know. Kealey hadn't slipped on one of the headsets he'd confiscated, because he hadn't wanted to be distracted.

The man stood behind Colin, his back to the floor-to-ceiling window, one arm locked around Colin's throat. The rest of the frightened, wide-eyed hostages had begun sliding to the other side of the room, creating a clear path between the man and Kealey.

"*Jebem ti mater!*" the gunman husked through his mask. "*Vi æte ga gledati umreti.*"

Kealey regarded him without expression. Still on his knees, he simultaneously hefted the dead man to his right and swung his own firearm around. He felt as if he'd been kicked through a dark, spiraling time warp. His lack of visible emotion gave no hint of his surprise and puzzlement. It had been over a decade since he'd heard Serbian spoken by a native, but he'd recognized it now, remembered the dialect from down in southern Kosovo, and understood the coarse profanity followed by an invitation to watch Colin die. No doubt the man hadn't expected Kealey to understand. It was just one of those spit-in-your-eye gestures so common to Eastern European insurgents. What was stranger, though, was that in the corridor minutes ago, when the other hostage takers had been shouting excitedly to one another, they had been speaking some other language entirely.

A moment passed. Another. Kealey stood there, pulling the long-unused vocabulary from his memory, giving its particular syntax a moment to click into place.

"*Steta ga i . . . da æ . . . biti ubi Jeni,*" he said at last. He was warning the man that he would also wind up dead if he tried anything. "*Ja ài te ubiti . . . sebe.*" Kealey was promising that he would make sure of it, would kill the man himself.

The man snorted. "*Yawa zhaba heskla bus nada!*"

Kealey didn't respond. That had not been Serbian.

It was the same language he'd heard from the others out in the corridor. *Pashto,* he thought.

What the hell is this? A convention of anti-American terrorists? Someone at Immigration and Naturalization was going to have a lot of explaining to do when, dead or alive, the gunmen were all ID'd.

Kealey kept staring into the room. Behind the gunman, the window shimmered a little as the lights of a hovering helicopter bounced off its tinted laminated glass, coming in almost horizontally over the church across the street. For a moment, the hostage taker and Colin were in stark silhouette. The helicopter was far enough away, at least a half mile, so that the sound did not intrude. Their gun-muffled hearing also worked to conceal its presence.

Shifting his gaze to Colin, Kealey was able to hear his rasping intakes of air. He looked at the weapon under Colin's chin, at the hand in the fingerless shooter's glove clenched around its stippled grip.

"I didn't come to play games," Kealey said at last. "What do you want with these people?"

The gunman laughed, shifting to English. "They say the more languages one speaks, the better one can know other men."

Kealey looked at him. "That doesn't answer my question."

"Who are you?" the man asked. "You do not seem FBI."

"I'm the janitor," Kealey said flatly.

"That doesn't answer *my* question," the man snapped. Without warning, he tightened his choke hold around Colin's neck, pushing his head up higher with the assault rifle. Colin gagged audibly, a sound like water draining through a clogged pipe.

"Who is out there? How many of you?" the man demanded.

"What's it matter?" Kealey asked. "You've lost."

"I have won!" he roared. "I enter your house to kill as many as I can, to send your people to the grave one after another."

There were muffled sobs from different places around the room.

"Even if it means joining them?" Kealey asked.

"If I accomplish my goal, yes."

Kealey felt his stomach wring tight with anger, but he just kept staring at him, his face a shield of calm. He needed to stall. Help was coming, but he had to make sure it came soon enough to save Colin.

"I remember Cuska after the massacre," Kealey said. "I saw what the Sakali did to the villagers. Do you know what I said to one of the killers?"

The man did not respond. Obviously, Kealey was not FBI. The references had caught him off guard.

"I told him that he would die in torment if he harmed anyone else." Kealey's voice dropped as he said, "I told him, '*Al sizvul.*' " He had chosen his words carefully, using the idiomatic Serbian phrase for "blood oath." "I say that now to you," Kealey went on, "and to whoever is working with you, and to whoever you leave behind. I will find them and make it my business to kill them. Or we can stop this now."

"You think I fear you?" the gunman yelled.

"It doesn't matter," Kealey said. "It's over."

They looked at each other, Colin between them.

Kealey kept his eyes steady, appearing to stare at the man while again letting his gaze travel past him to the window. Outside, the spotlight from the helicopter seemed to coat the church towers with molten gold as it washed over their high, curved roofs before splashing brightly up against the smooth glass wall of the convention center. But it was no longer shining on the window behind the gunman. And there was a good reason for that.

Recon was over.

Suddenly, the gunman's patience appeared to run out. The man jerked the arm he'd clamped around Colin's neck up with a sudden violent motion that audibly stopped his breath. The hostage taker began moving forward with the young man, who was gagging as he tried to walk on his toes.

Kealey felt his stomach constrict. He wished to hell *he* knew what was going on outside this room. Because the only option he seemed to have left was to take a shot at the man, drawing his fire and hoping he could kill the son of a bitch before he himself went down.

Chandra knelt on the wooden boards of the bell platform, the barrel of a Heckler & Koch PSG-1 sniper rifle cradled in his left hand, his right wrapped lightly around its grip, his elbows carefully balanced on the sill beneath the tower's window arch. Inhaling, exhaling, getting into the right breathing tempo, he peered through the weapon's powerful 6x42 telescopic sight, studying his target through the third-floor window of the convention center across the street.

There were good shooters, and there were snipers.

There were methods and formations that could make ordinary shooters better—by making a "figure eight" rotation with the barrel and firing at the peak of the second circle, or by firing in between breaths, but not actually *holding* your breath—but just how fast and how accurate a shooter was at making the calls and the shots, estimating a long-range target's distance, adjusting for conditions, stalking the prey to the point of invisibility, learning to live with discomfort in even the most serene terrains, and disguising himself to adapt to the most hell-sucking surroundings, anywhere and nowhere, and all while never existing in the enemy's eye, that was what demarcated a sniper. A sniper was as stealthy as his rifle was deadly.

Chandra was a city boy, recognized by his comrades more for his precision than his trail-hunting abilities; country boys were better known for tracking. But in either battlefield setting, it was imperative that scopes and muzzles remained invisible. If they couldn't see you, they couldn't hit you. Luckily for Chandra, urban environments were filled with glinting metal structures and flickering lights and windows. *Perfect cover for a sniper rifle.*

Beside him, in a nearly identical firing position, Alterman held a rifle of the same make and model, which gave them almost thirty thousand dollars' worth of precision ordnance to match the twenty years of training and experience between them here in the church tower. Both agents, in addition, wore tactical vests and black unis with the circular black and silver patch of the FBI's Hostage Rescue Team sewn onto their shoulders, though only Alterman, the pair's senior member, had on amber shooter's glasses.

In his flippant moments—and this was anything but one—the Indonesian-born Darma Chandra joked that the glasses were a sign of the other man's advancing decrepitude, Alterman being forty-three years old in comparison to his thirty. But Chandra knew his partner was the most capable and seasoned marksman in the unit, having been certified at the U.S. Marines Corps's 4th MEB antiterrorism school at Camp Lejeune, having done advanced recon in northern Afghanistan, then having been selected for diplomatic and embassy security in Kabul back in the days when Taliban assassins were a common roadside presence in and around the city.

Chandra didn't have quite as colorful a background, having spent his entire career stateside since joining the FBI fresh out of college—and with new citizenship. And while his top gun rating in the SWAT and sniper courses gave him cred among his peers, he willingly bowed to Alterman's expertise. After the president's executive ARI order had been received—All Resources In, overriding the allocation of sectors and jurisdictional red tape, and triggering the FBI-led assault—there had been not a word of discussion about who would execute the takeout. Alterman was boss all the way.

The BPD chopper had lighted the target before withdrawing, allowing their helmet cameras to grab an image for reference. The radio-linked gun laser locked on the target selected by the heads-up displays in the sharpshooters' glasses. The laser did not determine the actual trajectory; that was in the hands of the marksman. It simply created a circle, about the size of a wedding band, for aiming. The target discs were far more diffuse than the old single-point laser beams. It was unlikely that anyone inside the kill zone would see the circle unless they were looking.

Chandra's job would be to fire a heartbeat before Alterman, aiming slightly away from the target, breaking the window to leave a clear path for Alterman's bullet. Although with Chandra shooting through glass—the convention center architects had used a fairly standard glazed laminate for their floor-to-ceiling windows—it was always possible that his round would be sufficiently deflected to hit the mark.

But that wasn't something they expected. Made for precision shooting, their NATO Ball Special 7.62mm loads weren't especially frangible. They would not break up or lose their shape on impact with the layered glass. The church steeple itself was a good hide, offering them shade and concealment, and the torpid weather conditions eliminated wind as a variable in the bullets' trajectories. All factors considered, both snipers wouldn't need spotters. Second shots here were not an option. And both men knew it.

His cheek against the HK's black synthetic stock, Chandra saw the gunman continue to press his weapon into the hostage's throat while facing the Company guy, or whatever he was, who had come running into the conference room and had taken down one of the hostage takers in a slick, nasty bit of business. It did not look to Chandra like he was making any progress in getting the mark to surrender. Just moments before the Company guy had raised his assault rifle. Classic standoff. But with a weapon to the throat of a hostage and the SWAT teams already closing in, time was not on the snipers' side.

"Ready to do this?" Alterman said, as if reading his thoughts. They had been given full discretion on proceeding with the drop, and the senior agent was clearly in sync with him on the pointlessness of waiting.

"Yeah."

"On my count," Alterman said.

Chandra resumed his rhythmic breathing, centering the target in his crosshairs and then tilting the gun up by a tiny degree.

"Standby," Alterman said. "Four, three, two, one . . ."

Chandra exhaled on the *one,* aimed in the center of his own faint red circle and, at Alterman's fire command, gave the trigger of his rifle a smooth pull.

His full metal jacket NATO slug broke the conference room's sheet-glass window with a crack and drilled harmlessly into the wall above their mark's head. An imperceptible moment later, Alterman's full metal jacket round entered the room, twinkling as it passed through the down-turned chopper beacon.

Out in the corridor, Allison heard what sounded like the sharp *tak* of a stone bouncing off the windshield of a car, a high-pitched whine, and then the screams. The first cry came from Colin. She had heard that whoop at enough U of V Cavaliers basketball games to be sure of it. The rest of the yells came from many different people, men and women. But there were no sounds of gunfire, not from within the room.

She went rushing into the conference room. As Allison moved clumsily on cramped legs, she became aware of the rumbling of automatic weapons fire in the distance. It sounded different than what she and Kealey had heard before. This was rhythmic, deeper, somehow *coordinated*.

It was instantly forgotten as she swung into the room. She nearly tripped over the throat-cut guard at the door, splatting through the pool of his blood as she swerved around him, her eyes seeking Colin. She saw the people who'd been crowded together at one end of the room rising slowly, like time-lapse plants, looking as stunned and overwhelmed as she was. Then she saw Kealey crouched beside her nephew, comforting him. Colin was squatting and was covered with blood. It looked like he had been the loser in a paintball competition, and her first thought was that they had failed Colin, failed him totally and horribly. He was covered with such a massive quantity of blood that her mind initially refused to accept what she was seeing. She was a doctor; she'd seen people bleed. She was very aware that the five and a half quarts in a human body Colin's size was a *lot* of blood when you saw it draining out. But *this* much . . . How was he even awake? As she scurried forward, dropping the gun, her eyes scanned for a wound. Perhaps in his back, his shoulder . . .

"Colin!"

His eyes snapped toward her. He was sobbing openly, but not from pain. Something resembling a smile pulled at his mouth.

"He's okay," Kealey told her. His voice seemed far away, hollow, like he was in the bottom of a trash can.

Kealey helped Colin up by the arm.

And then, behind Colin, she saw the fallen gunman. He was lying facedown, splayed like a crime-scene chalk outline. The back of his head was gone, disintegrated, tiny bits of white showing around its gaping remnants like the pieces of a broken eggshell. There was the source of all the blood.

She was crying by the time she reached Colin. She threw her arms around him, felt his weight fall into them—but only for a moment, as he sought to stand on his own.

"I'm okay, Aunt Allison," he said, sounding like the little boy she used to hug, when he let her, on birthdays and holidays.

"I love you," she said. "I was so worried."

"Me too," he replied, weeping.

Her fingers feeling Colin's scalp just to be sure, she turned to Kealey while she held him. "Thank you," she sputtered.

"Wasn't all me," he said. Facing the exterior wall, he made a show of unshouldering his weapon and placing it on the floor before walking toward the shattered window. "We got some help. And I'm guessing there's more on the way."

"Those shots . . . ?" Alison asked.

"From the church," Kealey said as he reached the empty window frame and flashed a thumbs-up at the steeple. "It's the only place that has a direct line of sight."

Allison sought out the church, could barely see it in the dark. Then a helicopter moved in, throwing a bright white light across the steeple as it rotated toward the broken window. She looked away.

Kealey returned to her side a moment later. "I have to go," he said.

"Why?" she asked.

"I have to get upstairs to the ballroom. The one where Julie was supposed to give her speech."

Allison released her nephew. "Dear God, forgive me!" she said. "I forgot."

"No need to apologize," he said. He bent to retrieve the gun. "We've been thinking in little, bite-size pieces."

"But we don't even know if she's—"

"There's a lot we don't know," Kealey interrupted. "So let's take things one at a time. How are you?"

"Don't worry about me, Ryan."

He regarded her closely. "You sure?"

She nodded.

He looked at her nephew. "Colin?"

"Same here," Colin said, although his voice was tremulous. "Man, you did so good," he said. "You saved me."

"You got us here, and you stayed cool," Kealey said. "It was a team effort. You saved all these people, too," he added with a sweep of his arm behind him. "Your tweet said the hostages were in two groups. Where are the others?"

"They're in a room across the hall."

"How many altogether?"

"Fifteen, maybe twenty people. They separated us down the middle."

"The number of guards with them?"

"I don't know exactly."

"Your best guess," Kealey said. "It's important."

Colin looked thoughtful. "I think they split in half," he said. "There was *him,* you know"—he glanced back at the dead gunman's body—"and a second guy, who left the room when he heard the noise out there. The one you got with the knife. Then there was a third guy, who I'm guessing you shot at the door."

"So you're saying there were only a few in each room. That's it?"

"I think so, yeah."

"Ryan, I heard gunfire downstairs," Allison said.

"Those were point men for the hostage takers being picked off by SWAT personnel," Kealey said. "I heard it, too. The enemy was patrolling in twos, and there were a dozen bursts from FBI Glock twenty-twos. Nothing since. Our boys are working their way up here methodically, standard operating procedure, and they may not be in time. Not if the guys in the other room figure out they're licked."

He didn't have to finish the thought. Allison knew what he meant.

Kealey retrieved his weapon and slid his arm through the leather strap. He pulled in a breath, blew air out his cheeks, and turned toward the door. Everyone else in the room was standing there, looking at him, awaiting instructions.

"You're all going to stay put," he said. "Help is on the way. I'm—"

He stopped.

"What is it?" Allison asked.

Kealey held up a hand to silence her. He tilted his head toward the window, listening. Allison saw his expression go from thoughtful to sharply attentive.

"Ryan?"

"Hush!" he snapped.

She and Colin were silent.

Kealey listened some more, wanting to confirm

what he'd heard. The sounds were rapidly getting louder. They were overlapping in multiples, the telltale *whoop* of rotors accompanied by the whine of turbo-charged engines.

He turned back to Allison, saw the question on her face as she also picked up on the growing sound. Within seconds it had swelled to fill their ears.

"Ryan . . . ?"

Kealey looked at her. "Choppers," he said, throwing down his assault rifle an instant before the room was awash in white light. "Lose your weapon—fast."

CHAPTER 10

BALTIMORE, MARYLAND

Baltimore-Washington International Airport was the second embarkation point for the four Sikorsky UH-60M Black Hawk helicopters designated for the mission. The first was a closely guarded heliport at Marine Corps Base Quantico, which encompassed almost 75 square miles of forest in Prince William County, Virginia, and was also home to the FBI Academy, where the Bureau's elite Hostage Rescue Team was stationed as a major tactical component of the Critical Incident Response Group. Optimized for rapid force delivery capabilities, each of the choppers had been boarded by twenty heavily armed HRT personnel in full combat garb. A pair of MH-6 Little Birds had then accompanied them to BWI for final deployment; these nimble, lightweight choppers would provide aerial recon and fire support when the Black Hawks reached their target.

Only 9 miles south of downtown Baltimore, BWI was an ideal staging point for the second-front unit, the official order for which was issued by FBI director Charles Cluzot under the direct authorization of the president. The SWAT teams were officially designated first front because they were already on-site. However, their sweep-and-secure ingress would take time. If they met resistance, they might not be able to provide the kind of RTA—Rapid Target Attack—ordered by the commander in chief.

Honed and practiced in a realistic city mock-up constructed deep in the Prince William County woodlands, the HRT's swarm and penetration techniques relied on multiple elements acting in tight coordination: flooding the site with assault teams while snipers on adjacent rooftops—and gunners in so-called monkey harnesses riding the skids of the Little Birds—covered them from all sides.

The helicopters' arrival at the convention center was logged at 6:23 p.m. EST. Within a minute of that time, the lead Black Hawk had already banked in low over the building, delivering a stream of CS powder to clear it of hostiles who might be on the rooftop, a necessary precaution even though none had been observed by the AW139 already on-site. The windless conditions were favorable for use of the CS, limiting dispersal to the target area and thus making it unlikely that civilians would be affected.

After a brief interval the chopper returned with the others, all four lowering to stationary hovers above both the new and old sections of the convention center complex. Then hatches opened, rope lines dropped from their hoist brackets, and the rappel teams made their descent onto the rooftops, eighty of them sliding down one after another in swift succession.

Using safety handrails as anchor points, they strad-dled their ropes and began their descent with a spring-ing hop-skip, their backs straight, legs spread, bodies leaned outward from the sides of the building.

Meanwhile, radios crackling, the teams raced across the tar to previously identified access doors, breaching them with their rams.

In their dark gray uniforms, body armor, vests, hel-mets, and face shields, bristling with M16s and combat shotguns, tacs almost resembled warrior beetles to the pilots of the departing choppers as they packed into the service stairs and then hurried down toward the build-ing's fourth floor to begin their sweep.

Kealey was facing the window as the top-rappel team came sliding down in their harnesses, their boots flat against the side of the building. Kicking jagged edges of broken glass from around the steel window frame, a half dozen of them poured into the conference room in their tactical gear, machine guns leveled.

One of them shouted, "Toss your weapons onto the floor in front of me. Then put your hands up over your head!"

"We're unarmed," Kealey said. His hands were raised, and he used his toe to point to the MP5K on the floor. "Your sniper team in the church took this guy out. They can confirm."

"Everyone in the room, raise . . . your . . . hands!"

The man had drawn the last three words out as a way of giving them added emphasis. He couldn't have said them louder, since he was already yelling.

Kealey hadn't expected his pronouncement to change

ingress protocol. Nor this: "I'm Ryan Kealey. We sent the messages that brought you here."

A man picked up Kealey's gun. His face was invisible behind the black, skintight balaclava, which covered his face from the bridge of his nose down, and the goggles, which concealed the rest. He kept his weapon trained on Kealey.

With a reverse chop of his upraised forearm, one team leader signaled the other that this room was clear. He chopped forward to indicate to his unit to assume a file formation beside the door. The team leader who was staying behind had been talking into his throat mike. Finished, he walked over to Kealey. He did not remove his amber goggles or raise his balaclava.

"Who are you?" he demanded.

"Ryan Kealey—"

"Who are you *with?*"

"She's Company. I'm former," Kealey said. He had forgotten, for a moment, the priorities in securing a hot zone. It didn't matter what indigenous occupants were called, but where their loyalties lay. "We were here to attend the nursing dinner," he said. "Look, there may be more gunmen in the room across the hall. These guys and some of the dead men on the steps are Eastern European. I don't know why they're here or who they work for. I do know they've threatened to kill all the hostages—"

As he spoke, he heard the familiar sizzle of flash-bang grenades. Not only was the M84 designed to blind and deafen the enemy, but it also sent the equivalent of an electric shock through the eyes and into the brain, scrambling all thought, while simultaneously hammering each side of the skull with what felt like a mallet. The fluid of the ear was so severely compromised by the explosion, it was almost impossible to remain upright. The result was that if any of the hostiles in the vicinity of the blast had been holding a gun to a hostage's head, they would have been debilitated before they could fire. It would also have floored most of the hostages, keeping them below incoming gunfire. The two blasts were followed by the equally familiar pops of the M4 carbines the assault team had been carrying.

Six shots. There was no other gunfire. The ordeal was over.

"Please let us go there," Allison said. "Our friend Julie Harper—"

"I'm sorry, ma'am. You have to remain here," said the team leader.

"Or what?" she demanded.

Kealey answered before the team leader could. "Or they'll cuff and book you." He regarded the HRT officer. "The exhibition hall," Kealey said. "I'm sure the SWAT team has reached it by now."

"I can't provide you with any information—"

"I'm not asking for any. I'm *telling* you," Kealey said. "You'd be on your way down there if they hadn't."

The man shifted uncomfortably but said nothing.

"The president will want to know about the woman who was running the show there, Mrs. Julie Harper. Would you please get us clearance to check ASAP? It'll make our lives a helluva lot easier—mine now and yours later."

The tac studied Kealey for a long moment, then said into his throat mike, "Command, this is Griffith. I need a check on a Ryan Kealey. K, kilo . . . ?"

Kealey spelled it for him, and the team leader spelled it back, adding the appropriate radio jargon for clarity.

Kealey didn't blame the man for checking. But it reminded him why he had always been a solo operator and believed that looking into a person's eyes told you everything you needed to know, and more than any file could possibly tell you.

Before turning to organize triage, the young man identified himself to Kealey as Special Agent London Griffith. Kealey didn't ask about the name. Maybe over a beer one day he would. Right now he didn't care. Griffith had finally removed his goggles, and he left Kealey and Allison standing where they were while medics arrived to check on the former hostages. Colin went with them.

He gave his aunt a hug and Kealey a handshake before going to the cots that were being brought into the corridor. The dead men had been covered with black vinyl sheets, but they could not be moved until a postmortem team arrived to photograph the scene and—for purely tactical reasons—analyze the effectiveness of the steeple takedown and the flash-bang assault. It was felt that providing care for the hostages would be better accomplished where there were no dead bodies and where the air didn't smell of oily silica gel.

Kealey and Allison stood there in silence, holding hands. It was only an hour before that they were acting like tourists, chatting about fish, and looking forward to a relaxed evening and a little social triumph for their friend.

Now they didn't know whether or not she was even alive.

Griffith returned after a few minutes. He was an African American, about thirty, with soft brown eyes and a scar across his right cheek. He wore a strange, uncomfortable look that Kealey recognized.

"Mr. Kealey, sir, you and Ms. Dearborn are cleared for escort to the exhibition hall," he told them.

"Any word on casualties?" Kealey asked.

"They were described as considerable, sir," Griffith said. "If you'll follow Agent O'Neill, she will take you to the exhibition hall. After that, she will escort you outside the convention center."

A young woman had walked up behind them. At Griffith's command, she headed for the door. Kealey and Allison followed, still holding hands. Obviously, the matter had been booted up several levels—possibly to Jon Harper himself. They were to be permitted access and then gotten the hell out. Not for their safety, Kealey knew, but because he'd single-handedly done the job the FBI was supposed to have been handling. He was both a hero and an embarrassment. Kealey saw *that* in Griffith's expression.

They crammed hastily into the stairwell, Kealey and Allison entering behind O'Neill, other tacs in her detachment falling in at the rear as the group made their way to the next floor, moving as one, a multi-headed organism, their footfalls striking a rapid, un-echoing beat on the concrete steps.

The air had cleared somewhat, leaving a thin layer of white powder on the floor. It wasn't ash; it was matter that had been pulverized by the blast. The heat inside the convention center had caused it to rise, forming the tester Kealey and Allison had passed through earlier. But now that power was being restored and the air-conditioning was back in various sectors, now that gravity was overcoming the thermal lift, the particles were dropping.

There were probably fragments of human beings in the powder.

On the upper landing, O'Neill halted briefly by the metal fire door. Kealey heard Allison snatch in a breath and tried not to betray his own apprehension, but he could feel it tighten his chest from the inside like an expanding metal ring. O'Neill shouldered open the door, Kealey following her through, into what he guessed was the pre-function room.

Kealey felt his stomach slide as he realized the damage up here was as bad as anything he'd glimpsed elsewhere. He heard Allison groan behind him. It was too late to tell her to turn away. Every sickening piece of the tableau was seared instantly into memory. The odor of charred plastic, rubber, and flesh would never be forgotten.

They stood side by side, looking at the blasted walls; the collapsed, dripping ceiling panels; the light fixtures dangling from scorched and blackened clumps of electrical wire; the broken glasses and bottles and pieces of tables, chairs, and other smashed and over-turned furnishings that had been scattered around the cocktail area and ballroom. The microphone had melted on its stand and looked like ice cream that had pooled and been refrozen.

Kealey saw people lying on the slick, wet, debris-strewn floor, many of them dead, some with their bodies burned in spots to stiff, charred bone. From just inside the entrance it appeared the survivors outnumbered the fatalities, but whatever measure of comfort that gave

Kealey was tempered by the sight of all the wounded: they were everywhere, bleeding, moaning, ripped apart. Many had probably been deafened, permanently, by the blast.

Crouched over them, their clothes torn and soiled, dozens of men and women were tending to the injured. FBI tacs were circulating throughout the room, after having made their entries through the windows and stairs. They were trying to assist as best they could. O'Neill's detachment joined them.

Kealey felt Allison clutch his arm.

"Ryan, I see Julie," she said, pointing.

The horror had so overwhelmed him, he had forgotten why he was here. It was one thing to see destruction abroad, in the third world, among people you didn't know. This was a waking nightmare.

He followed her finger to a woman stretched out on the floor against one wall. A man was kneeling over her.

They made their way around O'Neill, quickly picking their way over and around the wreckage covering the floor. Partway over Kealey stepped on something soft, something that gave under his step—a hand. Just a hand. He kept going.

The man crouching beside Julie turned as he heard their approach, but he did not stop working.

Kealey crouched next to him. "She's a friend," he said. "We're here to help."

The man tilted his head sideways to the right. "Can't hear on that side!" he said.

Kealey shifted to the man's left, repeated what he had said.

"I'm José Colon, a doctor." He snickered mirthlessly. "Good thing those SOBs attacked a medical dinner."

Allison shuffled to his left. "You need to get it treated."

"I will," Colon said. "People who are bleeding go first."

Allison offered him a strained approximation of a smile, while Kealey looked at his patient. Her eyes were shut, her blouse was shredded, and her arms and chest were a patchwork of slashes and puncture wounds. The side of her head was matted with blood from a long gash that ran from behind her ear to the top of her head. Colon was treating that now with bottled water and dabbing it with a piece of Julie's blouse. There was a bloody length of material tied tight below her knee; two long, ragged wooden boards bracketed the leg.

The last two fingers of the woman's left hand were gone. Colon had tied off the wound with another piece of blouse. It was saturated with blood, but the stain did not appear to be increasing.

"Mild concussion?" Allison asked, kneeling at the top of Julie's head.

"I think so," Colon said. "Are you a doctor?"

"Psychiatrist," she replied.

"I gave her a GCS before I started on the leg," he said. "She's at two."

"The Glasgow Coma Scale registers neural activity," Allison explained to Kealey as she watched the doctor clean the wound. Two means reacts to painful stimuli and makes sounds."

"That's good?" he asked.

"Better than a one," she replied.

"I treated the hand and leg first because of the bleeding. She's got a compound fracture, but her vitals seem stable."

Allison reached around and carefully lifted Julie's wrist, feeling for a pulse. After a moment she laid it down. "Strong, all things considered." She said to Kealey, "Obviously, you can't know about internal injuries."

"But we do need to find out," Colon said. "I just wanted to stabilize her before they take her away. Can't do much for this without suturing."

"Look, I can finish here," Allison told him. "Please go and get yourself seen to."

Colon leaned back on his heels and nodded. With a final glance at his handiwork, he rose silently, like a wraith.

"Thank you," Allison said after him.

He did not appear to have heard.

"I'm going to have to stitch this up," Allison said. "See what you can get from the medics."

"Give me a minute," Kealey said, climbing awkwardly to his feet. His muscles were cramped and tired. The rest of him wasn't too hot, either.

Allison waited, cleaning the wound as best she could. She used the tips of her fingernails to pluck splinters of glass from Julie's flesh; they appeared to be the remnants of a faceted crystal goblet from someone's table. It took some doing to work them out; they'd hit with force that was sufficient to penetrate, but not pierce, her skull. Fresh blood pumped from the wound as she pulled them free. Allison applied gentle pressure to the cuts as best she could, laying a ribbon of blouse fabric across them and placing her thumb across it.

A minute or so later, Kealey returned with the pack she'd seen an FBI man remove from his vest. The large white print on its black outer fabric read FIELD TRAUMA.

"I need an antiseptic and a fresh dressing, Ryan," she said in a quiet voice.

Kealey crouched beside her. He unzipped the case, reached in, and produced a dressing roll and a packet labeled CELOX.

"I don't see any thread, just—"

"What you've got there will work for now," she interrupted. "Tear open the hemostatic packet."

Kealey pulled off the top and handed it to Allison, who applied the granulated agent to the wound after carefully brushing away Julie's hair. Hair that had been so carefully done earlier that day at the hotel salon. That was the last time they'd spoken. Julie had been anxious but excited about the way things were coming together. . . .

The Celox had the effect of cauterizing the cuts without heat. As soon as the bleeding stopped, Allison pressed the gauze to the wound. It was self-adhesive and large enough to cover nearly the entire side of Julie's head.

"It'll do for now," Allison said.

She looked up, and Kealey followed her gaze. O'Neill was standing behind him with two men and a collapsible gurney.

"We've been ordered to medevac her to GW," she said.

"I'm coming with her," Allison said.

"Yes, ma'am," O'Neill replied. "In fact, we've just received instructions to that effect." She regarded Kealey. "You too, sir."

"I'm a civilian—"

"The president has requested it personally," O'Neill replied. She grinned. "I was instructed to say that when you said what you did."

Kealey grinned back. It felt good to smile, even at something stupid. "I've got a car in the garage here—"

"It will be taken care of," O'Neill replied.

While they were talking, the gurney had been assembled and Julie carefully lifted onto it. Kealey excused himself to have a few words with Colin, who had made his way to the hall, and ten minutes later they were on board an FBI chopper, an intravenous saline drip in Julie's arm, and a transfusion bag feeding blood into the other from a separate line. Although she'd experienced no respiratory difficulties at any point, oxygen was being provided through a breather as a routine precaution. The techs had gone through the checklist of vital signs and had determined her to be in serious but stable condition.

As the helicopter rose smoothly into the night, Kealey looked back at the spotlit disaster zone that had once been the Baltimore Convention Center. Smoke was still curling from several areas as firefighters pumped water into sections from which personnel had been evacuated. Crowds of locals and tourists were gathered beyond the extensive police barricades, and Kealey could see the reds of braking lights, and the glare of headlights, as traffic was backed up for miles.

The ripples of disaster, he thought. Whether the disaster was natural or man-made, the impact came in waves, short term and longer term, keeping people physically and psychologically destabilized. The effect on the individual and on society was aggressively exponential, far surpassing the destructive force of the event itself.

Kealey sat back in the fold-down seat, let his head lean back against the gently vibrating headrest. There was nothing he could do about the big picture. His job had always been to focus on the triggers. Even now, his forensic soul was sifting through the rubble. As Allison looked down at the men who were redressing Julie's leg, he shut his eyes and replayed everything he knew.

The hostiles had been composed of Eastern European and Middle Eastern personnel. Probably the bombers as well. These were suicide attacks, from the look of it. Kealey had noticed what appeared to be the remnants of a body near the scorched epicenter of the ballroom blast. The dark blast radius and destructive swath suggested the attack had come near the entrance, not near the podium. Someone was hanging to the rear, probably near the open bar, where a suitcase or shopping bag could have been concealed.

How many people were involved? he wondered. The entire event had consisted of two waves of coordinated attacks: three bombings followed by the hostage taking. There were at least three bombers, multiple hostage takers, and who knew how many people in support roles, individuals who had not been apprehended.

It was big—at least the size of the September 11 attacks. How did something of that magnitude, with so many moving parts, get past the many watchful eyes of United States intelligence?

He didn't want to contemplate the logical answer. It was one of those worst-case scenarios that had always troubled his bosses at the Company.

What had scared them most was not the foreign jihadists or the homegrown terrorists, but what they had come to refer to as the Fort Hood scenario, named after the attack that killed twelve and injured twenty-nine in November 2009, when an army psychiatrist turned a .357 Magnum and an FN Five-seveN semiautomatic on his fellow soldiers.

An inside job.

Kealey was keen to know what the president and his team had uncovered. But he knew from experience that it was probably nothing that would bring them close to understanding the magnitude of the support system that was responsible for Baltimore.

And was probably planning something else.

CHAPTER 11
ATLANTA, GEORGIA

Jessica Muloni sat in a wood-paneled study, watching the convention center disaster on her iPhone.

She had been sitting in a deep armchair in the large room for over ninety minutes. The only person she'd seen was a man, about fifty, who had a very light step and wore a dark blue suit and tie. She met his feathery voice first as he buzzed her through the gate, then saw him briefly as he escorted her down a long, wide corridor notably devoid of ancestral oil paintings and lined instead with unfamiliar art by familiar American masters, like the Wyeths and O'Keeffe and Johns and Remington. Most of it was traditional, proud. The man showed her into this room; pointed out the beverage tray with its water, soda, ice; asked if she would like something to eat—she did not, thank you—then pointed to a phone by which he could be reached and closed the door silently.

She had accessed the CNN app on her phone, tucked it in her belt, and let it play as she moved around the room. About a half hour in, after she had looked at the collection of first editions and antique maps, she had almost called to ask for Liz to come by. Something about the woman intrigued her. Her poise was not an affectation. There seemed to be some steel in that woman's spine.

Muloni went through two cans of ginger ale, found a small lavatory behind a pocket door beside a massive fireplace, then sat in the armchair and closed her eyes. She resisted calling Langley for inside updates because she didn't want to leave a phone-to-phone e-trail. Her coworkers knew she was on special assignment; she didn't want any of them to try and find out exactly where.

The CNN broadcast became white noise, and she dozed lightly, a habit acquired from years in the field: both the ability to catch some sleep where she could, and to wake quickly and alert as needed.

The snap of footsteps in the hallway woke her. She had slumped slightly and sat up almost involuntarily. She poked off her phone, put it on the side table and rose as Trask entered the room. Muloni was standing before she was even fully awake. She wouldn't have fooled him, if that was her goal; she had noticed security cameras in the corners and in the hallway. Nothing happened here that Trask didn't know about.

He came forward behind an extended hand, a big smile, and an apologetic wince.

"So sorry," he said. "It was partly business, and partly . . . mea culpa . . . I lost track of the hour with all that's happening out there." He gestured vaguely toward one of the room's two big windows before clasping her hand in both of his.

"I understand," she said.

"I'm Jacob Trask. It's a pleasure."

"Jessica Muloni, sir," she said. "It's an honor."

She didn't know why, but she expected him to feign modesty and dismiss the compliment. He did not.

"Robinson and Elisabeth," he said, gesturing her back into the armchair while he sat in another. "They treated you well?"

"Very well, Mr. Trask. Liz—Elisabeth—in particular. She fascinated me."

"A remarkable woman," Trask agreed. "She's the former Athens-Clarke County sheriff, well connected among regional law enforcement. We knew each other through mutual political connections, and two months after retiring she came to work for me. She missed the excitement. And her patrol car." He chuckled. "She said she would go to the market on a scooter to save on gas and would feel . . . *Unempowered* was the word she used. No horsepower, no sidearm, no responsibility. Now she's a highly trained security chauffeur. She's had all the evasive and defensive training, and she carries a small arsenal in the glove compartment, under the dash, and upon her person."

Muloni smiled. Trask seemed personable enough, accessible—but there was still scrim of some kind, a line he wouldn't cross. She didn't know what it was.

He filled a glass with ice from the bucket, shaking each piece off before dropping it into a tall glass. Then he poured water. He did not offer her any, and then she knew what it was: he was being kind to an employee, but not servile. He did not offer her a refill, did not ask her about herself or her trip. His one question was about how his staff had treated her. Even his apology was by way of explanation, not actual regret.

"You are surprised to be here," he said.

"More than a little, sir," she confessed.

"What did your superiors tell you?"

"Nothing," she said. "If they knew why, they didn't share that information."

"They did not know why," he said. "It was strictly need to know."

The CIA doesn't know why I'm here, but a civilian does, she thought. That was a little unnerving. As if the legends were true, that all the events in the United States—indeed, the world—were understood and manipulated by just a handful of mega-powerful industrialists and financiers.

"Your prisoner of late, Yasmin Rassin, is no longer in captivity," he said. "Nor is she in Pakistan."

Muloni immediately superimposed that information with the attack on the convention center. It didn't fit— time-wise, in terms of her modus operandi, or pertinent to her skill set. Besides, she was a mercenary, not an ideologue.

The agent said nothing; she had nothing to add. She wondered how Trask knew and why he was telling her this, but asking wouldn't get him to say anything he wasn't already planning to tell her.

"While you process that, here's the rest," Trask went on. "We believe she is in the United States, possibly in New York. You are to find her and recapture her if you can, remove her if it's necessary. You will have the proper authorization, in writing, within the hour in your personal e-mail. Encryption code Date Three is being used."

Each agent assigned a date to the standard codes, an assignation known only to him- or herself and the high-security dispatcher. For Muloni, Date One was the day of her high school prom, Day Two was the day she saw Rush in concert, and Day Three was the day she had her appendix out. None of these were likely to be guessed by a hacker.

"The reason you are *here,* the reason I am telling you this, is that we believe she is in the custody of people who are in my employ. I have been watching them for some time, concerned that some of our technology was showing up in foreign weapons systems. Were their rogue status to become commonly known, the impact on my business—much of which involves government contracts that affect your own organization—would be disastrous. Your superiors have authorized you to be seconded to my own security team to track and eliminate my employees and their assassin. Your record is impressive and, now that I've met you, I believe what I have been told. You are someone that people know they can trust." He took a long drink, his steely eyes never leaving the agent. When he finished, he said, "And no. I do not know why they want her. But I can only assume one thing."

"They want to kill you," she said.

He regarded her, his gaze grown colder. "Why is that the first thing that came to your mind?"

She tensed, wishing she hadn't spoken. "I read the corporate file. There is no acknowledged successor. Removing you would create conflict, a distraction. I thought it might open your contracts to other bidders."

He nodded. "A reasonable guess. Most of my business *is* built on long-standing relationships. But I don't believe that I am the target. Besides, these men already have access to me."

"With her, their hands would be clean." She corrected herself quickly. "Clean*er*." They were already dirty to some degree. Otherwise, Trask wouldn't suspect them.

He considered this before dismissing it. "No. It is someone else and for some other purpose. They have access to our technology. They could take the company down by corrupting our resources."

"You found out you'd been compromised by reverse engineering the situation," she said. She was in this far with her pushing. She might as well go all the way. "How did you identify the personnel?"

He grinned. "Reverse engineering the situation," he said. "I like that. It's exactly what we did. Found our technology, and instead of suing the Chinese company, we infiltrated their plant, found the source of the leak, traced it back to our R & D division, known, ironically enough, as MoleS—Molecular Studies. They're responsible for making electronic relays from single molecules."

She probably looked as surprised as she felt. She thought single-molecule wires and conjugated molecular on-off switches were still mostly theory.

Back to silent mode, Muloni decided. She was out of her element on all fronts.

"We do not know if the industrial saboteurs are aware that *we* know what they've done," Trask went on. "What's more, though they have been watched here, their personal communications monitored, there appears to be only one connection between them and the escape of Ms. Rassin. The Pakistanis on board the in-coming flight were using our Minotaur secure phones. Two separate systems, interfaced internally, impossible to crack without the exact code because the compo-nents separate if there is any unauthorized access. The electronic bridge between receive and transmit literally breaks down, sealing memory from even the user. Those phones were hacked. The arrival time of the jet was known, the movements of the Pakistanis were also known, and they were slain inside the terminal where you searched the prisoner. Their bodies were found two hours after takeoff—by which time the jet had landed at JFK. We assume your target is still there. Otherwise, why fly her to such a heavily monitored area when a smaller airport in another city would have sufficed?"

Because it's easier to stay lost in a crowd, for one thing, she thought.

Trask drained the water glass. She had a sudden image of him as a cactus, lean and thirsty, with invisi-ble thorns. Maybe it wasn't just *noblesse oblige* this man was about. Maybe she was sensing something dangerous.

"If they are aware of us watching them, that does not mean they are aware of you," he went on. "Security personnel come and go frequently. That shouldn't raise any red flags."

"Unless someone links me to Rassin," she pointed out.

He grinned. "That will make your hunt a little eas-ier, not to mention more exciting. But I don't think that has happened. We had people at the airport, looking for anyone who might be tracking Elisabeth. Your pickup was clean. They will be there when you depart to make sure it stays that way."

He put the glass on the tray and rose. She did as well. Apparently, the audience was at an end.

"Thank you for making the trip," he said, offering both hands again. "I wanted to meet you and to tell you personally how important this is to me, to my business, and to our nation." He locked her hand in his again. "You will have whatever resources you need to carry out your assignment, the only caveat being that you keep this to yourself."

"Mr. Trask, there is someone I'd like to talk to."

His face and body locked. He did not release her hand. He was like a machine that had died suddenly. "Who?"

"I would like to consult with a colleague at the FBI about his operational checklists."

"You have none of your own?"

She smiled a little smile. "Our organization is not chartered for domestic surveillance as such. I don't want to miss any potential red flags the target may throw off."

"You may talk to your associate discretely," Trask said.

"Thank you, sir."

"You understand," Trask went on, his voice thicker, her hand still his prisoner, "we will be dealing with the industrial sabotage on our own. What I'm concerned about—all *you* need be concerned about—is your target. You will kill to protect it. You will die, if necessary, to protect it. *Those* points may not be in your friend's checklist."

"Fully understood," she replied. Something about the way he said that chilled her. Then again, everything about this man was a little off-putting. "But there may be tracking mechanisms embedded in the MoleS operation that can lead us to Rassin. Some angle, some component my colleague might think of. Something I can pass along to your people to investigate."

She said that a little stubbornly, she hoped.

It took a moment but Trask relaxed. The smile returned. He released her hand. He studied her for what felt like an interminably long time. "Do you understand the instructions, or must they come from your Director?"

A man did not go from being a wealthy dilettante to a major power broker without having a will of iron.

"I understand, Mr. Trask," she replied. She did not want her disobedience booted up to the director.

"And you'll follow those instructions?" he added. It wasn't so much a question as a command.

"Of course," she said—a little too obediently to sit well on the conscience, but that was what was needed. Muloni also appreciated—despite the part of her that hated the reality of it—that she was an African American woman of Muslim heritage who was being given an opportunity to land some very big game. That was the kind of takedown that made careers and helped to dispel Islamophobia inside the Company and out.

Trask continued smiling "You will wait at your hotel until we receive an update on your target."

"Hotel, sir?"

"In New York," he said. "There is no time to waste. Elisabeth has the details of your flight, your hotel, and the number of the taxicab that will be waiting for you. The driver's name is Shrevnitz. He will have a weapon for you. There are clothes and cash already in your room. There will also be a Minotaur phone in a desk drawer. Please use that for any calls pertinent to the mission."

"Yes, sir," Muloni said. She turned and retrieved her telephone. When she turned back, Trask was already at the door.

"Have a safe and successful trip," he said.

"Thank you," she replied to his back.

Robinson eased in as Trask strode out.

Something dangerous indeed, she thought. But then, people didn't achieve what he had by being sweet and yielding.

Still, it was her life that was at risk. And whether he liked it or not, she might need to contact Reed Bishop.

Trask went to his study, which was at the far end of a long corridor. His footsteps fell lightly, briskly on the cherrywood floor. On the walls of the corridor were historical documents signed by each of the fifty-six men who signed the Declaration of Independence, a collection that ranged from a ship's multi-language passport signed by John Adams to a receipt for hay signed by Arthur Middleton. Trask often stood in contemplation here, going from name to name, considering how these men of diverse backgrounds overcame their differences to agree on a defiant statement of liberty; how they risked their lives and the well-being of their families to turn a vision, an idea, into a reality.

That was how Jacob Trask had always lived his life, from the first aluminum spring trap he built as a young teenager to the fragmentation bullet he invented to help his sight-impaired grandfather bring down deer. That was what he was doing now.

He shut the heavy oak door and picked up the phone. He pressed a familiar speed-dial assignation.

"Yes, sir?" the voice on the other end answered.

"She's on her way," Trask told him. "Employ her as our lion if you can, as a lamb if it becomes necessary."

"She was deferential?"

"Only to a point, as you said," Trask told him. "She was prepared to challenge me on the mute order."

"Just like in the terminal in Quebec," the voice said. "A by-the-book team player . . . until she's not. We need to push her when she arrives."

"Agreed. It *must* be this agent Bishop, then," Trask said. "Are you certain you can get him?"

"Positive, Mr. Trask," he said. "We've been watching him because he was involved in similar operations."

"In what capacity?"

"Preventative, guarding against leaks on the inside," the voice said. "We needed to get his eyes somewhere else while we made our move."

"Why would the Bureau put a paper pusher on a field operation?" Trask asked.

"Because he is uniquely motivated for *this* job," the voice said.

"In what way?"

The voice said, "His daughter was killed in Baltimore. The Bureau would assume, correctly, that he was not involved in the attack."

The revelation about his daughter pinched. No suffering was greater than to see one's child dead or dying or incapacitated. He had witnessed his own daughter in anguish. As a young girl, Kate had become increasingly withdrawn. The "highs" of childhood were smothered by her frequent tetchiness and insoluble feelings of hopelessness. She would lash out over insignificant, everyday actions, at least Trask thought they were, like the occasional grinding of her mother's teeth during dinner or if she didn't get an immediate response to a question. And Kate would somehow manage to sustain that seductive anger throughout the next few weeks, and sometimes into months.

At first, Trask assumed it was just his lack of experience in nurturing a little girl's spirit, that perhaps as with his father, his stern comportment was better suited for rearing a boy. But as Kate developed and further removed herself from family, then friends, Trask noticed her issues begin to physically manifest themselves. She no longer had *oomph* throughout the day, and at night she had trouble sleeping, developing horrible, dark circles under her striking green eyes from staring through her angst all night. She would weep for hours and became increasingly paranoid that she was being analyzed and dissected by her parents. She stopped eating breakfast, then dinner, and lost alarming amounts of weight, when a girl her age should have begun blossoming. Trask and Eugenie could no longer ignore their daughter's problems, nor could they continue to be argued away. Trask needed to be a concerned father and salvage his fragile daughter's livelihood, to save her life

After many visits to the hospital for nutrient-infused intravenous therapy, among other recovery procedures, several doctors eventually concluded that she had an extreme case of hypomania: she was bipolar. Although relieved her condition wasn't something terminal, but rather treatable, Trask couldn't help but blame himself for her circumstances. Highs and lows were a fact of life he was familiar with, but he'd always had the tools to deal with those burdens, namely, projects and desires that kept him distracted from real life. Goals that kept his mind targeted on the bigger picture.

After many miserable months of trying to maintain Kate's temperament through heavy medicating, and after her almost successful suicide attempt by overdosing on her pills, Trask was loosely referred by a friend to the radical Dr. Ayesha Gillani, who was curing patients with hypnotherapy, connecting new passageways through the tunnels in their conflicted minds, straightening the lines of their internal communication by gradually guiding them through a seemingly self-actuated choose-your-own-adventure-type scenario. Trask had his doubts, but he also had his hopes.

Dr. Gillani wasn't too far removed from her Universität Heidelberg postgrad education at the time, a young woman in her early thirties whose light complexion, steel-blue eyes, and short dark hair, mixed with a spicy, almost cinnamon aroma, compounded her image into someone who could be trusted. She dressed professionally, wore very little makeup, no earrings or jewelry, apart from a classic Chanel watch. Simple and well manicured. And after only a few intricate sessions with Dr. Gillani, Kate's psychologically charged disposition had been virtually rewired. She had been cured. In his daughter's eyes, at least, Trask was now a hero.

But Trask had caused misery in the sons and daughters of others. Even the most hardened tribal warlord, refusing to become an informant, would change his mind when his young daughter was forced to watch her pet goat being skinned alive. Trask had studied the videotape that had been made of that little girl's face. *There* was the key to world peace. There was the inspiration for this undertaking. Not her agony, but the agony of the mothers and fathers of September 11, of the USS *Cole,* of the wars in Iraq and Afghanistan, where IEDs were used against good-hearted soldiers who were only trying to help packs of ignorant, thankless savages and their equally corrupt spawn.

"Mr. Trask?"

"I'm here," he said. "The loss of his daughter would suggest, Agent, that Mr. Bishop will be preoccupied."

"Not this man, sir," the voice assured him. "Not Reed Bishop. I had my eye on him before this. His wife died when he was in Mumbai, investigating an agent's death. He stayed with the case, and the funeral had to be postponed."

"Did he solve that case?"

"He did."

"Then you'd better be very, very careful," Trask warned.

"Of course, sir. The Yasmin angle will only strengthen our hand."

"All right," Trask said. "We'll talk later."

"Good afternoon, sir."

Trask hung up. The world around him was silent, conducive to reflection. It was a dangerous tactic they had embraced in the run-up to the mission, but Trask enjoyed the feeling it gave him. He hadn't had that sense of risk for a very long time. He looked at his desk, at the photos of his own family. His wife, Eugenie, whom he adored, and their daughter, Kate. He didn't know if he respected Bishop for that or found him despicable.

Not that it mattered. What was most important now was the corridor outside his study door. The men who had risked so much. The names to which he hoped one day, in all humility, to add one more.

His own.

CHAPTER 12

BALTIMORE, MARYLAND

*R*eed Bishop was cold when he woke.
Cold and very hard of hearing.

His right cheek was on the cool cherrywood floor, his lips were dry, and his lungs were rasping. His body was . . . naked, it felt like. His arms, legs, and back felt exposed.

And there was stuffing in his left ear. He moved his hand left, thinking to pull whatever was in there out, saw a cloud drift over.

What the hell? *he thought.*

Where was he? More importantly, where was his daughter? They had just been looking at someone, an older woman and her husband, talking to them. . . .

"Laura?" he said, though he wasn't convinced he had spoken. It sounded more like a thought.

Still thinking of his daughter, he placed his palms against the floor, pushed, and was suddenly surrounded by a cloud.

Did I do that? How?

He raised his head, looked through the haze, didn't see Laura to his left, didn't see much of anything that looked familiar, only a jumble of debris. His neck went numb, and he let gravity pull his face down with a hard slap so he was staring across the floor again. With effort, he turned slowly to the right.

There was Laura, *he thought with relief.*

It looked as though she was sleeping. But she was white, covered with what looked like confectioners' sugar. And . . .

What?

There was only half of her. The top half. He screamed. This time he was sure, because it punched through the thickness in his ears and caused his throat to shake and cleared his head so he could hear the sobs and wails of others. As the dust thinned, he saw them, and more debris, and bodies and parts of bodies and a glaze of blood across everything, which ridiculously reminded him of raspberry drizzle, except for the blood that had pooled around Laura, where her legs used to be. . . .

That was the last thing Bishop remembered until he was sitting in a metal chair in some other room, being examined by a medic.

He was no longer so cold. And he could hear.

"Mr. Bishop, do you have any pain?"

Bishop turned tear-blurred eyes toward the speaker. It was a young woman. She was wearing a look of grave concern. He wondered how she knew his name, until he saw her eyes looking at his chest and he remembered the name tag. He looked down. It hung incongruously from a piece of lapel on the remnants of the dinner jacket he still had on. An FBI-issue terrycloth wrap had been thrown around his shoulders.

"Do you understand me?" the woman asked.

He nodded. "No pain," he said.

"I'm going to leave you here," she said. "You have a few cuts and burns but—"

"What happened?" he asked stupidly.

"An explosion," she said. "If you'll wait here, I'm going to take care of someone else."

"I'll wait," he said. His eyes dropped to the floor. A dusty tile floor. There were planters nearby. He saw dark shops beyond. He had been through here earlier in the day, walking toward the ballroom with . . .

"Oh, Christ!" he cried. He tried to stand, dropped as his legs refused to cooperate, and sat, looking around.

He didn't remember the explosion, but he remembered the moments before it. He and Laura were sitting at their table, almost dead center in the big hall. They were talking pleasantly to people they didn't know, a couple who seemed enchanted with Laura, and waiting for Julie to step to the podium. Then the world went red and he felt as if he were flying.

He woke, briefly.

Bishop's thoughts drifted backward into waves of elapsed memories, of the times his daughter needed him. To be there. To show up. He summoned up the first words she'd been able to sound out for herself, during a short family trip to Florida when she was five, written on a bus window. *E-mer-gen-cy. Emergency exit.* He could still see her proud smile, her darling little legs cheerily kicking at opposite tempos, unable to reach the floor or the seat in front of her. Searching through the fog, he remembered the times he pretended to rise from the dead during her school's haunted hayride nights. Despite the thick, gnarled makeup he wore, she could always tell when it was her father clawing at the side of the wagon. And despite the multitude of shrill, shrieking children, he could always single out his daughter's excited squeal. He always made her the lucky victim, the most special rider of the night.

But he struggled to retain the thought of her face as it was then, as her present, more familiar features took hold of his delusional imagination.

Laura was glowing, her head turned slightly away from him, forward. Her light summer dress swaying proudly like a new flag, her hair flowing as if it were a tropical shore. He followed her as she slowly ran, silently along the slate pathway leading to their home, home toward her mother. Her mother. His wife. His late wife. She had been the embodiment of his future, of his daughter's future. His departed companion was the eternal bond between them, the rope connecting the climber to the cliff. And when that was detached, Bishop had to become Laura's security. His daughter's guide, her unconditional friend, her devoted supporter. Her father.

Bishop saw himself stop short only paces away from them. His family. The only links to what he could call real life. Laura embraced her mother like they were seeing each other for the last time, like only children know how to hold, except it was Bishop who couldn't stay there, who didn't feel right, and then she looked at her father as if to say, "Thank you."

He *had* been there for her. Whenever he could be, in

whatever shape the world had left him in. With whatever love he had protected for her inside his heart. It was always there. And always would be. And no one was ever going to remove that from him.

And now . . .

He looked for his wristwatch, saw that the pressure he felt there was his bandaged forearm. He had neither a wristwatch nor a shirtsleeve. He let the arm drop, then raised his hand in order to cry into it. He wasn't sure exactly why he was crying. But then a functioning part of his mind began putting it together. The medic had said there was an explosion of some kind. He had been knocked over and out, injured. His daughter . . .

"Dear God . . ."

He had an overpowering urge to see her, to hold her, but his body was trembling. Someone, one of the medics, saw him and came over to him, decided that he was not all right and that he needed to go to the hospital. He let himself be moved, lifted, wheeled for what seemed an interminable time. He was dropping, wheeled again. There were sights, shapes, sounds, but all he could see was his daughter's destroyed body lying next to him, her pale flesh so still.

He was crying again, shaking, and then there was a pinch in his arm and it was over.

CHAPTER 13

WASHINGTON, D.C.

The Situation Room was rank. All the energetic air-conditioning did was turn it into chilled rankness.

Ryan Kealey knew the primary ingredients of the smell: sweat and coffee. He could tell, almost to the half hour, how long the mix had been fermenting. He could also identify the *kind* of perspiration. It wasn't the surface sweat of exertion, the kind you pushed away with a sleeve on the basketball court. It was the deep, hot, stagnant sweat of pressure laced with fear.

"I liked it better when the air had smoke in it," Kealey said as Robert Andrews shook his hand.

"Sure used to hide that other stuff, didn't it?" the CIA chief said knowingly behind a crooked grin.

"Killed those nasal passages dead," Kealey answered, returning the smile.

Andrews extended a hand toward the seat that had been vacated by Jon Harper. It felt good to collapse into it. The president was not here, so Kealey had time to collect his thoughts.

The flight from the rooftop of the convention center to the parking lot of the George Washington University Hospital had taken a little over a half hour. The ride to the White House in a black Escalade had taken nearly twice as long due to police roadblocks and traffic. There had been more people leaving D.C. than usual, and it had nothing to do with the tail end of a busy commute. If anything, the traffic should have been lighter as the federal and local intelligence communities stayed at their desks, looking for clues about what had happened and what could happen next.

These are families leaving town, he'd thought as he noted the higher than usual percentage of minivans.

That was the curse of his profession. Noticing things. Both the conscious and subconscious mind were trained to record data. The vast amount of stored information—some of it unidentified because it was never tapped—was a phenomenon first studied after the September 11 attacks. Without naming names, mental health workers determined the percentage of New Yorkers who "knew something was wrong" by the wrong-way flight down the Hudson River of the first hijacked jet, American Airlines Flight 11. It was a staggering 59 percent. More than half the people who sought psychiatric counseling were subliminally aware of existing flight patterns by sight, but mostly by sound.

Kealey's entire existence was like that. It was one reason he had to get out. The vessel was full.

But it was never drained, he thought as he noticed that more office lights were on than usual, that street vendors were hawking more American flags than before, that helicopters were hovering, instead of passing over the capital. In many of those, onboard computers were comparing license plates to U-Haul databases and profiling renters by name; onboard cameras were watching approaches to the Capitol, the White House, and other institutions and using facial recognition software to match pedestrians to FBI, CIA, and Homeland Security "wanted" lists; onboard infrared and ultraviolet eyes were scanning backpacks and laptops, underwear and shoes, baby strollers and shopping bags for explosives or radiological material. One of them, Kealey knew, would be monitoring all cell phone communications in the city, watching for dialed numbers. Terrorists who planted improvised explosive devices triggered them with phone-to-phone calls. These phones were "short-term units" bought with cash off the rack, the pay-as-you-go variety. IDing buyers at domestic electronics stores, running their names for potential terror affiliations, was not enough; many of these phones came from overseas. Thus, Homeland Security had developed software to keep a record of every call made in the United States to and from "long-term units." Any call that was not on this list was instantly flagged. Between the time the first two digits of the receiving phone signaled an alert and the last two digits could be dialed, a computer on board the chopper activated Trask Industries' new KillButton. This was a directed electromagnetic pulse that would immediately shut down the receiving cell phone and pinpoint the caller for police.

All of that flashed through Kealey's brain as a new mental file was opened: D.C. in panic mode. He would always remember those details and would be able to apply them to any other city on the planet. Even if it was a place he had never been, he would know at once whether something was wrong.

"Helluva signal you worked out, Mr. Kealey," Homeland Security director Max Carlson said.

"Thanks. This morning I didn't even know what a user hashtag was."

There were knowing chuckles around the table. Kealey could tell that many of those present still didn't.

"How are Allison and the boy?" Andrews asked.

"Battered but unharmed."

"And Julie?"

Kealey made a face. He didn't feel it was his place to say. "Alive," was all he volunteered.

"Did you see Jon at the hospital?" Andrews asked.

Kealey shook his head. "He was running toward the chopper while I was being shown to an SUV."

All the conversation danced wide of the reason they were here. No one wanted to discuss the attack or Kealey's perspectives without the president in attendance. It was bad form; even a lame duck could ask for the resignation of a department head.

The president emerged from the Executive Conference Room with Jeff Dryfoos. Kealey went to rise, but Brenneman motioned him to stay where he was. The secretary of state departed, a leather case under his arm, and the president sat. He gestured to nearly empty plates of sandwiches in the middle of the conference table.

"Help yourself," he said.

Kealey was hungry. He obliged, placing a turkey wrap on a small ceramic plate and pulling it toward him.

"Thanks for coming," the president said. "Great work you did tonight. Everyone appreciates it."

It never sat quite right, having a body count referred to as "great work." Not that those guys at the convention center didn't deserve to die. It was just one of those actions that seemed to merit reflection, not a pat on the back. Besides, there wasn't a field agent alive who would feel in his or her heart that this was a job well done. The trick was to take the bastards out *before* they killed anyone.

Kealey thanked the president, anyway.

"Mr. Dryfoos is off to see some consuls general with fingerprints," the president said. "Bob, did you tell Ryan what we have?"

"Not yet, sir," Andrews said. He turned to Kealey.

"Eastern Europeans and Middle Eastern perps," Kealey said to save time. "INS confirms they were here legally."

It was as though someone had dropped a quilt on the room. No one spoke or moved for an eternity of seconds.

"Yeah," Andrews said at last.

"Not a big solve on my part," Kealey said. "I heard the languages, and you don't coordinate something this big with so many nationalities unless they've been on-site for a while. Planners couldn't risk even one illegal being turned up in an operation of this size."

The silence returned.

"This might be a good time for you to tell us what else you know," the president suggested.

"One question first, sir," Kealey said. "Has anyone taken credit for the attacks?"

"Not yet," Andrews said.

"Has anyone *denied* being behind the attacks?" Kealey asked, pressing.

Andrews shook his head. It was a gesture of admiration, not denial. "We were discussing that just before you arrived. The usual suspects, al-Qaeda and Hamas, among others, have issued Web statements of approval, but from the sidelines. They've all made a point of saying they had no operational involvement in this."

"Because they're all basically cowards and fear reprisals," said someone sitting across the table. He was Admiral Donald Breen, chairman of the Joint Chiefs of Staff. Kealey could tell he hadn't been here long; his uniform wasn't wrinkled.

No one disagreed with his assessment.

"It's more than that, Admiral," Kealey said.

"Oh?"

Andrews put a hand on Kealey's wrist. Obviously, the CIA director had figured it out, too, and felt it would go down better coming from him.

"That kind of distancing from multiple groups tells us that whoever planned this attack is a major new player," Kealey said. "If the other groups know who it was, then they do not want to claim credit for the accomplishment out of respect. It's a way of tipping their hat. If they do *not* know them, the same rule applies, though for a different reason. Al-Qaeda and the others want to show that they respect the accomplishment in the *hopes* of being asked to participate in future attacks."

Admiral Breen nodded thoughtfully. Kealey knew the man only by reputation. He had been appointed by the president because he believed in military solutions as a last resort. That meant hearing, and exhausting, all other opinions first.

"So we're agreed that we probably have a new mega-player on the scene?" the president asked. "Mr. Kealey?"

He nodded gravely. "People don't just rig themselves with explosive devices, infiltrate two major weekend events, and carry MP5K assault weapons without serious funding, preparation, and support."

"I'd go a step further and say it's unprecedented," Carlson added.

"Do we know anything about the kind of explosives they used?" Kealey asked.

"Preliminary field analysis of the residue indicates both C-four and Semtex," Carlson told him.

"Suggesting diverse sources," Kealey said. "One of them gets closed down, they still have another. What about their physical construction?"

"The one in the ballroom appears to have been a briefcase bomb, and the individual who blew himself up in the hotel wore an explosive belt. We're not sure of the third, the one inside the food area."

"I saw that area myself," Kealey said. "It was totaled. That's where Colin Dearborn was. I asked him about it before I left. He said it was a massive white blast."

"Magnesium component," Andrews said.

Kealey nodded. "Right. The only reason he survived, and without so much as a scratch, was because he leaned against a column to tweet."

"Max, is the magnesium significant?" the president asked. He was careful to pitch that one to Homeland Security. With Andrews and Kealey present, he clearly didn't want this to become too much of a CIA show.

"Burns," Carlson said. "In powdered form it becomes and remains extremely hot. In addition to shrapnel, it's a way of ramping up the pain and damage."

The president shook his head. He looked tired to Kealey—not today, but generally—yet at the same time he seemed more focused and energized than in the old days.

"Mr. President, while you were out, we picked up some intel," Sandy Mathis said.

"Go ahead," Brenneman said, swiveling his chair slightly.

Kealey turned toward the video monitor. He had noticed that it was on but hadn't really paid any attention. Kealey did not know this man by name or reputation.

"A bartender at the Hilton came forward with information about a man named Michael, or so the individual claimed," Mathis said. "Thirtyish, blue sports jacket, white shirt, dark pants. He'd stopped in a short while before the explosions, ordered an iced tea. He was carrying a briefcase and said that he was an attendee of Julie's nursing conference. According to the bartender, he was sweating, flushed. *Nervous* was the word the bartender used."

Kealey waited in silence. He could tell there was more.

"This man, sounds like Michael Lohani, the man Julie Harper mentioned to her husband," Mathis went on. "The one she called security on."

"Do you know anything about Lohani?" the president asked.

"He checked into the Hilton last night at seven twenty," Mathis read from a laptop. "The reservation was prebooked by a travel agent who made it on behalf of a Yemeni firm, International Pharmaceuticals. Neither the company nor any of its principals are on any hot lists."

"It's Yemen," Carlson said angrily. "What are the odds that it can be one hundred percent clean?"

There was an uncomfortable silence. Brenneman had resisted imposing stricter sanctions on the terrorist hotbed for fear—as he put it in an executive white paper on policy in Yemen—of "poking the cat with sticks." Brenneman had even crossed out the original word, *dog,* for fear of insulting Sana'a.

"What about the hostage takers?" Kealey asked. "Anything come up with the fingerprints?"

"Nothing," replied Andrews.

Kealey took a belated bite of his sandwich. "Damned strange. The guys I faced were well trained."

"They could have been mercs," Admiral Breen offered.

"Possibly," Kealey said. "They certainly didn't seem as anxious as that Lohani guy. The problem with that, though, is that not only did they seem ready to die, but it looked to me like they were planning on it, going out in a firefight."

"How is that any different from the Taliban or the Chechens or the mujahideen?" the president asked.

"These men were a disparate group of nationals on foreign soil," Kealey said. "You just don't see that level of cooperation, skill and, frankly, intelligence in that kind of fighter. They are angry, knee-jerk reactionaries. One man I spoke with said words to the effect, 'The more languages one speaks, the better one knows other men.' "

"A goddamn philosopher," Carlson snickered.

"Exactly," Kealey said. "Not your garden-variety crazy."

"He could have been quoting the Koran," Andrews pointed out.

"The man was clean shaven," Kealey said. "He just didn't have a jihadist vibe."

"Here's something else, Mr. President," Mathis said. "A month ago, a room at the Hilton was booked for this weekend by an Iranian expat named Amal Geybullah. He was a poli-sci student at Georgetown, graduated in twenty ten, and has been working as the manager of the hotel gift shop."

"That's an odd career choice," Carlson remarked.

"Not if you're looking to get legitimized and to network before putting yourself in a venue that has international clientele," Kealey said.

Carlson sat back, grumping. He did not seem pleased to have been corrected. Especially by someone who had no real standing here.

"Where is Amal now?" Andrews asked.

"He hasn't been back at his apartment since this morning," Mathis said. "We checked. He has a roommate, someone who found the place on Craigslist. Says he doesn't know much about him."

"Could be a civilian casualty," Kealey suggested.

"It's possible," Andrews agreed. "They've only just begun clearing away the sky bridge."

"Do we know who stayed in that room?" Carlson asked.

"Amal told a clerk his family was coming to visit him," Mathis said. "He requested a total of five swipe cards."

"That didn't seem unusual?" the president asked.

"Apparently not, sir," Mathis said. "A lot of tourists get keys for each family member."

"Is the room intact?" Kealey asked.

"As far as we know," Mathis said. "Except for smoke, that section of the hotel doesn't seem to have been affected. A couple of agents are en route."

"Anything else?" the president asked the table.

No one spoke. Brenneman regarded Kealey. "You were the only one on-site while all this was going on. What's your gut tell you?"

Kealey had taken another bite of his sandwich. He chewed thoughtfully before answering. "Mr. President, the entire time I was in there, I did not feel that I was facing a terrorist attack. It felt more like a deployment."

"You don't mean tactically, do you?" Admiral Breen asked. There was a knowing look in his eyes.

"No, Admiral," Kealey said. "It was well executed, yes. But it didn't have the mission zeitgeist you get from taking a hill or securing a compound."

"You lost me," Carlson said. "Mission zeitgeist?"

"The spirit of the thing," the admiral said, his eyes fixed admiringly on Kealey. "I believe Mr. Kealey is referring to a missing sense of completeness. Every battle has that, even a losing one."

"Exactly, sir," Kealey said. "We haven't seen anything about this online, and probably won't, because I don't believe these killers were there to die for a stated cause."

"I'm still not following," Carlson said.

Kealey leaned forward. He regarded Brenneman. "Frankly, Mr. President, this felt to me like a beachhead. The big opening salvo of a war."

* * *

He had made his way up the stairwell of the hotel, the half mask of the PBA pressed to his face. The soft, flexible silicone piece conformed to his face and provided a double exhalation valve system that minimized resistance. The oxygen for the portable breathing apparatus was attached to his back, on top of the black bulletproof vest.

The young man moved quickly, a .45-caliber semi-automatic in his black-gloved right hand, pointed at a low angle, his eyes alert. Arriving at the third floor, he pushed slowly through the fireproof door. Ordinarily locked from this side to prevent ingress, the heavy steel doors opened automatically in the event of a fire.

The hallway was empty. He glanced up at the nearest corner. As promised, there were no security cameras here. Because the stairwell doors were locked, there was no need. The only cameras were located at the elevator.

He turned left, as instructed, and made his way to room 306. Upon arriving, he pulled the swipe key from his vest pocket and popped the door. His breathing loud in his ears, he entered, shutting the door behind him and swinging the security lock into place. He replaced the swipe key and removed the mask. Except for the smell, the air didn't seem dangerous.

The room was empty, but he moved through it cautiously, checking the bathroom and closet before making his way to the dresser. Crouching, he opened the bottom drawer. There were three marbles inside. Removing them, he dropped them in the same pocket as the key. After checking the other drawers—they were all empty—he went back to the door. He stood behind it, a foot or so into the room.

There were voices in the hallway. He went to the door, listened. Though he was half expecting it, he started as he heard the swipe key shoved into the lock. The door clicked, one of the people pushed, and it caught on the lock.

"What the hell?" said one of the people outside the door, his voice muffled. He was also wearing a face-piece. He was either FBI or Baltimore FD.

Shit. How did they find it so fast? thought the young man in the room.

He moved quietly to the window. It was too big a drop to the street, and there were people outside.

He swore again to himself. He had come here to make sure the room was clean. Now there was only one way he was getting out. And it had to be fast.

He put the mask back on and returned to the door. It was still open about an inch and a half. He jumped back as a pair of shoulders hit it.

The jamb cracked but did not give. He had only moments. . . .

Rushing to the door, he shoved the .45 through the opening and fired four times. There were muted cries, the sound of fabric dragging along the metal door, and then two simultaneous thuds. He listened, heard moaning. He leaned out the newly widened opening, aimed at the moaning bundle, and shot it through the mask.

Shoving hard against the door to shut it—there was about 400 pounds of FBI agents lying on the other side—he managed to push it far enough to slip the security lock. Then he let the door swing in, jumped over the bodies, and ran back to the stairwell. Before entering it, he took a last look back to make sure no one else was in the hall.

It was empty, save for the dead men.

He turned and was gone, relieved to have gotten out with the goods. What had happened shouldn't affect anything: the FBI wouldn't find anything in the room, and the dead men would only confirm what they already suspected, that the room was somehow involved in today's attack.

And since the man who had rented it was clean— and dead—that wouldn't tell them a damn thing.

CHAPTER 14

NEW YORK, NEW YORK

The world's finance funneled into Manhattan, and Manhattan funneled that into a few square blocks of Lower Manhattan. Within a few blocks of one another were the New York Stock Exchange, the American Stock Exchange, and a headquarters of every major financial institution on earth.

Lower Manhattan was also rife with skyscraper apartments, home to many of the financiers and attorneys who serviced those institutions. Residents didn't need a car; they could walk to work. The beach and amusement park on Brooklyn's Coney Island were an endurable subway ride away. The proximity to a great park, Battery Park, to a beautifully landscaped esplanade that ran up much of the west side of the island, to world-class restaurants, to the Statue of Liberty, to a major airport—Newark Liberty, just fifteen minutes across the Hudson River—and to the rising colossus of the new World Trade Center site also made this one of the most desirable places to live in the city.

None of which was known to Yasmin Rassin, or mattered.

After crossing an old iron bridge, the car moved through the thin nighttime traffic among the zigzagging canyons. The buildings flashed by, some of them stone titans, others spindly giants of glass, all of them lit with squares of light, window after window, stack after stack. The woman had been in cities before—London, Istanbul, Shanghai, Sydney, and others—but none of them had created the same strong impression of a place that could have been designed by an assassin or a sociopath. So many people, so many dark streets, so many vantage points. It was a miracle civilization existed in this place, let alone thrived. Money clearly was a root of evil, but not the murderous kind. It was a shield against evil.

Two men sat on either side of Yasmin. En route, they had changed into street clothes. They resembled nothing so much as young businessmen. It concerned her more than a little that her escorts had not sought to blindfold or handcuff her. They were letting her know where she was going, which meant one of two things. First, they expected her to be entirely cooperative. And second, they did not anticipate her leaving. These men had been in the room with the American woman at the airport. They knew about her daughter. Perhaps they also knew that was all the leverage they needed.

Though she saw her only two or three times a year, Kamilah was the center of her life. She was the product of a situation Yasmin had created for herself twelve years earlier. She was Cara Sumaida'ie then. An orphan, a young "pleasure girl" for the Syrian police, she had given herself to those men in their barracks—or in a lavatory or an alley or an automobile, wherever they happened to be. In exchange, they had shown her how to use firearms because she was oh, so afraid for her security in the poor neighborhood in Damascus where she lived, a ghetto overrun with Iraqis and Pakistanis looking to escape war and sectarian violence in what was then a relatively peaceful nation. That was how she had come there, with an uncle. He was an automobile mechanic; she was barely able to read. When he was killed in a robbery—only his tools were stolen—she was left alone.

She was twelve when he died. Two years of poverty, of begging, of digging through trash for food, of being threatened by police, drove her to their embrace. It wasn't that she felt safe with these men; to the contrary, they did not understand rules or boundaries. More often than not she left with fresh bruises, sore and bleeding, her back raked raw by whatever she had been lying on. But at least she could eat and she was able to sleep in something other than a doorway or a cart.

And something more, something that came to dominate her thoughts, her actions. Their weapons. Not just the guns, but the batons, the knives, the garrotes.

These men were feared because they had the power of life and death, liberty and captivity. People were not frightened of them, because the police patrolled in packs. These groups were like the sea, usually calm, usually motorized, moving through a place and leaving. It was the individual, the rogue, the angry breakaway, the religious fanatic who civilians avoided. Yasmin envied that power. Not because she yearned to dominate others, but because she wanted to control her own life, her own safe zone.

She spent all her unrestricted time learning everything she could about weapons and tactics. She learned the basics of shooting. She was a natural marksman with a supernaturally steady hand. She helped some of her mentors win bets that she could knock a bottle from a wall or pick off a bird in flight. She also learned how to stab and strangle. The police thought it was cute, adorable, to see her choke a rubber dummy or stab a bale of hay tied in the shape of a man. She retained her ability to please, and to convey enthusiasm she did not feel, just so she could stay among them. When they were not instructing her, she was watching them train, even as she lay on her back with the sergeant in his office, moaning and looking out the window at the compound.

She was all alone. Except for one ally. A former Israeli Defense agent, Abrahem Bär. Bär was not an exceptional man: he stood several inches under six feet; had thick, dark hair with a low hairline, a rough face with a matching beard, and thick chapped lips; and his skin was gritty and tanned from spending years in isolated combat zones. He was merely a good man who had been trained well by his country. Perhaps too well.

Disagreeing with orders he'd been given to remove the presence of peaceful civilian demonstrators near his post near Kiryat Shmona, Bär had gone AWOL from the IDF and had met Cara while he was hiding out in the slums of Damascus, waiting for the heat from his desertion to die down. In spite of her past experiences, Cara was remarkably genial at the time, her hair was much longer, she kept it combed and delicate for her many mature handlers, and her body had only recently developed into womanhood. Bär had propositioned the then nearly sixteen-year-old girl, and when she met with him for what she thought would be intercourse, the multilingual, twenty-eight-year-old Israeli explained that he intended only to take Cara under his wing, to help her along what, in his eyes, seemed to be a serrated road she was traveling down.

Listening to her lurid stories of abuse, rape, and torture and disgusted by the treatment she was receiving, but unable to help her financially or even afford her a safe place to stay, Bär helped her to train harder, to find her self-worth, to fight for herself. *To fight back.*

In the early mornings, before the sun broke over the horizon, the pair would trot alongside each other for miles into the desert, where Bär would work with Cara to perfect her long-range shooting ability. She learned to recognize her surrounding conditions and adjust accordingly—something as slight as the direction and intensity that a target's hair was blowing started to give her killer insight. She learned to be a one-woman militia, a sniper without need of a spotter, a captain without the assistance of soldiers, a killer without use of her conscience. Some mornings consisted of simply skull dragging for hours in the desert heat. Moving slowly, undetected, dragging her stomach, legs, and face in the dirt and sand to get close enough to her target, a true test of her will. On more than one occasion Bär would spot Cara moving too quickly, or moving at all, and would send her back to the starting point. Although she sometimes thought he was being cruel, this proved to be an invaluable technique.

Between the jogging in and the walking out of the improvised training grounds, it wasn't long before their teacher-student relationship crossed their respective barriers and the two became romantically involved. This was the first time a young Cara felt that sex could be enjoyable for the female, too, that it wasn't just about letting a wolf feed off the remains of a carcass, but about finding a rhythm with a partner and working together to match strides and momentum. Making love. Making mistakes met with laughter rather than hostility.

During their many nights together he taught her how to contain her impulsive rage and maintain focus by using Krav Maga techniques he had learned throughout his IDF training to concentrate on pinpoint precision, counterattacks, and neutralizing her enemies without losing crystal clear awareness of her surroundings.

"The hardest part is the escape. Don't ever lose sight of that. Or your target," he'd tell her. Bär's friendly eyes would crinkle and his crooked smile would actually make her lose focus when he joked. But he never distracted her for too long before giving her something else to consider. Bär loved her because she was rough like him. She was beautiful, but in many ways she was ugly, and he was fond of that, too.

He always reminded Cara to attack before being attacked, which was ironic because Bär would be shot in the back of the head by a jealous Barzeh police officer who wanted a piece of Cara. He would have told her to learn from his mistake.

Her name, Cara, meant *fortress,* and that was what the young woman became. Emotionally closed off, she was single-minded in her purpose. Shortly after Bär was killed, Cara realized that she was pregnant. Desperately hoping it was his, she put all of her accumulated hostility into killing a courier for the Central Bank of Syria, stealing the ten thousand in *al-līra assīriyya* he was carrying, and used the currency to buy her way into Egypt. People had compassion for a pregnant girl on her own, and money bought those for whom that wasn't enough. It was there that she gave birth to her daughter, in the hovel of a midwife who was recommended to her. She was barely seventeen.

Egypt's capital was a place where one could find— or be—anything one wanted. What Cara wanted was a new life. She began with a new name. She drew it from separate articles on the front page of a newspaper she found in the trash. The compost pile seemed a fitting place from which the new woman, Yasmin Rassin, should arise.

In retrospect, that had been a terrible, possibly fatal error.

Who could have known that one day newspapers would be searchable online? she thought. Inputting her name would not only place her in Cairo at that time, on that day, but it would suggest, strongly, that she had been there under another name. Most likely in a poor section, if she was looking to start over and picked her name from a newspaper without bothering to change it legally.

The midwife, Akila Fazari, was probably still delivering babies there. The CIA had Yasmin's photograph from when she was captured by the British. That could have been how they learned about her daughter.

Will either of us ever be free of the Americans now? she wondered.

The car stopped across the street from Battery Park, an open area at the foot of Manhattan. Yasmin saw Castle Clinton, a circular fortress whose function was once to defend New York from the British. Beyond it stood the Statue of Liberty, aglow in the spotlights that surrounded her. Yasmin felt that this symbol of freedom should mean something to her; it did not. She was a captive here, most likely about to be coerced into killing. The irony was that if the Americans had simply been true to their capitalistic nature, they could have hired her to do their dirty work. They didn't have to threaten her daughter.

A chill rolled from her shoulders down her back.

What if that isn't why you're here?

"Here."

Yasmin looked to her right. The man to her right held a plastic water bottle. Beyond him she saw a short block of tall old buildings.

"I'm not thirsty," she said.

"I don't care," he told her. "You're to drink it all."

She noticed the top was not sealed. The water had been spiked. They wouldn't have driven her this far to kill her, and they also knew she was going to cooperate. Why drug her?

And then it occurred to her: it wasn't water. The men had a scenario to enact.

She drained the vodka, sat back, and waited for it to take effect.

Blurry snippets of image and sound flashed through Yasmin's mind. A solicitous doorman, a look of concern as they helped their inebriated friend to the front desk.

He didn't know them. He had to call up to announce them.

A walk through a lobby whose ceiling reminded her of the Sistine Chapel's, but with a maritime theme. The *bing* of several elevators coming and leaving, the three of them waiting for one. It arrived. They emerged. There was a floral-pattern carpet on the floor. Then it was above her, then below again. . . .

You're just dizzy.

She was being carried now. There was darkness. Then she was motionless, lying on something soft. Her arms and legs were being moved. . . .

Yasmin awoke in absolute darkness. Her head hurt on the left side, above the eyebrow, like someone was striking the inside of her skull with a brick.

Hangover.

She tried to move; that was when she remembered being bound. With leather, she could tell from the feel of it. She did not bother to struggle, but lay back. She was on some kind of foam that conformed to her body. She did not sink deeply into it, but she moved her hips slightly from side to side and felt it give with her motion, like soft clay.

She had not been brought here to rest.

Yasmin thought through the pain, realized that she was no longer wearing the clothes in which she had arrived. She was in what felt like flannel pajamas. She did not feel as if she'd been violated. Yasmin was obviously here for a test or experiment of some kind; whoever was behind it wanted her to feel as if she could trust them.

She became aware of a slight pressure on her chest, over her heart. Yasmin rolled her left shoulder several times. There appeared to be something hard in her shirt pocket. She was able to increase the pressure on the fabric by raising herself from the foam slightly. Yasmin felt an object in her pocket, and it was round. It moved slightly. She arched as far as she could in a failed attempt to let it roll out. After a moment she relaxed.

All right, she thought. At least nothing had been implanted in her flesh.

The idea of giving herself to the police in Cairo or to the American authorities now in exchange for something made it still a matter of choice. But being fitted with a device that could stop her heart or explode against her rib cage—that was untenable to her, the idea of it miserably suffocating. She did not know how she would react to what spies called an "off switch." She had always assumed that if she were captured, it would be by some legitimate, rule-of-law agency, like Interpol.

The hammering in her skull drew her attention once more, and she lay back, listening to the hollow silence around her. She wiggled from side to side; whatever she was on was fixed to the floor. Even that level of restraint gave her some anxiety.

Was that part of the reason for incarceration? she wondered. *To distract me and break me down?*

The headache prevented her from falling back asleep. Yasmin lay back again, with her eyes shut. She had no idea how long she lay there. She tried the wristbands again, giving little tugs, then an extended pull, and finally putting all her will into a long, fruitless struggle—first up, then sideways in both directions, then slumping.

"Hey!" she shouted.

Yasmin didn't expect anyone to answer, but she thought the sound of her voice might tell her something about the size or composition of the room.

Her voice sounded unusually flat.

Sound-absorbent material, she thought. Her captors didn't want her to be heard outside the room.

She looked around as far as she could see to both sides, raised her head to gaze between her feet. There was no light, anywhere. Maybe the soundproofing was black curtains. For all she knew, they could be hanging just a few feet away. She didn't feel a breeze, any kind of stirring, heard no exterior sounds, even though she was in Manhattan. She was definitely closed off *within* a room.

She flopped back and folded her thumbs in, squeezing her hands into narrow wedges. She tried to draw them through the restraints. The leather was too tight. Like the shouting, that, too, had been anticipated. She noticed then that even her nails had been trimmed. It was tougher to dig into someone's eyes this way.

Over the years, Yasmin had evolved a three-tiered approach to captivity. Until she was apprehended at

Heathrow, it had been theoretical. First, try to escape. Failing that, play on their compassion. Failing *that,* pretend to cooperate. Escape had failed. She sucked air through her open mouth several times to tighten her throat.

"Please!" she cried. "Anyone? I thirst."

No one came. She repeated the plea. She did not even hear the shuffling of feet, the click of a light switch, the beep of a cell phone or a computer, the chug of a water pipe, the hum of an elevator, the passing of an airplane. She might just as well be locked in a coffin buried in six feet of frozen earth.

Her thoughts about captivity had always been about what she would do to get free, not about what someone would do to *her*. Women were sexually abused by jailers, and she was mentally prepared for that. It wasn't about a man taking her; it was about a man putting himself close to her so she could hurt him. She had learned that from studying kung fu during an extended mission in Hong Kong. When someone presented his body in an aggressive way, any part of it, you let him in. And by locks and strikes you kept him from getting away. Even bound as she was, she had teeth, fingers, her head, affected submission, the vanity of the male lover who wanted to win legitimately what he had taken.

She had not contemplated isolation. Were the men from the plane waiting for someone to arrive or trying to unnerve her? She considered both with increasing anxiety. Though she realized that weakening her was probably the goal, she couldn't help herself. Either one accepted a situation and thought about something else or one tried to accumulate information, understand motivation, replay what had been seen and heard in search of clues.

She did the latter, for what seemed like an hour or more, long enough for her headache to subside somewhat.

And then the world went suddenly, painfully white.

"**H**e's breathing!"
The words shot through the FBI radio system like a bullet. While four agents secured room 306 in the Hilton Hotel, two others performed crude field triage on the agent who lay in front of the broken door. His partner on the advance team was dead, with a bullet wound to the head, but this man was alive, with three holes in his left side.

Medics arrived in less than a minute, pulling off the bulletproof vest, which was putting pressure on the chest and increasing blood flow to the injuries. While one prepared an IV to replace the blood that was dripping onto the carpet, the other turned a pocket flashlight on the wounds.

"Point of entry—no serrations," he said.

The other man nodded and said into his shoulder radio, "Debrief on site."

There was a crackled acknowledgment. The medic continued with his work. The clean wounds suggested not just a point-blank assault but a high-velocity penetrating intra-abdominal injury. In addition to the damage caused by the bullets themselves, the kinetic energy each one had generated would have caused severe trauma to adjoining organs. One of them had entered under the armpit and could not have avoided passing near the heart. The organ was probably already swelling. That injury alone was likely fatal.

The medics refused to think about anything beyond each passing second. The goal was to keep the victim alive as long as possible. His life was important, of course. So was information. Epinephrine would be part of the cocktail being administered.

The victim's breathing was shallow. There was a bubbling sound deep in his throat. Blood. There was no point to surgical management. Adhesive bandages were placed on the wounds. A second medical unit arrived with a stretcher, along with a senior agent, an intelligence specialist.

The dead agent had been covered with a sheet from the hotel room. The IS knelt beside him, leaning close to his partner.

"Did you zap him?" he asked the medics.

"Just now," said the agent with the IV. "Heavy dose. Give him a few seconds."

A terrible quiet lay upon the hallway. The gurgling in the agent's throat gave way to a sudden, vacuum-like inhalation. Then he gagged, coughed, lay still, wheezed, and opened his eyes.

He was not looking at anyone in particular. Perhaps he was peering into the near future or into the past. They would never know. He said just one thing before he died, spoken clearly and without equivocation.

"One . . . of . . . us."

CHAPTER 16

WASHINGTON, D.C.

Located in the heart of Washington, D.C., the century-old George Washington University Hospital was fully renovated in 2002, transforming it into one of the finest multi-care medical facilities in the nation. With a medical staff of over fifteen hundred doctors and nurses and nearly ninety thousand outpatients a year, the hospital boasted of many successes. Julie Harper, whose surname was then Deas, had previously been one of those success stories.

After she met Jon unpredictably at the notorious 1983 Peace Now rally in Jerusalem, where support of Israeli-Palestinian peace ended with a protester's grenade killing peace advocate Emil Grunzweig, the political pair had agreed to reunite when they returned to "home field," as they lightheartedly referred to anywhere peaceful.

The following month Julie finally received the promised phone call, and with it, Jon's formal invitation to dinner. Julie, however, had another proposal, and Jon arrived at her home for a casual, no-fuss, intimate evening together. Pouring him a glass of 1978 Louis Roederer Cristal Champagne while she finished preparing her simplified version of an off-season Thanksgiving dinner, Julie had the misfortune of slicing into her left hand's pointer finger, leaving the soft tip amid the turkey and other trimmings. She swore, but nothing more, as Jon swallowed what would be his last sip of champagne before rushing her off to the ER at the George Washington University Hospital.

Several stitches and a healthy injection of lidocaine later, Julie was released into Jon's loyal care, and the pair returned to "home field," where they nibbled on the uncontaminated side dishes, finished their bottle of lukewarm champagne, and watched the stunning D.C. sunrise. It would be the last one they'd share as strangers.

The meeting with the president ended around 8:00 p.m.—at least Ryan Kealey's part in it did—and he cabbed over to the hospital. He had been offered a staff car but preferred to make his own way. For one thing, he didn't like accepting gifts from these guys, not even a lift from one of their meetings. It was a matter of expressing your independence. That was important in Washington. Otherwise, people assumed they owned you. For another, he needed to be around real people, starting with a short walk across Lafayette Park to the Hay-Adams Hotel, which was where he got his ride.

The mood of the evening tourists in the park, and of the people in the hotel lobby, was one of somnambulism. Not disbelief. Americans knew what terrorists were capable of. That the bad guys had gotten through again, however, was still a blow. Even the cabdriver was silent and listening to the radio.

Jon Harper was sitting in the hospital's main waiting room on Twenty-Third Street, NW. Someone with Harper's connections and stature would certainly have been offered a private office to wait in. But someone of Harper's personal stature would not have accepted special treatment. Which was why Kealey knew exactly where to find him.

Harper was slumped in a plastic seat, staring at his lap. The CIA official didn't look up until Kealey was on top of him.

Harper didn't say anything at first. He smiled weakly, then rose and put his arms around his colleague.

"I'm glad you're all right," Harper said.

"I made 'em pay," Kealey said into the man's ear.

He felt Harper's grip tighten. "Thanks for what you did, buddy. Thank you."

Kealey didn't respond. It wasn't a moment for words.

"Allison all right?" Harper asked, taking a step back.

"Yeah. Her nephew, too. He was lucky."

Harper's face was tight, fighting something more than tears. He cleared his briefcase from the adjoining seat, and Kealey sat. He looked around. The room was crowded, but not packed. It would be hours before the overflow from Baltimore began arriving.

"I heard," Harper began, then choked, started again. "I heard some doctors talking. Seems that until the air force gives an all clear on medevac pilots, some of the injured are being brought here via hospital boat."

Washington, D.C., had an automatic lockdown protocol in the event of a terrorist attack. The airways were closed, and incoming vehicular traffic was severely restricted. The perpetrators would expect a loosening of flyover regulations for medical aircraft. If they had compromised a pilot of one of these aircraft, how better to hit the nation's capital?

"I can't imagine that Ninety-five is real crowded in this direction," Kealey said. "People will stay put or get the hell out of town."

"I heard they still need the ambulances up there," Harper said. "They're finding people in the rubble."

Kealey wondered if there had been further collapses since he'd been ferried away, weakened structures collapsing at the convention center, maybe more in the hotel. That was what happened after the World Trade Center attacks when, late in the afternoon, the weakened and burning 7 World Trade Center collapsed and slid onto the rubble.

Harper didn't ask about the meeting. He knew that Kealey wouldn't tell him anything in public.

"What's the latest with Julie?" Kealey asked.

Harper shrugged helplessly. "She's in surgery. Bone fragments on the brain. They told me that'll be about five hours. When they can, they have to cut open her leg and close the flaps where her fingers used to be. . . ."

He stopped again, on the verge of losing it.

Kealey sat still, giving him time and space and also picking through his own thoughts. He had called the attack a beachhead, and to a man—even Andrews—the president's other advisors had cautioned Brenneman that there was no evidence of that. Kealey agreed. Nonetheless, the kind of training the commandos had had did not come from a training camp in the mountains of Afghanistan. The weapons were new and, worse, current. They hadn't been captured from fallen Russian or American soldiers. And the strike was complex, with more moving parts than September 11 or any other attack. No group put that kind of effort into an operation, then failed to take credit for it.

Unless they weren't through.

It was flimsy, Kealey had to admit, but it wasn't what the Company classified as an "unreasonable assumption," the kind of spitballing agents did when they were looking for links in disparate enemy activity and chatter, overlapping names, places, timing, or objectives that might signal the coming together of a plan.

"When the hell does it end?" Harper asked.

"It will, Jon."

"How? When?"

"Like the cavalry used to say out West, 'When the renegades are taken or destroyed.'"

"It's not the same," Harper said. "The Indians had nowhere to go. We boxed them in and cut them down. This is like playing goddamn Whac-a-Mole with the whole damn world."

"Not really," Kealey replied. "You take out enough Osamas, you Tomahawk missile enough cars with top terror brass, and eventually the movement runs out of gas."

"Jesus, Ryan. Do you really believe that?"

"I do."

Harper shook his head dejectedly. "We do that, these killers just go on the Internet and recruit more."

"They try," Kealey said. "You remember that white paper Allison worked on?"

Harper thought for a moment and then actually chuckled. "You mean Project Pond Scum?"

"That's the one. A small amount of algae is unavoidable, but after you skim the pond, you can keep most of it from coming back."

"Algae doesn't communicate via the Internet."

"You obviously didn't pay attention to what three million bucks and sixteen months told us," Kealey said. "I had a long plane flight to South Africa to read it. Whether it's terror or porn, yes, the Internet allows people to communicate and find kindred souls. But it doesn't increase their ranks at the rate they're being thinned by arrests and death."

"Right, and that was what? Three years ago? We've got kids growing up with a sense of virtual community, a sense of video-game invulnerability, and an aggressive tribal mentality because of all that. Their minds calcify into something hardcore, into small agile pockets of twisted little sociopaths. I don't share your optimism. I see packs that are tougher to track and destroy."

"You've gotten too close to the daily intel briefings," Kealey said quietly. "When I've been abroad, I see mothers who still don't want to see their kids blow themselves up. And I see kids who mostly want Nikes and PlayStations."

"Not the kids in hate schools in Yemen and Somalia," Harper said.

Kealey chuckled. "Hell, Jon. When did *you* ever pay attention to anything your teacher said?"

Harper considered that. He shrugged, sighed, and deflated.

"Having a vision is one thing, but getting shot at opens your eyes," Kealey said. "For all the righteous indignation and out-of-the-box heroics, where would the Libyan rebels have been without NATO? For that matter, how long would the French Resistance have survived without D-day?"

And he wondered if that was what didn't sit right today, the sense he got from the attackers and their matériel that there *was* a supply line, a logistical support system. What bothered him almost as much as the feeling was now knowing, whether he was frustrated or relieved, that none of this was his responsibility.

"You're probably knocked out," Harper said. "You also need a shower. You smell of firefight and Situation Room."

Kealey smiled. He was about to remark, "Hey, the ladies really go for it" when he thought of Julie and bit it off. "Yeah," he said instead.

Kealey rose. So did Harper. They hugged again, and the deputy director thanked him once more for everything. He was still struggling to hold it together.

"Call me if you hear anything," Kealey told him. "Or even if you don't and just want to talk."

Harper promised that he would.

Kealey left and got in the cab, which was still sitting at the curb.

"Hope you don't mind me spying on you," the driver said. "Saw you go in, figured you might not be long." He poked a thumb at the radio. "Nobody calling to go anywhere tonight, and Union Station was dead."

"No, I'm glad," Kealey said. The cabbie was a young African American with an accent that sounded like Arkansas. Kealey gave him the address.

"Courtesy call?" the driver asked as he pulled away.

"Something like that," Kealey responded.

"Probably a lot of that today," the driver remarked.

"Yeah," Kealey replied.

People were always friendlier in a crisis, wanting to make a connection. On the way over the driver had been too preoccupied with negotiating the streets blocked off with police vehicles to do more than mutter unhappily about the detours. D.C. cabbies were paid by the sector, not the mileage, and he was burning a lot of extra gas.

Kealey didn't want to be rude, but he was too tired, too preoccupied to chat. He sat there, acutely aware now of the odors. That bothered him. He still had the old instincts for combat—those never left, even if the joints stiffened a little—but Kealey realized he was definitely out of practice. He hadn't noticed the smells until Harper said something. That was the kind of slipup that could get someone killed in the field. He had always been alert to that after meeting a source overseas who smoked a distinctive tobacco or served him food that stayed on the breath for hours. Having Handi Wipes and flavored gum in his pocket was as important as having his passport and *balisong*.

His eyelids drooped as he sat there. The streetlights became smears; the outside world dreamlike. He just now understood what Harper had meant but hadn't quite been able to articulate: since 2001 life itself had seemed unreal. Attacks or the threat of them. Anthrax in envelopes. Constant war.

Might as well call it what it is, he thought in his strangely lucid state. *World War III on a slow burn.*

Each time one of these events happened, here or in Madrid, London, Israel, Kealey privately hoped it would be the tipping point, the event that caused the globe to scream, "Enough!" There had been another white paper, one prepared by the Department of Defense, called Operation Tripod. It was named for a code word ascribed to the theoretical next world war. The précis—which itself ran seventy-four pages, just one one-hundredth of the document's entire length—described unprecedented bombing runs around Middle Eastern oil facilities and pipelines to cut them off, followed by a massive airdrop of personnel and matériel to protect them and the construction of secure spans to get the oil out. The idea was that without petrodollars the enemy would starve. Starving, he would be forced to attack for supplies. Attacking, he would be cut down. The most radical part of the proposal was the section called Dewdrop. Radical or fence-straddling regimes that did not instantly fall in line, from Iran to Pakistan, would have their capitals razed by MOABs, Massive Ordnance Air Blasts, bombs that delivered the destructive force of the smallest nuclear devices but without the radiation.

A horrible scenario with countless innocent casualties, yes, Kealey reflected. *But worth the price for normalcy, of an end to the Dark Ages nipping at the world's extremities?*

He didn't know. And, fortunately, it wasn't his decision to make.

And as he was thinking about that, his phone beeped. He checked the text message and frowned.

"Driver," he said, "I've got a change of plans."

"Yes, sir?"

"Take me to Lafayette Square, please."

"Hello, Yasmin."

The soft voice, speaking Arabic, came from all around her. There were probably speakers nearby.

Clever, she had to admit. The blinding light her captors had turned on forced her to close her eyes, to pay attention.

"As you may have realized, there is a marble in the pocket of your blouse," the voice went on. "We will release your left wrist from the restraint. You are then going to remove the marble and hold it in your left hand. You will close your fingers tightly around it. You are to squeeze the marble. If you relax your hand, my voice will be replaced with a less pleasant sound and we will have to begin again. Do you understand?"

"I do," she said. For now, this was one of those plan-three responses to captivity: in the absence of any other option, pretend to cooperate.

There was a low hum and a *snap*. Her restraints were electromagnetic. Her left wrist had just been released. She reached for the marble and placed it in her left hand.

"You are not to speak unless a question is asked. Do you understand?"

"Yes," she said.

"The light will be dimmed. You will keep your eyes closed."

The bright red-orange hue of her eyelids darkened to a burnt sienna and then to deep brown.

"We are going to give you a series of instructions. If you fail to obey any of them, we will know."

There was a long pause. When the voice returned, it was softer. Nearer, as though there were headphones a few centimeters from her ears.

"You are to tell us the first thing that comes to your mind," the voice said. "Do not open your eyes. Do not think about your answer. Give us an immediate response. Do you understand?"

"Yes."

There was another pause. When she heard the voice again, it was a little softer, a little nearer.

"Imagine that you are lying someplace. Where are you?"

"On a beach," she replied.

"Imagine you turn to your left. What do you see?"

"The ocean."

"What color is the water?"

"Blue."

"Clear?"

"Yes."

"Calm?"

"Yes."

"What do you smell?"

"Salt in the air."

"What else?"

"A moldy piece of wood."

"Where is it?"

"At my feet. From a boat. An old boat."

"Is it near the water?"

"Yes. Partly buried in the sand."

"You turn to your right. What do you see?"

"A cliff."

"Look up the cliff. What do you see?"

"A fortress."

"Is it yours?"

"Yes."

"Imagine you are standing beside it. What do you see?"

"A great wooden door."

"Is it windy?"

"Yes. Up here."

"Are the skies clear?"

"Perfectly."

"Do you wish to enter?"

"Yes."

"What do you say?"

" 'Guard, let me in.' "

"The guard asks, 'Who are you?' What do you answer?"

"I tell him that I am Princess Yasmin," she said.

"You enter," the voice told her. "What do you see directly in front of you?"

"My father." She smiled. "The king."

"He embraces you. How do you feel?"

"Wonderful."

"What does he say to you?"

" 'Did you enjoy the beach?' "

"What do you tell him?"

" 'Very much, Father . . .' "

Two men and a woman were watching Yasmin on a monitor. The forty-two-inch LED screen sat on a glass-topped desk against a bare wall. A third man sat in a converted bathroom at the far end of the room. He was watching the same image on a laptop. A translation program was running the exhange in English along the left side of the screen with just a two-second delay. The room they were in was less than 300 square feet, with white walls and a bank of windows that looked out on the Hudson River thirty-six floors below. The glass was double thick as a buffer against street noise from the West Side Highway. The room on the laptop was a third that size, with only a gurney and an attendant. The big man was standing off in the shadows, well behind the gurney.

One of the men, Franklin May, was assistant director of the FBI's Directorate of Intelligence. He did not know who the subject really was; a volunteer from NYU, born in New Delhi, raped as a child, he was told. The other, Alexander Hunt, was assistant director of the New York field office. He knew exactly who was on the table. May was sipping black coffee, and Hunt stood beside him with his arms crossed.

"The disassociation is working perfectly," the woman said in a voice barely above a whisper.

"How can you tell?" asked May. He was short, balding, and was dressed in a black Brooks Brothers suit with a tightly knotted red tie. His whisper was like a rasp. "It's been less than two minutes."

"You witnessed the point at which she actually joined the altered reality," the woman said. "When she spoke of the board and the smell. It was the first time she took the initiative to elaborate and explain. He kept talking to her to see if she would expand on it, go further into that reality. But the wood, stuck in the sand, was a dead end, so he moved her away from it. But she was there."

"Not to doubt your expertise, Doctor, but you got that from her talking about a board?"

"And her expressions," the woman said with a trace of annoyance. "It isn't just one nexus that informs us of success, but many. You saw the way she went on to personalize the princess as herself?"

"Okay—"

"All people have repressed desires," the woman went on. "Family, society, our jobs, our financial status do that to us. When we go deep enough into our psyche and are given not just the freedom to express those desires but also a command to do so, people invariably, willingly submit. It is liberating. The id welcomes that freedom. It's only a question of how long it takes. Someone in this woman's situation—an impoverished, lonely childhood—is particularly susceptible. You see her hand, the one with the marble?"

The man said he did.

"Despite our orders, she relaxed her grip. She forgot that because of the very strong reality we impressed upon her. She abrogated her responsibility because of the power of the vision she's creating for herself."

"You told her you'd start again if she did that."

"That was to emphasize how important it was," the woman said. "Yet she still succumbed. That's another way we know the hypnosis is working."

"And yet the marble will remind her of this session."

"It will do much more than that," the woman told him. "It will keep her in the session, functioning outwardly as her old self, but inwardly focused on that object. It is called cognitive sublimation."

"So there is no 'less pleasant sound,' I think your associate called it?"

"Oh yes," the woman said. "There is definitely a less pleasant sound. It's not something you want to hear."

May continued to peer into the adjoining room. The voice of Dr. Emile Samson, the moderator of the session, had already taken this Indian rani from the courtyard to the palace itself.

"How do you know she's not faking?" May asked.

"Because we have seen virtually this same pattern in all the subjects who have come through here," the woman replied.

The woman, Dr. Ayesha Gillani, had been introduced to May as the "brilliant hypnotherapist" who had treated Jacob Trask's bipolar daughter in Atlanta. Trask was so impressed that he'd hired her to work in Xana, his psyops R & D division. It was named after a fairy-tale character Trask remembered from a childhood storybook, a nymph who was the keeper of a great treasure.

"It's remarkable, Frank," the other man said. Special Agent Hunt was in his early thirties. Square shouldered and six foot one, he was wearing a button-down white shirt, sleeves rolled up, knotted black tie pulled to one side at the neck.

May nodded in agreement. "And when you're finished with the process, in two days, this woman's traumatic memories will be gone."

"That is correct," said Dr. Gillani.

"We've proven it numerous times," said Hunt. He laid a hand on the other man's shoulder. "But that's not the beauty of it. We can turn the Gillani Technique into a goddamn assembly line at Guantánamo Bay, send those miserable SOBs back home to spy for us."

May shook his head. "It *is* amazing, and I'd back it in a New York minute. But I don't see how I'll ever get the director to go along with it."

"Why? Congress? The ACLU?"

"For starters, but also Brenneman," May said. "He's not going to want to leave office under an indictment from the Justice Department for torturing detainees."

Hunt laughed. "Torture? Christ, everyone will be thrilled that we're finally going to clear out Gitmo! Hell, we can turn it into a petting zoo for the Cubans, win the hearts and minds of those poor people."

The assistant director regarded his subordinate with a curious, wary expression. "The zoo I like. The rest of it is admirable, and some of the assistant directors may want to keep it going at a low burn. But I can't see Cluzot going along with it. Hell, you've got her strapped down—"

"In case she has a post-traumatic episode," Hunt lied. The woman was a killer. They had to keep her bound in case she slipped from their control.

"And if she does? And hurts herself in our custody, goes out one of these windows?"

"We'll board them," Hunt said. His eyes were hard, fixed on the other man. "Give us more time. We weren't expecting you. We can clean this up, Frank."

"Alex, look. I see the merits of the process. I do."

"It's not *costing* us anything!"

"That's part of the problem and the main reason I came down early. A lot of people in D.C. don't want Trask crossing from the military to the Feds. That's too much influence in one place. Cluzot is being pressured to demonopolize, to sever ties like that." May's eyes were sympathetic. "You're doing great work here, the three of you. Hell of an achievement. Beats all hell out of waterboarding. But frankly, speaking personally now, this is more CIA than FBI."

"I'm really not sure I follow that reasoning," Hunt replied. His voice was taut. His hand was still on his superior's shoulder. "One, protect the United States from terrorist attack. Two, protect the United States against foreign intelligence operations and espionage. Three, protect the United States against—"

"I know the charter—"

"Cyber-based attacks and high-technology crimes. Four, combat transnational-national criminal organizations and enterprises. Five, freakin' upgrade technology to successfully perform the FBI's mission."

May slowly shrugged off Hunt's hand. His voice was still quiet, but there was an agitated little wire somewhere inside it. "You forgot the most important. These activities must have a proper purpose and may not undermine activities protected by the Constitution of the United States."

"I haven't forgotten it," Hunt said. "It just doesn't apply to scum who want to kill us."

The men regarded one another. May shook his head. "I will recommend to the director that he communicate to Mr. Trask that the Bureau was extremely impressed by the remarkable work of the Xana team, and Dr. Gillani in particular," he said. "But I will also strongly suggest that we do not add this procedure to our field operations."

"You'll sink us," Hunt said.

"I'm sorry." He looked back at the monitor. Yasmin Rassin was smiling. She was rolling the marble lightly between thumb and index finger. "Has the marble become something else in her little fantasy?"

"Yes," Dr. Gillani replied, apparently unmoved by the conversation that had taken place behind her. "She is being told that it is the world, her world. I will soon go back inside and take it from her. To get it back, she will have to do as she is told in the next session."

"Will she sleep like this from now until then?"

"This is not sleep, but a sensitized waking state, and no. When my colleague, Dr. Samson, brings her out of this, she will remember having the marble in her pocket and waiting for something to happen. Her wrist will be restrained, and she will be hungry, thirsty, and tired. I will feed her, and she will be allowed to sleep. Then we will begin again."

"Fascinating," May said. He finished his coffee, then turned and offered Hunt his hand. "You've done an excellent job here, and I'll be sure to highlight that in my report."

"Thank you," Hunt replied, without enthusiasm. "Well, let's get you over to Penn Station so I can go back to the office to close out the file. I'll walk you to the subway."

May thanked Dr. Gillani. She responded with a little smile but did not look back or leave her post.

"She's watching for facial signals and muscular reactions along her body," Hunt explained. "It's being recorded, but this way she can give Dr. Samson instructions."

"I see."

The men were silent as they left the corner penthouse and walked to the elevator. Dr. Gillani had rented two of the ten apartments on the floor, using Trask's money. She had her hypnotherapy practice in one—this one—and lived in the other next door.

May checked his cell phone on the way down. The assistant director held the phone straight in front of him. If there were overhead cameras in the elevator, they would not be able to see the screen.

The iPhone was not equipped with encryption software, so messages were either oblique or coded with "words of the day." This was a simple substitution dictionary physically downloaded via USB each morning and overwritten the following morning. The user had to check any unclear words manually so that anyone scanning the Wi-Fi signal would not be able to intercept the dictionary.

"Damn," he said.

Hunt looked at him. He didn't have to ask what it was about. "Update?"

"Yeah."

The door opened, and they crossed the lobby in silence. A few people moved around them, some tenants taking their dogs for a walk, deliverymen arriving with dinner for others. A few were sitting in the chairs along the walls, working on laptops. May had admired the maritime murals when he entered an hour before. He didn't notice them now.

"Two agents were killed at the hotel," May said when they were outside. "By another agent."

"Obviously an impostor," Hunt said.

They walked east, turned north on Washington Street. Hunt walked slightly apart from May, to his left. He was still decrypting the message as they passed the dark edifice of One Western Union International Plaza, which was also on the left. To the right was the deep, sloping entranceway to the Brooklyn Battery Tunnel. A block ahead, a footbridge over the tunnel ramp led to the subway entrance.

The building had a large overhang supported by columns. A homeless man was huddled against the locked doors of the twenty-story black tower. While May was concentrating on the phone, Hunt stopped and walked over to the older African American, who was huddled in a worn blanket. There were no security cameras under here. They were all on the street, watching the street. Hunt had avoided them by walking close to the building. All they would show was May.

Hunt kicked the man hard in the face with the bottom of his shoe. The homeless man yelped. May looked over.

"Alex! What are you—"

"Goddamn beggar!" Hunt snarled. He stomped on the cheek of the fallen man.

May shoved his phone in his pocket as he ran over. He bear-hugged the bigger man, but Hunt was ready for him. He was *expecting* him.

Hunt gave May a hard elbow to the chest, breaking the hold, then turned. He swung hard at the man's face, catching him against his left ear. He threw an uppercut to his jaw, then jabbed his nose. May staggered back against the black tile wall. Hunt had taken pains to hit him square, never punching down, so it would look like a shorter man—which the homeless person was— had hit him. While May sucked blood up his nose, Hunt drove his knuckles repeatedly into his windpipe. Then he scratched his eyes, his cheeks, his neck as he went down.

He had to make it look like a scrap.

When May hit the sidewalk, Hunt pulled an old boot from the dazed beggar, slipped his fist inside, and pounded the heel hard, repeatedly, into May's face. Then he put the boot, covered with blood, back on the homeless man, bent over May, grabbed his ears, and drove his head hard into the concrete.

Brain tissue clung to the pavement. May was no longer breathing.

Hunt glanced behind him to make sure no one was walking by. The street was empty. He had been down this road often enough to know that dog walkers preferred Battery Park across the street. Except for people coming in from the subway—and there were few this time of night—the street was largely untraveled. Even if anyone came by, the darkness beside the office building was thick. Because of the high fence beside the tunnel entrance, the street was invisible from the buildings across the way on Trinity Place.

Pulling a handkerchief from his pocket, he fished May's wallet from his inside jacket pocket and tucked it in the bundle of garments that was the homeless man.

"Wha—"

"Shut up, pig," Hunt said to the groggy man.

Then he took off May's big college ring and punched the man again, leaving an impression on his jaw. He hit him several times in the side of the head, until blood oozed from his ear. Then he wiped his prints off and put the ring back on May's dead finger. The cops would conclude that there had been an attempted mugging, a struggle, and mutual assured destruction.

Hunt walked to the street and made a final check. No one was around. He walked quickly back to his building.

You had to make a visit now, he thought angrily.

They'd needed the cover of a legitimate FBI project to justify Hunt's presence. But they also needed a little more time to finish. May had not recognized Yasmin Rassin, but then he did not know Veil was not on her way to Pakistan as planned. When he learned that back at his office, when he saw her photograph, he would have put things together.

And then there was this latest news. Of all the goddamn luck, to have someone "made" at the hotel. The man at the hotel wasn't real FBI; he was a Saudi medical student at Johns Hopkins. Unlike the "Indian rani," he had actually volunteered to be part of Gillani's bogus trauma mitigation studies. Still, that would put the Bureau in Baltimore under all kinds of scrutiny. If they found the kid, he would remember nothing, but they would learn from e-mails that he had been to New York, that he had been here.

All they needed was another day. Hopefully, the kid would return to his daily life and would remain hidden for that long.

Hunt walked through the revolving door at One

West. He looked at the concierge and shook his head. "Text, text, text."

"Sir?"

"My friend," Hunt said. "I got tired of waiting. Pointed to the subway. He can find it himself."

"I don't blame you." The doorman smiled. "It's the same with my kids."

"Hey, how are they?"

"Good, sir. Thank you for asking."

Hunt smiled until he passed the reception desk. He liked the young man as far as that went, but he couldn't worry about anything but the mission right now. All he wanted was the doorman's good will and something resembling an alibi. Even if the police called him in as part of their investigation, they wouldn't have cause to arrest him in time. Not before the second part of the operation put everything else in the city—in the nation—on hold.

He took the penthouse elevator and returned to the laboratory. He was not about to let a premature review of the FBI's investment in the Xana project jeopardize the program, not when they were so close to realizing their goal.

"Is everything all right?" Dr. Gillani asked when he stepped up behind her.

"It's been taken care of," he assured her.

"Functionaries," she said disdainfully. "It is their job to collect enough small minds to stop larger ones."

Hunt liked that. He looked at the contented subject on the video monitor. When Trask recruited him, the billionaire had described bureaucrats as the monkey bars from which the rest of us swing.

"Sometimes monkeys get aggressive," Trask had told him.

That was how he had come to the industrialist's attention, a newspaper article about an unusually violent pursuit of a terror suspect into a mosque. The media had come down on him for ignoring the sanctuary of holy ground in pursuit of a terror suspect. He was forced to undergo sensitivity training. All *that* did was make him hate the sycophants even more, living under the umbrella of American freedom so they could undo it. The worldview he shared with Trask was why Hunt had agreed to be the industrialist's inside man at the Bureau. In return, Trask had promised to give him what he wanted most.

America. Whole, safe, *sane*.

That prize would not come for free, of course. But then, it was supposed to hurt. A quote from Thomas Jefferson had stuck in his brain when he was still in high school, and it had become his bold personal motto, typed and carried on a slip of paper folded into his wallet: *God forbid we should ever be twenty years without such a rebellion. . . . And what country can preserve its liberties, if its rulers are not warned from time to time, that this people preserve the spirit of resistance? . . . What signify a few lives lost in a century or two? The tree of liberty must be refreshed from time to time, with the blood of patriots and tyrants. It is its natural manure.*

Today had been a costly beginning. The next event would carry a higher price tag in blood and treasure.

Hunt left to go clean himself up, get dinner, and take a nap. Dr. Gillani barely noticed that he was gone. She was observing the process carefully, watching Yasmin's movements, listening to Dr. Samson's prompts, paying special attention to the subject's responses.

A normal sleep consisted of five stages. The first was a light sleep, in which the brain threw off waking agitation in the form of theta waves. Theta brain waves were also generated during states of high creativity and emotional excitement; they were the source of daydreams. It had been Dr. Gillani's belief, during her studies at Universität Heidelberg, that phobias, habits, and even mental illness could be treated by riding what she called "counter-instructions" into the brain on the peaks of those outgoing theta waves, almost like surfing, as she put it in her doctoral thesis.

Her paper was greeted with reactions ranging from cautious interest to condemnation. The sheer bulk of overwritten instructions was deemed too large to be simply slipped into the mind. But Dr. Gillani's goal was not to assault, but to invade, like a Trojan horse. To relax the subject and have him or her take the new instructions right to the part of the brain that was least defended, the home of the most pleasant thoughts.

Mild hypnosis simulated stage one sleep, stimulated theta production. The voice kept the subject locked in that phase, relaxed but only nominally asleep, never allowing him or her to go to stage two. Together, the subject and the voice went to an idyllic spot. There, the voice walked the subject through new instructions. It introduced the subject to the marble, which was his or her real-world connection to the hypnotic suggestion. In the case of "cures," as they had done with Jacob Trask's daughter, no personal contact was necessary. The marble was sufficient to keep the suggestion alive, an object small enough to be carried, to be inconspicuous, to keep the owner attached to the commands they carried inside their head. In the case of "phased actions," the rules were different. A phone call from the control voice, from Dr. Samson—a fellow student in Germany—would direct the individual to the marble and return him or her to the Trojan instructions.

Though relatively straightforward, this was a delicate procedure. Pushing any individual too hard, too fast, in a direction that did not seem natural would cause the process to derail entirely and they would have to begin again—but with new, subconscious barriers against intrusion.

There was also the likely potential of leaving subjects "unglued," an informal, more descriptive word she preferred over the technical terminology. Should subjects not receive the full series of treatments, it left them deeply in tune with their darker "Jekyll" side and out of touch with their two or three other, more passive character personas. People "worked" because their various characters performed together in harmony. But subjects, having exercised and strengthened these mental pathways, could easily access and give preference to their dominant, more negative character at will, with very little instigation, and the other parts of their personality did not have the means or power to break free from the dominant character's almighty grasp.

As was the case early in Dr. Gillani's studies with a local German author, whom she referred to in her paper as patient 8R. He was insistently curious about her cerebral process and wanted to personally experience the effects of her, at that time, mind-regression techniques. Making him aware of the "bad idea" quotient of his request, Dr. Gillani reluctantly agreed to give him a private demonstration and she arranged to meet 8R off campus, at his home across the river in Dossenheim.

During his first consenting hypnosis session with Dr. Gillani, she accidentally accessed and provoked 8R's heavily charged creative side, his dominant, darkest nature, to the point where it was necessary for Dr. Gillani to leave the room, then completely exit the house for a few minutes to simply remove her presence from the enraged subject. Patient 8R believed he was a ten-year-old boy, not in present times, who had injured his younger sister and was being punished by his father, a role Dr. Gillani played in his mind, and he wasn't going to allow himself to be harmed by him again. Of course, 8R no longer realized he had the strength of a grown man and was lashing out like a wild child.

Against her better judgment, Dr. Gillani returned inside to fully awaken and disengage the subject, who remained still somewhat unrepressed after she did so. Agreeing to meet again at a later date for successive sessions to correct her oversights, 8R was temporarily released back into his everyday routine. Dr. Gillani never heard back from patient 8R.

Several weeks later Dr. Gillani learned that 8R had perfunctorily punched his way through his bathroom door to get at his mother and didn't stop until her skull was as fractured as the plywood barrier. While Dr. Gillani had always been secretly, scientifically curious to see the consequences of leaving someone divided and unchecked, it ultimately became a necessary operating procedure for her to restrain patients, to hold them against their will if necessary, and she privately vowed to never again leave a patient unfinished. Unglued.

Like the subject in Baltimore, Yasmin had to be done right. Compared to those others, however, they had less time and more instructions to convey.

The scientist watched intently. Dr. Samson had guided Yasmin through the palace with gentle nudges. The movement had to be her own choice; otherwise, her brain would sense that it was being manipulated. Now Samson needed to get her to a bookmark, a place where they could bed her, put her briefly into a REM sleep, during which she would be given a control word. In case something went wrong, the word would take her back there instantly.

Dr. Gillani leaned toward the microphone connected to her colleague's headphones.

"Emile, try to jump her."

"All right," Dr. Samson replied. He spoke to Yasmin. "What do you see inside the tower?"

"A great many stairs," Yasmin told him.

"You don't need to climb them," the voice told her.

"Oh?"

"You're a princess, remember?"

"Yes . . ."

"In a fairy tale," he coaxed. "A magical fairy tale."

"Oh yes."

"Just *go* there," he told her. "Think of the top of the tower."

The young woman was silent for several moments. "I see! It worked. I'm there now."

"Very well done. Look around. What do you see?"

"A beautiful room with white furniture. A dresser. A bed with a gossamer canopy. A full-length mirror. I see pictures of my parents framed in gold."

Dr. Gillani told him, "Take her to the marble first."

"All right." To Yasmin he said, "Go to the dresser."

"Can I cross the rug? It seems so fragile."

"What do you want to do?"

"I want to go around it," she said. "It's such a lovely design. I want to admire it."

"Go ahead."

The scientists watched as she smiled, as her eyes moved beneath her lids.

"Are you still looking at the rug?" Dr. Samson asked.

"Yes."

"Look ahead of you now. What do you see?"

"I'm at the dresser. So many lovely things on top."

"Tell me about them."

"There is a brush with a silver handle. A hand mirror. A jewelry box—"

"Open it." The voice waited a moment. "What do you see?"

"Necklaces. Rings. Jewels."

"Do you see a bracelet?"

"No—"

"Are you certain?"

"I don't see it."

The voice hesitated. "Do you see a watch?"

"Let me look. Yes, there is a watch."

"Very good. Take it out and put it on."

"All right."

The voice waited again. "Is it on?"

"Yes. It sparkles in the sunlight."

"There is a marble in your hand," the voice went on. "Do you feel it?"

"I do."

"It will sparkle, too."

"Let me see." Her wrist moved up. She admired the object through closed eyes. "It's so . . . mysterious."

"Put it on the face of the watch."

Yasmin frowned slightly. "I don't understand."

"Be careful," Dr. Gillani warned. "You mustn't confuse her." That would take Yasmin to a problem-solving corner of the brain. We should have gone to the bed first, she thought. But connection to the marble was a bigger prize, would cut the need for a bookmark and an hour of sleep from the process.

"The marble is like a little sun, is it not?" Dr. Samson asked.

A smile played across Yasmin's lips. "Yellow . . . gleaming." The smile stayed. "Yes."

Dr. Gillani exhaled. Her colleague had kept Yasmin in the illusion.

"If you take that little sun and place it on top of the crystal, it will stay there."

"It will?"

"Yes. The light of both will merge into something beautiful, something worthy of a princess, something you will like very, very much. Don't release it when you put it there. Continue to hold it so you can feel its warmth."

"All right," Yasmin said.

Dr. Gillani pressed a button on the console in front of her. The magnetic strap around Yasmin's right hand was released. She watched as Yasmin moved her wrist to the marble, held it there.

"Oh, yes!" Yasmin said. "I am holding the sun!"

Until she relaxed, Dr. Gillani did not realize how tightly her shoulders had been tensed. The rest of the process should go relatively quickly now. Dr. Samson would suggest that Yasmin change into something regal and would lead her to the closet. There, as she went through the gowns, she would find a chest. In that chest would be the items she would need for the mission. They would be made an anachronistic part of her fantasy, one in which—with Dr. Samson's guidance—she would come to believe the palace was under attack.

Yasmin would defend it.

To the death.

CHAPTER 18

WASHINGTON, D.C.

The meeting had moved to the Oval Office.

Kealey learned that after arriving at Lafayette Square, walking to the White House, and making his way to the West Wing, where he passed through a metal detector at the door and another at the far end of the lobby just before he made a left past the Roosevelt Room. A right at the Cabinet Room brought him to the last leg of his journey. He was escorted by a Secret Service officer and a self-important aide who couldn't have been more than twenty-six. Kealey learned from Erin Enslin, personal secretary to the president, that he was, in fact, twenty-five and the son of the Speaker of the House. Ms. Enslin presented Kealey to Richard Meyers, special assistant to the president and personal aide. Meyers sat right outside the Oval Office. He phoned inside, and at last, like a pail of water in a bucket brigade, Kealey was tossed on the blaze.

Kealey knew all the people present and waved a general hello before the president directed him to an armchair. In addition to Brenneman and CIA director Andrews, the others in attendance were FBI director Charles Cluzot, Homeland Security director Max Carlson, and Press Secretary Andrea Stempel. They were arrayed on two mustard-colored sofas that faced each other just short of the presidential seal in the carpet. Kealey's armchair was not quite between the sofas on the opposite side, just in front of the unlit fireplace.

The hot seat, he reflected.

There were no military brass, cabinet members, other than Carlson, or what Kealey called "the briefers," people like the FBI's Sandy Mathis. They didn't need the multimedia extravaganza that was the Situation Room. That told Kealey they weren't here to analyze findings or put pieces together. There was a plan to discuss, and it involved him.

Andrews's slightly amused eyes confirmed that. He was seated nearest to Kealey, on the right.

"Mr. Kealey, we would like you to accept a temporary reactivation to service," the president said.

The president did not ask him to *consider* a TRS. This was a fiat. It was too bad, Kealey thought—even though part of him resented being the recipient of this—that all presidents didn't govern their entire term with the assertiveness of a lame duck.

"What's the assignment, Mr. President?"

"Is that an acceptance, Ryan?" Andrews asked. "We need to be clear about that before we go on."

Now Kealey was amused. Andrews knew him too well. It wasn't an acceptance, not really. He had said it firmly, which gave that impression to the president and the others.

"I'm accepting," Kealey replied.

Andrews smiled with satisfaction.

"Thank you for clarifying that," the president said. "Charlie?"

The FBI director was on the end of the sofa on the left, nearer to the president. He leaned forward and angled himself toward Kealey. He was a distinguished-looking man, square-jawed and steel-eyed, with broad shoulders and an unfortunate comb-over.

"Two of our agents were shot and killed while attempting to enter what appears to have been the staging area at the Baltimore Hilton," he said. "Before he died, one of them said that he was shot by one of our own agents."

"FBI," Andrews clarified.

"That's correct," Cluzot said. "Insiders at the Bureau, and perhaps elsewhere"—he said that with a glance at Andrews—"would help to explain how the terrorists were able to mount such a large-scale action without anyone catching a whiff of it."

"And you want me because you don't know who to trust," Kealey said. "Problem is, I don't know my way around—"

"We'll be pairing you with an IA agent we know we can trust," Cluzot went on. "Reed Bishop."

"You know we can trust him how?" Kealey asked.

Cluzot's smug half smile told Kealey that he'd been bushwhacked, that his renowned I'm-from-Missouriness had somehow backfired. It underscored what he had witnessed a moment earlier in the exchange between Cluzot and Andrews, that despite the mandated interdepartmental cooperation since 2001, there was still a sharp, enduring rivalry between the intelligence branches.

"Agent Bishop was with his daughter at the convention center," Cluzot said. "She was killed in the explosion."

The words hung like a toxic cloud. Kealey actually felt sick. Andrews saved him.

"Who's spoken with Agent Bishop?" he asked.

"I did." Cluzot raised a hand. "He flew back with the special agent in charge up there, who will be briefing me about ongoing operations"—he popped the pocket watch he carried—"at midnight."

"Does the SAC know why Bishop was summoned?" Andrews asked.

"Courtesy to a brother who has suffered a loss," Cluzot replied. "That's all."

As he was speaking, both the phone on the president's desk and the FBI director's cell beeped. They exchanged looks. Kealey knew why. They were probably getting the same message. He was guessing it wasn't good.

Cluzot rose from the sofa and walked to the recessed door. The president picked up. They listened without comment to whatever was being said. The room was like church, full of purposeful silence.

The calls finished at nearly the same time. Cluzot deferred to the president.

"New York?" Brenneman asked him.

"Yes, sir," the FBI director replied.

"Go ahead," the president said. He sat back in his leather chair, looking reflective and disgusted, like someone who just wanted to push every damn thing off the table.

Cluzot took a long breath. This was obviously personal to him. "Franklin May, our assistant director of the DI, was found beaten to death on a Manhattan street," the director said gravely. "It appears to have been the work of a homeless man, but the NYPD is investigating."

"Was the AD on assignment at that location?" Andrews asked.

"He was checking the progress of psyops research," Cluzot replied. "It happened near Battery Park, less than a block away from our lab." He regarded Brenneman. "If you'll excuse me, Mr. President, I'd like to see what our people down there know. The NYPD is asking."

"Of course," Brenneman replied. "Use my study."

"Thank you, sir."

Cluzot made his way to the door between the fireplace and the main entrance. This was where presidents went for breakaway talks during meetings, to smoke, or to meet clandestinely for reasons that were rarely discussed on the outside. The FBI director did not shut the door behind him but walked toward the dining area beyond the study. No one said what was on the unhappy faces and busily working minds of everyone present, that this was somehow related to the events of the day. Everyone slipped into reflection while they waited for Cluzot. Only the press secretary seemed fully present. That was understandable. She was listening carefully to everything that was said. When standing before the press corps, it was just as important to know what not to say as it was what *to* say.

"How's everyone holding up?" the president asked. The question seemed calculated more to break the silence than to pump up energy levels.

There were indecipherable murmurs and vague nods.

"Would anyone like—where are we?—dinner or breakfast?" he asked, gesturing to a small table that had been set up on the other side of the desk.

There were insincere chuckles. It didn't look as though anything had been touched, other than the coffee. There were half-emptied cups on the coffee table between the sofas. The Oval Office attendees had been too tired, too shell-shocked, too focused to think about eating.

The president went over, poured himself coffee from an antique coffee pot, and selected half a turkey sandwich. He sat on the corner of his desk and held the plate while he ate.

"I'll be meeting with the Joint Chiefs at one a.m.," Brenneman said. He lofted the coffee as if he were making a toast.

"That stuff'll float a horseshoe, Mr. President," Carlson remarked.

"That's what I need," the president replied. "I don't think that meeting will be brief."

The chuckles were even less enthusiastic now.

The president didn't have to explain to this group what Admiral Breen was doing. The Office of the Chairman of the Joint Chiefs would be collating its own satellite data, phone intercepts, and reports from international intelligence teams, all of which were being funneled through Homeland Security. If they came up with anything that showed the attacks were rooted somewhere overseas, they were going to have to respond. The best-case scenario was a city in an allied nation, like Germany or England. Arrests could be made there, with no attacks. If it turned out the terrorists had plotted in a hostile nation, that nation would be bombed.

That was informally referred to as the Kissinger Mandate, and Kealey agreed with it. In the hours after the September 11 attacks, the former secretary of state was the first official to go on record saying that a military target must be found and hit. That was necessary not only for the psyche of the nation but also to show the enemy that they couldn't bloody our nose and get away with it. Not in the short term, and certainly not in the long term. It was also a bone to the military. As an army colonel had said to Kealey after the attacks, "What the hell are they waiting for? Just send us over, with fixed bayonets, shoulder to shoulder, and let us march from one end of that goddamn country to the other."

Cluzot returned before that could become a topic of discussion.

"One of our guys walked him downstairs from the lab, pointed him in the direction of the subway, came back," the FBI director said. He looked at notes he had made on a small notepad; he would shred those before leaving the Oval Office. "The man in question is Alexander Hunt, assistant director of the New York field office. He was the only other Bureau man on scene. Eight-year veteran, fast-track rise. Psych tagged him as an 'aggressive patriot' because of actions against some of his Muslim coworkers, but no other blemishes. Concierge at the building confirms that he was in and out."

"Surveillance?" Andrews asked.

"Solid except for about a half a block, zero of the crime scene."

That set off alarms in Kealey's brain. In a high-security area like Lower Manhattan that kind of a precision "mugging" was just too neat to be an accident. "What do we know about the lab?"

"We are presently running twenty-nine separate R & D projects in psych alone," Cluzot said. "I wasn't following this one."

"Who was?" the president asked.

Cluzot replied, "May and Hunt."

"Terrific," Press Secretary Stempel piped in.

"Andrea, the idea is to keep information contained," Cluzot said. "That's the strength *and* the weakness of these programs."

She raised her hands defensively. "That wasn't a knock, Mr. Director. It's just another question I can't answer at a press conference. Every time I say an operation is 'classified,' we get ten conspiracy theory sites online."

"Well, we can't go asking Hunt," Kealey said. "Not until we're sure about him. He might torch the place."

Cluzot looked at him. He didn't seem pleased by the suggestion.

"You said he was . . . What was the phrase?" Kealey asked. "An aggressive patriot? That place is about five blocks from the World Trade Center site, eight blocks from the Ground Zero mosque. That kind of proximity does things to people."

"Agreed, but we still have to debrief him," Andrews said.

"No argument. Recommendation?" the president asked.

"I suggest that Mr. Kealey and Mr. Bishop go up

there and talk to AD Hunt and the people at Xana, that is the name of the team at the lab," Cluzot said.

There was a short, crushing silence. Kealey had always been a Hail Mary pass, not a first responder. He wondered if things had gone farther than Cluzot was letting on.

"Won't that tell them someone is onto them?" the president asked, obviously wrestling with a little of what Kealey was thinking.

"I think, Mr. President, that's kind of the idea," Kealey said. He looked at Cluzot. "I'm sure, if he tried real hard, the director could find one trustworthy soul at the Bureau. Someone in accounting or data processing, someone with no connection to Xana."

"Mr. Kealey, that option wasn't presented to me—"

"No, I was presented to you," Kealey said. "A red flag to wave at the bull."

"Gentlemen, I'm a little tired and a little confused," the president said. "What the hell's going on here?"

"Sir, we're not just investigators," Kealey told him. "We're bait."

"That's a little strong, Mr. Kealey," Cluzot said.

"No, it's exactly right," Kealey said. "And it's okay. I've been there before. It would just be nice if we were all up front about it."

There was a point in any meeting with the president when it was over for one or more of the participants. Someone would upset the delicate balance by speaking his or her mind a little too frankly and way above his or her pay grade. For Kealey, that moment had arrived. He was a former mid-level agent who had effectively called a department head a liar. Before things could escalate, Andrews rose, saying he'd see Kealey out.

"Of course," the president said. He looked at Kealey. "I'm not interested in whatever was behind this little flare-up. We have a situation, and we need results. You're the man to bring us those results. Are you on board with that?"

"Very." The former agent had gotten to his feet as Andrews was speaking.

"Then thank you again," the President said, "and please keep Bob in the loop."

"I will, and thank you, Mr. President," Kealey said without looking at Cluzot.

"Let us know if there are any names or resources you need, Mr. Kealey," the FBI director said to his back.

That was as good and sincere a send-off as Kealey was going to get. He left the Oval Office ahead of Andrews's extended arm.

They walked down the hallway that took them past the outside wall of the study toward the reception area. Tired staff, fewer than in the daytime—but not by much—moved between doorways that ended with the office of the chief of staff. His own door was opened as aides came and went, helping him to coordinate the intelligence briefings that would be presented to the president prior to his meeting with Admiral Breen.

"Still can't play along," Andrews said quietly as they made their way along the narrow hallway.

"I hate that goddamn sandbox."

"No. Really?"

"Anyway, Cluzot will survive," Kealey said.

"Not the point," Andrews said. "His organization is the one that got blindsided and humped. You could've cut him slack."

Kealey stopped. "And I'm the guy going up there to *be* humped. He could have been up front about that. You already made the point that I was accepting the assignment—for which push, thank you very much, by the way."

"Again, beside the point. You know the way the totem is stacked, and you know how the game is played."

"Yeah," Kealey said. "You done?"

"I think so."

The men continued walking. Whether Kealey liked it or not, Andrews would apologize for his snippiness when he went back to the Oval Office. For his own self-respect, Kealey decided to make it "or not."

"You need a ride?" Andrews asked.

"No thanks."

"I'll have Mei make the arrangements. She'll e-mail the itinerary. Figure on a six a.m. flight."

"Figuring away," Kealey said. "Only book me on the Acela. The train is less hassle with more legroom. And it'll give me time to prep."

"Okay."

They stopped at the exit. Andrews didn't look happy, but he wasn't angry, either. "It's been a long day for everyone," he said. "And all of the bullshit aside, what you did in Baltimore was exemplary."

"I know you mean it," Kealey said. "That's a commendation-level word."

Andrews showed a little smile. "Honestly, Ryan? I don't know how you lasted as long as you did."

"My exemplary deeds." He grinned back. He sighed. "I'm tired, Bob. Not just of the work and the egos, but of the responsibility."

"I hear you."

"And the pain, always up close and too personal," he added. "I went to see Jon."

"Shit. I meant to call—"

"It's okay. He's pretty out of it. Julie's facing a couple of surgeries. There was no word on any of them."

"Thanks for doing that," Andrews said. "And for going along with this. It's a little seat of the pants for my taste."

"That's okay," Kealey said, his smile broadening as he turned to go past the guard. "It's what I do."

CHAPTER 19

NEW YORK, NEW YORK

The "Canyon of Heroes" is the short section of Broadway that runs from city hall to Bowling Green, located just a few blocks from the bottom of Manhattan. It is the traditional site of the city's ticker-tape parades, which are staged to honor national and international heroes. Plaques set in the sidewalks commemorate the names and dates of each parade.

In the aftermath of the World Trade Center attacks, there was another kind of hero at the midpoint of the parade route. Stationed near historic Trinity Church, where the likes of inventor Robert Fulton and founding father Alexander Hamilton were interred, a unit of police officers stood beside steel barricades erected on the east side of Broadway. Their job was to pull over and examine any vehicles—typically vans and U-Hauls—which they deemed to be suspicious. Stopping a van or truck loaded with explosives, of course, would cause the driver to trigger the device prematurely, killing them. But the police stopped the vehicles just the same, as part of their oath to preserve and protect.

The Trask Industries van was pulled over as it rolled down Broadway. A name was easy enough to fake, so the Atlanta tags would have to be checked along with the contents.

Police sergeant Dario Russo approached the driver's side. It was a warm morning, and the van's window was already down. There were two men inside, both African American. They looked hot and tired.

"Good morning," the fifteen-year veteran said to the driver. "May I have your registration and manifest please?"

"Sure thing, Officer."

The driver, a powerfully built man in his late forties with short gray hair, pulled the documents from a folder in the glove compartment and handed them over. The other man, in his early forties, was in the passenger's seat.

"You're not running the air-conditioning," the officer observed.

"We're from Atlanta, sir," the driver said with a smile. "This weather is what we call cool cucumbers."

"I see. Would you open the rear of the vehicle please?" the officer asked humorlessly as he scanned the papers.

The driver got out and followed the sergeant. He was met by another officer in the rear, a young man whose name tag said HEMMINGS.

"Good morning," the driver said.

"Good morning," the young policeman said back.

The driver selected the key from a ring in his pocket

and opened the back door. Sergeant Russo handed the bill of lading to his companion and took the registration to the squad car that was parked just outside the barricade.

"Most of these are going to our HQ," the officer said, mildly surprised and slightly more alert.

"Two blocks down."

"You've made the run before?"

"Just once," the driver said. "Last winter. After a snowstorm. But the tech upgrades had to get through."

"We appreciate it."

"Enough to let me stay parked here so I can just walk the stuff over?" the driver joked. "Those side streets are a bear."

"Sorry," Hemmings replied.

The officer leaned in and checked the marked contents against the bill of lading. The NYPD's Counterterrorism Division was located in a secure block of office buildings, in a modern skyscraper. The bill of lading said the boxes were upgraded radiation detectors for the technology and construction section. That was the division responsible for the Lower Manhattan Security Initiative. Routes to the Wall Street area were already watched by streetlight-mounted boxes of technology designed to prevent even a well-shielded dirty bomb from being brought in. They were programmed to watch for radiation, as well, as the chemical signatures of containers in which radiological devices would be stored.

Everything looked to be in order. It was impossible to dismantle all the contents of every vehicle, but officers used the quick check—as well as common sense and profiling—to ascertain whether cargo represented a plausible threat.

The driver seemed relaxed. His accent seemed to fit where he said he was from. The van's license checked out; the cargo looked right.

The vehicle was allowed to go on its way.

Contrary to his concerns, Absalom "Abbie" Bell found a parking spot on Exchange Plaza, a side street that bordered 55 Broadway, the police building. Two workers were sent down with dollies to accept the packages. A third came along to supervise. That left Bell with nothing to do. He offered to accompany his "copilot," John Scroggins, on his delivery.

"Why don't you get us some lunch instead?" Scroggins suggested.

"You ate in New Jersey."

"And I intend to eat again when we get out of this maze. Might as well have some decent food, instead of rest-stop junk. All the Pennsylvania roadside is bad, and it only gets worse as we head west."

Bell agreed that was a decent idea.

While Bell set out toward Broadway in search of something that didn't sound like a chain, Scroggins took his own dolly from the forward section of the van and loaded it with a pair of crates that had been tucked beneath a canvas tarp. The other men were too busy to pay him any attention.

Scroggins easily off-loaded the crates one at a time, banded them to the dolly, and walked it west, to Trinity Place. It was amazing how the dolly seemed to have a will of its own due to the sloping, lopsided streets. They had seemed to the eye to be fairly level.

Just like people, he thought and chuckled to himself as he looked at the people heading to work. *You never know what's inside.*

His eye caught the reflective glass of One World Trade to his right, the titan rising from the long-gone ruins of the World Trade Center. The tallest skyscraper in the hemisphere was a beautiful sight, its reflective glass skin aglow in the morning sun. He paused to take a cell phone picture. That site, too, seemed so level and firm. Looking at it, there was no way to know the trauma that probably still resonated in the granite below and the buildings all around it. Scroggins was looking forward to getting a better look at the site as they drove by on their way up the West Side as they started home. He only wished there were time to visit the memorial and museum. But staff drivers for Trask were constantly on the move, rarely having time to visit their families, let alone tour cities they visited.

He continued along Trinity to Battery Place and made a right. The wind from the harbor carried the smell of the Atlantic Ocean. He drew it deep into his lungs and smiled. You just didn't get that in Atlanta or New Mexico or Chicago or Colorado or any of the other places they drove. In the park, to his left, was *The Sphere,* the large metal globe that once stood in the plaza between the World Trade Center towers. Though dented and torn, the Fritz Koenig sculpture was still readily identifiable. It choked Scroggins up to see it there, standing behind an eternal flame that had been lit on the first anniversary of the attacks, tourists pausing to pay their respects or marvel at something that had survived the destruction.

He continued west until he reached his destination. Arriving before the century-old white stone building, he stopped, pulled out his cell phone, and called a number he had been given.

"Dr. Gillani?"

"It is."

"John Scroggins from Trask Industries," he told her. "I have a pair of crates for you."

"Thank you," she said. "I will send someone."

"Yes, ma'am. His name will be?"

"Excuse me?"

"For security. Who am I meeting?"

"Oh. Chuck Lancaster."

"Thank you, ma'am."

Scroggins folded away the phone and stood in the warm sunshine. It had been a long, nonstop drive, and as always, it felt good to have arrived. He felt as though he and Bell had earned their pay. Their coworkers at Trask did not refer to what he did as blue collar. So many of them were software geeks that they described his work as "analog labor." He actually liked the sound of that. It was like LPs and movie film. He liked them, too. They were old but real.

He was thinking that thought just as his eyes wandered across the park to the harbor, where they settled on the Statue of Liberty. She had been whited out by the storm the last time they were here. It had been over twenty years since he'd seen the old analog girl.

"Nice to see you're still here," he said from the heart. He took another picture to show his wife. Eva had never been out of Georgia. If he was analog, she was just . . . log. Like a native who loved her ancient village and didn't see any good reason to leave it. She said she was happy to live through him.

"Mr. Scroggins?"

The deliveryman turned as a burly man in a white lab coat came down the front steps.

"That's me," Scroggins said.

"I'm Chuck Lancaster," the man said, flipping out a college ID.

"Yes, you are," Scroggins said with a smile.

The young man showed him to the small service elevator just to the west of the door. They loaded the crates together.

"Not as heavy as they look," Scroggins said.

The man in the white coat was silent. Years of sitting in a truck cab had made Scroggins comfortable with not talking. But that wasn't the same as being antisocial. Scroggins believed in always making an effort.

"Some kind of equipment, but you'd never guess it," the deliveryman said amiably. "Most of that stuff is transistorized and microchipped. Not like the brutes I used to handle for TI."

"I'll take it from here," the big man said.

So that's how it is gonna be, Scroggins thought. *Okay. You tried.*

"Great. All you need to do is sign, please." Scroggins took an electronic device from a loop on his belt. He held it out.

The man looked down at the tiny screen. "What do I do?"

"Thumbprint anywhere on the monitor," Scroggins

said. "That way, if it doesn't get where it's supposed to, we know who to look for."

He had said it as a joke, but he wasn't kidding. The other man didn't laugh. He just pressed his thumb to the screen, immediately heard a little chime, and stood next to a metal door, the service elevator access.

Ten minutes later, after Scroggins used his Minotaur phone to text his progress to dispatch—and received the go-ahead to proceed—he and Bell were back on the road, heading north past the World Trade Center site. Scroggins got only a glimpse as they swiftly headed uptown while the heavy commuter traffic crawled downtown to his left. The west side of the great tower, away from the sun, was comparatively dark and silent. It looked like a monument making the site seem mute and sacred. It choked him up, and he had to look away.

The drivers were actually saner here than they were in Atlanta. He looked forward to being away from all that. They were headed west now, to New Mexico. Neither he nor Bell had been told why. Presumably to pick something up, since the van was empty. It didn't matter to him. They had a couple thousand miles of open road, his iPod was loaded with Dixieland jazz, and a generous expense account had been allotted for food and lodging. Because the van was empty, they wouldn't actually have to sleep in it, as they did on many trips.

Scroggins was still reflecting on the things he'd just seen, on how cooperative and accommodating the police had been. Not so much that Chuck Lancaster, but he was young. He wouldn't have remembered. A lot of people said that it was 2001 that changed New Yorkers, made them more aware of their surroundings but also of their neighbors. Maybe that was true, the same way that his father said World War II brought everyone to-gether.

"Especially when they realized that Coloreds could fight for our country as well as everyone else," Pop had said.

John Scroggins found it sad that brotherhood should come at such a price. Though it was a good thing to have, he mouthed a little prayer that nothing like those tragedies happened again.

Chuck Lancaster did not go immediately to the penthouse. He went to the parking garage, where he loaded one of the crates in the trunk of a beaten-up 2005 BMW. There was a rusted dolly already in the trunk. He had to shuffle the latter around to make room. It was not a car anyone was likely to steal. Even if they wanted to, the spark plugs had been removed. They were upstairs and would be restored at the proper time.

As soon as the crate was loaded, the man went back to the elevator and took the other crate to the pent-house. He was still thinking about his thumbprint and understood why the doc had made sure he did not have a criminal record before hiring him. She wouldn't want an ex-con signing for equipment being used for exper-iments in mind control.

Not that an ex-con would know what to do *with that equipment,* the big man thought. He was an undergrad-uate psych student at Columbia. He had been working with Dr. Gillani for three months, watching her and Dr.

Samson with intense interest, and he still didn't know what to do with it.

But he was learning. That was why he worked here. He hoped he would be able to continue when the semester started again. Dr. Gillani had said the crate he had just off-loaded was going to a new facility up the river. If it wasn't too far out of town, he would still be able to commute from the university.

That was still months away, though. No need to worry about it now. He was eager to get back and see how Princess Yasmin fared in the next phase of her evolution.

Dr. Gillani called Alex Hunt to let him know that the packages had arrived. She asked again what they were.

"Need to know," he told her again.

The agent had been asleep in his Hell's Kitchen apartment, exhausted by the previous day's events and the long night of answering questions from the police and his own people. The police seemed satisfied that he had left Franklin May standing on a street corner and had gone right back to Dr. Gillani's lab. He couldn't tell what his own boss thought. The assistant director in charge, Samantha Lennon had been pulled from a squash tournament to deal with the situation. She had always been suspicious of Hunt because he did not seem to be after her job. Paranoia was a funny thing. The truth was, he liked having all access to information and resources without the responsibility of running the field office.

Hunt showered and grabbed a coffee at the corner of

Forty-Fifth and Eighth Avenue before heading to the subway. He took the One train downtown, emerging at Rector Street and walking to the lab.

He felt almost guilty about how easily the packages had got into Manhattan. The Trask name, an oblivious and innocent driver, cargo bound for the NYPD. It guaranteed there would be sharp scrutiny of the handiest packages, and an assumption that the rest were more of the same. Why wouldn't they be?

Hunt crossed the narrow footbridge and passed the site where he had left Franklin May. The area was still marked off with yellow police tape, and an officer was standing guard. Employees were entering the building, some clearly unaware of what had happened right outside their door.

Hunt didn't smile. He didn't feel anything. He had done what had to be done.

And in two days, after nearly two years of groundwork, after a nearly flawless execution in Baltimore, he would finally finish the job.

So the larger mission could begin.

CHAPTER 20

WASHINGTON, D.C.

K ealey could have slept for a month.

He woke with the alarm, moving to the bathroom before he was really awake, giving himself the luxury of a few seconds to remember why he was up and what he was supposed to be doing. At least he knew his way around the bedroom in the dark. Kealey had slept in so many beds over the years that that in itself was a small, happy miracle.

In fact, he thought as he snapped on the bathroom light, the time he'd spent in this rented house might be the longest he'd stayed put since he was a kid.

Rented house, he thought. Not a rented *home.* His life had not wanted for excitement, for travel—often to places most people had never heard of—and even for romance. But home was something that had eluded him. The desk jockeys, the informants, even the politicians he had known all seemed to envy him his freedom. CIA field guys listened a lot more than they divulged, and Kealey wasn't a talker to begin with. So he never told them, told anyone except Allison, how much he missed having anything approaching roots.

"Your stability is all self-generated," she had told him in one of their recent therapy sessions.

She was right. But what he told her, half joking, was also true: "Boy howdy," he'd said, "bootstrapping does wear you down."

Hot water was waiting for Kealey after his shower and shave. He had smelled nothing brewing and swore when he saw it. He had set the Krups timer the night before but had forgotten to put coffee in the filter. So he had Lipton to go. It failed to satisfy, but Kealey got the caffeine kick start he needed. He grabbed the ticket he'd printed out and the overnight bag he'd also packed the previous night. He hoped he hadn't forgotten to put anything important in it. Like his Glock, hidden in a leather toiletries bag. That was the real reason he preferred to travel by train. It was the only mode of public transportation that was relatively unchanged since it was invented: schedules were an approximation and security was nonexistent. There were no bag checks, and the gun stayed with him.

The drive to Union Station took a little longer than he'd expected, with checkpoints and roadblocks still in effect. It would be that way for at least a week, until Homeland Security had determined there were no in-motion or pending threats against the nation's capital. Kealey wasn't surprised to see them, to have to show his license and registration to beat cops; he'd simply forgotten.

Sometimes you get so deep into something, you forget what it does to the real world, he thought as he finally reached the station.

Long-term parking was at 50 Massachusetts Avenue, NE. It cost twenty dollars a day and wasn't really worth it. But since Andrews was paying, Kealey indulged. The station's beautifully refurbished lobby was cavernously empty. Anyone who was getting out of the city had done so the night before; anyone who was already out wasn't coming back.

Kealey checked the arrival/departure board, noted his track, and went to it. The IA man he was traveling with was already there, waiting at the open gate. He was dressed in a black raincoat and a dusty, badly rumpled suit. Kealey had never met Reed Bishop, but he knew him at a glance.

He was a man who looked like he'd just lost his daughter.

Kealey didn't go directly over. He stopped at a coffee shop that was just opening, waited to go in, then got himself a tall black hazelnut and a couple of biscotti. He washed the tea taste from his mouth, then walked over to the gate.

"Reed?" he asked.

The man was staring at a color tablet. Kealey caught a glance before Bishop clicked it off. He was reading the *Christian Science Monitor*. Kealey knew the paper well. More than a few times he'd tucked himself in a corner of one of their reading rooms around the globe. For some reason, the kind of people who ended up searching for CIA agents never thought to look there. Maybe they thought it was a temple, a sanctuary. Or maybe they thought Company men couldn't read.

A pair of heavily lidded red eyes looked up. They were set in a pale face that seemed even whiter because the owner hadn't shaved. "Yes, I'm Reed," the man said numbly. "Mr. Kealey?"

"Ryan." He set the bag of biscotti on his carry-on, offered his free hand. Bishop took it mechanically. "Can I get you a coffee? You look like you could use one."

"No thanks," he said. "I've given up . . . well, smoking."

Kealey looked at him. "Okay. I'm guessing you can't have coffee without a smoke?"

Bishop smiled weakly. "Since I was thirteen."

"That's a helluva double whammy. Most people would have trouble with just one or the other."

"I know. But I promised."

Kealey didn't pursue the discussion. He saw the ticket in Bishop's hand and suggested they board.

The Acela—Amtrak's equivalent of a bullet train—made the Washington-to-Boston round-trip several times a day, hitting Baltimore, Philadelphia, and New York, among other stops, along the way. As he and Bishop walked along the platform, Kealey did not see a lot of heads in the train's windows or people on the platform. The conductors were standing beside an open door, chatting.

"Looks like we may have a car to ourselves," Kealey remarked.

Bishop glanced over and nodded. He was carrying a small gray cabin bag that didn't seem especially full. It had wheels, but he didn't use them. Kealey felt the guy was trying hard to be present, but he recognized the mechanical movements, the programmed responses. He hoped Bishop would snap out of it enough to be of some use. He would need help in New York, not extra baggage.

The first-class car wasn't empty, but it was nearly so. They had the forward section to themselves. There were facing chairs and side-by-side chairs; Kealey selected the former, with a small table between them, close to the door. He didn't want anyone overhearing what they had to say. That was another advantage trains had over airplanes.

Not that they had anything to say, immediately. Bishop stared out the window as the train moved through the station. Kealey finished his coffee, ate a few bites of a biscotto, and tried to imagine what he was thinking. *What* does *one think when his child dies? In a terrorist attack that he survives.*

"You want to talk about it?" Kealey asked.

"Not really." Realizing that had sounded more dismissive than he'd obviously intended, Bishop looked at him and said, "No thanks."

"I was there," Kealey said.

That got Bishop's attention. "At the convention center?"

Kealey nodded. "I was there for Julie Harper's dinner."

Bishop leaned forward. "What do you know?" His eyes were open now, alert.

"Only what you do, I'm guessing," Kealey said. He leaned into the table. "Reports of an inside job. G-man killed last night near a Trask lab. And . . . I'm sorry, truly sorry for what you're going through."

That caught Bishop off guard. He had gone into professional mode, not thinking of his own loss.

"Thank you," he said.

"If it's any consolation, even a small one, I took some of those SOBs out personally," Kealey told him.

"Not at the dinner," Bishop said. "I was there."

"No. We were in the parking garage when it all started. Armed myself from my little trunk arsenal, made our way in through a kind of back door."

"We?"

"My date, sort of. Allison Dearborn, a Company shrink. Her nephew—"

"Was the one who tweeted," Bishop said. "I heard about that. Your idea?"

"We all pitched in."

"Well done," Bishop said. "That's why you're on this job. Couple of directors playing who-can-you-trust."

"Pretty much. What about you?"

"You mean, how did I get picked?" Bishop asked. He shrugged a shoulder. "Who knows why the higher-ups do what they do. I spent most of my career behind a desk. Then, suddenly, I got a field assignment." Bishop smiled thinly and looked down. "It does matter, Ryan."

"Sorry?"

"What you did in Baltimore," Bishop said. "You got a chance to act. I've never felt so goddamn helpless."

"It's only temporary," Kealey assured him. "We're going to find these guys, and we're gonna skin them."

Bishop nodded. "You ever smoke?"

"No. I'm vice free."

"Really?"

"Sure. Unless we're including the Ten Commandments."

That drew a little smile from Bishop. "I promised my daughter I'd quit. Just when I need one most."

Bishop looked like he was about to lose it, and Kealey sat back to give him space. Bishop rallied when the conductor came by for their tickets, followed by a porter, who asked them if they wanted anything to eat or drink. Kealey hoped he didn't ask for anything hard. He didn't. All he wanted was water and a bran muffin. Kealey was guessing that would be the first food he'd had in a lot of hours.

There was usually a lot of get-to-know-you chat on an almost three-hour train ride, but not this time. Kealey didn't think Bishop was snubbing him when he went back to his tablet and checked e-mails. But it also didn't help Kealey get to know the man on whom his life could possibly depend. That was important. He didn't want to be relying on a man—even a thorough-going professional—whose thoughts were elsewhere.

"I probably know the answer, but why did you agree to this?" Kealey asked.

"You mean, now?"

Kealey nodded.

"I could ask you the same thing," Bishop said. His reply wasn't challenging; it was a simple statement.

"I don't follow," Kealey said. "I didn't lose any-one—"

"If you were still officially a Company man, you would have been given mandatory leave. You killed people in Baltimore. Enemy combatants as far as we know, but there's been no investigation. The good fortune of you being in the right place at the right time, and armed, has not been questioned."

Kealey made a face. "I don't think I like that."

"You misunderstand," Bishop said. "Or maybe I'm not making myself clear. I don't doubt you. But standard operating procedure has gone out the window. It always does in these situations."

"I'm here because the president asked me to be," Kealey replied. "I have a habit of saying what's on my mind, which is one reason I'm *not* a Company man anymore. Brenneman obviously felt the situation required that kind of outside point of view."

"And someone who was already primed by action, maybe even a little hair trigger after the day's events," Bishop said. "The president wanted a pit bull and not a bloodhound. I've seen hundreds of psych profiles over the years to understand how people get into one of the 'triple o' situations, where they overreact, overreach, or overcompensate. That's why ninety percent of my subjects go bad. Not because they *are* bad, but because they shouldn't have been doing what they were."

"Are you saying I'm a good witch or a bad one?"

"Neither, Ryan. I don't know you. I'm saying that I understand why the president picked you," Bishop replied. "Since I got the call last night, I've been zeroing in on what we have here. The scope of this suggests we're dealing with the 'other' ten percent. A person or persons who are bad because they *are* bad. That's why I'm here. Because truly bad men don't just take cash from the evidence locker or shoot someone because they're angry at their spouse. They don't just kill my daughter. They kill a *lot* of daughters. That's not going to happen on my watch, if I can prevent it."

Kealey took a moment to reflect on what Bishop had said. "I like that. But there's something that doesn't jibe."

Bishop regarded him. "What's that?"

"We don't know that New York has anything to do with Baltimore. Shouldn't you be there, where the FBI poser was ID'd?"

Bishop smiled thinly. "Touché. There's something else."

Goddamn it, Kealey thought. *Nothing ever changes, except to get worse.* "What didn't the sons of bitches tell me?" he asked.

"It came in very early this morning, and I'm sure they didn't want to wake you," Bishop said.

"I'm sure they just didn't want to tell me," Kealey said. "What is it?"

Bishop touched the tablet several times, then handed it over. It was an eyes-only message from FBI director Cluzot:

Cargo from Quebec hijacked. Believed to be in NYC.

"What cargo?" Kealey asked. A frisson of fear rolled up his spine. His first thought was of a nuclear weapon.

Bishop leaned over and tapped another button. A color photograph came up. It was a mug shot with an RCMP stamp in the corner.

"Top assassin, Pakistani born, spent her teenage years in Damascus and Cairo" he said quietly. He touched a button, and the screen dissolved. It would take a password to get back in. "Heartless merc, no apparent ideology. A CIA agent and I put her on a private jet up there with three Pakistani caretakers. At least, we thought they were. We don't know what happened, except that three Pakistanis were found dead at the airport after we left, the plane ended up in New York, it was on the ground for under an hour, and then it headed out over the Atlantic."

"To where?"

"We don't know that, either," Bishop said. "The transponder was shut off, and either it was blown up at sea or some pretty sophisticated technology was apparently employed to erase the image from radar. We're still looking into that."

"Who was the agent in on the transfer?"

"Someone from Rendition Group One," Bishop said. "I tried to contact her. No response. When I called her boss this morning, he told me she was in New York on special assignment. He was not at liberty to reveal its nature. Frankly, I don't think he knew."

"You suspect she's looking for the missing cargo?" Kealey said.

"I hope so." He didn't have to add, "Either that, or she's in on the escape." "I've got a call in to the powers-that-be but they haven't returned it."

Kealey considered this. "There's something a little off," he said.

"The timing?"

"Yeah."

Bishop nodded. "Why was she involved before I was informed?"

"Right. I can see that it wasn't an IA issue, but as a matter of course, they would have wanted a debrief of everyone who was on-site."

"Ordinarily," Bishop agreed.

He didn't have to finish.

"Yet they called you for this," Kealey said.

"They did. When you think you've got a mole or a renegade, who do you go to?"

"Right." He didn't have to say it. *You go to someone their actions impacted. Someone who values the take-down more than their own security.* Like Kealey, someone who was hair trigger.

Kealey felt more comfortable with Bishop after that. He wasn't being critical. What the G-man had said before about Kealey also applied to himself.

"Do they suspect your RG colleague of being involved with what happened in Quebec?" Kealey asked.

"They don't *not* suspect her," Bishop said. "That's one of the things I'm going to have to find out."

Kealey leaned back into the seat to think about what Bishop had said. He fell asleep instead. The next thing he knew, they were arriving at Penn Station.

CHAPTER 21
NEW YORK, NEW YORK

New York's Penn Station was a bunker that used to be a palace.

When the original station was ripped down and replaced with the new Penn Station and Madison Square Garden—under the theory that commuters would be more inclined to go to events if they were held right above trains to Long Island and New Jersey—the city lost a glorious and majestic landmark. That architectural disaster, in 1963, was one of the triggers for the creation of the city's Landmarks Preservation Commission.

The current station was a pair of below-ground hives without character or interest. Since the attacks of 2001, there had been a permanent presence of military reservists there, in addition to the police. Kealey respected their mission, while at the same time seeing hole after hole in the security. It was no different in Washington or at virtually any other train station in the country. Bags went unexamined, were not even spot-

checked; tickets to board were glanced at cursorily by
conductors as people moved down escalators to the
tracks; dozens of shops received deliveries, probably
daily, which might not contain bagels or I ♥ NEW YORK
T-shirts or magazines. This, in addition to the fact that
tracks were accessible from the outside before trains
passed under the Hudson and East Rivers. Kealey
guessed that the backgrounds of porters and employees
were only superficially examined.

Of course, as the NYPD and Homeland Security
knew, applying manpower to what law enforcement
called those "open doors" would be a large commit-
ment of resources with low-yield results. The lone
bombers, the homegrown terrorists, would invariably
find a way to slip through. The cops and soldiers were
eyes on-site for aberrant behavior, and that was the
best that could be done. Kealey knew what law enforcement also knew: that the al-Qaidas of the world,
the real terrorists, were looking to strike in ways that
the West hadn't considered or had not yet faced. That
was the unfortunate nature of this war: the only way to
catch them was on the intel side, with HUMNIT and
ELINT, the people who infiltrated enemy groups or
watched their movements from places of concealment,
the digital eavesdroppers who listened for cell phone
calls and watched computer posts.

It was for all those reasons that Kealey was not entirely surprised by what happened as they left the station.

He and Bishop were booked in rooms across Seventh Avenue, at Hotel Pennsylvania. Scaffolding had
been erected along the Thirty-third Street side of the
building, where workers were doing the initial prep

work before dismantling the hotel, which was to be replaced by the city's third largest building.

The sidewalk was jammed with commuters and tourists, some waiting for taxis at the stand to the left, others going to work in the city's once-thriving garment district. The first muted crack came after a woman had been spun 180 degrees just a few steps in front of Kealey. He had been unaware of her back, her yellow jacket, until she spun with a raw red hole in her forehead and dropped to the sidewalk, on top of her shoulder bag.

A second crack followed a cabbie's head exploding inside his vehicle as he pulled from the curb. The car, with its screaming occupants, turned into Seventh Avenue and collided with a hollow crunch against several other vehicles.

From the first shot Kealey was on high alert, his instincts registering the attack before his mind had processed it. He pulled Bishop down flat, crouched for a moment, then ran to a trash can several steps ahead. He pulled down a young man in a business suit who was standing beside it; pieces of the man's heart blew out his back as Kealey acted.

This is for us, he thought angrily. The cab was to block traffic, but the deaths were to show that the victims could just as easily have been Kealey or Bishop. The gunman was a helluva marksman.

Even though Kealey realized where the sniper was situated, there was nothing he could do about it. Even if he could get to his bag—he'd left it beside Bishop—his handgun didn't have this kind of range. The shots were from very high up.

Cops were gathering, and as soon as the first two

went down, the rest withdrew to the safety of the station to await armored reinforcement.

Kealey knew the gunman would leave before choppers could arrive. He had to get to the hotel. The killer might be expecting that but did not desire it; otherwise, the shots would have been aimed to Kealey's rear, a signal he should head forward.

Sirens broke through the terrified shrieks and sobs and the honking horns that were all around him. Traffic was trying to maneuver around the disabled taxi, to pull to the curb or down one of the side streets. The police and emergency units were converging from all directions. His ear attuned to them, Kealey heard police radios rasping behind him.

The gunfire had stopped. People were beginning to rise as a terrible calm spread across the scene. They were in pockets behind the concrete walls of Madison Square Garden or behind the newspaper stand or the line of cabs. They were alone, rushing to get back into the station or into the arena.

And then a flurry of awful gunfire cut through them. It came from the same place, from a bolt-action weapon, judging from the delay, a slashing death that took down bodies alternately to the left and right of Kealey.

The gunman was swinging from side to side, sighting and taking down targets in a heartbeat. It was formidable.

Then everything was silent again. Kealey knew the killer was done. He hadn't had time to get his gun from his bag, but Bishop was ahead of him: he had assumed the former agent was carrying one and had retrieved it. He flipped it over.

Kealey acknowledged this with a hasty salute as he tucked the Glock in his belt. He pulled out his shirt to conceal the weapon so he wouldn't be shot by police. Then he ran through the now-halted traffic, Bishop close behind.

Yasmin climbed through the window she had broken to reach the scaffolding. She tossed aside the blanket she'd pulled from the bed to conceal herself, sidestepped the occupant—a young flight attendant whose spinal cord she had cut from behind—and stuffed her XM2010 Enhanced Sniper Rifle into a vinyl wardrobe bag. She had already donned the woman's blouse and skirt while waiting for her audience to arrive from Washington. Cutting the woman's neck in the back had prevented her from bleeding out on the garments. A deeper cut to get through the sinew and vertebrae, but as soon as the cord was cut, the woman fell, quite lifeless.

Yasmin passed the bed on which she had dropped the key stolen from the housekeeper. The woman lay dead in a hall utility closet, the cheap pen bearing the Hotel Pennsylvania logo that was plucked from her cleaning cart still stuck a good 4 inches into her carotid artery. Less mess would have been ideal, but there just hadn't been enough time. She glanced at the mirror to muss her hair and assume a look of panic, then grabbed her garment bag and rushed into the hall. Security here was little more than a few cameras, and it didn't matter if they had captured her likeness. They would know who was responsible for this.

That was the point, she thought—though the thought

was not her own. All the young woman had to do was keep from being caught.

She was in the stairwell and on the nineteenth floor before the first police officers reached the room. She was in the lobby and then on the street before the block had been surrounded. She did not see the men whose attention she had been sent to attract. She did not know who they were, only that the spotter in the station had called her cell phone and told her to start.

Yasmin walked over to Broadway to catch a cab headed downtown. She kept the garment bag with her for the ride downtown, instead of putting it in the trunk. She wanted the gun handy, just in case.

The gun and the marble set in a bracelet on her left wrist.

The hotel lobby was jammed with people who had come in from the street. They stood awaiting some kind of instruction, from anyone. Mobs were like that: big, burly, and impotent until someone struck a match.

Kealey knew it was probably safe, but he wasn't going to be the one to tell them so. Not because he thought they were safer here—they might not be; the gunman could have herded them here to set off a bomb—but because Bishop had a job to do.

"Stay here and look for your cargo," Kealey said. Bishop had caught up to him as Kealey started weaving through the packed room.

"How certain are you that she's the one?"

"Call it a strong hunch," he said. It was a little more than that: the way the line of fire had skipped them during the sweeping barrage was a hallmark of her precision work. "I doubt she'll come out this way, but we need to be sure."

Bishop agreed as Kealey literally shoved his way through.

He asked a bellhop for directions and took the stairs. He felt that would be his best chance of running into her, or at least of finding anything she'd discarded. He drew his Glock and held it close to his ribs as he ascended.

Breathless, his legs aching, he reached the twentieth floor and entered the hallway. He had approximated within a floor in either direction that that was where the shots had come from. He was right. Apparently alerted by guests who saw blood seeping from a utility closet, hotel personnel had just discovered the housekeeper's body.

Kealey stopped and looked around.

"I need the key to that door," he said to one of the young executives. He was pointing to a door at the end of this section of hallway.

"Is that your—"

"It's where the sniper was," Kealey said. "Let me have the key."

"Shouldn't we wait for—"

Kealey showed his Glock. "Give me the goddamn key."

The man obliged. Kealey ran over. He felt the wall to the side of the door. It seemed solid enough. He leaned against it as he swiped the plastic key. The lock clicked. There was no gunfire. Relatively certain she would not be inside, Kealey nudged open the door with his foot. It swung in to reveal the dead flight attendant lying in her underwear on the blood-soaked carpet and the broken window.

"Oh Christ!" someone shouted from behind him.

Kealey shut the door. He didn't have long before the police arrived, and he didn't want to answer questions. Still breathing heavily, he looked around the body without disturbing it. Killed from behind, bled out from there. He walked over to the window. It was an old-fashioned type, wood framed, but a lock had been added at the top, so it opened only a crack. Rather than unscrew the little metal piece, she had smashed the window. He looked around. Saw shards on a discarded pillowcase.

With her fist inside that. He looked out. Large pieces of glass were lying on the scaffolding. She had kicked those out, no doubt.

He took the pillowcase, turned it inside out, crumpled it in a ball, and left the room. The police sirens were screaming from directly below. He tucked the room key in his pocket so he wouldn't leave prints behind, put the gun back in his belt, and went to the stairs. He ran up to the twenty-first floor and took the elevator down. He did not encounter any police until he reached the lobby. They were directing people to leave by the side doors. The front of the building was a cordoned-off crime scene.

Kealey found Bishop standing on the north side of Thirty-third Street, watching for him. He had both of their travel bags. Traffic had been stopped on the side street, and Kealey crossed. He cocked his head toward Broadway, and they hooked up as they continued east. The street was a wall of stalled traffic and people either flowing west or staring east. Heads had emerged from windows to look at the carnage. Kealey glanced back. The police were already out on the scaffolding.

"She was in the room of a flight attendant, probably picked her out in the lobby and followed her," Kealey told Bishop. "Killed a maid to gain entrance, then took the flight attendant's clothes to get out."

"So we're looking for a—"

"No," Kealey said. "She'd stay in the uniform only for as long as it took to get away from the hotel. And then only for a short subway or probably cab ride. She knows the cops will be looking for a flight attendant."

"Right."

"What's more significant is that our killer had an accomplice on the ground," Kealey asserted.

"How do you know?"

"She broke the window in the hotel room instead of taking time to unscrew the lock," Kealey told him. "That meant she didn't have a lot of time. A dime, a nail file would have done the trick. Someone saw that our train had arrived, eyeballed us, told her we were coming, and she started firing as soon as we came up for air."

"So she was already in the hotel."

"Yes."

"How did they know we would come out this side?" Bishop asked. "We could have gotten out on Eighth Avenue."

"Not likely," Kealey said. "They knew either that we were booked in that hotel or that we were going to catch a cab headed downtown."

"Shit."

"Exactly. This was for us, to tell us they know we're here."

"But they couldn't kill us," Bishop added. "They couldn't afford to have another dead agent."

"That, plus making it seem random is going to have a major chilling effect on transportation," Kealey pointed out.

"To what end?" Bishop asked. "I mean, I understand the *theory* of it. Terror."

"This wasn't terror," Kealey said.

"That's my point," Bishop said. "Assuming this action is related to Baltimore, and accepting that they were sending us some kind of message, why pile one atop the other? What's their endgame?"

"That, obviously, is what we need to find out," Kealey said. He didn't add, "Quickly." They both knew that.

"Those poor innocents," Bishop thought aloud as they reached Broadway.

Kealey also hurt for the wrong-place-at-the-wrong-time victims. But he couldn't think about them now.

Who knows we are here? Kealey thought. *Everyone in the president's office and the people who made the travel plans. Whoever sent Bishop data on his missing cargo. The NYFO personnel they were supposed to meet and, most likely, everyone in their office.*

It was a nightmare of possibilities with too little evidence. What was more, the perpetrators knew where *they* were, most likely were watching them now, but they had no idea where those eyes might be.

"I'm guessing we shouldn't go back to the hotel," Bishop said.

"So they know exactly where to find us while we sleep? No," Kealey agreed. Standing on a street corner, he felt like a tourist in Italy learning that a couple of strikes had just been called. *What do you do? Where do you go?* He looked at Bishop. "You got anything you really need in there?"

Bishop regarded him for a moment. He opened the cabin bag from the top, removed the iPad. "No."

"Good," Kealey said. "Let's leave these here as a message for whoever's still watching us. They're going to have to work for their pay."

They stacked the luggage against a cornerstone at Broadway and Thirty-third then walked south on Broadway to catch a cab at Thirty-second Street, that had made it though the jam-up feeding into Thirty-third Street. They headed downtown, the driver chattering into his cell phone in what sounded to Kealey like standard Hindi. As Kealey glanced back to see if anyone else had grabbed a taxi and was following— they weren't—there was something strangely reassuring about that.

The city was just attacked, the nation was just attacked again, *but life goes on*.

Kealey could not remember when life had been that simple for him, when choices had been so clear, when the pressure had not been so absolute and crushing. He wasn't lamenting that; he had chosen this life. But there were times like these when there was a clock ticking in his head, when he really did wish he could convince someone like Allison Dearborn to bag her life, too, and just find a jungle somewhere, build a tree house near a lake, and worry about nothing more re-

mote or abstract than snaring a rabbit for the next
meal. . . .

Jessica Muloni could not believe what she had seen.

After an excruciatingly slow drive into the city, her
driver had finally arrived at the hotel. She expected for-
hire cabbies to take the costly scenic route, but this one
worked for Trask. Her driver, Shrevnitz, also obeyed
the speed limit and stopped at yellow lights.

He doesn't want to be stopped by cops, she decided.
Not with an armed passenger.

She'd remained at Hotel Pennsylvania, awaiting instructions. She'd ordered room service breakfast. She'd
checked e-mails. Word had finally come shortly after
9:00 a.m., a text message on the Minotaur phone.

Suspect believed to be in vicinity. Face recognition software at Penn may have picked her up at 7th Avenue.

Muloni had hurried downstairs to Seventh Avenue.
The station had only recently been equipped with FRS,
which had been deployed for several years in London.
Cameras scanned the faces of everyone walking
through the terminal. Nothing was recorded, so the
ACLU couldn't squawk about privacy being invaded;
but if the computers got a match with their criminal
database, the transit police were quickly notified.

As she was waiting to cross the street, the attack
began. She saw gunfire knock people down, but before
she could turn to ascertain where the shooting was
coming from, she saw Reed Bishop. He and another
man were crouched in front of Madison Square Garden. They seemed immune to the assault. It was a hor-

rifying thing to behold; it was as though they were shielded, behind a force field, as people died around them. Their omission as targets was *that* striking.

How could Bishop be a part of this? she wondered in shocked silence. Yet how else could Veil have gotten away in Canada? *And he's here within a day of the death of his daughter*. That was monstrous.

The gunfire was over within a few moments, coming in two quick salvos. Muloni weighed running back into the hotel to chase Veil and waiting to see what Bishop did.

She decided to wait. If Veil and Bishop were in league, staying with the FBI agent would take her to the assassin. She wondered if Trask had suspected him; maybe that was why he didn't want her to contact him. If that were the case, it would have been nice if he'd shared the information.

Muloni watched from behind a streetlight as Bishop flipped the other man a gun. The armed man came toward the hotel. Possibly to cover her retreat. Bishop went across Thirty-third Street with two pieces of luggage. Muloni watched him as he waited. Mobs milled around her, fleeing toward Penn Station, into the hotel, out to Broadway. She did not see Veil—nor did she expect to—but after a few minutes she did see the other man. He rejoined Bishop, and they moved toward Broadway. She followed. They got into a cab.

Obviously, Trask was not the target as she had thought back in Atlanta. The City of New York was the target, she realized.

Muloni was blocked in by a mob with no chance of tracking the sniper. She had pulled the number off the cab but hadn't been able to follow it. They were smart, her colleague and his partner. There was a queue of traffic stretching across Broadway, stranded there because they were blocked from going west. There was only a narrow passage for downtown traffic. Bishop and his partner had gotten a ride on the other side.

She punched a number into the Minotaur phone the driver had given her. It was the Bureau's main number. She asked to be connected to Domestic Tracking and Identification. She provided her ID number. The intel associate would know from the call who and where she was. That couldn't be helped. She asked the agent to get into the NY Taxi and Limousine Commission database, find out where that cab had gone. New security regulations required New York cab drivers to enter their destinations for GPS tracking. The American Civil Liberties Union had opposed the law but the New York City Taxi and Limousine Commission put the safety of their workers above privacy concerns and endorsed the measure.

"They're headed to One West Street," the agent said. "That's at the corner of West Street and Battery Place."

"Thank you," she said and hung up.

Muloni had been walking south along Broadway as she placed the call, getting herself below the traffic jam. But traffic was backed up in all directions. She knew she would never get into Penn Station, so she walked four blocks to Twenty-eighth Street then back west to Seventh Avenue to catch the One train downtown. She had a feeling that people would be leaving the city after an event like this, not coming into it. The One terminated at the bottom of Manhattan. Few people would be going there. They'd be going to Penn Station, or else uptown to Grand Central to catch a train to Connecticut, or to the Port Authority Bus Terminal to head for New Jersey.

Muloni was right. Within five minutes she was on her way downtown in a near-empty subway car.

Watching Fox News and pacing anxiously in the lab, Hunt glared at the phone when it beeped. It was Shrevnitz.

"Go!" Hunt said, almost angrily. He did not like waiting under ordinary circumstances. And these circumstances were not ordinary.

"She saw them," reported the driver, who was also the team's eyes on at Penn Station. "Everyone is in motion."

"Details."

"The men are in a cab headed down Broadway. Muloni is in the subway, the One downtown."

"The subway?" Hunt said.

"That's right," Shrevnitz replied. "Traffic up here is hell."

Jessica Muloni obviously knew where Bishop and Kealey were going. That had been the plan, of course. Shrevnitz had timed everything so she would be in the area when the gunfire began. She would look over, of course, and couldn't miss them. Recognizing Bishop, knowing there was a mole, knowing how absurd it was for a grieving father even to *be* there, she would have done what she was trained to do: suspect him. Follow him without making contact. She must have taken the subway to circumvent the traffic. That meant she'd be getting off at either the Rector Street or the South Ferry stop. She might even beat the other two down here.

"Thank you." Hunt hung up. He'd have to arrange for her to regain sight of the targets.

He turned to Dr. Gillani. "Where is Yasmin?"

"She phoned while you were talking," the woman replied. "She is in position."

"Tell her to hold," Hunt said. "This is going to take a little finessing. I'll call you when it's time."

Hunt decided to go downstairs and wait for them, see if he could spot Muloni. He couldn't start without her. The best place for her to observe would be from Battery Park, across the street. He didn't think there would be a lot of tourists headed for the Statue of Liberty right now, but there were trees and kiosks she could lurk behind. She wouldn't have to see Bishop's face; a good agent would have noticed what he was wearing.

And Jessica Muloni was a good agent, he thought, which was one of the reasons she had been selected for this important task. Handpicked by Mr. Trask.

As Hunt waited for the penthouse elevator, he thought back to his own meeting with the industrial juggernaut two years before, when he underwent a psychiatric evaluation after expressing his disappointment with Muslims *to* a Muslim coworker. It was in response to an alert received by the NYFO that the NYPD was providing 24/7 police protection to the so-called Ground Zero mosque.

"They didn't do that for the Jewish museum around the corner when someone painted swastikas on the wall," Hunt had noted.

The coworker was offended. Hunt was forced to undergo sensitivity training. The two-week course turned up a general attitudinal problem toward Muslims. Not enough to require further attention, but enough to bear watching.

Trask was one of those who was watching. He requested that Hunt be part of a team that was evaluating new electromagnetic vests, designed to slow the velocity of incoming projectiles. Satisfied with Hunt's worldview and his trustworthiness, Trask had taken him into his confidence. Put him in charge of what might prove to be the most important operation in American history since D-day.

Hunt still got chills down his spine when he thought of the honor he had been accorded. It was humbling. And *nothing* was going to derail it.

Within minutes he was standing in the sunshine outside the building. The streets were eerily empty, the loudest sounds coming from helicopters that were circling six and a half miles to the north.

Leaning against the brass handrail that ran down the center of the short flight of steps, his cell phone in his hand, he saw a woman walking across the street. She stopped to study a poster around the Pier A restoration project that showed Lower Manhattan early in the twentieth century. She looked back toward the building, then back toward the poster. She turned away. She moseyed as if enjoying the day. Never once did she look across the harbor, where most people looked, toward the Statue of Liberty.

That had to be Muloni.

A single cab made the right turn from Broadway, which was three blocks away. It moved along an empty street toward his building. It was moving slowly, as if looking for a number.

That had to be Bishop and his ex-CIA companion.

The cab pulled up to the curb. Hunt speed dialed upstairs. Dr. Gillani answered.

"It's time," Hunt said and hung up.

CHAPTER 22

NEW YORK, NEW YORK

The UPS truck was parked on South Street, just below Catherine Slip. The driver was dead in the front, from a knife wound through the right eye and into his brain.

There was nowhere a young, attractive woman could not go.

She had taken the taxi to exit 2 of the FDR Drive. There Yasmin had discarded her flight attendant's jacket and donned a red blazer she had in the wardrobe bag. There was a Realtor's logo on the front. She had approached the coffee-breaking driver, cell phone in one hand, knife hidden up her sleeve, pretending to ask for directions. He didn't even feel the hot thermos as it spilled over his lap.

Yasmin removed the man's shirt and trousers and changed into them in the back. This time, it didn't matter if the front was bloody. All that was important was that she blended in, briefly, with the top of the truck. She noticed the bracelet as she was changing, the one with the marble. She knew it, knew it so well, but she could not recall why. Nor did it matter. She had a job to do.

She lay down with her rifle in front of her, looked through the 4X telescopic sight at the Brooklyn Bridge. These weren't like the last ones, rats smoked from a hole and picked off, *pop, pop, pop,* like she used to do in Cairo. These were bottles on a wall, heads moving across the walkway. A lot of heads, all leaving New York. Ironically, they were probably eager to get away from the city after that morning's attack.

No, not bottles, she thought without knowing why. *Invaders. At the moat.*

Her phone pinged. She looked at the text message.

Go.

She slipped her finger over the trigger, picked a head at random, watched until it cleared the meshwork of wires that distinguished the sides of the stone edifice, then fired.

Walking home across the wooden planks of the bridge, June Furst never got used to the incessant wobble caused by the automobile traffic passing below. Or the bicycles shooting by in lanes that ran alongside the too-narrow pedestrian walkway. With most of the traffic moving in one direction—east, away from Manhattan—the bridge almost seemed lopsided. But that might have been just a visual response to the solid mass under and beside her and the relative emptiness to the south.

If the traffic was a constant hum and shudder, the people around her were always different. In two years, the twenty-five-year-old fashion designer couldn't remember ever having seen the same person twice on her walks to and from work. . . .

At first she thought someone, a workman, had dropped a can of red paint from above. Then she saw the man in front of her cartwheel to the same side the crimson splash had gone. It wasn't exactly a cartwheel; his body turned, but his arms were like noodles, spindly and whipping as he moved.

The screams from behind her told June that it was not paint and not an acrobatic stunt. A muted crack reached her ears a moment later.

"Someone's shooting!" a man screamed.

June dropped to her knees as she turned, looking for whoever had shouted while at the same time seeking to get behind the fat cables that ran up the span in a gentle slope. It took only an instant, and it was an instant that saved her life. The person to her right lost the left side of his head. It came away in fragments, riding another wave of red, as the older woman did a half-corkscrew turn before dropping. A bride who had been posing with her husband for wedding photos was slashed across the throat as her mouth, tongue, and neck spat blood sideways across his tuxedo and forward down her own white gown. She grabbed at her throat like it was the recently tossed bouquet.

Then people began dropping everywhere, each under a ruddy plume, their blood continuing to pump as they lay still or twitching.

June flopped on her chest, pressed herself as low as she could while sidling over to the cables, to protection. She slid across something wet. Her face was turned to the south, and she heard the screams, watched the death, with a kind of disconnected horror, as if this were a movie. She could do that, feeling she was no longer at risk. Even when the bodies stopped being knocked down, when the distant pops faded like the last echo of holiday fireworks, she lay on the unvarnished wooden floor of the bridge, trembling from more than just the traffic, promising her dead mother that she would go home to Montana and work at the family bridal gown shop and never leave, as she had once been warned.

She had no idea how long it was before people started moving again, most of them running, some of them crawling, toward the Brooklyn side of the bridge. When she saw them move, she got up.

An elderly Hasidic Jew, hurrying by, turned toward her.

"Are you all right?" he asked, showing concern.

"I'm sorry?"

He pointed to her blouse, which was covered with blood.

"Oh, no," she said, smiling stupidly, as if she were declining sidewalk literature. "It's not mine."

He gave her a funny look and moved on.

As did she.

Slowly, tentatively, before fainting.

Alexander Hunt's cell phone chirped as Bishop and his partner walked toward the building. He checked the message, though he knew what it must be.

From: Notify NYC swnalert@sendwordnow.com
To: Alexander Hunt
Sent: Mon, May 20, 2013, 9:59 a.m.
Subject: Notify NYC - Notification
Notification issued 5/20/13. Gunshots fired at
Brooklyn Bridge from Manhattan. All traffic,
pedestrian and vehicular, is being diverted from
FDR to Pearl.

For show, Hunt pretended to study the message intently, then shook his head and swore. He "happened"
to look up as the men swung by him.

"Are you Reed Bishop?" Hunt asked, turning to
catch the men as they moved up the stairs.

"Yes."

"I'm Agent Hunt," he said, turning back to snag the
cab as it pulled away. It screeched to a stop. "You'd better come with me."

"Where?" Bishop asked.

"There's been another sniper attack, at the Brooklyn
Bridge."

Hunt jogged to the curb, the men running behind.
They climbed in the back of the cab, Bishop in the center. Hunt gave the cabbie their destination, and he
made a U turn on Battery Place and headed north on
Greenwich Street.

"See if you can get us to the foot of the bridge," Hunt
told the driver as they sped north.

"Why? Is something going on?" the driver asked.

Hunt slapped his ID against the plastic partition.
"Nothing you need to worry about," he said and sat
back.

The driver sped up, either enjoying a moment of importance or immunity from a speeding ticket.

Introductions were made, after which Hunt said to Bishop, "I'm very sorry for your loss."

"Thank you. What the hell *is* happening here?"

Hunt showed them the e-mail. "I'm guessing it has to do with the individual you met in Quebec. You heard about that?"

Bishop nodded.

"Is she *on* the bridge?" Kealey asked.

"I don't know any more than this," Hunt said, still holding up the phone. There was a drumming noise overhead, passing west to east. "Choppers heading to the scene." He cranked down the window, looked up before they vanished behind the waterfront towers. "Disbursal pattern, fanning out. A search."

"Hey, am I gonna be in some kind of danger over there?" the cabbie asked.

"Not anymore," Kealey said as a second wave of police and coast guard choppers flew behind them, following the harbor to the East River. "Safest place on the planet."

The ride was quick until they reached Park Row. Then it stopped moving, with the bottleneck from the closed bridge spilling in all directions.

"We'll get out here," Hunt said, tossing the driver a twenty-dollar bill and getting out across from St Paul's Chapel.

Bishop thanked the driver and told him to stay safe.

"Thanks," the cabbie said. "You too."

The men rushed toward the bridge, Hunt's credentials getting them through the police barricade. Hunt slowed as he saw someone else from his field office. Kealey and Bishop did likewise.

Kealey looked around. In the air, on the ground, and now in the water, it looked as though all of New York law enforcement was arriving. He even noticed the WhisprWave, the NYPD Harbor Unit's sleek, new, seventy-two-foot, high-tech antiterror vessel.

"What do you think about all this?" Kealey asked. Even though there was little chance of being overheard with the police shouting and ambulance sirens shrieking toward them, he spoke softly.

"Sniping people on the bridge? That's at the top of her skill set," Bishop said.

"Pull back from the bridge, from the hotel," Kealey suggested. "What does it look like to you?"

"I don't follow."

"The larger picture," Kealey said, "because to me it doesn't add up. The minute we get to New York, there's an attack that dances all around us. We arrive to interview Hunt, and he gets pulled away by a second attack. It's all too damn neat."

"It's unusual, but why bother?"

"That's what I want to know," Kealey said. "Tell me what you know, going back to Quebec."

"About Veil?"

"Yeah. Was that her code name or yours?"

"Ours. It was meant to be ironic, something a Middle Eastern lady, a *shaykhah,* would wear."

"She came from poverty? She wasn't a pampered sociopath like bin Laden?"

"As far as we can tell," Bishop said.

He and Kealey had stopped, while Hunt moved

ahead, up the walkway on the Manhattan side of the bridge.

"Go on," Kealey said.

"The Gulfstream had landed from Pakistan before we got there. We never really met the escorts. She arrived with a group of Mounties by car, we took custody with the Pakistanis, and an agent from Rendition Group One, Jessica Muloni, let her know that we knew she had a daughter, knew where she was, and expected her complete cooperation."

"Let her know how? Photos? Details?"

"Her name and information about the midwife," Bishop said. "Veil believed her."

"Where is the daughter?" Kealey asked.

"Pakistan."

Kealey shook his head. "This doesn't make sense, then. Veil had a ride home. Why go on a rampage here, especially when she knows that her daughter can be used as leverage to stop her?"

"Do you think someone else has the girl?"

"If *we* found out, someone else could have," Kealey said. "They got to the Pakistani escort, hijacked the plane."

"You're right, though—that doesn't make sense. It's a lot of effort to go through. Snipers are easy enough to buy."

"What about Jessica Muloni? Do you know her well?"

"Rendition Group and internal affairs wouldn't have many encounters. Tough to find common ground. But she seemed square."

Kealey looked at the pieces he knew. As in Baltimore, the shootings here were acts of terror. A city of some ten million citizens and a good chunk of the world's commerce had been paralyzed in the space of less than an hour. Their presence could have been a coincidence. It made sense that a killer would target incoming and outgoing commuters. But he had to assume there was a connection.

"What if someone helped to arrange it so that two upstanding agents were brought here just to be stonewalled?" Kealey said as he glanced at Hunt and his colleagues. "There are other boots on the ground, but the Oval Office can't trust any of them, not with a potential traitor at the Bureau. He or she could pollute everything, even intel going to otherwise clean divisions, like the NYPD antiterror units."

Bishop considered this. "The president is more or less made to sit on his hands until . . . what?"

"Exactly. What? Another attack in another city? What does he do then? Dispatch another team? The pattern could go on for days."

"So simple," Bishop said. "It's like a computer virus—with people."

"We've got to take charge of this," Kealey said. "What do you think about going back to the psyops project office where we were supposed to meet Hunt? Get up there, find out what he was working on, what May had been checking on?"

"Sounds good," Bishop said. He looked to where Hunt was talking with the other members of his field office. They were pointing up South Street, presumably in the direction from which the gunfire had come. Helicopters were circling that area as well. "Check in if you've got anything. I'll do the same."

Kealey gave him a look. "How are you holding up, Reed?" He was concerned about Bishop personally, but also—and this was a hard fact of their line of work—he had to know that he could count on the man to stay focused.

"Everything seems surreal," Bishop told him. "Short answer, I can function as long as I don't think about it."

He didn't have to tell Bishop that what they were doing here was for all the Lauras of the nation. He could see in the man's resolute expression that he grasped that.

Kealey gave the agent a supportive clap on the shoulder as he turned and went back in the direction of Centre Street.

Police were moving everywhere to try and clear the massive tangle that reached from the Brooklyn Bridge to Broadway and city hall. More people were standing still than moving; they didn't know where to go. Many were shouting into cell phones, trying to hear above the sirens and choppers and the endless honking of horns. Other people were texting. Some were just sitting on benches or steps, alone or in pairs, talking, sobbing, or just resting with their head on their knees. A few were praying. People were asking the police if the subways were running, the PATH trains, the buses on Church Street. Some were trying to find out if the shootings at Penn Station had shut down the commuter lines. The officers, showing remarkable patience, did not know the answers as they tried to direct all foot traffic north. They just wanted to clear the area so vehicles could be moved. The FDR Drive and South Street were also at a standstill heading downtown. Bishop realized the best way to get back to Battery Park was to walk the mile or so. He knew he had to pick his way southwest and decided that once he left the on-ramp of the bridge, he'd turn down Park Row.

Brooklyn-bound pedestrians were still making for the bridge, dodging police who were trying to preserve the multiple crime scenes and rubbernecking as they passed. They were the most orderly group, like metal filings being drawn by a magnet. They obviously felt it was safe enough to cross now that the shooting was over and the sniper had apparently fled. Bishop had to weave his way through the mob. In spite of everything that had happened, he found himself smiling when he remembered being with his wife and daughter at Disney World on a holiday about eight years ago. It was packed solid, as these streets were, and he was holding both of their hands as he spearheaded an exit from the park. His hands closed beside him, and he could almost feel their soft, loving, trusting grip.

I miss you both, he thought.

He shouldered his way through people, twisted his way through cars, even climbed over fenders that were nearly touching. And then he froze. Among the stopped cars was a cab. Getting out less than 20 feet from him was someone he knew. It seemed surreal seeing her here, but when their eyes met, there was no question who it was, because she recognized him, too.

It was Jessica Muloni.

CHAPTER 23

ATLANTA, GEORGIA

Trask Industries AMRAD Division—advanced munitions research and development—was located beneath a boxy white warehouse in the Atlanta Industrial Park. Sitting at the dead end of Atlanta Industrial Drive NW, the four-thousand-square-foot, two-story structure was completely rebuilt in 2011. It generally resembled the others in the park. What set it apart was that the grounds were entirely surrounded by a fence. The thin iron bars were ten feet high, were painted white, and resembled spears on top. One would have to touch them to discover that there were ten thousand volts of electricity running through every bar. That was the maximum allowed by international law, as likely to kill as to render unconscious. There were signs warning of the danger, though it was unlikely anyone would get close enough to read them. The surveillance cameras that lined the barricade every 10 feet—backed by a guard station on the roof, staffed 24/7—alerted a corps of security personnel to any individual who made the turn off Atlanta Industrial Way NW, which was the only way in. The day's scheduled arrivals had already been logged by their license numbers. If the cameras and computers didn't match a vehicle with its license number, security converged at the gate and a spike plate rotated points up from the road. The plate did not just deflate the tires; it pierced the rims and stopped even a speeding car bomb.

After the attacks in Baltimore and New York, the chief of security at the facility received preliminary reports from the FBI on the type of weapons used. He and his team reviewed the estimated yield from the explosives at the convention center, studied photographs of the damage, and saw no reason to expand the existing protection of the facility. They were an unlikely target. Few people outside the industrial park knew Trask had a facility here, and no one beyond the staff knew it was the AMRAD Division. Still, the unlikely targets were the ones that were usually caught with their shorts around their ankles. So the team met, did its review, and was satisfied that nothing needed to be done.

Even if all the systems failed, even if a hijacker crashed an Airbus into the facility, the cost would be in human life and property, but not ordnance. The above-ground structure was comprised entirely of executive offices. The real research facilities—the labs, the molding shops, the low-yield ordnance ranges, the storage facilities—were all located on four belowground levels, each of them protected on the top, bottom, and sides by steel-lined concrete 10 inches thick. The steel was ribbed with wires that created an electronic web: in the milliseconds after an explosion, a strong electromagnetic force would be generated to disburse the concussive wave, minimizing the impact in any one spot. If something exploded upstairs, it was unlikely to penetrate the ceiling of the first sublevel. If something exploded down here, it was unlikely anyone upstairs would hear it.

Within this system was another series of protections designed to circumvent industrial espionage. Every vial of nitroglycerin, every packet of gunpowder, every bar of steel or silver used by the molding shops, every tin filled with .3mm screws had to be logged out from the OCQ—the Office of the Central Quartermaster. When he had established his company, Trask had realized that to sell to the military, he had to appeal to the military mentality. Using an army term to describe what was simply a disbursement center gave him an advantage over a rival with a purely functional "stockpile" or "repository" or "distribution center," which made them sound like Wal-Mart or Best Buy, and not an arms developer.

Within the OCQ were the MCs—the munitions caches. These small, guarded warehouses were located side by side on sublevel four and were numbered from one to eleven, from small-caliber armaments to long-range missiles. There were also two lettered divisions: A and Z, as they were unofficially known. These were in a separate, isolated section of the basement. Officially, they were Division Alpha and Division Omega. Division Alpha experimented with high-yield bunker-busting devices, like the air-to-ground, laser-guided Enhanced Paveway III bombs, which were used by NATO to pummel Gadhafi in the Libyan uprising.

Division Omega was different. It created weapons that had never been used in combat. To date, only a handful had even been tested at the military's White Sands range in south-central New Mexico. Division Omega designed EPWs—earth-penetrating weapons. These were all nuclear in nature. Unlike atom or hydrogen bombs, which had to be dropped from airplanes, or the much-feared but unwieldy and impractical "suitcase nukes," these weapons were designed to be portable and precise.

And two of them were missing.

They had been checked out legitimately two days before. Tom Brehm remembered that clearly. Trask Earth Penetrator 1 and 2 were the only crates that had left the room in nearly a month. According to the manifest, they were bound to Site Green at White Sands via road, Absalom Bell, driver. They were due to arrive today. Except there was a problem—an alert Brehm had received that morning from the Department of Defense. It was directed to everyone involved with weapons testing:

    EYES ONLY
    DoD Command Center Dispatch A894D
    SENT: 5:20:13—8:22 a.m.
    RECIPIENTS: SECURITY LEVEL 4, W-PROJECTS
    STATUS: *URGENT*
    NOTIFICATION: UNTIL FURTHER NOTICE ALL
    NUCLEAR AND EPW WEAPONS TESTS ARE
    ON HOLD. RDUs ON HIGH ALERT FOR PO-
    TENTIAL MOVEMENT OF ENEMY
    ORDNANCE.

RDUs were radiological detection units. In test runs using low-level contraband, these radiation sensors, hidden throughout the nation in likely targets—ports, airports, financial and transportation centers, sports arenas—had been successful in identifying low-level radiation, as low as one hundred counts per minute. That technology assumed that in getting such material into the United States on board a boat or plane, the containers had taken a jostling and were leaking, even slightly. But no one in the DoD or at Homeland Security was willing to bet a city on that good fortune.

Thus, a secondary technology, the CIP—the Containment Identification Profile—was secretly deployed in 2009 on highways, on major bridges, at tunnel entrances, and elsewhere. It used fluoroscopic technology to search for lead containers: anything the beams could not penetrate was labeled suspect. Homeland Security had opted to keep the CIP program secret not just to prevent a general alarm—though people were constantly moving through the crosshairs, they received exposure on par with a dental X-ray—but also so potential terrorists would move slowly and confidently to and through cities until they could be quietly apprehended. These early warning systems allowed for a measured police response to prevent terrorists from panicking and triggering their devices prematurely.

The reason the DoD had instituted the A894D alert was to freeze lawful radioactive ordnance so that law enforcement could stay focused on radiation and radiation containers that might actually represent a threat.

The problem, Brehm noted, was that Absalom Bell was just entering Texas and was still on the move. His dispatcher, who would also have received this alert, should have notified him instantly to pull over and stay pulled over.

Protocol required that any anomaly in the system be reported not only to appropriate officials in the local system—Trask executives—but also to Homeland Security. Tom Brehm did so at once.

Brehm did not contact Bell directly. He was not authorized to do so, and a quick check of the system indicated that the problem was on the driver's end: the stop order had been dispatched and ignored.

Most likely the entire thing was a careless oversight. Inexcusable, but not immediately dangerous.

In the event that that wasn't the case, however, Brehm notified the Texas State Police. He did not provide them with any information about the contents of the vehicle; he gave them only the GPS data and alerted them that a Trask Industries van should be eyeballed with possible prejudice. That would put the NMSP in a position to act in the event, however unlikely, that at some point in its cross-country passage a van armed with a pair of tactical nuclear weapons had been hijacked.

Brehm kept an eye on the computer, watching for updates, as he went about the day's business. But it was difficult to stay focused. Perhaps it was a reaction to what had happened in Baltimore and New York, perhaps it was his own bent toward devil's advocacy and Murphy's Law—*What can possibly go wrong, and did it?*—or perhaps it was a combination of those. But he couldn't shake a nagging sense that something had gone bad here.

Bad with the potential to be *very* bad.

*   *   *

Jacob Trask was at his desk in his study, reading CNN online and having a breakfast of homegrown fruit and coffee. He had had an uncharacteristically restless night, not only because the goal was finally in sight but also because he feared possible blowback from Hunt's actions in New York and the discovery— now being reported as breaking news—that the FBI might have been infiltrated prior to the attack. They didn't need a lot of time to finish what they had started, but they did need today. They needed to distract an entire city, keep the eyes in the sky away from the target and on likely targets. When Yasmin Rassin was ID'd, she must be dead, not poised to perform her final act of marksmanship.

That was when he saw the high-priority alert come in from Division Z. He read it, then read the original DoD dispatch, then stared at the monitor while he felt his heart begin to race. He didn't realize he was squeezing the handle of his ceramic mug until he heard it snap at the bottom. He pushed the coffee aside, pushed the bowl of fruit away, looked at the computer clock, and did a quick mental calculation.

Time, as always, was the adversary. Time and speed. He had been forced to move slowly. It had been necessary to test the Gillani Technique in the lab, test it in the field with random acts of violence, test it in Baltimore with a coordinated act, and now maneuver crowds of people *out* of position while he prepared for the final act. He had to keep law enforcement moving in an amoebic mass all around New York, like a herd of elephants dancing around a mouse that had already gone to ground in the high grasses. . . .

"The driver," Trask said through his teeth. *The goddamned driver*. It was not the driver's fault he had ignored the alert; he did not know he had ever been carrying nuclear materials. Dispatch knew he had been carrying them. White Sands thought he had been carrying them, but he was always going to take the fall before he got there. . . .

It will have to happen sooner rather than later, Trask thought. *Before he can reveal where he brought the crates.*

Trask phoned Brigadier General Arthur Gilbert, the commanding general at the White Sands Missile Range. This was a direct call to his secure cell phone, one that was not used unless there was an emergency.

General Gilbert answered at once. He did not know about Trask's personal project; it had not been necessary to involve him, nor was it remotely possible that he would have participated. Still, the brigadier general would be useful.

"Jacob, what have we got?"

"Pony Express."

"Aw, Christ." The code name indicated that nuclear materials had been passed from one vehicle to another. "Where was the handoff?"

"We're trying to find out."

"The crates' GPS locators?"

"Presumably disabled by Shotgun while the driver was checking in." That was the assignation for whatever man was in the passenger's seat. Trask checked the latest data. "The source is en route to you, on Interstate Thirty just outside of Texarkana. The Texas Highway Patrol has been notified, but we need him to *not* be taken. This is not a due process situation."

"No, sir, it is not," the general agreed. "I'm drafting an order for the garrison commander to execute a SAD ASAP. We will have birds in the air in a quarter hour."

A seize and detain order was a benefit of the Patriot Act. It allowed the military to capture a suspected enemy combatant without a warrant or anything in hand other than circumstantial evidence that suggested "cause or motivation." It was legalese that allowed the government to act with the same powers and impunity as the secret police in any nation on earth.

Knowing that General Gilbert was on the case made Trask feel better. He would take the men into custody, hold them incommunicado until one million dollars was found in each of their bank accounts, money they were paid to turn over the two nuclear weapons.

It was 10:00 a.m.

All they needed was another eight hours. Not only had Trask seen the DoD white paper, but he had helped to write it as a distinguished civilian advisor. When the next act had concluded, there would be no question what the nation—and the world—should do.

As soon as he hung up with White Sands, Trask went to the FBI Web site and typed in Hunt's data to gain access to the domestic tracking requests. Finding the information he needed, he picked up the phone. There was something else he needed to make happen.

CHAPTER 24

NEW YORK, NEW YORK

Hunt had no interest in what his colleagues from the New York field office were saying. He knew what had happened here; he'd helped to plan it. He knew what they would do in response, and it was unfolding around him. The FBI was the perfect reaction machine. Something happened, they checked the playbook, and they deployed.

That kind of thinking was what had brought Hunt to this point. He had grown up in a family of cops. He remembered his grandfather's frustration when Miranda suddenly became more than just the surname of a Brazilian samba singer. Suspects, even those caught in the act, suddenly had more than just their constitutional rights. Those rights had to be spelled out while the perps spit and swore at you. Hunt's father was young enough to adjust—and was pushed backward into oncoming traffic on Philadelphia's Broad Street by a mugger whose rights he was reciting. The elder Hunt never walked again.

Hunt had grown up believing in preventative action, which was why he'd joined the Bureau. He thought he would have the opportunity to infiltrate criminal organizations, sniff out terrorists in their communities, track clearly unrehabilitated felons as they returned to their previous lives. Hunt wanted to do it all with the fidelity, bravery, and integrity that was the FBI motto. He also had his own subset of that, his own personal marching orders: foresight, boldness, and imagination. His father and grandfather often spoke of the sixth sense a lawman had or acquired for knowing who was square and who was not. Hunt possessed that instinct. It didn't matter to him who had to be put down to protect "the good." It had never mattered to him.

Even in the more trivial times of his youth, he'd learned that winning was just the beginning of success. Young Alex had been playing king of the hill in the backyard when his neighbor's Doberman, Sergeant Pepper, was let out, and spurred on by the rowdiness of the kids, it impulsively jumped the fence and went on the attack. Terrified, the other boys scattered toward the house, but it was Alexander, the king, who stayed and faced the canine head-on. His mind quickly chose a different battlefield.

Hunt ran down the hill, across the street, and channeled the pursuing dog into the small cemetery on the adjacent block, where he industriously picked up a collapsed tombstone and used it brazenly to crush the dog's back before it could fully latch on to his leg.

Sergeant didn't die instantly, but instead wriggled and whimpered on the manicured lawn while Alexander's friends slowly congregated and then celebrated their safety with applause and taunts to the now debilitated, squirming creature. Hunt challenged any one of them to finish the job, to match the strike he had been forced to make. And no one stepped forward. Having sustained only a scratched ankle and calf from the initial chase, Hunt took a deep breath and brought his foot down heavily on the creature's chest, crushing the remaining life out of it. *Checkmate*. He then methodically dug a hole with his hands and buried the remains under a nearby willow tree, the other boys uselessly stomping the earth down afterward, and then Alex went home without saying another word. His friends kept quiet about the missing dog. The deed was done and couldn't be undone, no matter what sentence was passed—nor did they wish to answer to Hunt if they spoke up. His equanimity had protected not only him, but them. And to them, the small fee of silence was worth the price of security. And Alex's reward of preserved loyalty, however useless his cohorts were at the time, taught him to start choosing his associates more carefully. *Friends with better hits*.

It seemed to Hunt that humankind had become apprehensive and could no longer keep pace with an exceptional willingness to prevail. To stand one's ground. To fight inflexibly for sovereignty. And sacrifices just became footnotes to his many Bureau successes, casualties of his inviolable crusade for better traction. For the greatest advantage.

Because of the rules, because the Federal Bureau of Investigation was so concerned with rights and with not offending this group or that by profiling, by eschewing critical eyes on the borders, on mosques, on ethnic neighborhoods, or on markedly nonethnic neighborhoods where white supremacists were known to dwell, the FBI had lost the all-important first-strike capacity.

And so the United States of America became the giant who had to take the jabs while waiting for the opportunity to kayo an opponent. That was true at home, and it was true abroad, where most of the hate was nurtured. Trask had said it best in their first meeting.

"No more surgical strikes, no more military body bags," he'd said. "We'll turn the desert to glass and clean up with Windex."

Getting to that point would come with an awful price. But it was necessary. And before Hunt's father died, the AD wanted to be able to go to his bedside and say, "Dad, we went on offense, big-time." He wanted to see the old man smile before he died.

Hunt had walked over to the agents to stall his guests. But he was watching them, and when he saw Bishop peel off, he had a good idea where he was going. Hunt was about to excuse himself when his Minotaur beeped. He stepped from the others, watching Bishop, while he took the call.

"Where is Muloni?" the caller asked.

"She was across the street from the lab," Hunt said behind his cupped hand. He had begun walking briskly toward the retreating Bishop. The crowd would keep him from getting too far. Kealey was watching Hunt. There was no getting around him, and Hunt motioned for the man to move in that direction.

"I checked domestic tracking and ID," Trask said. "She requested two cab destinations today. The second was to your location."

"That's standard operating—"

"I don't care," Trask interrupted. "It's time the renegade was eliminated."

For Baltimore, for Franklin May, Hunt had assumed a philosophical attitude toward killing: the good of the many outweighed the needs of the few. That made what he was ordered to do palatable.

"I'll take care of it, sir," he said as he folded away the phone.

Hunt carried a Sig Sauer P220 Equinox. The Sigs were being phased out in favor of Glocks, with their smoother trigger action, but the AD was fond of his .45 semiautomatic. He didn't reach for the weapon in his deep shoulder holster, not yet. But he was folding and unfolding his fingers, his eyes zeroing in on Bishop as he walked, watching the area around him—and making sure, all the while, that he stayed wide of Kealey.

And then Hunt saw Bishop come to a hard stop at the foot of Spruce Street. Kealey was slightly behind him. He couldn't risk drawing now; the CIA expat was certainly packing, as well. Hunt waited until he was at the edge of the crowd, which thickened as he neared City Hall Park, where the people he put behind him would shield him.

There was not enough room between the cab and the car ahead of it for Bishop to stand in front of the cab. Since he didn't want it to go anywhere, he yanked open the passenger door.

"Hey, it's *occupado!*" the driver shouted.

"It's okay," the passenger told him. "I'm getting out." She pushed a twenty into the plastic tray and slid from the cab.

The driver muttered his thanks for being stranded in a no-go zone as she slammed the door. Bishop was staring at her.

"You first," he said.

"That's not how it's going down," she replied.

Bishop was perplexed. He assumed she was here tracking Veil. He hadn't wanted to say anything until he knew for sure that *she* knew. That was SOP packaged inside IA über-caution. But what Jessica Muloni had just said to him was something else entirely. It wasn't a prelude to information exchange. It was a command, as if Bishop were a suspect and she was the arresting agent.

Muloni pulled him away from traffic, toward the sidewalk. They stood beside the Pace University building. It was less crowded here, beside the bridge.

"Put your hands in your front pockets," she said. Her voice and eyes were steel, and her right hand was behind her. He felt sick. She had a piece in her belt, under her shirt, and she was prepared to pull it on him.

"What?"

"Do it!"

He obliged.

"Tell me everything, now," she ordered.

"What the hell's going on?"

"Just goddamn answer me!" she snapped. "Your little girl was killed *yesterday!* What are you *doing* here, Reed?"

Bishop regarded her sadly. "Jessica, how did Veil get away?"

"You tell me!" she shot back.

"I have no idea, and for the record, I'm not here alone."

"I know."

It was then that Bishop realized how careful Muloni had been. She had situated them so that his left side was facing the bridge. He was looking uselessly out in the direction of the South Street Seaport. She, on the other hand, could see the surging crowds. She was also a step and a half away from him. Basic FBI training included disarming a gunman with a grab and twist of the hand while turning and stepping aside; he would need two steps to execute the maneuver, time enough for her to draw and fire.

"Where is she, Reed? Bishop was silent. It was obvious that Muloni had been following him. It took only a moment for him to consider the ways she could have known he was here. He wished he had asked Kealey who else knew the president requested him to go to New York. Was it possible that someone at a cabinet level, at a director's level, was involved in this? Were there secretaries taking notes, or was it all being digitally recorded, as all official meetings in the Oval Office were? That wasn't just for reference. It was for blackmail of chatty, duplicitous, or even drunk world leaders. It wasn't that Bishop refused to believe there was duplicity at that level; he had seen all kinds of corruption and perversion of purpose in his years with IA. Considering all options came with the job. He simply didn't want to believe it.

More likely, Muloni was the problem. Had she been at One West, working with Hunt? Was she the AD's backup? Had she spotted them at Penn Station?

But this was a secret mission. How did she find out? he thought.

What did he miss? Where did he slip up? What would he have done had he not been here?

Funeral arrangements.

The Bureau would have created a death notice, which was standard for family members. That would have been circulated internally at the Bureau. But there would have been no funeral home attached.

That, plus Veil had escaped. Maybe someone put the two together, reasoned he had agreed to be involved with the trackdown, watched him, saw him get onto the train. . . .

"I asked you a question," Muloni said thickly.

"You're way off base, Jessica," Bishop replied.

"You're here with a former Company man, a lone wolf. Way outside the Bureau comfort zone."

"Cluzot had to—"

"Enough! Everyone around you was gunned down at the station this morning. Left, right, behind, in front. But not you."

"I don't know why that happened, either—"

"*Bullshit!* I will put a bullet in your leg and step on it when you're down," she said. "You *will* tell me what you know."

"While your crony Alexander Hunt keeps the cops away," Bishop said. "He's the bad egg, Jessica—"

"Really?" She looked past him. "You can tell him that to his face. He's on the way over now."

"Don't trust him, Jessica. There's something wrong with his operation—"

The young woman brought the firearm around, held it in both hands, pointing down in front of her. "Last chance."

If Hunt *were* coming, Bishop was certain that Kealey would be right behind him. He needed to stall.

"If you let me get my cell, I'll show you what I know about Veil," he said.

"Left hand," she said.

"I know the drill."

Bishop slipped his left hand from his pocket. He used his thumb and index finger to reach across his waist slowly and remove the cell phone from his belt. He held his left arm in front of him, removed his right hand from his pocket, raised it palm up, then brought his index finger over and accessed his e-mails. He scrolled slowly to the one he had received on the train that morning. He turned the phone toward her.

"Read it," she said.

As he expected, Muloni didn't want to come forward or take her eyes from him until Hunt arrived.

Bishop turned the phone toward him and read: "Cargo from Quebec hijacked. Believed to be in NYC."

Her lips drew back in a tense, straight line. She cocked the hammer of her .38. "I got that, too. I'm going to count to three. One . . . two . . ."

"She's working for the Bureau," Bishop lied.

Muloni regarded him suspiciously. "Killing civilians?"

"No," he said, his mind racing to think of an answer she would buy. "Hunting the sniper who is doing that."

Muloni didn't release the hammer. "Who is this other sniper?"

Christ, she seemed sincere, Bishop thought. Was it possible she really didn't know anything?

Bishop was about to give her a story about a Hezbollah sharpshooter attacking Jewish centers of activity when Muloni's eyes suddenly went very wide. Her back arched, thrusting her chest forward, and her chest spewed blood and organs in a column. Some of it struck Bishop in the chin and throat.

An instant later he heard the delayed crack of a single gunshot. It rolled over him, echoing down the narrow street. As the woman fell to the pavement, Bishop could see what her body had been blocking. He saw the people freeze and look ahead, to the west. At the head of the mob was Assistant Director Hunt.

The prick, Bishop thought. He didn't come the way Muloni had been expecting. He had come up behind her. Bad luck on her part—or because I would have been in the way? he wondered.

As Hunt jogged forward, Kealey emerged from the mob right behind him. He charged forward, shoulders hunched, obviously not certain whether the AD was finished shooting. Bishop believed he was. Hunt was holding his weapon pointed down in his right hand while he drew his credentials with his left.

"Are you all right?" Hunt yelled ahead. "I saw her draw a weapon."

Bishop didn't answer. He heard footsteps behind him, raised his hands to show he wasn't holding a weapon, turned as a quartet of NYPD officers converged on the spot.

"FBI business!" Hunt shouted, keeping the gun down but raising his ID. "She was in league with the sniper!"

Hunt was a bad apple, all right. Shouting that second part broke every rule there was. The identity of any suspect was need to know. Either he was trying to get the police to stand down ASAP or he was trying to put that information out there.

Why, you bastard?"

Just as important, what was Muloni doing here? Even if the Bureau put two agents on Veil without letting the other know—because of the leak—how did she get here when the notice went out only hours before?

Hunt arrived, breathing heavily. His eyes were on Muloni. He nudged her weapon aside with his foot, checked her pulse.

"She isn't getting up," Bishop said.

"No," Hunt agreed. He picked up the gun with a handkerchief, put it in the inside pocket of his blazer. The cops arrived at the same time as Kealey. The AD showed his badge around without looking up. He put it away, patted the body down.

One of the officers called in the shooting. He described it as "an FBI action against an armed terror suspect."

"You okay?" Kealey asked, circling around Hunt and Muloni.

"Yeah." There was disgust in Bishop's voice and in Kealey's expression.

"Who are you two?" one of the cops asked.

Bishop held up his hand to show he was going to reach for something. He drew out his own ID. Kealey did the same.

"This card is expired, sir," one of the cops said to Kealey.

"Call President Brenneman," he said. "He'll vouch for me."

Kealey was looking at Hunt when he said that. The AD's eyes rolled up. He knew the name had been dropped for his benefit. Hunt rose. Bishop had watched as he'd confiscated Muloni's phone. He'd palmed it carefully, but not carefully enough. Bishop knew what it was. Bishop removed his jacket, knelt, and laid it on top of Muloni.

"These men are fine," Hunt said.

The policemen exchanged looks. Kealey's ID was returned. The cop who had spoken to Kealey, Officer Ratner, still seemed unconvinced.

Hunt faced him impatiently. "Don't you have *traffic* to clear so we can get a meat wagon to pick up this individual?"

"Don't get belligerent, sir," the young officer replied.

"Christ Jesus, we've got a sniper running around *with* accomplices, and you don't think I should be *yelling* at you?"

"What I think," the cop said stubbornly, "is that you just shot a woman in the back, and I'm supposed to take your word about who, what, and why."

"Did you see the gun?"

The cop didn't answer.

"Was it pointed at this individual?"

Officer Ratner remained silent.

"Let's go," one of the other officers said. "We'll check in with the FBI field office, see if he's kosher."

"Tell them it's Assistant Director Hunt you're asking about," he snapped. "Do you need me to spell any of that for you?"

"No, we've got it," the other officer replied.

The others started to go. Ratner remained where he

was; one of the others reached back and drew him away by the arm.

The scene was incongruous to Bishop. Two men alpha dogging over a dead woman and a growing puddle of blood. He glanced at Kealey, who handed him a handkerchief, indicated the blood on his chin. Bishop wiped it away.

Hunt calmed slowly. He was perspiring, possibly from having run over in the heat, possibly from something else.

Kealey was watching the AD carefully. "How about putting the gun away?"

The remark drew a sharp reaction from Hunt. "Are you challenging me, too?"

"Not at all. I'm trying to get you back to center," Kealey replied. "You just killed someone."

"In the execution of my duties—"

"Yes, and now the shooting is over—"

"I saved your partner!"

"Thank you," Bishop said evenly, hoping he didn't sound overly solicitous. He was with Kealey on this: he didn't like the way Hunt was looking at them. "Mr. Hunt, you know as well as I do, the rule book says if you discharge your weapon, you have to surrender it. We're not going there. All Mr. Kealey asked is that you holster the firearm. Otherwise, I *do* have the authority to confiscate it."

Hunt considered this, then shoved the weapon in its holster. He looked at the IA officer. "Sorry, but you walked into a situation that has been ongoing."

"What do you mean?" Bishop asked.

"We've been watching this agent for several months.

We believe she is—was—a sympathizer with radical Muslim causes."

"Was she?" Bishop asked, staring at him. "I watched her rough up a Muslim assassin in Quebec. She didn't seem very sympathetic."

"Veil was bait," Hunt said. "We believe Muloni engineered Veil's escape."

"Speaking of Veil," Kealey said, "do you mind if we forgo the trip to the lab right now? Maybe nose around and see what we can find out?"

Hunt relaxed noticeably. "Not at all. In fact, I'd appreciate the assist."

"Great. Tell us what to do," Kealey said.

"They've found the body of a UPS driver about a half mile up South Street," he said. "Why don't you head over there, see if you can figure out where she went or what surveillance cameras might have seen her?"

"Sure thing," Kealey said.

Leaving the corpse behind—she would have to wait her turn to be picked up—the men separated, Hunt going east while Kealey and Bishop headed north. The two men made their way up Centre Street, past the bridge, then cut over to the east.

"There's a guy on the edge," Kealey said.

"He's also full of it," Bishop said when they set out.

"Which part?" Kealey asked.

"About Muloni being a sympathizer."

"Was she going to shoot you? She looked like it from where I was standing."

"Very possibly," Bishop said. "That's the thing. She was tailing us. She was convinced that *we're* in league with Veil. And I don't think she was kidding."

"Well, that's a dead end now. The bigger problem is I don't think Veil is done. These feel like sideshows."

"Killing dozens of people, shutting down a major city—that's a sideshow?"

"It's a short-term hit," Kealey said. "People will be back in a few days. A couple of businesses will decentralize, like they did after September eleven. That doesn't generate fundamental change. It isn't reason enough for someone to have gone through the trouble of springing this particular assassin."

"Why not? She's evading capture while—"

Even as he was saying it, Bishop realized that Kealey was right.

"While she's dragging the NYPD and the FBI all across Manhattan," Kealey said, finishing the thought for him. "Midtown west, now Lower Manhattan."

"Right," Bishop said. "A distraction. But why don't you think she's finished?"

"There's one more meaty target," Kealey said. "People are evacuating fast, en masse, so she'll probably hit Grand Central Terminal or the Port Authority Bus Terminal before she or her sponsors move on to the next step."

"Yeah, the more I think about this, the more I don't think she's acting solo," Bishop said. "I was there when Muloni mentioned her daughter. That registered big-time. If Veil engineered an escape, she would have gone to Pakistan to get her into hiding. It is more likely someone wanted her here. Maybe someone else who had access to the kid."

"There's something else," Kealey said. "Did you happen to see the phone Hunt took from Muloni?"

"Yes."

"It's a Minotaur," Kealey said. "The latest high-security uplink. Someone at her pay grade wouldn't need one."

"She was sent here," Bishop said. "And not to watch for Veil. Jesus, Ryan. Who the hell is setting us up?"

"I don't know," Kealey admitted. "The Minotaur is not standard issue to anyone in government service. It costs about a half million per unit. The CIA wouldn't be giving one out to an undercover agent. It's conceivable, though, that the manufacturer would."

"Who's that?"

Kealey answered, "Trask Industries."

Bishop considered this. "We need a double-dog op."

"Hunt?"

"Got no one else," Bishop said. "He took the phone. He's the closest to 'suspicious' we've got."

"All right," Kealey said. "I'll take point on this. You stay with him. I'll go to Grand Central. After that, I'll hit One West."

"Gotcha," Bishop said.

"Get something to eat, too," Kealey told him. "Fast. These vendors look like they're selling out down here."

Bishop offered a halfhearted grin. "Capitalism. Gotta love it."

CHAPTER 25

NEW BOSTON, TEXAS

John Scroggins was dozing in his seat after his dawn-to-ten shift at the wheel. Absalom Bell had made the White Sands run before, but Scroggins was primarily a Florida-to-Maine man for Trask Industries. The flatness of the land, the will-sapping heat just outside the door, the whitewash bluntness of the sun—none of these were for him.

"You might as well be driving through hell," he had told Bell when he turned over the wheel a few minutes before.

The sameness of the world around him included the sounds—the whoosh of air moving past at 80 mph, the tuning-fork sound of the hybrid engine, the hollow whisper of the tires on the road. Save for a vintage hot rod that passed them, there was nothing new.

Until there wasn't.

Scroggins felt the dull drumming before he heard it.

"Is the engine okay?" he asked without opening his eyes.

"That ain't us," Bell said. "It's them."

"Eh?" Scroggins cracked an eye. It took a moment before he could see through the white glare of the windshield. The pale blue of the sky formed beyond it, and in that sky he saw three silver-white bugs. They were low on the horizon, just above the dashboard, and getting larger—and finally louder—by the moment. He felt as if he were sitting in a vibrating chair in a furniture showroom.

"Definitely not a traffic copter eye in the sky," Bell said, sipping coffee.

"Must be some kind of maneuvers," Scroggins said.

"How-to-fly-in-a-triangle training," Bell joked and chuckled.

The Bell-Boeing V-22 Ospreys continued in a straight, sinister line along the interstate. They grew larger as they approached, their tilt-rotor pylons rippling like snakes in the heat rising from the asphalt.

Scroggins shifted uneasily, glanced in the side-view mirror, sat up, drummed anxiously on his knees. "Maybe you ought to pull over," he suggested.

"What for? They ain't the damn highway patrol."

"No, but they are," Scroggins said.

Bell looked in his mirror. Just coming over the horizon was a line of Ford Police Interceptors, their dark chassis blending with the asphalt in a way that made their white tops and red and blue lights seem to float forward.

"You running guns?" Scroggins asked.

"No. Heroin," Bell replied.

"Don't joke," Scroggins said. "They may have some kind of listening shit."

"Well, what kinda dumb question is that?"

"The kind that makes me wonder why we've got the law and the air force converging on our asses."

"Maybe they're after each other," Bell said. "Some kinda drill. And they're navy, not air force."

"Excuse me all to hell," Scroggins said.

The driver slowed and pulled off the road. The men watched as the THP vehicles neared—there were four of them—and the choppers formed a line in front of them, straddling the interstate. Their six main rotors were literally shaking their insides from waist to throat now, the propellers churning dirt from the plains below them. The brush struck Scroggins as ancient peoples waving and swaying before their gods. He wished he felt more like a god and less like a cactus.

The VTOL aircraft on the right descended. It set down ahead of them, beside the road, while the other two hovered at around 200 feet. The THP vehicles arrived almost simultaneously, spinning off the road, two on either side. Men with rifles got out and stood behind the open doors.

"Holy shit," Scroggins said. "It *is* us."

"Man, I swear I don't know what's goin' on."

"Don't tell it to *me,*" Scroggins said.

"Yeah? How do I know this *ain't* about you?"

"I confess, brother. I'm a mule."

"I'm serious—"

"And I ain't, man," Scroggins said. "Maybe you should call HQ."

Bell nodded. The Minotaur was at his side, and he picked it up.

"Put your hands on the dashboard!" a mechanical-sounding voice blared from behind him. "Both of you, *now!*"

Scroggins put his hands ahead of him slowly. Bell raised his, then rotated them down to the padded vinyl. The men didn't know whether to look ahead or into the mirror. Armed men were emerging from the Osprey. They were covered head to foot, crouched behind raised weapons as they approached. It looked to Scroggins as if some of the automatic rifles were aimed beyond them.

"Lower your weapons!" shouted an amped voice from the Osprey.

"This definitely ain't no drill," Bell said.

"Just thinkin' that myself," Scroggins replied. "I'm sure hopin' they're mad at each other and we just got caught in—"

"Persons in the Trask vehicle," said the voice from the Osprey. "Open both doors and emerge slowly."

"I'm guessin' that means we have to take our hands *off* the dashboard," Scroggins said. "On three?"

"Huh?" Bell said.

"We gettin' out?"

"Oh, yeah," he said. "Shit, I just can't figure this."

"I think we're way past trying figuring anything," Scroggins said. "One . . . two . . ."

On three, both men reached out and pushed open the doors.

"Nobody go shootin' us!" Scroggins yelled as he swiveled in his seat and leaned his head out. His hands were raised as he stepped from the cab. "You guys hear me? Which way do we face?"

The Osprey decided that for them. The rotor wash from the transport was pelting them with dead foliage, sand, and pebbles. Both men turned their backs to the air force detachment. Scroggins didn't like what he saw ahead of them. It reminded him of pictures he had seen at the Atlanta History Center from the turn-of-the-century South: early police cars and armed officers ready to face bootleggers, bank robbers, and black men. Though his brain told him he'd done nothing wrong, he started to pray.

"What do you want with these individuals?" someone in front of him said through a bullhorn.

"That is classified," replied a voice from behind. "Stand down."

"Stand down? Hell, we just got here," the bullhorn replied.

"We repeat. Stand down!"

Lord Jesus, Scroggins thought. *You don't talk to Texas lawmen like that.*

The military unit continued to advance. Scroggins saw the men behind the doors growing restless.

"Gentlemen, I'm just going to step from the line of fire," Scroggins said.

"You stay where you are!" the Texan bullhorn shouted back.

"You will *step backward* and surrender, or we will seize you with whatever force is required!" the airman insisted.

"I'm going to do what *that* guy says!" Scroggins pointed both thumbs backward after considering the two commands. The one from the air force definitely had a colder sound. He glanced at Bell, who nodded.

The two men started walking back. Several airmen moved around them, toward the van. They were dressed in what had to be miserably hot long-sleeve camouflage uniforms with bulletproof vests, helmets, munitions belts, high boots, and goggles. There were four men in all. While two kept their weapons trained on the THP vehicles, the others opened the back of the van and went inside. They came out less than ten seconds later. One of them stepped wide, faced the mission leader, and ran his hand sideways across his throat. Scroggins guessed that meant what he could have told them if they'd asked: the cargo bay was empty. The four men rejoined the others.

Scroggins continued moving backward. He was watching the Texans closely, his heart a solid mass in his throat. He saw one man—the man with the bull-horn—lean toward the man beside him. They seemed to be conferring.

"Oh, man, tell me they ain't gonna rush us," Bell said to Scroggins as they cleared the front of the van.

"If they do, dive for the fender and hug that baby."

Suddenly, a pair of Texans shouldered their wea-pons—one from behind each of the two nearest police vehicles. They rose from behind the doors with their hands raised shoulder high and started walking for-ward.

"Now what the hell do they want?" Scroggins asked.

He never found out. He heard boots clomp on the ground behind him, felt hands grab the fabric of his shirt at the shoulders and arms and remain there. He was turned around and found himself facing a pair of fliers with M4 carbines pointed past them—ugly little mosquito-looking black guns with barrels that made his knees turn to liquid. He was glad the hands were prop-ping him up.

The guns jerked in little sweeping motions. "Move!" one of the men behind him said.

Bell and Scroggins half walked, half stumbled forward on liquid legs. Scroggins squinted into the hurricane winds caused by the rotors, tucked his chin into his chest, and pursed his lips tightly as he felt the dust and pieces of twig bite his face. He was helped up a step into the helicopter, still not looking, only feeling the darkness enfold him. The prickling pain stopped, and the noise changed from something harsh to something deep and throaty. Even as he was thrust into a seat and felt himself rising and tilting, he thought of something his grandmother had once told him after a tornado hit her Arkansas community: "Something ain't so bad if you live to get a good story out of it."

He was praying again, hard, that this was something that would impress his grandkids one day.

Lt. Samuel Calvin of the Texas Highway Patrol Intelligence and Counterterrorism Division lowered his hands as the choppers took off. Behind his dark aviator glasses his blue eyes remained fixed on the Ospreys, with a look that was somewhere between contempt and amusement.

"Everyone stand down!" he said, half turning and shouting over his shoulders. "Except you, Munson."

"Yes, sir, Chief."

The men got to their feet, stretching cramped legs. They lowered their weapons, reached for bottled water, and stood at ease. Only Letty Munson remained where she was. She was still crouched, watching the retreating Ospreys through her binoculars, shielding them with one hand so the lenses wouldn't catch and reflect the sun.

"Doesn't look like they're taking any action," she reported. "Those boys are headed home."

Calvin nodded. Low on his to-do list was hanging around—let alone walking over to the van—as the choppers cut loose with incendiary ordnance of some kind.

"You were right, Lieutenant," said the other man.

"Appears so."

The two officers were standing behind the Trask Industries vehicle, one man on either side, their crisp light brown uniforms stained with perspiration under the armpits and around the collar.

"They follow orders like they were written by the finger of God Himself," the thirty-one-year-old said. "Sent for two individuals. They go back with two individuals." The blue eyes lowered as he turned his sun-leathered face toward the van. "Check the cargo back, would you, Patrolman?"

"Yes, sir."

Calvin was on the driver's side and walked around it. *People don't always have the information you want, or else they lie,* he thought with satisfaction as he approached the open door. *Evidence does not.*

From the moment the THP came within visual contact of the van—and the Ospreys—Calvin knew what he wanted. The van had Georgia plates. The men had been on the road awhile. Whatever they had done, whatever the navy wanted them for, it had most likely taken place during that drive. That meant the van would bear the fingerprints of whatever was at issue here. The military didn't confiscate it because, Calvin—a veteran of four years in army intelligence—knew, HUMINT was prized above all. Get prisoners to talk. And they

clearly didn't want a showdown with the THP. Whoever was in charge of the operation snared the targets
and got out.

Calvin bent and looked into the driver's side. He saw
what he expected to see: soda cans, candy wrappers, coffee cups, two newspapers, and an iPod. The GPS was still
on. He checked their route. Atlanta to New York to
White Sands.

They were headed there, anyway, Calvin thought.
Why the rush? To keep them out of our hands, he decided.

"The bay is clean except for muddy footprints," the
officer reported.

"That's why they were so shiny."

"Sir?"

"The Ospreys," he said. "They were cleaning them.
Got the order to deploy real sudden."

He grinned. *High school kids at a car wash.* "Thank
you, Carter. Go back to the vehicle. I'll be there in a
minute."

The patrolman left and Calvin climbed in. He took
the keys; never knew what else they might open. He
checked the glove compartment. No one used it for
maps anymore. There was a flashlight and a small tool
kit. A first-aid kit was attached to the underside of the
dashboard.

There was one thing more. It was in the small compartment between the seats, along with a packet of registration material and a St. Christopher's medallion. A
cell phone, one unlike any Calvin had ever seen. He
took it, and the charger, then used his Swiss Army
knife to unscrew the GPS. He tucked it under his arm
and went back to his own prowler. He was most curi

ous about the phone but did not want to risk turning it on and triggering some kind of data self-destruct code in the phone's program.

"Take us back to division," he said to the driver. "On the double."

The driver signaled the turnaround to the others, adding, "And put the spurs to the flanks."

Calvin didn't know what he had in his little trophy, but he knew that it made him smile. He imagined one of two things would happen next: the choppers would come back when HQ found out they hadn't swept the vehicle, or they'd dispense with the vehicular pat down and toast it from the air.

Either way, Calvin scored that one for what his grandfather used to call "us Texicans." But as the glow of their success faded, he began to wonder what was really behind the apprehension of two men who didn't appear to have a clue what was happening. In light of what had occurred in Baltimore and New York, followed by the alert from Trask Industries, plus the emptiness of the cargo bay—it all suggested nothing good.

He hoped to have some of those answers when they reached the mobile unit in New Boston. In the meantime, he texted a brief on-site report to the division leader so that Washington could be alerted.

CHAPTER 26

WASHINGTON, D.C.

The Oval Office meeting broke at 3:00 a.m. with word that a young student at Georgetown University had been found dead in his dorm room of a self-inflicted gunshot wound. He was a Lebanese citizen, and an FBI uniform was found in a burning pile in the bathtub. The smoke detector was what had triggered the security guard to break in.

The only things found in the uniform were marbles.

The president grabbed a few hours' sleep upstairs, in the master bedroom, was showered, shaved, and about to go back to work when word of the Penn Station shootings reached him. He hurried down to the Oval Office. There were no new briefing folders on the president's desk. In situations where intel was streaming and constantly changing, updates were typically delivered by the department heads.

An intern arrived with a tray of coffee for the president. A second tray arrived and was placed on the coffee table for the others. FBI director Charles Cluzot was already there, along with Homeland Security chief Max Carlson and the CIA's Bob Andrews. The press secretary had already convened her staff to discuss the talking points for her 10:00 a.m. appointment in the Briefing Room.

That was postponed until noon after the first sniper attack. It was postponed again indefinitely after the second attack.

National Security director Bruce Perry was also in attendance. He had flown back from London, where he had been meeting with his counterpart, Britain's National Security advisor Sir Peter Gurney.

The Oval Office became a clearinghouse, as information was received by the three intelligence directors and shared with each other and the president. It frustrated Brenneman and the others that no larger pattern seemed to be emerging. The events in two cities appeared to be random acts of terror, albeit most likely coordinated.

"So we've got our FBI impostor," Andrews said. "Another man of Arab descent with no priors and no apparent radical affiliations."

"What still bothers me," Carlson said, "is that no one has claimed credit for any of these. Even the guys who claim credit for everything they *didn't* do were caught flat-footed."

"Hold on a second," the fifty-two-year-old Perry said. "This isn't good."

Brenneman looked over the edge of his coffee cup at the bald-headed NSD. Perry was the former director of the nonpartisan National Assured Salvation think tank based in Savannah, Georgia. His appointment had taken a lot of heat from civil rights groups because

NAS was an outgrowth of the Confederate group Assured Salvation, which was responsible for evacuating civilians of all races from war zones. Though many blacks had been saved, they were saved as slaves. Many who wished to wait for the Northern troops were forced out. For Perry—and for Brenneman—the Civil War was over and population centers were prime targets for terror. That was Perry's specialty.

Perry was not an alarmist. When he said that something wasn't good, it was the equivalent of "Dear God in Heaven!" from other lips.

"What is it, Bruce?" the president asked.

"Sir, you are probably aware of DoD Protocol Eleven, in which all high-yield weapon transports are locked down in the event of an enemy attack," he said. "The DoD issued a temporary alert after Baltimore, then lifted it for ordnance already in motion, then reissued it yesterday at eight twenty-two in the morning. It is still in effect."

"What's on the hoof?" Cluzot asked.

"The Texas Highway Patrol was alerted by Trask Industries AMRAD Division that a pair of prototype EPWs—earth-penetrating weapons—were en route to White Sands," Perry said.

"Hell's silver bells," Andrews said, sitting back.

"Yeah," Perry said. "A report from THP Intelligence and Counterterrorism says that the van went from Atlanta to New York with cargo for the NYPD. The GPS showed no stops other than Arkadelphia, Arkansas. When the vehicle was detained outside New Boston by a trio of Ospreys, it was empty and the crew was taken away."

"To White Sands?" the president asked.

"Presumably," Perry replied.

"Who's in command there?" the president demanded.

"Looking, sir," Andrews said as he studied his laptop. "Brigadier General Arthur Gilbert, since two thousand nine—"

"Get him," Brenneman said.

For a long moment no one moved. That was typically the role of the executive secretary, but the president hadn't asked her. He'd kept it in the room. There was no established pecking order, and no one wanted to take that ride down the totem.

"I've got the number here, sir," Andrews said before the president had noticed the hesitation. He moved to the phone. He had said it to the others in the room, using it to save face. He reached for the phone on the coffee table.

"Could there have been an exchange at the motel?" the president asked.

"I was just texting the THP to find out what the GPS says," Perry said. "That may not help, though. Satellite coverage at night . . . We don't do a lot of it along those remote stretches." He finished the message and sent it. "The FR also indicates that the THP recovered a secure cell phone from the cab of the van," Perry went on. "A Minotaur, standard issue for classified transport."

"Are they cleared to access the cell records?" the president asked.

"If you sign a directive, they are," Perry replied.

"Draft it," he told Perry. "The day I can't trust a Texas lawman, the nation's done, anyway."

"Yes, sir."

The president moved to the laptop on his desk to await the document. He would sign it electronically and forward it to the Texas Department of Intelligence and Counterterrorism.

Andrews's personal phone beeped as he was placing the call to White Sands. He checked the number, stopped the outgoing call.

"Mr. President, it's Ryan Kealey," he said.

"Put it on speaker," Brenneman ordered.

Andrews answered the phone as he walked to the president's desk. It wasn't a secure line, but there was no time to worry about that. Anything they knew, the enemy already knew.

"Ryan? You're on speaker—"

"Good. Sorry I haven't checked in. A lot's been going on. The guy we were supposed to meet here, AD Alex Hunt, just shot and killed CIA agent Jessica Muloni of Rendition Group One. Said she was a suspected Muslim sympathizer. I can't say if she was or wasn't, but he shot to kill."

"This is Cluzot. With cause?"

"She had her weapon drawn, was interrogating Reed Bishop, who she seemed to think had helped the assassin Veil escape," Kealey said. "Sir, have you been notified about the shooting?"

"No," Cluzot said.

"I'm not surprised. I think Hunt may be our man. He's certainly dragging his feet on letting us near the lab and keeping his people in the loop. One thing that surprised me, though. He took a cell phone from Muloni. Snuck it away. A Minotaur."

The president was looking at the phone. He had a strange thought then: that it was his enemy, like some kind of mischief maker in the myths he loved to read as a kid. During his first term in office, technology was not so omnipresent, and information not quite so immediate and unfiltered. The data was compounding to weigh the group down and confuse the hell out of them.

"Hold on, Ryan," the president said. He looked at Cluzot. "Charles?"

The FBI director shook his head. "Not standard issue."

"Is there any chance Hunt was right about her?"

"It's possible," Cluzot said. "Veil disappeared on her watch."

"Mr. Cluzot," Kealey said, "Mr. Bishop impressed on me that Agent Muloni seemed genuinely convinced that *he* was responsible for the assassin's escape. She pointed out something else, something I'd noticed, too. The shooting at Penn Station started virtually the minute we walked onto the street. The gunfire took down people all around us, and I mean every side. We were left alone."

"She was watching you?" Andrews asked.

"Apparently," Kealey said.

"Then, and I'm sorry to say this," the president said, "how do we know that Bishop *isn't* a part of this? Maybe his daughter was an unintended casualty."

"I don't think so, Mr. President," Kealey said. "He's been on board with me from the start, letting me run the show. He comes alive when we're on the trail of these killers."

Brenneman looked at the others, his expression asking them if they were okay with Kealey's explanation. All of them nodded.

"What are you doing now?" Brenneman asked.

"I'm leaving the bridge and heading uptown—on foot until I clear the traffic. I have a feeling we may take one more hit here. People are being fed through bottlenecks out of the city. That's too tempting a target to ignore. It'll either be the Port Authority Bus Terminal or Grand Central Station. I'm betting on the latter."

"Why?" Andrews asked.

"High perches and easy getaway to the side streets," he said.

"All right," the president said. "Do you want support there?"

"The NYPD is pretty high alert right now," he said. "I'm sure the National Guard at both locations is the same. Not much more we can do on that front. And there's no point clustering even more high-value security targets in one place."

"True," Brenneman agreed.

"I'm going to see this through, then get downtown for a belated look at Hunt's project," Kealey said.

"How is Bishop?" Carlson asked.

"All right. Focused. I have him checking on something. Is anything new there?"

"Nothing that would help you," Andrews said.

Kealey would understand that to be code for "There's no significant data, so don't bother going out of the way to find a secure location." And they would understand that he was not in a position to tell them where Bishop had gone. Not on an open line. The president presumed it was to the FBI lab at One West Street.

Andrews hung up and went back to placing the call to Brigadier General Gilbert.

"THP reports that the van stopped west of Interstate Thirty, on Pine Street," Perry reported. "Showing an Arklight Dome Lodge there."

"Bob, hold on," the president said.

Andrews and the others all looked at him.

"White Sands is not the issue," Brenneman said. "You had cargo off-loaded in New York, and possibly in Arkadelphia."

"Hell, they could have stopped anywhere," Carlson said.

"That's true," the president agreed, "but we need to at least alert the police in Little Rock and Dallas. Bruce?"

"On it, sir."

Cluzot seemed surprised. "Only the police?"

"Unless we freeze out your AD Hunt, I don't think we can risk notifying any field offices, Chuck."

"Sir, we'll need all eyes on this that we can get—"

"Those cities have terrorist units, good ones," Brenneman said. "I know. I signed the funding bill."

"Mr. President, why don't we want to talk to General Gilbert?" Andrews asked.

"Let's see if he files an action memo," Brenneman said. "He apprehended civilians. That should be coming in soon. If he doesn't, we'll know he's running black ops and we'll need to find out why."

"I'll tell the chairman of the JCS to let us know the instant that comes in," NSA chief Perry said.

The thought was chilling. That this was a domestic-based action was frightening enough; even the hint that the military could be involved made it that much worse. One could be aggressively fought; the other could, at best, be aggressively defended against. There was a potentially devastating difference between the two.

As the president finished his coffee, he turned to the computer monitor to have a look at the online edition of the *Washington Post*. What he saw caused him to forget the cup, the room, the passage of time. He said nothing until he heard Perry's voice.

"Mr. President . . . another situation."

CHAPTER 27

NEW YORK, NEW YORK

The Port Authority Bus Terminal was a grim, inelegant structure that blotted Eighth Avenue between Fortieth and Forty-second Streets. Shadowed by its own latticed box of elevated bus lanes and mostly surrounded by old New York buildings that offered relatively little gaiety, it was primarily a way station between Manhattan and New Jersey, or a point of departure for people who couldn't afford the more expensive trains that departed a few blocks south from Penn Station or who lived in the smaller towns serviced by the eighteen different carriers.

The large, impersonal interior space was like a crab carapace with spindly legs extending outward. Commuters patronized the food and beverage stands, magazine and book stalls, trinket shops, and other impersonal stores. The lower level was primarily a waiting area, cramped and claustrophobic.

Shameen Al Dhahrani passed the statue of Ralph Kramden as he headed for the terminal entrance. A freshman student at NYU, the Saudi had never heard of *The Honeymooners,* but he would not have been surprised to learn that Americans had erected a statue to a fictional bus driver from a television show. Americans lionized false gods. These hollow deities took the place of true faith and morality, which was one of the reasons he was racing to catch a bus. There was to be a rally outside a shopping mall in Wayne, New Jersey. It seemed a suitable venue to demand the payment of reparations to detainees at Guantánamo Bay. He carried a leather case thick with flyers he would hand out to shoppers or place on car windshields. A psychology major, he would remind himself with each rejection that these people had been conditioned by their news media, by their televisions, to believe that wrong was right. They had been brainwashed to insensitivity, to self-absorption.

The doors slid open to admit him. He looked at his watch to see how much time he had. He had purchased his ticket online, so all he needed to do was grab a cup of tea if there was time and make his way to the departure gate.

He saw the nickel-plated brass wristband where his watch should have been. Set in the band was a blue and white marble. He slowed, but he did not stop. He looked into the cavernous lobby—ahead, to the sides. He blinked. It was as if a creamy film had gummed his eyesight. He blinked harder.

The haze cleared, and he saw an arena. There were people in the stands. A sandy surface lay ahead of him. He approached a large circle of guards, dressed in military uniforms, standing watch—around what? They were standing far enough apart so that if Shameen moved his head slightly to the right, he could see between them. There was a man standing beyond them. He was dressed in a loose-fitting white *thobe,* a full-length skirted garment, with a red and white checkered *kūfīya* around his head. The ends of the cloth were pulled across the lower half of his face, forming a mask.

The man held a saber.

Someone was kneeling before him, facing away. A woman. She wore a white burka, which had been pulled around her shoulders. On her head she wore a black *hijab,* which was raised from her neck by pins.

An execution. A beheading.

Shameen circled the soldiers so he could see the woman. He saw her shoulders moving—in prayer or sobbing, he could not be sure. She was wearing a black cloth over her eyes. Were those tears or perspiration trickling from beneath?

She turned at the sound of his footsteps on the sand.

Sand, to soak up the blood.

As she moved, the mask fell away. Her large, dark eyes were red. Her pale cheeks were radiant with tears. She bit her lower lip so she wouldn't cry, or cry out.

"Mother?"

Fawza Al Dhahrani had been accused of witchcraft. It was said that this poor woman from the Al Shmeisi neighborhood in Riyadh had enchanted the son of a prominent diplomat, had bade him marry her, had used him to elevate herself from poverty. His father, Ubayd Al Dhahrani had agreed to raise the child of their union, but only if the unholy marriage were terminated.

It was about to be.

Shameen was suddenly aware of the bulge in his leather satchel. He remembered what he had placed there before leaving his room. He had purchased it from a policeman who had confiscated it from a radical who had surrendered during a raid. The young officer had said he needed the money.

And you wanted to save your mother from this unjust and horrible fate, Shameen told himself.

As he continued around the circle of police, he unzipped the satchel. He reached in, withdrew the Steyr AUG A2 with a short-barrel carbine configuration. It snagged a little as he tried to withdraw it, and he was forced to wriggle it a bit before it came free. His finger was already inside, on the trigger, and he blew away part of the leather side as he screamed inarticulately, aimed high—above his poor mother's head—and began cutting down the policemen, getting them out of the way so he could kill the executioner, who had already raised his sword prior to delivering the death stroke.

The men in their khaki-colored uniforms and black caps went down, spinning, tumbling, crashing one into the other and spraying blood on the sand.

Shameen felt a punch in the back of his leg, in his side. The hits burned almost at once. He felt another in his shoulder. His right arm, the arm with the gun, went numb. The weapon dropped. He felt something slash through his chest from the front, and there was something hard hitting his knees. . . .

The tile floor.

He had fallen. The world turned strangely around him, like a carousel that was turning and also tilting wildly up, down, up, down. The milky haze returned, he thought briefly about the bus he had to catch, and then he fell forward in a growing stain of his own blood.

Kealey had finally managed to secure a cab near Canal Street and Lafayette. And only because he stood in front of it. The driver was off duty and had not intended to take on a passenger.

"Mister, unless you're goin' to Astoria—"

"I'm going to Grand Central," he said, coming around to the window but holding the door handle so the cab couldn't hurry away. He glanced at the driver's ID on the dash. "Norm, you look like old school. Whatever happened to the 'neither rain nor snow'—"

"That's the post office."

"Fifty bucks," Kealey said.

Horns screamed behind them.

The driver agreed to the terms with an exasperated nod.

Kealey didn't release the handle until he had the back door open. "Thanks," he said and slumped in the back.

"All I can say is, these terrorists know how to mess with us," the driver said.

"How so?"

"They hit when people are comin' in. Makes it tough for people to get out."

That was true, and the man had arrived at that with zero security clearance. It reinforced what Kealey had always said about intelligence. It was well and good to have ELINT, electronic intelligence, eavesdropping on cell phones and computers. But without HUMINT, human intelligence, eyes on the scene, a complete picture was not possible. That was where the United States lost its edge in the 1990s, until 2001, when it put all its faith—and resources—into satellites and hackers. That was one reason the Israelis rarely got caught with their pants down. Using Druze citizens—Arabs loyal to their adopted nation—they were able to infiltrate Hamas, Hezbollah, and other enemy groups.

Kealey took advantage of the moment to call Allison. She had called four times since last night; he felt guilty about not having checked in before this.

"Where are you?" were the first words out of her mouth.

"In a New York taxicab," he replied.

He gave her a moment to process that, to not ask what she knew he couldn't answer, and then say, "Oh."

"Where are you?" he asked.

"At the office," she said. "No reason to be, though. My morning slate was wiped clean. People are busy trying to figure this out."

"How is Colin?" Kealey inquired.

"He seems fine," Allison said. "I've been waiting for a shoe to drop, and it hasn't. And *don't* tell me that kids are resilient. He was taken hostage and saw people murdered. If that's not a recipe for post-traumatic stress, I don't know what is."

"No, you're probably right," Kealey said, though the first killings he saw in his early twenties were pretty brutal, as well, and he was still waiting for some kind of emotional blowback, as well. It hadn't happened. Maybe it just manifested itself differently in some people, perhaps driving them to stay in the crosshairs because they liked the all-or-nothing scenarios. "How are you?" he asked. "You were also in the belly of the beast."

"My memory is blissfully hazy," she said. "Or maybe it's just a lack of sleep, or both. As long as I don't let myself slip back there, I'm fine."

"Eyes front," he said. "That's true about everything."

"And you?" Allison asked. "Is your being there related to the shootings?"

"It wasn't when I left, but it is now," he replied.

"Are they finished? Do you know?"

"I hope so, but I don't think so," he said.

She was silent for a moment. "Did you get any sleep last night?"

"I did," he said. That wasn't a lie. Over the years, on missions, Kealey had to sleep whenever he had the time, wherever he was.

"Would it be a complete waste of breath to tell you to be careful?" she asked.

"Probably. But it's good to hear."

"Do you have any idea when you're coming back?"

"I'm guessing it'll be soon," he said. He didn't have to add, "Or not at all."

This was beginning to feel like more than doctor-client concern to him. Or maybe he was wishing it was. A crisis produced strange bonds. It also brushed away the posturing and forced real feelings to the forefront.

The cab had just reached Park Avenue and Seventeenth Street when they heard sirens screaming to the west. They were headed uptown.

"Now what?" the driver muttered.

"Ryan," Allison began, then stopped.

"What's happening?" he asked.

"FoxNews.com says there's been another shooting in New York."

"Where?"

"Port Authority Bus Terminal."

Kealey leaned toward the open partition. "I need to get to Fortieth and Eighth," he said.

"Something happening there?"

"I think there is," Kealey said.

"I'll take you as far as Times Square. Then I'm goin' home to Queens," the driver said. "Sorry."

"That's fine," Kealey said. "Allison? I'll call you later."

"Make sure you do—"

"Okay. Bye."

He clicked off. His head was no longer in the conversation.

As far away as Thirty-fourth Street, Kealey could already see traffic starting to back up ahead.

"Mister, I'm thinkin' this is as far as—"

Kealey thrust the fifty and another twenty through the window. "Cut over to Sixth, go up to Fortieth, you can leave me there. Deal?"

The driver took the money and headed up Sixth Avenue. He made it as far as Thirty-fourth Street before police—still on duty at Penn Station—directed them to turn east.

"Sorry," the driver said, passing back the twenty.

"Keep it," Kealey said as he opened the door.

"Thanks! Take care of yourself, G-man."

Kealey grinned. The driver winked back.

HUMINT, Kealey thought. *Nothing like it.*

Kealey went up to Thirty-seventh and ran west. The

street was the least crowded of all those he'd looked down. He paused only long enough to eavesdrop on something that was coming over a policeman's shoulder radio.

"Reports the shooter is down, according to Port Authority dispatch."

Kealey wasn't convinced. Breathing hard, he hurried ahead, showing his expired credentials quickly to gain access to Eighth Avenue, then again to get by the cordon of blue surrounding the bus terminal.

He knew at once this was far from over.

CHAPTER 28

WHITE SANDS, NEW MEXICO

White Sands Missile Range was America's largest military facility, covering nearly 3,200 square miles carved from terrain as harsh as its history. On April 6 and 7, 1880, it was the site of the fiercest battle of the Victorio War, between the U.S. cavalry and the Apaches. Even before that it was the site of countless mining operations, ambitious individuals and large corporations staking claims in the rough-hewn mountains adjoining the salt-white sands.

The navy came to the blistering range in June 1946 to join the army in testing V-2 rockets captured from the Germans during World War II. At the time, the navy was interested in expanding the power of its Viking rocket with V-2 technology, the first supersonic rocket to run off of liquid fuel, which resulted in the development of the sleeker, more powerful Aerobee, a small rocket originally introduced in the fifties that was designed for high atmospheric research. Today the Naval Surface Warfare Center, Port Hueneme Division, White Sands Detachment, was an independent group at the army-operated range. One of its charges was to develop weapons for America's Strategic Defense Initiative. This sprawling blanket of technology included the Terrier and Tartar missiles and the Aegis weapons system, Rolling Airframe surface-to-air missiles, Vertical Launch Anti-Submarine Rockets, Tomahawk and Sea Sparrow missiles, high energy laser devices, and the Mid-Infrared Advanced Chemical Laser and the Sealite Beam Director.

One of its key projects was the Sea Burst, a six-inch guided projectile designed to be fired from the shoulder-mounted Windjammer rocket-propelled grenade launcher. Unlike previous antisubmarine and anti-shipping RPGs, the Sea Burst was a thermonuclear device. At 35 pounds, it was the lightest such device ever designed, packing .009 kilotons of destructive power. By contrast, the "Little Boy" gravity bomb that was dropped on Hiroshima had the destructive force of approximately 13 KT of TNT. But "Little Boy" was not a focused explosion. It destroyed buildings across a two-mile diameter. The unleashed shock wave, moving faster than the speed of sound, turned structural debris created by the blast into shrapnel, which extended the field of destruction even farther.

It was an extremely effective weapon. However, if used in combat against a nearby boat or fleet, the blowback and fallout would not do the parent battleship any good. Even fired from a safe distance at a port city, it would destroy the port and the city both. Such results were not in the navy's best interests.

The Sea Burst was designed to surgically obliterate a target with a minimum of collateral radioactive contamination. The delivery system itself had been tested at White Sands with conventional explosions. There were jokes in the bunkers about the comical little "pops" they produced, even though those blasts would be sufficient to punch a hole in 12 inches of alloy steel.

Brigadier General Arthur Gilbert was United States Army, not navy. But daily top secret briefing memos told him everything that was going on at the installation. He had been following the Sea Burst with particular interest because the applications for portable nuclear grenades impacted all branches of the military. It would enable special ops forces deployed in mountainous regions to employ bunker-busting force, rather than having to call in air raids, during which time their targets could relocate. It could enable a single paratrooper, dropped into a city at night, to take out the entire electrical grid of that city.

In the wrong hands, however . . .

Interrogations at White Sands typically involved amateur archaeologists looking for shell casings from the Apache war or for mining memorabilia. One woman, the fifty-five-year-old editor of the Canine Defenders of Freedom Web site, was looking for memorabilia from the Range Instrumentation Development Division's dog program. In the early 1960s, it was necessary for engineers to recover small missile parts to ascertain why tests succeeded or failed. Ground crews would spend hours, sometimes days, recovering this material, which was often buried in the sands by the force of the test. That was before scientists came up with the idea of using canines in the recovery effort. The key missile components were coated with shark-liver oil. Specially trained dogs could smell it from 100 yards away. What took training was not smelling the squalene, but keeping the dogs from running after desert wildlife. The editor was searching for remnants of the terry-cloth jackets worn by the dogs, the pockets of which were stuffed with ice during the summer to keep the dogs from overheating.

The program was discontinued in 1965, when word got out that the dogs were also being used to recover materials from nuclear testing sites. The United States military went back to sending scientists.

Like many high-ranking officers, people who had spent their adult lives in uniform, General Gilbert had little use for civilian values and ideology. The inter-service rivalry was intense but, like any tribal organization, they closed ranks when it came to facing outside forces. And for all the value they provided, the American industrialists were a pain. Whatever machismo the individual soldier possessed; whatever alpha-dog qualities an officer developed or had innately; whatever vanity soldiers possessed about their bodies, the press of their uniforms, the medals they displayed, they were patriots first. Even a president could not stand opposed to a unified wall of military will. When the Joint Chiefs wanted surges in Iraq and Afghanistan, they got them. When the United States Central Command wanted to expand operations from Afghanistan to Pakistan, it was done. No president could risk worst-case scenario commencement addresses given by secretaries of defense. No administration wanted dire outcomes whispered in the ears of hawkish senators of its own party.

Conversely, industrialists all had boards of directors and stockholders. They might be patriots, but they were capitalists first.

Except for Jacob Trask.

Gilbert had first met him in the late 1970s, at a conference involving the role of the military in urban security. It wasn't simply a matter of civil unrest, like the kind that had rocked the Watts neighborhood of Los Angeles in 1965. It was about the bankruptcy New York City faced and the role technology could play in safeguarding streets with a skeletal police force. Trask had presented a slide show of his company's plans to adapt discarded U-2 spy plane technology to urban patrols. Gilbert and many others liked the idea, but the ACLU learned of it and pressured Congress not to fund any broad domestic eavesdropping programs.

"Well, what do you expect?" Trask had said to him during a visit to White Sands with other private-sector captains of industry. "They're the people who voted to let Reds in the organization."

At the time, Gilbert was a liaison between the U.S. Army Command sergeant major Victor Houston and Commander Matt Lewis, deputy for navy of the White Sands Detachment, Naval Surface Warfare Center, Port Hueneme Division. When Gilbert replaced Houston in 1984, Trask became his go-to advisor on civilian matters. There was not a more passionate American than Trask. His company was privately held, and from Reconstruction to the present day the family business was about making the nation the greatest power, the greatest explorer, the greatest melting pot the globe had ever seen.

Gilbert trusted Trask. He had never known the industrialist's honor and duty to be in conflict. Those qualities were not mutually bonded: a soldier could be asked to make an object lesson of a tribal leader by killing him in front of his people. For a civilian, the conflict could appear only in the form of treason. Nine times out of ten, traitors were motivated by money. That was not Jacob Trask.

But something else was true about Trask. He was a passionate man, especially about his country. He had ramped up the Trask Industries war machine in 2001 to provide ordnance for an attack against the Taliban and, later, for the invasion of Iraq. He did that without firm orders from the Department of Defense and, indeed, ended up producing nothing that could be used for traditional carpet bombing: he had filled the bombs with napalm that was left over from the Persian Gulf War. He did not share the concern of the Bush administration that civilians might be caught in the strategic waste laying of vast stretches of the tribal regions. The loss ran to tens of millions of dollars. He had told Gilbert that was the price of preparedness.

Gilbert had been impressed by that. Yet today, when they spoke on the way to the office, Trask said nothing about Baltimore. He had been awakened by alerts about New York; Trask hadn't mentioned that, either. Gilbert's sole concern was to take these men into custody.

Gilbert went directly to the interrogation room with the idea that if there was a problem, the problem was with one of the two men—probably both—who were being held in Conference Room B. The innocuous-sounding designation was known internally as the Bastille, since it was soundproofed, wired for video, had a teak door lined with iron mesh, no windows, and could be used to hold a person or persons indefinitely.

There was an antechamber with a gunmetal desk

outside and three computer monitors on it. Two of them were for the cameras located in opposite corners of the square room. Gilbert saw that the men had been given bottled water and nothing more. Audio was streaming through an overhead speaker. The guests were silent. The door to the room was to the right, a guard stationed before it. A pair of naval intelligence officers were manning the computers. From there, they could access civilian and government databases. That information was displayed on the third monitor. Right now it was displaying the motor vehicle data and police records of each man.

There was one cell phone on the desk.

"Mr. Jenkins, only one of them had a phone?" Gilbert asked.

"On him, sir," the intel officer replied.

"Nothing was recovered from the vehicle? The GPS?"

"Those weren't part of the orders," Jenkins replied. "Only the recovery of the men."

"Brilliant," Gilbert said.

"In defense of the team, there was a showdown of sorts with the Texas Highway Patrol. Lieutenant Delguercio thought it best not to let the situation escalate. Marley?"

"We've sent a team back to the vehicle and requisitioned whatever might have been recovered from the vehicle by local authorities," the other officer said. "I'll be monitoring that effort."

"Who's going to talk to these men?"

"Colonel Murray is on her way," Jenkins said. "Command Sergeant Mintz thought it best to have an African American interrogator on this."

As they spoke, the door to the antechamber opened. A young army officer strode in, saluted the brigadier general without stopping, and walked directly to the door of the Bastille. Jenkins buzzed her in.

"Efficient," Gilbert said.

"You don't know her, sir?"

"Only by dossier," he replied.

It was going to be interesting, Gilbert thought. She would have seen the same data that was on the screen: these guys were clean.

Those were exactly the kind of men one would want to hire to hijack nuclear weapons.

Gilbert watched the monitors as Colonel Kathy Murray put her electronic tablet on the table, glanced at it, then regarded the men.

"Mr. Bell, Mr. Scroggins," the woman said without preamble, "crates with nuclear materials, earmarked for delivery here by you, are missing. I want to know where they are. Mr. Bell?"

"Ma'am—"

"Colonel."

He made a gesture of apology. "Colonel, I have no idea what you're talking about. As I've been sayin' to everyone who has had a hand in putting me here—"

"Thank you. Mr. Scroggins?"

The other man regarded her before answering. "I'd like to know who says there were nukes—"

"I'll repeat the question if you like."

"Colonel, we delivered electronic components," Scroggins said.

"The address?"

"One was to the NYPD Counterterrorism office at 55 Broadway. The other was to an FBI lab at One West

Street. Abbie handled the NYPD delivery, then went to get us lunch. I walked the other crates over to One West."

She regarded Bell. "Earlier today you ignored an alert from your dispatcher."

"It didn't apply to us," Bell said. "Because . . . we *weren't* carrying nukes."

"Did you make any stops?"

"A few rest areas for a few minutes and then at a lodge in Arkadelphia," Bell said. "You can check the—"

"We know what to do. Name?"

"The Arklight Dome Lodge."

"How did you disable the tracers?"

Bell shook his head. "We didn't. There were no—"

"Mr. Scroggins?"

"What Abbie said," he replied.

"What do you know about disabling a weapon-specific GPS device?"

Scroggins made a face. "I don't know. You mean, like smashing it with a hammer?"

"What do you know about disabling a weapon-specific GPS device, Mr. Scroggins?"

"Shit, Colonel. I know shit about it."

"We couldn't even get to 'em if we wanted to," Bell said.

Her dark eyes shifted to him. "Explain."

"They told us in orientation that those gadgets get tied to the mechanism, inside. If the primary one isn't working, the backup one goes on."

"When the weapon is turned on," she clarified.

"I don't know about weapons, but for our gadgets, that's my understanding," Bell said.

Gilbert listened with detached interest. Col. Murray

was going by the book: fast hits, no backtracking, keep them off balance and carried along by your agenda, not their own. But it wasn't producing results. General Gilbert already knew that these systems had a backup. They gave you exactly one minute of warm-up before the weapon was fired. That was not a lot of time to prevent it from being used, because that was not the function of the timer. Someone on-site had to target and fire the weapon. The exact location was fluid because of external circumstances, like the repositioning of enemy security, patrols or, in the case of an airfield, the target itself. The idea was that a waiting chopper or vehicle could locate the signal, reposition itself, and get to the shooter in that minute, remove him from immediate-proximity danger. The air-to-ground nuclear rockets had an additional one-minute countdown detonator to give the team extra time before the shock wave or radioactive cloud hit. There was no need for a concussion explosion with a nuke: there was no way anyone at the target could shut it down or contain the blast.

His gut told him the guys weren't hiding anything.

"Call me if something comes up," Gilbert said.

"Yes, sir." Jenkins replied.

Gilbert left the antechamber and walked to his office. Assuming the two men were telling the truth, he reverse engineered what might have occurred. Someone wanted nukes. Trask wanted to make sure they got them for reasons yet to be determined. The drivers were told they were delivering electronic devices. What if that information were false? What if someone at Trask—not the Shotgun—had disconnected the GPS devices on the Sea Burst prototypes? Fewer people would have to be involved with stealing two hot devices than with arming two "dummy" devices to make them hot.

But what about the missing inventory alert?

Was that an oversight, a screwup that some in-house nuke-stealing son of a bitch was supposed to have covered? Or hadn't it been worth the bother? The loss of the nukes would have been discovered when the van got to White Sands in another day or so. The drivers would have been blamed, interrogated, and would have said exactly what they were saying now.

But what if "tomorrow" had been too late to take any action? What if someone was planning to transport—or worse, use—the nukes before then?

Had the nukes even been *on* the van, or was that a misdirection, as well? Were they going to be used in Atlanta? Were they in somebody's van, headed for Washington, D.C.?

The devil's advocacy was starting fires of suspicion rather than dousing them. As soon as he reached his office, Gilbert called Trask on his private line. The call was sent to the industrialist's voice mail.

Gilbert hung up without leaving a message.

It was then that he allowed himself to contemplate something that made his gut burn. It was something about which studies had been conducted and white papers written: what if someone on the civilian side of things decided to use their military wherewithal to start or assemble an underground army, like al-Qaeda or Hezbollah, only with a great deal of money and a solid command structure? Was *that* what this was? The first major weapons delivery to a nonnational source?

Unless Trask talked to him, there was no way Gilbert could find that out. The only military oversight of the industrial, civilian world was what the industrial, civilian world allowed. He couldn't even authorize an examination of the crates that were delivered to the two New York addresses: he would have to pass that information along to local law enforcement.

For the first time in his life, Brigadier General Arthur Gilbert wished to hell he was dead wrong about something. But all of that wouldn't change the fact that for whatever reason, there were two nuclear weapons that could not be accounted for.

CHAPTER 29
NEW YORK, NEW YORK

Kealey did not have to study the scene to know that the situation was not contained and far from over.

He took it in at a glance, saw that the weapon the dead man carried was not the same that had been used for the Penn Station and Brooklyn Bridge shootings. He left the terminal and hurried along Forty-second Street as he called Andrews.

"We just heard about—"

"It's a sideshow," Kealey told him. "Different gunman. I'm heading back to Grand Central."

"Do you have any information about—"

"Zip," Kealey said. "But I can't think of anywhere else she'd go. Make sure someone tells the cops there not to stand down. There's still a potential risk from the original shooter."

Kealey waited while Andrews informed the president and the others, put the information out there. He was alarmed at how many people were being funneled along this one route—and he was still five avenues away. Vehicular traffic was down to a single lane as pedestrians clogged the streets.

It was a shooting gallery.

As he waited for Andrews to get back on, Kealey thought about the attacks this morning. Something was not making sense. Why would the enemy use a skilled killer for two attacks, drop in a ringer, then pick up again with the pro? Why sacrifice the Port Authority killer to take a sniper off the radar—and then put her back on again?

You wouldn't, he thought. *You'd take the opportunity to get her out with the crush of commuters. Send her somewhere else.*

Or put her on another project. The one she had really been freed to undertake. The one that not just any adequate marksman could pull off.

Kealey slowed.

What the hell are they planning?

When Andrews came back on, Kealey shared the thought with him.

"We were just kicking that around ourselves," Andrews said. "We just received an action memo from Brigadier General Arthur Gilbert at White Sands. A pair of prototype nukes that were en route to the installation never made it."

"Projectiles?" Kealey asked.

"Damn. How did you know?"

"Just an ugly hunch," he replied. "How are they fired?"

"Shoulder-mounted."

"Shit."

"They may be in New York," Andrews said. "The drivers are in custody. They swear everything they had was off-loaded downtown."

"Let me guess," Kealey said. "One West Street?"

"Yeah. That was one of the addresses."

Kealey had stopped on the corner of Fifth Avenue. The four miles from where he needed to be suddenly felt like a hundred. "Bishop is still downtown," Kealey said. "I'm going to send him over. I'll call you when I can."

As he was clicking off, he heard Andrews say, "Thanks, and Godspeed."

Reed Bishop felt like a corked bottle on the sea. He would shift and move, not always forward, as people shifted around him. And it was in one of those backward pitches, as a fire truck moved in front of him, that he lost Assistant Director Hunt.

The maneuver might have been intentional; Hunt was there and then gone. It was too clean. He had to be watching for the opportunity.

Bishop charged in that direction, shouldering through people when there wasn't an opening. He fished out his badge, apologizing and flashing it at the same time; he didn't want to have to stop and explain what he was doing to anyone, police or civilian. He was moving against the human wave on Frankfort Street, as people who had walked along the East River resumed making their way to and across the Brooklyn Bridge. He couldn't imagine that all these people lived in the borough of Brooklyn; Bishop had the feeling that people just wanted to get out of Manhattan.

Or were being driven out? he wondered.

An air of relief seemed to pass over the crowd as people chattered about a gunman having been slain at the bus terminal. Bishop took out his phone, was about to call Kealey as he weaved his way past the Manhattan base of the bridge.

The phone beeped. It was Kealey.

"What happened?" Bishop said as he answered.

Kealey told him about the shooting. "I think we have a bigger problem," he said then he proceeded to tell about the missing nukes. "Where's Hunt?"

"Gone," Bishop told him. "I lost him when traffic got between us."

"Where are you now?"

"Nearly at the East River," Bishop said. "I want to see if I can spot him."

"Whether you see him or not, you need to get to the lab. There's no way I can get down there now."

"Yeah, I hear that," Bishop said. He was nearly a half block from South Street. The broad avenue, which followed the river, looked like the top half of an hourglass with human sand pouring down. People were making the loop down Frankfort up to the entrance ramp to the bridge. Vehicular traffic was basically halted now, with horns voicing their displeasure. "Man, I don't see how somebody in a hurry would go any way *but* the direction from which I was coming."

"Could Hunt have ducked down a side street?"

"That would have put him in the mess by City Hall Park," Bishop said. "I could have run into him the same way I did Agent Muloni." Bishop pushed harder as he neared the bottleneck. "Oh, shit."

"What?"

"Hold on." Bishop stopped being polite. He stiff-armed his way forward, shoving and driving his hip against anyone who was in his way. "FBI!" he repeated, with his badge raised. "Please step aside."

There were isolated protests, but for the most part, people made faces and tried to accommodate him. He finally reached South Street, crossed it, went to the esplanade that followed the river. It was packed with humanity, but he wasn't looking for Hunt. Not there. He looked north, then south along the river.

It was packed with maritime traffic. Most of the boats were ferries—water taxis and even private vessels—which were pulling up to the seawall. Most were doing this for free; some were charging people anywhere from twenty to one hundred dollars to cross to Brooklyn. Times were tougher and citizens were more polarized than they were in 2001, when all civilian vessels provided this service for free.

"My insurance company won't let me do this," one tug captain was saying as he asked for 120 dollars. "You gotta make it worth my while."

He had some passengers already. The exploitation made Bishop sick.

There was other traffic moving up and down the river, mostly police and coast guard ships.

Except for one. It was speeding toward the harbor.

"What's going on?" Kealey asked.

"The river," Bishop said. "I'm guessing that's how he's getting back to One West."

"Is there anything there you can commandeer?"

"I can try, but there's no way I'm going to catch him."

"He wouldn't be going back to clean the place," Kealey said. "He could do that with a phone call. He must be—" Kealey stopped.

"What?"

"The crates," he said.

"What target?" Bishop asked. "The Statue of Liberty?"

"Doesn't fit," Kealey said. "He wouldn't need the punching power of a nuke to cut her in two."

"Speaking of 'two,' why would he need two?" Bishop said. Though he knew the answer even as he said it.

"Double jeopardy," Kealey said. "He's pulled the police all over Manhattan so they can't organize to stop him. They're too busy with goddamn crowd control."

'Look, I'm going to hoof it," Bishop said. "I can cut across from the Staten Island Ferry terminal, get there faster than on the river. If he's going to the West Side—"

"I'm on it," Kealey said. "I'm going to need Brenneman's muscle for that. Call me when you get to the building. Don't pull in any cops unless you need to. There isn't time to get a search warrant."

"Agreed," Bishop said.

Kealey was gone, and Bishop turned and headed downtown. He was tired, but he was focused now.

However much his cramped legs protested, he couldn't afford to rest.

Not if Baltimore was only a warm-up for something written on a much larger canvas with a much stronger pen.

CHAPTER 30

WASHINGTON, D.C.

"I need a helicopter, now. With firepower. I'd like Twenty-three."

In government circles Kealey's request—put on speaker—was what was known as a torpedo. It had the effect of sinking whatever was in front of it.

The president and his team had been sifting through the IDs of the Baltimore bombers and the FBI impostor, hoping to find a common link. There was nothing, save what their fingerprints told them: they were all Muslims here on visas, mostly students, from different world hot spots where hatred of the United States was high: Kosovo, Yemen, Somalia, Libya, and the like. As with so many other things in these past two days, it seemed too pat to be real. They had been debating whether the attacks had been designed to be conclusion driven—individuals recruited to guarantee that blame attached itself in a particular way—when Kealey called.

"Sorry, what's that?" the president asked. "The high-tech surveillance chopper?"

"Yes, sir," Max Carlson said. "It went into service in two thousand eight. Named for the number of officers killed in the World Trade Center attacks."

"What do you plan to do with any chopper?" Andrews asked.

"Bishop thinks Hunt may have escaped by sea, to get to One West and the nukes may be there."

"Bishop thinks that," Cluzot said.

"He's your man, Mr. Director," Carlson pointed out.

"He's internal affairs!" Cluzot said. "A desk jockey. What does he base that on, Mr. Kealey?"

"Suspicious activity, reasonable assessment."

"SARA is not sufficient for the president to make this call," Cluzot said.

"Where did he get a boat?" Andrews asked.

"He probably had it there, waiting," Kealey said. "He knew there was going to be an attack on the bridge. He knew he'd be going over there with us. Hell, the timing of *both* attacks seems to have been built around us. That and the death of Agent Muloni."

Cluzot made a face. "You and Bishop are the new Ground Zero?"

"Hey, if I'm wrong, you can put me in the corner. That SOB knew we were going to be stranded on the far side of a big goddamn crowd. Even if we knew how he got away, we wouldn't be able to follow. Everything he's done has been to buy himself or someone else time. And right now we're giving it to him."

"You know where he's going?" the president asked.

"Yes, sir, and he's already halfway there, with me unable to find him. Bishop's on his way. In case he doesn't make it in time, or if things don't break our way, we need a Plan B. The chopper is it."

"Do you know what kind of boat he's in?" Cluzot asked. "We can phone that information to—"

"We don't know for sure if we've even got this *right!*" Kealey admitted. "We can't have the NYPD storming the river, looking for him. That could scare Hunt into doing whatever he's planning."

"It could also stop him!" Cluzot said. "The NYPD has a pretty good antiterror unit."

"That isn't the point. What they don't have are facts. Maybe the second nuke is support in case the NYPD *does* pursue. Or maybe that's the sniper's job, to start taking down aircraft over the boat. We just don't know. That's why I have to get up there, watch from a distance, with the ability to act if necessary. That chopper's got facial recognition software. We'll need that. You want to summon the cavalry, I'm happy to back the play when it's appropriate. But let's make sure of our target first!"

The president did not have the authority to commandeer an NYPD resource. He could not tell the police commissioner why he wanted it. He would have to put his reputation on the chopping block and make the strong request.

"Is there any other bird we can get over there?" the president asked his team. "Maybe something from Joint Base McGuire-Dix-Lakehurst."

"Not without having to explain *that* to the NYPD," Andrews said.

"Mr. President, I'm on my way back to the West Side," Kealey said. "That chopper is in the air twenty-four-seven. Please have it meet me at the West Thirtieth Street Heliport."

The president looked at Andrews. The CIA director nodded. He looked over at Carlson. The Homeland Security chief cocked his head to one side, then, with reluctance, nodded once.

"I'll make the call," Brenneman told Kealey. "Bob will let you know what the NYPD says."

"Thank you, Mr. President," Kealey said.

Andrews ended the call. Brenneman looked at him. "I'm not completely sold on this, but I was afraid your boy would take a chopper at gunpoint."

"Sir, your concern is not unfounded," Andrews replied with a half smile.

Brenneman picked up the phone.

"Mr. Meyers," the president said, "get me commissioner Lee Strand. I'll hold."

"Yes, sir," his special assistant replied.

"Thank you." The president looked at the others in the room. "I want us to get ahead of this damn thing. Kealey's got the only option on the table. Andrea, we know how this plays if it works. If it doesn't . . . ?"

"If it doesn't, Ryan Kealey's not a lone-wolf operator anymore," the press secretary replied. "This call puts the go-ahead on your shoulders, sir. There will be questions from both sides of the aisle about why you didn't put massive force in the field to find a pair of missing nuclear weapons, as Director Cluzot suggested."

"My uncle Bernard once drove a hay truck off the road because there was a yellow jacket in the cab," the president said. "If he'd been surrounded by horses or sheep, he'd've just stopped and waited for them to move on."

"The herds wouldn't have been looking for him," Cluzot pointed out.

"Neither was the hornet," the president said. "Point is, it was on him before he could react."

Commissioner Strand got on the line. Brenneman did not put the call on speaker.

"Good morning, Mr. President."

"How are things up there, Commissioner Strand?"

"Calm for the moment, sir. You've probably heard we got a shooter. We're not sure he's working alone."

"We've reached that same conclusion," the president said.

"Mr. President, forgive me, but we've been hearing disturbing rumors about missing nuclear weapons."

"They appear to be true," the president replied. "We have two men on the ground who we believe are on the trail of a pair of highly classified projectiles with nuclear explosives. We need to get one of those people in the air. Can you lend us Twenty-three?"

"Will this protect my city?"

"We believe the action has a good chance of doing that," the president said.

"Is there anything you can share with us, sir? Was the deceased FBI agent a part of the sniper's support system?"

Brenneman did not look at the others. He turned his chair, glanced out at the Rose Garden. "We believe she was framed by the individual who *is* behind this. We also believe he is in possession of the weapons."

"Where and when do you need Twenty-three, sir?"

"The heliport on West Thirtieth Street. Our man is on his way."

"Name?"

"Ryan Kealey. K-e-a-l-e-y."

"Any special expertise, sir?"

"Yes," the president said. "He wants to see this bastard dead."

"Those are the kind of credentials I admire, sir. The chopper will be there."

"One more thing, Commissioner." The president looked at his notepad. "Our second man, Reed Bishop, is on his way to One West Street."

"Around the corner from the killing yesterday."

"Yes. If you get any nine-one-ones from a research lab at that location, you would do well to delay responding."

"That's against our policy, of course. But we *are* spread thin," Strand replied.

"Thanks to the individuals we're pursuing," the president said. "I'll be in touch."

"Thank you, sir."

The president hung up, then swiveled back to look at the faces of the other four people in the room. His press secretary looked the grimmest. "Andrea?"

"You are personally *very* far out on a limb, sir," Stempel pointed out.

The president's eyes shifted to Cluzot. "Chuck?"

"The comment about nine-one-one . . . if it ever got out . . ."

"That's what I was thinking," Stempel said.

"If that happens," the president replied thoughtfully, "it will pour gas on the debate about the rights of suspected terrorists, and I'll have the Justice Department on my back for a few months for some violation of equal protection statutes. You know what? I'll take my chances. I want to stop trailing these bastards. I want to get ahead of them."

"I like it," Andrews said. "I like it a lot."

"That's the good thing about being a lame duck," Brenneman said. "Sometimes you get to do what you think is the right thing for its own sake."

"Besides, Commissioner Strand has his eye on my job," the Homeland Security director said. "He won't tell tales out of school."

"Amen. If it works, he'll take credit for it," Andrews said.

The president chuckled. It broke the tension slightly.

Stempel shut her laptop. "It's ten past eleven. I've got to tell the press when I'm going to talk to them. How does one o'clock sound, Mr. President?"

"I have a feeling this will be over by then," he said.

"This part of it," Cluzot said.

Except for Andrews, the others looked at him. The CIA director was nodding in agreement.

"What do you mean?" the president asked.

"Let's assume—only for the sake of this discussion—that the two nukes are the finale of this wave of terror," Cluzot said. "Someone, some group, put them into play. Someone got to my people and turned at least one of them. If Kealey is right, someone was watching him and Bishop. In short, someone has access to our playbook—or enough of it to cobble together a response."

It was an unpleasant thought. They had all been so focused on current events that they hadn't given any consideration to the befores and afters.

"Mr. President, I think we should continue to keep our thoughts in this room," Andrews said. "If we start putting together DSTs, we may do exactly what we're trying to prevent, which is continue to give the party or parties access."

Data strike teams were the new first wave of defense against potential terror threats. Each group had one: CIA, FBI, NSA, and the military intelligence branches. They took raw intel gathered by HUMINT and ELINT resources, saw if the pieces fit. If two or more went together, that DI—data image—was fed to the other intel units to see if they had any pieces that belonged there. It was an efficient coordination of resources grouped under the Homeland Security tent.

"Everyone in agreement?" the president asked.

That was his way of indicating he backed the play. Otherwise he would have said, "Thoughts?" Anyone without a strong dissenting opinion and the facts to back it was likely to get smacked down in the first moments of debate.

The president called Meyers, told him they were going back downstairs.

"I want a live feed from the NYPD Counterterrorism Division, and I want streaming updates from the Baltimore Convention Center," the president said.

"Something may turn up there that can help us in New York."

"Yes, sir."

"And see if you can put us inside the NYPD chopper Twenty-three," he added. "Audio is fine if that's all we can get."

"On it, sir," Meyers replied.

The president rose, followed by the others.

"Fifteen-minute break. Then we're back in the hole," the president said.

He turned once more, opened the doors to the Rose Garden, stepped onto the patio to take in the daylight and the clean, non-ventilated air while he still could. Press Secretary Stempel stuck her head out.

"How are you doing, sir?" she asked.

"All right," he said. "I was just thinking . . . I read an anecdote—I honestly can't remember where— about the British Admiralty hunting for the *Bismarck* during World War II. The men and women in charge of the operation were down in their bombproof bunker in London for days, receiving data and plotting strategy with this big, table-sized map, moving wooden planes and boats around as updates came in. When they finally crippled the battleship and sent her to the bottom of the sea, the Admiralty's chief of operations looked at the clock and said he was going upstairs for a proper dinner. He got outside and saw that it was eight in the morning, not evening." The president squinted into the sunlight. "I pray to God, Andrea, that we are not down there long enough to lose track of time."

"I didn't know him before today," Stempel said,

"but I got the very strong impression that Ryan Kealey is not the sort of man to let things drag on."

"No, he is not," the president agreed.

Andrea Stempel left, the president said his silent prayer, and then he turned and walked through the empty Oval Office to the West Wing elevator.

CHAPTER 31

NEW YORK, NEW YORK

Yasmin was walking down West Broadway, just crossing Chambers Street, thinking about the morning.

She hadn't eaten. She stopped in the Amish Market to get a sandwich. Large sections of the store had been bought clean: evacuees had picked up beverages and snacks, and locals had already been in to buy essentials.

She bought a Greek yogurt and some kind of power juice, warm. Then she continued down the avenue to Vesey Street, then over to Church for the last leg of her walk. She had no idea how she had gotten to West Broadway. The last thing she recalled, she was over by South Street, walking toward a UPS truck.

All she knew was that it was okay. She had been where she wanted to be, where she was supposed to be, and was headed back to where she was staying. Except for the memory lapse, she didn't feel as if anything was wrong. Hooked on a finger and slung over her shoulder, Yasmin was carrying the garment bag she had left the apartment with early that morning. She knew there was a weapon inside. She detected, very faintly, the burned gunpowder and knew it had been fired.

You're an assassin. It's what you do. You've smelled that odor many, many times before.

But she simply couldn't remember who it had been fired *at*. What was more, she was strangely ambivalent about not knowing. It was as if, not remembering, she simultaneously had nothing to worry about. Except the fact that she couldn't remember, but that, too, didn't bother her much.

Downtown seemed oddly deserted. It wasn't just un-populated; it was as though it'd been swept clean of life and activity, like the shelves in the market. She sat in the park in front of 7 World Trade Center to eat. It was the last building that had fallen on September 11 and the first to be rebuilt as a great silver rhomboid.

She ate the yogurt, was sorry she didn't have bread to fling to the pigeons. The birds were respectful at least, not like in some cities, where they came up and sat on your shoulder to try and pick at whatever you were eating. She drank the tart-tasting juice concoction as she continued to One West. The finger holding the garment bag was beginning to cramp. When she was finished with the drink, she threw the bag over her arm. It didn't fold.

Right, she thought. *There's a rifle inside.* She hugged the bag to her. She was an assassin. She packed wea-pons the way an electrician packed a toolbox or an at-torney packed legal documents.

Church Street was barren. Century 21, one of the city's busiest clothing stores, looked as if it were closed. There were no police. With a mounting sense of alarm, she quickened her pace. There were no tourists in Battery Park, but the seawall was lined with people waiting for boats. The harbor was filled with traffic, some of it police, some of it private, most of it commercial. All of it was in motion, to New Jersey and Staten Island, some of it up the Hudson to Midtown.

She saw a few policemen here, most of them trying to move the traffic along Battery Place and West Street. All of it was funneling into the lanes that opened into the Brooklyn Battery Tunnel. She looked at her watch. It was nearly lunchtime, but everyone was going home.

This isn't holiday traffic, she told herself. *Something's wrong.*

Yasmin went to a cop who was standing with her hands on her hips, waiting for a signal from up the street to let more traffic onto West Street.

"What's going on, Officer?" Yasmin asked.

"You been asleep?" the woman asked.

"Apparently," Yasmin replied.

"Sniper attacks uptown and on the Lower East Side," she said. "If you live near here, get there now."

"Thanks," Yasmin said.

She walked to her destination, the tall, century-old building on the corner. Sniper attacks. She was a sniper. Was this about something she'd done?

Why can't I remember?

She went inside, was announced by the concierge, and took the penthouse elevator to the top floor. There was something she needed to do. She frowned. What was it?

The drawbridge lowered, and she crossed it, walking the narrow passageway into the palace. It wasn't *what* she needed to do; there was someone she needed to see. Her cousin, Nabi Bakhsh.

So smart, she thought, *but so arrogant. He doesn't think his little cousin is a threat. He doesn't think she can stop him.*

She paused before the palace door and laid her saddlebag on the carpet. She drew a nine-inch blade from a leather sheath inside. There was already blood on it from the guards she had killed earlier, making her way into the usurper's city. She closed the saddlebag, left it on the carpet, held the knife behind her back, blade down, and turned the door handle. It was unlocked. She entered, saw the princeling in his regal garb, talking to her own informants. He smiled at her. She smiled at him. She went to embrace him. He seemed surprised and backed away.

"You aren't going anywhere, Nabi Bakhsh," she said.

"What are you talking about?" he replied.

She swung the knife around and pushed it into the soft tissue just behind his chin. The blade was slanted toward the back of his head. The steel went through flesh, tongue, soft palate, and sinus cavity. Blood washed her wrist; and air, sucked through the wound, caused it to bubble. He gurgled down air as he reached for her hand, tried to pull the knife away. But she was pushing him back, twisting as she did, ripping a cavity at the base of his brain. His arms went limp, and he hung there on the knife, deadweight increasing by the moment.

She drew her arm back and let him fall.

"You will not be taking the throne from my father," she said defiantly.

The princess became aware of her informants moving around her in a wide circle. They were coming toward the body, not away from it. One of them, the woman, was placing her saddlebags on the floor. The other, a man, came over and gently, quietly, took the knife from her hand.

"You have done well," the man told her.

"Thank you."

"As we discussed, all that remains is to make sure the moat cannot be crossed again," he said.

"Yes," she said.

The man turned her toward the closet to her left, beside the window. The woman opened the accordion door. There was a weapon inside, nearly as long as the other woman was tall. It was a narrow tube with a trigger, a sighting device, and a sleek, flattened arrowhead on the upright end.

"You know the target, where it is," the man said. "We've shown it to you."

"I remember."

He set a cell phone on the table. He held her hand, raised it so she could see the bracelet with the marble. "You will wait here until the phone rings. That will let you know it is time. Then you know what to do?"

"Take that rocket launcher, go to the roof, and make certain the moat cannot be crossed."

The man smiled. "And when you are finished?"

"I will come back here, locate the highest point, and keep a lookout for my father."

The smile vanished. He looked at the other woman in the room. She nodded, cocked her head to the door. "Why don't you sit beside the phone and wait for it to ring?"

"All right."

The woman grabbed keys and her shoulder bag from the table and took a final look around. The man waited for her at the door.

They left without a word.

Drs. Ayesha Gillani and Emile Samson took the elevator to the lobby and walked to the parking garage. While Samson restored the spark plugs, Gillani got behind the wheel of the old BMW. Once they had pulled onto West Street, a police officer helped them cut across the tunnel-bound traffic to get to the virtually empty uptown lane. She swung west toward the World Financial Center and the marina. She pulled as far onto Rector Place as the cul-de-sac would allow, and then Samson went to the trunk.

He took the dolly from the trunk and placed the crate on it. Then he yanked a canvas blanket from underneath and threw it over. The box said TRASK INDUSTRIES. That was not something they wanted a cop to notice. Not that any would be here, on the esplanade that led to the marina. The people who lived in adjoining Battery Park City—a complex that had been built on landfill pulled from the original construction of the World Trade Center—were already home, very few taking advantage of the beautiful day to jog or fish along the river.

Hunt had arrived there shortly before the two doctors. He had arrived in an FBI first responder counterterrorism launch, which was tied to an iron fence pole at the mouth of the marina. The New York field office kept one at the NYPD Harbor Unit marina at Gover-

nors Island, off the tip of Manhattan. Hunt had hitched
a ride with the East River Patrol Division earlier that
morning and had moved the launch to a berth at the
South Street Seaport. It was just a short jog from the
Brooklyn Bridge.

He was standing on the deck of a larger vessel, a
sky-blue, twenty-eight-foot runabout with an extended
triple cockpit. A canvas top with detachable aluminum
poles covered the open area behind the seats. He was
wearing a black FBI Windbreaker. He handed two
more to the others.

"You're late," he said with annoyance.

"She was late," Gillani replied. "You can't program
every minute with the time we had available."

"Did she take care of the boy?"

"Her cousin? Yes," the scientist replied.

There was no joy in her eyes, no satisfaction in her
voice. It was a task that had to be done; that was all.
Like this one.

Hunt hurried onto the concrete walkway and helped
Samson with the crate.

"Just leave this," Hunt said, knocking the dolly out
from under it as he picked up one end of the crate. The
men carried it onto the runabout, laying it in the open
area behind the three forward seats. Hunt picked up a
crowbar.

"The key's in the ignition," the AD told Samson.
"Get us out of here."

Samson slid behind the wheel, while Hunt pried
open the crate. The pine lid came away easily, revealing a steel container inside. There was a keypad on top
of it. Hunt had memorized the code Trask had given
him, inputted it, and the lid popped open.

The codes for this container and the other had cost five million dollars each. That was what Trask had to pay the inside man at his company. For the same price he threw in turning off the GPS signal built into the container. It was a big price, but then only a handful of Trask's eleven thousand employees had access to that kind of information. And he found one who had kids in college and a house near foreclosure.

The mercs who took out the Pakistanis in Quebec were a bargain compared to that, he thought. They were just a million each.

Hunt removed the launcher. The 15-pound tube was assembled, save for the placement of the nuclear RPG. That was in a separate box with a thumbprint code. Hunt put on a latex glove with the print from Brigadier General Gilbert. The AD had lifted it from a beer bottle Trask had collected during a post-think-tank cookout in Atlanta.

The smaller steel box snapped open. Hunt removed the silver projectile from its formfitting polyurethane bed. The device was 13 inches long, 7 inches of which contained the warhead and fit snuggly against the barrel of the launcher. The maximum range of the projectile was 3,000 feet, almost twice the reach of a normal rocket-propelled grenade. The added distance had been necessary, if the shooter was going to be evacuated before the radioactive cloud from the explosion reached him. In their case, they would be racing up the Hudson when he fired, already well past the target. The winds there blew primarily to the south. That was a key part of their planning.

The major cities within 50 miles—New York; Newark, New Jersey; Stamford, Connecticut; and Bridgeport, Connecticut—would not be so lucky. They were all in the radius of the prevailing winds and the radiation. Not just from the RPG blast, but from the target.

Hunt laid the assembled weapon beside the crate. He sat in the middle seat of the three, watched the thinning water traffic as the boat sped north, past Chelsea, past Midtown on the right, past the New Jersey Palisades on the left. The air felt good. He didn't realize how much he had been perspiring until the cool wind chilled his chest, his arms, his face.

He looked at his watch. It was time to call the cell phone, put the first part of the operation into action. He drew his phone from his inside blazer pocket and handed it to Samson. All the months of planning were about to come together, seamlessly. And then the second part of the greater mission could begin.

The phone on the table beeped. Yasmin, sitting calmly beside it, answered.

"Yes?"

"It's time," Emile Samson told her.

"I know." She hung up. Yasmin took a Glock from the top shelf of the closet, then picked up the rocket launcher. There were two grips on the underside; she grabbed the forward one and went to the door. There was something familiar in the air. A hint of fragrance she recognized. Where was she? Where had she been? Beside the door, arranged neatly in a vase, were chrysanthemum flowers. *Why do I care? Why do I want them?* Suddenly she was back in Damascus. There was a man; he was reaching out to her. She knew him and wanted to reach back. She extended her arm toward the flowers and caught a glimpse of her marble bracelet, of her world. It was in trouble. Turning to open the door, she glanced at her cousin's body before leaving.

"You never win by betraying your own people," she said and walked into the hallway.

She held the firearm in her right hand as she slung the rocket launcher to her left shoulder. If anyone tried to stop her, they would be shot. The safety of the palace was too important. There was no time to deal with anyone who might be loyal to Nabi Bakhsh.

There was a stairwell at the end of the hallway. She tucked the gun in her pants, threw the door open wide, and stepped through. She walked the single flight to the roof. The surface was covered with concrete tiles and afforded a 360-degree view of the city. To the south she could see the harbor, all the way out to the Verrazano-Narrows Bridge. Westward, planes were coming and going from Newark Liberty International Airport. She saw the Statue of Liberty, Ellis Island, and the line of red lights on cars heading toward the entrance to the Brooklyn Battery Tunnel. To the east were the skyscrapers of finance, the Trump Building at 40 Wall Street and the AIG Building at 70 Pine Street. Classic structures from the previous century, bought and rebranded, but not repurposed. They were still, all these things, the emblems of a kingdom. The kingdom her cousin had wanted to usurp.

The kingdom she was to protect.

Helicopters moved up and down the river, behind her in the harbor, and well to the east, above the Brooklyn Bridge. This building was alone at the end of the island, bordered by a park, not a high-security concern. Yasmin made her way to the north side of the building. The former Downtown Athletic Club was the only structure there, looming high but slightly to the east of her position. She had a clear line of sight to her target.

She crouched on the tiles. She looked behind her, saw large slabs of concrete that had been removed by work crews repairing the ornate façade of the old building. She wondered if that might cause blowback, which would singe her back when the weapon discharged.

Possibly. Instead, she went over to one of the boulder-size fragments of concrete and laid the back of the rocket launcher on it. That would spare her and give her added support. She took out the Glock, laid it beside her within easy reach. She held the forward grip of the rocket launcher with her left hand, the center grip with her right. She rested the rear section of the tube on her right shoulder—there was a plastic cushion under the weapon for that purpose, two-thirds of the way back—and looked through the sight. Her aim was a little high: all she could see was the midsection of the 1,776-foot-tall One World Trade Center Tower, one of the five skyscrapers that were rising at the site of the complex where the slightly shorter Twin Towers once stood. She lowered the weapon. She still couldn't quite see the target. She looked around.

The turret . . .

The image returned to her. She was supposed to climb the highest wall of the palace. There was a water tower on the southern side of the building. It rose about 30 or 40 feet above the point where she was now. There was a ladder on the side.

Rising, she kept the rocket launcher on her shoulder as she strode to the steps that led to the base of the water tower. She lowered the weapon to her side when she began to climb the ladder. Reaching the top, she climbed onto the narrow area between the peaked top and the low rail that surrounded it. The view was commanding—and perfect. She raised the weapon and found her target on the western side of the site.

There was nothing there, which was exactly what she expected. Her job was to expand the moat so it would encircle the palace. To do that, she needed to put a hole in the foundation of the pit, the concrete bathtub in which the Twin Towers once stood. The slurry walls kept the Hudson River—and that harbor that nourished it, and the Atlantic Ocean beyond that—from filling the dry underground passages through which the trains moved. Trains that could carry enemy troops, who would soon learn of the death of their prince.

Yasmin's slender finger slipped between the trigger and the trigger guard. There was no timetable for her action; she had been told to fire when she was ready.

She exhaled slowly, just as she had done on the scaffolding by the train station, just as she had done on top of the UPS truck.

She was ready.

Beside the trigger was a button. When she pressed it and held it down, the projectile and the launcher would be one. Ready to be fired, ready to defend the realm.

She pressed it.

Breathless and struggling on feet that had turned to deadweight, Reed Bishop arrived at One West Street.

Cars were backed up to Broadway, trying to get onto West Street, but the sidewalks were eerily empty, there was no one there except a man walking his dog. Four police officers were literally feeding cars into the tunnel entrance one at a time.

Bishop needed the brass handrail to help him get up the stairs. He went through the revolving door and showed his ID to the concierge.

" I work with an FBI guy. Hunt. You know him?"

"Yes, sir."

"Where does he work when he's here?"

"Penthouse."

"I need to get there, fast."

"None of the tenants are there," the young man told him. "I saw Drs. Gillani and Samson leave—"

"I need to get up there *now,*" Bishop said.

The concierge hesitated, but only for a moment. He picked up a walkie-talkie. Bishop slipped his gun from his pocket and placed it on the countertop.

"You call for help, I shoot you."

The concierge said into the walkie-talkie, "Michel? I need you to take someone up to the penthouse." He regarded Bishop. "Michel Buñuel. The handyman. May be packing a putty knife."

Bishop huffed. "Sorry. It's been that kind of day."

"Go to the freight elevator, straight ahead. Middle door. Michel will take you up. You, uh . . . you got a search warrant?"

Bishop picked up the gun.

"Yeah, that's what I thought," the concierge said. "Michel will let you in if you need it. Just be . . . I dunno. Careful with stuff?"

"Thanks," Bishop replied. "Anybody else been up there?"

"Just a lady," the concierge said. "Got here about a half hour, forty-five minutes ago. Up there now."

Bishop felt acid in the back of his throat. "Dark skinned? About five foot, slender?"

"That's the gal."

Bishop started running through the lobby. "Get me that goddamn elevator ASAP," he shouted back. "Now!"

The ten-million-dollar NYPD 23 was a sleek silver chopper with parallel red and blue stripes running along its tail section and turning down halfway across the cabin. Inside was a crew of three: a pilot, a copilot, and an intelligence officer, who watched one of the three flat-screen monitors mounted on a slender tabletop. With sophisticated cameras mounted around the helicopter, the chopper could read faces and license plates on the ground below; it could also watch every exterior section of John F. Kennedy and LaGuardia airports. If the TSA flagged an exiting passenger, or ground crews reported suspicious activity around any of the fuel lines or tanker trunks, the helicopter could watch them without leaving Manhattan airspace. And still had two cameras turned elsewhere.

The helicopter carried only one weapon: an XM29 Objective Individual Combat Weapon with a laser range finder. The operator of the thick, relatively compact weapon had the ability to place a 20mm shell at a

target up to .6 miles away. It was an extremely powerful weapon that could take down an aircraft, directed
only by the police commissioner or the assistant police
chief in charge of the aviation division.

There was not enough room in the equipment-
packed helicopter for four passengers; as the helicopter
set down, the copilot exited and Kealey took his place.
The intelligence officer had rudimentary flying skills
and would be able to land the bird if necessary.

"Mike Perlman," the crew chief said, offering his
hand as Kealey came aboard.

"Ron Sagal," the pilot said.

Kealey introduced himself as the exiting copilot
shut the door. The chopper rose instantly. In any helicopter, there was a sensation of the bottom dropping
out when you rose; the amount of hardware in this one,
the weight of the reinforced airframe, made the sense
of the bottom about to drop out even stronger. And it
was more cramped than any aircraft Kealey had ever
flown in. Surrounded by hardware and tubes filled with
cables, it was literally impossible to turn to either side
in some sections of the helicopter.

Kealey slipped on the headphones offered by Sagal.
Otherwise, he wouldn't be able to hear.

"Where are we going?" Sagal asked.

Kealey adjusted the microphone. "We're checking
the Hudson for a launch that will be headed somewhere in a hurry," he said.

"Is that all you got for us?" Perlman asked.

"No," Kealey added. "We think it's carrying a nuke
that can be fired from a rocket launcher. I've got that."

The men were instantly focused as the chopper
rose.

"Any way we can patch my cell into these?" Kealey tapped the headphones.

The crew chief nodded. He plugged a jack into the phone, pasted a Velcro strip to the back, pressed it on a patch on the console beside him. "When it rings, I'll hit TALK. You want me to cut Ron and me out?"

"No," Kealey told him. "I'm hoping it's the FBI. One of their guys is chasing a second nuke."

"Mother of God," the pilot said.

"The good news is, both weapons have GPS locators," Kealey went on. "The bad news is, they'll only be active thirty seconds before the weapon can be fired. How do you scan for signals like that?"

"The signals come from the satellites to the cars, cell phones, etcetera, on the ground," Sagal told him. "Those are just passive receivers."

"Okay, so we're looking for an incoming signal. The weapon won't activate without it—"

"The weapon will have to be in the open," Perlman said. "Signals can be intermittent in those canyons." He pointed to the city, which was falling beneath them.

"River or top of a building, then," Kealey said. "How do we find two goddamn signals?"

"Are the weapons identical?" Perlman asked.

"Twins."

"So we're looking for one signal in two places," Perlman said. "Anything data the manufacturer can provide?"

"Negative," Kealey said. He didn't bother explaining that people at Trask were probably involved.

"Is this DoD ordnance?" Perlman asked.

"Yes."

"Well, that's a break," he said. "We'll watch for the Y-code."

"Which is?"

"It's an encryption sequence designed to prevent spoofing—mucking with military signals," he said. "The normal satellite-to-earth signal is a P-code, a precision code. That's used to piggyback a modulated W-code, which creates a Y-code."

"Can you block the Y-code? That will shut the weapon down."

"No," Perlman said. "The W vacillates, so you can't pin a tail on that donkey. But the W is about fifteen times slower than the five hundred kHz of the P. Not a lot of those footdraggers bouncing about. We can watch for that. Narrows the field to a manageable number."

"Do it," Kealey said.

"We going to circle or pick a direction?" Sagal asked.

"Not sure," Kealey said. There was a pair of binoculars in a case at the side of the seat. He took them out and looked at the river, some 2,000 feet below. There was still a lot of traffic going to New Jersey, upriver, out of Manhattan. He looked south, hoping to catch sight of the boat Bishop had described.

"Shit," he said.

"What is it?" Sagal asked.

"South, by the marina. There's a launch just sitting there."

"The one you're looking for?" the pilot asked.

"Possibly," Kealey said. It was empty. He looked around the area. A man with a rocket launcher would not be inconspicuous, especially in a city on high alert.

So where the hell would he go?

* * *

The freight elevator opened next to the mechanical room, the housing for the elevator equipment. Bishop stepped out, followed by the short, elderly handyman. He was dressed in a blue janitorial uniform splattered with white paint. There was, indeed, a putty knife in his back pocket.

"Is that door locked?" Bishop asked.

Buñuel tried it, nodded.

"Where's the apartment with the lab?"

"This way," the handyman said, pointing around a corner.

"I need to get in. Hurry."

Bishop drew his gun as he followed Buñuel. He had no idea what he would find there. And then he saw the bloody footsteps on the hall carpet. They went in the opposite direction a few paces before vanishing.

"Sweet Jesus Christ," the handyman cried.

"Where do those footprints in the hallway lead?"

"To the stairwell, it looks like," Buñuel replied.

"Up as well as down?"

"Yes."

Someone opened their apartment door, peeked out. "Is everything all right, Michel?" the young woman asked.

"It's fine," Bishop answered, waving with the gun. "Back inside, please." The door slammed.

The two men hurried, then stopped by the lab door. Bishop held up a hand before the handyman could use his master key. He listened. There was no sound inside. He looked along the jamb. He couldn't see any wiring, smell any putty. That didn't mean there weren't plastic explosives on the other side. It just meant he couldn't detect any.

"Okay, Michel. Open it. Then get behind me," Bishop said.

Buñuel did so and stepped back. Bishop tapped the door with the base of his toe, allowed it to swing in. He immediately saw the body on the floor, the empty room. He stepped in cautiously, took a quick look around. He noticed the open crate with a Trask Industries stencil on the outside. He saw the garment bag with a distinctive outline pressing against the vinyl. He went to the latter.

A sniper rifle. Fired fairly recently, from the smell of it. He took another look around. There was a window, a gurney, a booth. . . .

What the hell were you doing up here, Hunt?

There was no time now to try and figure that out. He looked out the window, saw the Hudson. At the edge of the window he saw the western corner of the World Trade Center site. He looked up at the ceiling. The roof was above them. He looked back at the Hudson, thought for a moment. Then he swore as he grabbed the rifle. He ran into the hallway.

"Michel, call nine-one-one," Bishop said. "Tell them we need a bomb squad, and tell them to go to the roof."

"Sir?"

"Just do it. Inform them we've got a dead body in the penthouse. Make sure you tell them to take the stairs, not to come in by chopper, and to hurry like hell." He started down the hall, then stopped. "Also, tell them *not* to take out the guy with the rifle. That will be me. I'm on their side."

Bishop turned to his left, and followed the bloody footprints to the stairwell. He had no idea what the configuration of the roof was like, where she might have positioned herself. If seconds mattered, he wanted to have the range of a rifle.

There was only a single flight of concrete stairs between the thirty-sixth floor and the roof. He opened the door quietly; he didn't want her to hear him and fire prematurely. He peered out. From where he stood, he could see most of the roof to the north. It was covered with cement tiles 3 feet square, and it was empty. He took a few steps out, looked around, and cleared the dormer-like exit that blocked the view to the south.

That was when he saw the shadow of the water tower before him, and an irregular shape on top of it. Such an unusual contour was what snipers referred to as "tree cancer," an abnormal growth on an otherwise ordinary object. Bishop crouched, looked up, peered through the telescopic sight at the tower itself. He recognized the assassin instantly. His heart beating thick and fast, he put her in the crosshairs.

"Yasmin! Put down the weapon!"

He watched her shoulder. There would be a slight flexing if she intended to shoot. He started to squeeze the trigger. . . .

The woman looked back. He relaxed his grip on the trigger, but slightly.

"Yasmin, raise your right hand now, or I *will* shoot!"

"Who are you?" she asked.

"Agent Reed Bishop. We met at the Quebec airport," he told her. "Come down now. You can't get away!"

She hesitated. "The airport?"

"I was there with another agent," he said. "We went to a room, talked about your daughter."

She shook her head. "You're wrong. I have no . . ."

Yasmin didn't bother to finish. She looked away, re-sighted the rocket launcher, hunkered into the rocket launcher.

Damn you, Bishop thought. Her head, in profile, filled the circular scope. He dropped the site very slightly; a head shot could still cause a reflex action in her finger. He remembered that much from basic weapons training. He aimed at her shoulder and squeezed the trigger. There was a pop, a recoil, the gun site exploding in red before it kicked up toward the soft blue sky.

Bishop lowered the rifle just in time to see her jerk toward the tower. He laid the weapon down, took out his handgun, and ran to the base of the water tower. He could hear her groaning, see her feet kicking at nothing, like those of a wounded animal, as they hung over the edge. He couldn't see her hands or the rocket launcher. He hurried up the ladder, gun at the ready. When he reached the top, he saw her lying on her side, the rocket launcher at an angle beneath her. She was trying to reach the trigger, but her right arm was hanging on by sinewy strings, the flesh ripped and the shoulder shattered, the side of her face coated with blood. The blood on her face was not from her shoulder: the bullet had glanced hard from her temple upon exiting. It was still there, nestled in a raw hole in her skull.

Bishop tasted bile, swallowed hard as he walked over and carefully moved the tube from under her. He did not want to touch anything. He laid it gently beside her and knelt, called for an ambulance. He was told there would be a wait of forty minutes or more. He didn't think that would matter.

He kept the phone out. "I'm sorry, Yasmin," he said.

She looked up at him with uncomprehending eyes. "Where . . ."

He didn't answer. He saw her good hand pawing at her broken arm. At a bracelet with a marble. She hadn't had that in Quebec. He slipped it from her wrist. Then he searched her for a cell phone. There wasn't any.

Yasmin shut her eyes. "Kamilah," she sighed. "God. Oh, my God. I want . . . to . . . go . . . home."

Bishop didn't know what to say. He took her good hand. He understood what they had been doing in the lab. He held the fingers that had caused so many deaths. After a moment her eyes rolled back slightly and the fingers relaxed. He laid her hand on her side.

Bishop looked out at the sparkling waters of the Hudson as he called Kealey.

"Reed, where are you?"

"On the roof at One West," Bishop told him. "I got Yasmin and her nuke."

"Nice work. Real nice." There was a slight pause. "I see you. By the water tower."

"Right." Bishop looked up, saw the silver 23 hovering over the World Financial Center a few blocks north.

"I think the Xana project was about brainwashing," Bishop said. "After I shot her, Yasmin had no idea where she was or what she was doing."

"Wipe killers' minds, you've got plausible deniability," Kealey said. "Any idea what her target was?"

"Given where she was aiming, I'd guess the bathtub of the World Trade Center site, west wall," he said looking north toward the site. "If she'd popped that, Manhattan would've been cooked. The subways, Penn Station, Grand Central . . . There would have been endless miles for the river to empty into."

"Jesus."

"Exactly. The nuke is armed, but I've got the bomb squad—"

"Leave it," Kealey said.

"What?"

"For just a minute, I mean. We need to get its GPS signature so we can find the other one."

"Roger that."

There was muted talk on the other end of the phone. Bishop looked down at the woman he'd killed. She was paling quickly as blood and life left her. He had never shot anyone. It had been easy to pull the trigger; the rest, he imagined—whatever degree of sadness, regret, revulsion—would come later, if at all. The big pain was that despite having hunted one participant down and prevented unimaginable slaughter, he didn't feel a damn bit better about the loss of his daughter. He glanced at the bracelet. Did that have something to do with Kamilah, or was it something else? Maybe Veil's mind was impacted by the gunshot wound, or maybe it was something else. But Bishop got the feeling that this woman truly had no idea what had just happened to her.

Like so many of your victims over the years, he thought, *if they were even permitted to have a final thought.*

Kealey got back on. "We got it, Reed. Listen, can you see the marina from there?"

"Negative. World Financial tower's in the way."

"Okay. I'm going to send you a photo of a launch at the marina. Tell me if that's the one you saw."

The sun was high and hot to his left, over the harbor. Bishop shielded the phone from the glare and waited for the e-mail. The sun felt good. Life felt good. *Damn these people . . . damn them*. Tears streamed along his cheeks as he thought of Laura and the days and sunlight she would never know. The graduations, books, dates, children . . . *Damn them all for eternity*.

The phone pinged, and Bishop opened the attachment.

"That looks like the one," Bishop told Kealey. "So he's on foot? With a nuclear-tipped rocket launcher?"

"I doubt it," Kealey replied.

"Right, of course," Bishop said. Being spotted wasn't the issue. Hunt was expecting Veil's bomb to go off. He would have wanted to be as far away as possible.

"I'm sure he's skipped town, and there's one other thing I'm sure of," Kealey said. "That SOB will have been expecting to hear a blast by now. We need to intercept Plan B."

The speeding runabout passed below the George Washington Bridge as it left New York City.

Hunt looked at his watch. He exhaled loudly. "Was it your work or did they screw up our plan?" he asked Dr. Gillani.

"I do not believe the fault was mine," she insisted.

"No, of course not," Hunt rasped.

"She's right," Dr. Samson said as he steered the runabout north. "The programming worked straight down the line. There's no reason to think it broke now. We spent the most time on this part of it. She was solid."

Hunt shook his head. The years of work and planning, from Pakistan to here, and it ended up on his shoulders, after all. His one consolation was that if they took Yasmin prisoner, she would remember nothing. If they killed her, the effect would be the same: another Muslim had participated in a wave of Muslim attacks against the United States. That also meant the lab would not be destroyed. Even if they got in there— *And they wouldn't have much time to do that*, he thought—even if they checked all the records, everything would point back to another Muslim, Dr. Gillani. A call to her from Scroggins's phone would tie them together; the men would take the blame for the nukes. Trask would see to that. The drivers would disappear into a cell at any number of secret government prisons for weeks.

By then it would be too late.

As for himself, he would say that he was undercover, trying to sniff out this Muslim brainwasher. Dr. Samson was the voice of her process, knew how it worked. He was all they'd need. In one hour, she would be the last victim of this necessary evil.

Except for the ten million people of New York. That, too, was a tragic requirement for the liberation of the world.

"You store your city views?" Kealey asked.
"For twenty-four hours," Perlman said.

"What have you got of the marina from the last hour or two?"

Perlman opened the video library, typed in the street he needed, brought up a fuzzy video of the marina from an hour before.

"That's the best we've got," he said. "We were over Midtown, between Thirty-fourth and Forty-second Street."

The FBI launch had not yet arrived. There were several boats that did not appear to be there now, yachts mostly. They would probably have headed out to sea, where there was room to maneuver, up-the-coast or down-the-coast choices available.

"Can you pick me a good frame and print it out?" Kealey asked.

Perlman stepped through the video, selected an image, enhanced it as best he could, then handed Kealey an eight-by-ten glossy. Kealey looked at it. Any one of them would be a suitable, anonymous strike ship. They would have to look for all of them, listen for the GPS signal, hope to hell they could get to it in time.

"You don't happen to have grenades on board?" Kealey asked.

Perlman shook his head. "Just the OICW."

"You better keep it handy," Kealey said.

"We need authorization from Aviation HQ just to take it off the—"

Kealey took the handgun from his jacket. "I don't have time for bureaucracy. I'll shoot the bastard with this if I have to, but no one is going to fire a nuke on my watch."

Sagal and Perlman exchanged looks. Sagal nodded.

Perlman angled awkwardly behind him and unscrewed the wing-nut bracket from the stock and barrel of the weapon. He kept it in his lap.

"Thanks," Kealey said.

The intelligence officer nodded.

Times Square, Herald Square, Grand Central Station, the United Nations, the Empire State Building—those were obvious targets for a sniper. Some would make meaty bull's-eyes for a nuke. If that were the case, though, why did Hunt head south toward the harbor? Why circle the island? He could have had the nuke left somewhere in that vicinity, in a van or car trunk or a storage unit.

Kealey considered the other options. Aside from the Verrazano-Narrows Bridge or Statue of Liberty, which he'd already determined could be destroyed by conventional weapons, Staten Island, Brooklyn, and the Atlantic Ocean were the closest southern targets. He didn't think those made sense. Farther south were Philadelphia and Washington, but Kealey didn't believe Hunt would want that kind of exposure for the time it would take to reach them. North was . . . what? The George Washington Bridge. Highways clogged with cars trying to get out. A pair of baseball stadiums, which would be empty in light of what had happened that morning.

There was a map on a monitor that sat on a thin metal arm beside the seat.

"How do I work this?" Kealey asked.

Perlman held up an index finger, wagged it up and down.

Kealey nodded, used his finger to scroll the map. It responded faster than MapQuest on his laptop.

"You can expand the view using your thumb and index finger," Perlman said.

"Got it. Thanks."

Kealey followed the river north, out of the city and into Westchester, Putnam, Dutchess counties. Nothing jumped out. He magnified the image and went back toward the city slowly.

"Shit," Kealey said suddenly.

"What is it?" Perlman asked.

"They may not be going after people this time."

He expanded a view. Perlman looked at it on his screen.

Save for the *whapping* sound of the rotors, the cabin was very quiet.

"We need to stop this," Perlman said.

"We do," Kealey agreed. "But if we commit to going north, and he isn't there, we're screwed."

"I can take us to the GW Bridge and wait for the ping," Sagal said. "That'll put us more or less equidistant, in reach of him north and south."

"In reach or on top of him?" Kealey asked. "We won't have a lot of leeway here, about thirty seconds."

Sagal shook his head. "No way to answer that, Mr. Kealey. It depends where he plants himself. If he goes ashore, tucks himself under a bridge or tunnel—"

"Of course." Kealey considered their options. They hadn't any. "Let your aviation unit know. They have other choppers they can put on this?"

"Yeah, plus maritime," Sagal told him.

"But we're the only ones that can hear the GPS signal."

"In time to act," Perlman said. "It'll have to go through channels to turn all our ears on this."

"Time is something we don't have," Kealey said. "Let's get other eyes up there and head for the bridge."

Sagal gave him a thumbs-up and turned the helicopter north along the river.

CHAPTER 33

BUCHANAN, NEW YORK

It was called the Indian Point Energy Center because *nuclear power plant* had an unfashionable connotation that summoned images of Chernobyl and Fukushima. In operation since September 1962, the facility had undergone many upgrades since then, some in response to geological concerns, others as a result of terrorism 38 miles to the south, in New York City.

The red buildings with their yellow-golden domes were a familiar and inherently ominous sight to local residents. Despite assurances from Entergy Corporation, which owned the facility, the truth was that no nuclear power plant could ever be made entirely safe.

Though the plant had received the Nuclear Regulatory Commission's top safety rating, and there was a National Guard base a mile away, Alexander Hunt had read the reports from the New York State Department of Environmental Conservation and Columbia University's Lamont-Doherty Earth Observatory findings that the power plant was nonetheless vulnerable to earthquakes and megaton-level attacks. With the sophisticated radiation detection systems attached to any nuclear plant, no one was anticipating anyone being able to smuggle even a well-protected nuke into the vicinity.

Hunt had also read a 2003 report prepared for then governor George Pataki, which noted that radiological response systems were inadequate to protect the citizens of three states from radiation that could be released from Indian Point in a worst-case scenario. Yasmin's mission was to be a one-time hit. This one would be a lingering and constant reminder that the Muslim world represented an ongoing and inevitably catastrophic danger. The sooner they were dealt with, the quicker the world could move from the present Dark Age.

The runabout entered Haverstraw Bay, which carried them northwest around the promontory that preceded the plant. There were other boats moving through the area, some of them pleasure vessels, others patrol ships on alert because of the events in New York. As long as Hunt kept them moving north, they would be fine. No one would think to stop a vessel that had already passed by the facility.

The facility was on the northeastern side of the large outcrop of land; the first part of it that became visible was the white smokestack with its distinctive red bands. It sat between the three domes.

Like an ace of clubs, Hunt thought as the entire complex rolled past. He had instructed Samson to take them to the western side of the river, where 202 broke off from Old Ayers Road, the route that ran along the Hudson. He would fire the rocket from that point, and they would move farther up the river to West Point.

That was where Dr. Samson would leave and a heroic FBI officer would shoot the monstrous Dr. Gillani. She was sitting placidly beside him, playing absently with a drawstring on the Windbreaker she had donned against the brisk river breeze. A cloud cover had rolled in, and the wind had a bit of a nip. The scientist was probably trying to figure out how things had gone wrong with Yasmin Rassin. Maybe they hadn't. It was possible that Bishop or Kealey had caught up with her at One West, prevented her from completing her mission. That was why they needed two nukes. As with the rest of her mission, Yasmin was there to keep the authorities moving, distracted, focused on someone who was more or less a sideshow. The irony was that all those people she had chased from Manhattan with her sniping—*all* of them would be even more vulnerable to the radiation cloud that would spew from the reactors. Most of them were closer now, in their suburban homes.

"Any place in particular suit you?" Samson asked.

Hunt looked over at the shore. "That cluster of trees," he said, pointing to a row of oaks along the shore. "We'll tie up there."

He needed the cover of the canvas top, but Hunt wanted the boat to be secured when he fired. There were yachts and motorboats moving mostly north along the river, along with the private security boat hired by the plant, which ran by every ten minutes or so. He didn't want the wake of one of those to cause him to miss one of the domes. The blast was guaranteed to kick down the door, but only if it landed squarely.

Samson maneuvered the runabout toward the shore.

"Wait until the security boat has passed," Hunt said,

watching as the black and white speedboat sliced by, close to the opposite shore. He didn't catch the glint of sunlight off binoculars, but that didn't mean the men on board weren't watching. If something had happened to Yasmin, the NYPD might have put out an alert to watch out for another nuke. They might even be told to watch out for a rogue FBI agent, though he wouldn't be expected to announce himself. A crew of three agents would probably get a pass.

If not, then a security unit would die, Hunt thought.

Samson powered down the runabout as he nosed toward shore. The current carried it sideways, and he brought them to a low sandstone cliff. Branches hung over the water. Samson took the towline that was attached to the bow ring and slung it over a limb. Hunt went to the back of the cockpit.

Excitement burned in his belly.

While Samson took the spare fuel and filled the tank for a rapid getaway—and to provide a reason for them being there, in case anyone looked over—Hunt went to the open area of the cockpit and picked up the rocket launcher. He knelt, as if in prayer, as he raised it to his shoulder.

"Let me know when you're ready," he told Samson.

"It'll be a minute," the scientist told him.

There was no one near enough to stop him. He smiled. They had done it.

This was going to happen.

Kealey was a restless, unhappy passenger.

It was a rule of the field that, in the absence of intel,

staying put was a good idea. The operative got a chance to know his or her immediate vicinity, find the strengths and weaknesses, plan a quick-exit strategy if necessary. Even though the enemy might know where to find him or her, so did allies or extraction teams. For Kealey, it wasn't the chopper sitting over the George Washington Bridge that gnawed at him. It was not having intel flowing in.

He had contacted Andrews, who had the National Reconnaissance Office turn their space eyes on the river. They could see boats in the breaks of cloud cover. But the angle of the Taurus 9 geosynchronous satellite gave them only the east side of the river, the side with the power plant. It would take time to move another set of eyes into place. The sporadic cloud cover didn't help.

"What about the plant?" Kealey asked Perlman. "They've got to have cameras on the river."

"They do," the intelligence officer replied. "Access code changes daily. I'm trying to get it, while my tech team is working to hack it. One way or another, we'll get in. Just may take some doing."

Kealey shook his head. Goddamn bureaucracy. It was one reason he got out of this game. *You hire people to do a job, let them do it.* Meanwhile, one of their trusted insiders, Assistant Director Alexander Hunt, had turned rotten and was about to blow them a new "mole hole," as the CIA called it. The big damage radius caused by someone with an all-access pass.

Kealey looked out the windshield, saw moisture rippling from the middle to the top of the sloping glass. It was condensation from the clouds just above.

"Is rotor wash doing that?" Kealey asked.

"No, sir," Sagal replied. "That gets deflected around us. That's a southeasterly air movement."

Kealey's heart was running at full throttle. *You hire people to do a job, let them do it,* he thought again. "Mr. Sagal, let's head up to Indian Point."

"Are you sure?"

"Yeah. The wind is blowing toward the city. Toward Newark. Toward all of Westchester County and part of Connecticut. If I were a bad guy, I'd want killer doses of radiation riding that stream."

"If we do that—"

"We leave the city open. I know."

Nothing more was said. Sagal nosed into the wind and headed north.

Kealey watched the river on the monitor next to his station. There was a built-in mouse so he could scroll the nose camera, zoom in or out, look ahead. He had the printout of the boats in his lap, watching for any of them. He thought he saw one of the yachts, checked it on the monitor, did not see anything that suggested either great haste or a weapon. He did not see Hunt on deck, or a porthole that would accommodate a rocket launcher without blowing out the inside of the vessel. He didn't think the AD was prepared to die for this.

"I've got you into the IP security camera," Perlman said. "Not legally, but we're in. Sending it over."

"Thanks."

Kealey was looking at a view of the river from a slightly elevated point. The camera was either on one of the domes or the smokestack. It was slowly panning north to south, then back again.

"I don't suppose we've hijacked the zoom capability," Kealey said.

"Afraid not. But if you see something you want to look at, we might be able to do that from here."

Kealey watched the screen. Perspiration was dripping into his eyes. He blinked it away, bent closer to the screen. "Slow" had never been so frustrating. He saw trees. He saw rust-colored rocks. He saw river and boat traffic, a security vessel. . . .

"Whoa. Can you grab this image?"

"Yes." Perlman hit a button, froze the screen. "Enlarge it?"

"Yeah. You see—"

"The blue runabout tied to the branch."

"FBI jackets," Kealey said. "Magnify on the woman sitting in the cockpit."

Perlman did so.

"Her torso," Kealey said.

The picture blurred, then sharpened. It wasn't perfectly clear, but it was enough to see what he wanted: she wasn't wearing a holster, shoulder or hip.

"She's not FBI," Perlman said. "And that canvas top . . . perfect cover."

Kealey did not have to give the order. Sagal pushed the helicopter ahead as Kealey and Perlman went back to the live view.

"I'm going to call this in," Perlman asserted.

"No!" Kealey barked.

"Mr. Kealey, they have people on-site—"

"If anyone approaches him, he will fire. He has to think he's safe until we're in range."

"HQ is going to ask where we're racing. We're not exactly off the grid," said Sagal, stating the obvious.

"Don't answer," he said.

"That's not going to work," Sagal told him.

"We don't have a *choice!*" Kealey insisted. "You tell them, they tell Indian Point, and hired-hand security charges in. Unless they're going to gun this guy down, he—"

The conversation was cut short by a dinging sound.

"That's him," Perlman said gravely. "The weapon's been activated."

There was no more talk. Kealey had a sense of motion like nothing he'd ever experienced, not even in an F-16. The cockpit of a fighter was aloof from the air, the elements. This helicopter was pushing against that barrier, slamming it hard, not letting the air roll around a streamlined design.

"I need the OICW," Kealey said.

Perlman looked at him.

"We've got seconds, not minutes," he said. "Please."

The officer handed him the weapon. Kealey threw off the safety, kept it pointed down. The contours of the Hudson shores were winding past, like separately undulating snakes. He saw the domes of the plant. The western bank curved in a way that did not allow him to see the site from the surveillance camera.

"Take us down," Kealey said.

The chopper dived forward. Kealey put a hand on the door. The power plant was coming into view.

That also meant Hunt couldn't see them, though he'd hear them approaching. Hopefully, he would be too focused on his target, on waiting for the go-ahead signal from the rocket launcher. . . .

"As soon as that boat comes into view, you're going

to have to hit the brakes and turn me toward it," Kealey said.

"Don't open the door till I do that," Sagal said.

"Yeah." If Kealey thought that by flying from the chopper, he could stop Hunt, he would gladly take the flier.

"He's hot in ten . . . nine . . . eight . . . ," Perlman said.

They were about a half mile downriver and 1,000 feet too high.

"*Push it!*" Kealey shouted.

"Seven . . . six . . ."

Kealey felt the harness dig into his chest as the helicopter screamed forward. It didn't matter if Hunt knew they were there. He couldn't fire for another few seconds. . . .

"Five . . . four . . ."

The chopper came out of the half-parabolic dive, just skimming the Hudson.

"*Brake, now!*" Kealey yelled.

Kealey grabbed the door handle hard. The turn was so sharp that Kealey was thrown against the left side of the harness, but he retained his grip. As the chopper leveled, he yanked the handle, popped the harness, and put his foot to the door.

"Three . . . two . . ."

As he kicked open the door, he raised the 20mm and fired. He was short, raised it, peppered the canvas roof of the runabout.

"One!"

Kealey continued firing at the covering, turning the ivory-colored surface black with holes and smoldering fringe. Flaps fell away as he emptied the clip. He saw a man in the cockpit move toward the back; Kealey cut him down. A woman in the front seat had dropped to her knees with her hands raised.

Kealey was out of ammunition.

"Take us down," he said and drew his handgun.

Sagal was on the loudspeaker system. "NYPD anti-terror action. Stand down!" His voice rang across the river, and he repeated the announcement several times. That was for any security forces who might not notice the big NYPD on the side of the chopper and opened fire. Hourly security was like that.

The chopper lowered itself directly above the runabout. Kealey leaned out. Hunt was lying facedown, a mass of red splotches. The other man was on his back, with blood running from the top of his head. Kealey climbed onto the landing strut. The woman was looking out. He motioned toward the shore with his handgun. She nodded and made for the shore with her hands raised.

The black and white security boat was racing over.

"Put down your weapon!" someone shouted.

Sagal said, "You gettin' off?"

Kealey grinned back and nodded. He glanced back at Perlman. "We're gonna need bomb guys from the National Guard station."

"Already called it in."

Sagal turned the chopper around so Kealey was over the shore. He jumped from the chopper and landed near the train tracks that ran between the river and the road. The woman was standing there with her hands up.

"I said drop your weapon!" the voice from the boat repeated.

"I've got this," Sagal said into the mike. He moved the chopper sideways and dropped it between the security boat and the runabout, a few yards above the water. The black-and-white had to make a hard turn to avoid a collision. "I said stand down," he repeated.

The security boat stayed where it was.

Kealey told the woman to lie facedown on the track bed. She listened. He knew Perlman would be watching her, and he went to the runabout.

Hunt was dead. So was the other man. The nuke was active, alive. He didn't want to read too much into that, but that had been the state of the world since Hiroshima: the players changed, died, and were replaced. The threat remained the same.

He called the update in to Andrews as he walked back to the train tracks.

There were cries of relief on the other end.

Kealey said he'd call when he was en route. Then he phoned Bishop.

"Ryan . . . ?"

"We got him," Kealey said.

"Jesus Christ."

"With time to spare. What's going on there?"

"Bomb squad shut down the nuke. I'm giving them a report."

"Well, smoke 'em if you got 'em."

"Can't," Bishop said. "Made someone a promise."

Kealey understood. *Good man,* he thought. "Can you meet me at the Thirtieth Street helipad in an hour?"

"Probably. What's up?"

"I'm going to get these boys to give us a lift to LaGuardia."

"Debrief hell," Bishop said.

"Yeah, but not yet."

"What do you mean?"

"We have a stop to make first," Kealey said. "I'll tell you about it en route." He clicked off, walked over to the woman. "Who are you?" Kealey asked.

"I will not answer your questions."

Kealey went to the runabout, found her shoulder bag, retrieved her wallet. She was Dr. Ayesha Gillani. Affiliated with universities, hospitals, high-powered organizations.

He threw it back in the bag and looked back at her. Behind him, local police choppers and maritime units were converging. The NYPD chopper found a spot to set down.

Kealey was going to sit this one out, let them work out all the who did what and why.

A psychiatrist. A medical doctor. Obviously, World War II didn't teach some members of the profession a damn thing about morality. Or maybe it was just a percentage of the general population itself that had corrupted data files in their head—Hunt and his dead companions included. *Fortunately, there's more of us than them,* he thought. *Un*fortunately, all it took was five or six of them to let loose the dogs of destruction.

Well, at least there were fewer. And soon—very soon—there would be fewer still.

CHAPTER 34

ATLANTA, GEORGIA

"Mr. Trask," said the voice from the intercom, "there are people to see you."

He turned to the box mounted to the wall of the greenhouse. "Who are they?"

Before the voice could answer, the door behind him opened. Six FBI agents in SWAT gear entered, their weapons trained on the industrialist. The four agents on the outside held .45-caliber Springfields; the agents on the inside were holding M4 carbines.

The two men who entered after them were not holding weapons, nor were they wearing SWAT black.

"Jacob Trask," said Reed Bishop, unbuttoning his blazer, "you're under arrest."

Trask placed the shears in the box of soil. He turned to face the men, his hands on the planter. "The charge?"

Bishop continued to walk toward him alone. "Accessory to murder."

"Based on what evidence?"

"The testimony of your chauffeur, Elisabeth Kent,"

he said. "She went to the Atlanta PD when she learned that the woman you sent to New York, Agent Jessica Muloni, had been murdered."

Trask smiled. "That's ridiculous."

"Ms. Kent, the former sheriff, gave us security footage." Bishop stopped less than a foot from Trask. There was a Glock tucked in the agent's belt. "Ridiculous or not, the charges will give us the twenty-four hours we'll need to get you on federal terrorism offenses."

He held out his hands. "Your charges will have me back here, tending my tulips, before they require watering. As for the other—"

"You killed my daughter, you miserable man," Bishop said. "You're going to answer for that."

"I'm sorry, but I don't know you or your daughter," Trask said. There was no hostility in his voice, no emotion whatsoever. "But I do know that your accusation is harassment. That will get me back here even sooner."

Bishop looked like a mannequin, his skin pale and blank. Kealey walked up behind him, pulled him back. "I'd like to be alone in here," he told the team.

"We can't do that, Mr. Kealey," said one of the masked figures, the special agent in charge.

"You can search the premises. You have a warrant," Kealey said. "Agent Bishop will take responsibility for the prisoner."

The agent hesitated. Bishop looked back at him. The IA officer nodded once.

"All right," the team leader said. "We will be back here for the prisoner in fifteen minutes."

"Thank you," Kealey said. "Close the door behind you."

The agent hesitated again, then complied. Trask regarded Kealey.

"Former CIA agent Ryan Kealey," Trask said. "I've seen your name in DoD reports—"

"Don't," Kealey said.

"You need to *hear* this," Trask went on. "*You* understand what's out there. You know how the enemy is inoculated, protected by political correctness, but free to portray us as racists, haters, Christian soldiers, imperialists. They run labels up the flagpole like amens at a prayer meeting. Their poison is to make us hate ourselves. It has to *stop!*"

"What I need to do—what *we* need to do—is arrest you," Kealey said. "And not just for a day. Agent Bishop and I were the ones who took down your nukes. Your team. And before you deny it, Minotaur phones were recovered from Hunt and the Texas Highway Patrol. The Bureau labs have them now. I'm betting they're going to show that there were calls to—and from—your home phone." Kealey moved closer now. "You see, Mr. Trask, the bad guys *can* be brought down legally."

Trask's expression turned ugly; he grabbed the Glock from Bishop's belt and threw all three safeties as he slid away along the planter.

Bishop moved between Trask and Kealey. "Go on," he said. "You took everything else from me."

"It wasn't *about* you!" Trask said. "I'm sorry your daughter was collateral damage. Very, very sorry. But you understand why it had to be done—"

"I don't!" Bishop yelled. "No way do I, you sick bastard! But you can explain it in open court and keep explaining it right up until they strap you to the gurney."

"That won't happen—"

"It *will*. You want to kill me? They'll get you for murder, and it ends the same way. As long as it puts an end to you, it's all good to me."

Trask was shaking his head. "I am a patriot! It doesn't end this way!"

"You're a piece of shit, and you're done," Bishop said through his teeth.

"No. I can shoot you and leave by the garden door—"

"On foot?" Bishop said. "The grounds are surrounded. There's only one play that gets you out of here without cuffs. The one I let you take."

Kealey was trailing Bishop. He had picked up the industrialist's shears and was holding them at his side, his eye on the Glock. Bishop had hidden the gun behind his buttoned blazer until his back was to the SWAT team. Kealey had not supported the agent's plan, but he respected it.

Trask was shaking his head. "All the planning . . . I gave Hunt and his team *every* advantage! *I* won't be a failure!"

"You failed the day you stopped trusting the system," Bishop said. "It always self-corrects. It was *designed* to do that!"

Trask reached the sweating glass wall of the greenhouse. He held the gun waist high.

"I accomplish more in a day than men like you achieve in a lifetime."

"Not this day," Bishop said, stepping up to the barrel.

"Yes, today," Trask replied. "Today I leave the dying body of America to the dogs."

His eyes burned into Bishop's as he raised the gun to his own right temple and fired. Bishop didn't flinch as the impact slapped Trask to his left, smearing the clean spray of blood even as it struck the glass. Trask landed on a row of empty pots, shattering them. The two men looked down at the ruin of an industrial titan.

"I told you I wouldn't need the backup," Bishop said.

"He could have killed you instead," Kealey said.

"He already had," Bishop replied. "He knew it, too. This was his only play."

There was no sense of triumph in his voice. There was only sadness as he looked down at the crumpled shell that had caused so much suffering.

Kealey wiped the shears on his shirt, put them back on the planter's soil. He didn't want anyone finding his fingerprints, thinking he'd forced Trask to do this.

It took just seconds for the nearest of the SWAT team members to reach them. They ran in, stopped, pulled up their masks.

"He had a gun under the table," Kealey said. He raised and lowered his shoulders. "Nothing we could do."

The special agent in charge came over, squatted over the gun—which had fallen from Trask's hand—and made a face. "Weapons maker had a Glock . . . with no serial number?"

"Guy was a traitor, right down to his gun," Bishop told him.

"So you say."

Bishop and Kealey just stood there.

The team leader frowned but said nothing more as he ordered his team to secure the crime scene. He told one of the agents to escort Bishop and Kealey out. They walked down the corridor past the autographs and accompanying portraits of the signers of the Declaration of Independence.

Kealey laid a hand on Bishop's shoulder. "You're not dead, you know."

"Yeah. I hurt too much to be deceased."

"I meant that you still have a lot to do, a lot to offer."

"Maybe."

"You saved a couple of million lives. That's not an end. It's a beginning."

Bishop grinned. Kealey smiled back. "I don't mean you have to top that, Reed."

"I know what you meant." Bishop cocked his head noncommittally as he looked at the respectfully lit documents. "But I believe what I said back there about the system working." He added quietly, "How do I justify what I did?"

Kealey stopped and faced him. The agent escorting them stopped several paces back, gave them space.

"Trask declared war on this nation, and you responded," Kealey said quietly. "You gave him a choice as to how the end played out. That's more than he gave anyone else. That, to me, is one of the things we're about. Americans. It may not be in any document, but it's here." He touched a hand to his own chest.

Bishop held it together a moment longer, then put his face in his hand, sobbing. Kealey turned and joined the agent. There would be time enough for embraces and words of comfort. Bishop knew he wasn't alone, and right now all Kealey wanted was to give the man his privacy.

He looked over at the wall, at a painting of Thomas Jefferson standing beside a pedestal with the Declaration scrolled over the side.

Help him find peace, Mr. President, Kealey thought. *Some things* are *that black and white, aren't they?*

CHAPTER 35

SILVER SPRING, MARYLAND

The funeral for Laura Bishop was held at the Holy Sepulchre Cemetery. It was where her mother was buried. She would be laid to rest in a plot Bishop had bought for himself.

Bishop's brother, his brother's wife, and their children were there to support him. So was his mother. Harper, Andrews, Cluzot, and Carlson were in attendance, as were select members of both houses. Along with the funeral of FBI agent Jessica Muloni, this was one of the few services President Brenneman attended as a result of the so-called "16 Hour" attacks. That was the name the media had given the time span covered by the two days of terror. Even in the administration there had been some debate about how to refer to the two bloody days. No one wanted to refer to it by the dates; not even the most lurid elements of the media wanted to create the impression that attacks against the nation were an ongoing series.

The media were not invited to the service or the interment. The burial was beneath spotless blue skies, where the priest remembered Laura as a young girl who cared not only for her father's health but also for the health of others, just like her mother had.

"Young Laura was always making healthy-eating posters for the church and for her school," the clergyman recalled. "She once asked me about the fat content of the Communion wafers and whether the holy water was spring or tap. Her interest in people, in caregiving, was one of the reasons she was with her father among the nurses and doctors who held such a high place in her heart. We know she was happy then, and that is how we must remember her. For we also know that, reunited with her mother, they are both happy now."

Kealey didn't know if he embraced that idea, and he took no solace from it. He had seen enough evil and suffering to doubt the existence of God Himself. Yet it never failed that these reminiscences spoken to celebrate a life were invariably the most painful part of saying good-bye. Or maybe they were intended to do just the opposite—to prevent us from leaving everything behind, to help us to hold on to the soul of a loved one.

After paying their respects to Laura's mother, the Bishop family went back to their limousines alone, the officials leaving in their cars. Harper lingered long enough to tell Kealey, Allison, and Andrews that Julie was conscious, though still in a fog.

"It'll be a while before she's anything close to being herself again," he said. "But she'll get there. Hell, she'll probably turn it into a platform to talk about courage."

"Healing isn't just about the body," Allison said. "What she's been through *will* help many others."

Harper excused himself, leaving the others under an old oak tree. Standing there, seeing the play of light, feeling the nearly imperceptible dampness, caused Kealey to flash to the runabout under its limb.

Healing the mind? he thought. They had been one second away from a nuclear holocaust. Kealey didn't know if his brain would ever process how many lives, how many faces on the news, would have been scratched in his soul had they failed. He had been thinking about that since they left Trask's mansion, about the words that Jefferson had chosen to conclude the Declaration: ". . . with a firm reliance on the protection of divine Providence . . ."

Maybe. Or maybe it was luck. Whatever it was, Kealey would be thinking about it for the rest of his life.

"I figured you were sleeping late this morning," Andrews said, "so I didn't bother to call you. But we got a lot of data off those two phones. It's going to help us round up the mercs and close the book on Hunt and Trask."

"What about the drivers?" Kealey asked.

"Bell and Scroggins? Free. They were dupes in this whole thing. So were all the poor students who had volunteered to be subjects and interns with the Xana project. They were selected to foster Islamophobia, like the Muslim terrorist nations were piling on."

"What's going to happen to Dr. Gillani?" Allison asked.

Andrews smirked. "Do you really want to know?"

"I don't know. Do I?"

"I can answer that," Kealey said. "She'll end up working for us, just like the Nazi rocket scientists did after World War II."

"From the first debrief I saw this morning, she's got a helluva technique, with marbles as controls. Once they were hypnotized, the victims were told to associate the marble with that world. Touching them, looking at them, was good for about an hour. They would act normally, not arousing suspicion until it was time for them to act. A phone call and Dr. Samson's voice sent them to the marble and then back into a trance. With Yasmin, wearing it kept her under constantly when the demands of the timetable kicked in."

"That's pretty incredible," Allison agreed.

"If we had a snowball's chance of getting the White House onboard, we could get a lot of intel by setting loose our Guantánamo guests with that kind of cooperation."

Kealey didn't disagree, but he also wasn't in the mood for this. He was done—again. He would go back to the university and pick up where he left off.

Either that or find an atoll somewhere and live off fish and crustaceans for the rest of my life.

"By the way," Andrews said, "when you're ready, Ryan, the president wants to see you and Reed. He was real proud of you both."

"Thanks," Kealey said. "He made some tough calls there. Backed us."

"You know you can come back if you want."

"Thanks, but I'm too old for the field and too restless for a desk," Kealey said.

"Too old?" Allison said.

"There isn't a part of me that doesn't hurt," he said.

"Just the hit I took opening the door of the helicopter. Those shoulder harnesses are unforgiving."

Andrews laughed. "The offer will always be on the table."

"I appreciate it, but I've been thinking a lot about how close we came to *not* pulling this out. I'm not a big believer in karma, but I think I'll quit while the scales are still in my favor."

The conversation ranged after that from Colin to changes in Company and Bureau policy to watch out for rogues. They returned to their cars, which were alone along the tree-lined street in the cemetery, and headed out—Andrews and Allison to Langley, Kealey to I-95. He did not go south to Washington, but south to parts unknown. He knew he would not find an atoll in that direction, but it was okay. He just wanted a long coastline of open road, away from government, out among the people he had always served.

Just him and ordinary citizens, not the Trasks and Hunts or even the well-meaning bureaucrats, but those whom the rest of Jefferson's phrase so aptly described: the men and women who "mutually pledge to each other our Lives, our Fortunes and our sacred Honor."

EPILOGUE
SUKKUR, PAKISTAN

I t figured.
   Of course.

Sukkur, the Pakistani city in which Reed Bishop found himself, was one of the region's largest centers for the production of tobacco. He had smiled as the "big green cow with wheels for feet"—as the nickname for the bus was loosely translated—entered the town and he saw the proud billboard of a farmer harvesting plants.

You're testing me, aren't you, honey? He laughed. *That's all right.* He had stopped smoking, at first, when he was around her. He was around her now, always. He would never smoke again.

Bishop emerged from the rusting, lopsided conveyance that had brought him from Islamabad. He had a bet with another American that the circa 1950 vehicle—with a hole in the floor that allowed them to watch the dirt roads crunch by—the bus would never finish the journey.

Bishop was wrong. They didn't even get a flat. And they arrived on time.

"There's a point at which components become so mutually dependent, they become a sort of closed system," the other American passenger said, collecting Bishop's five dollars.

The man was a mid-level diplomat. Bishop guessed that if anyone knew how tough it was to stop any force that had been in motion for so long, it was him.

The provincial attaché had also given him a tip on how to get what he wanted here.

"Dollars or technology," he'd said. "Those are your best currency."

What he wanted was to take the information Cluzot had obtained for him and put a face on it. The driver gave Bishop his two bags off the top of the bus—he was surprised to find them there—after which the American stopped in a local teahouse to clear the dust of travel from his throat, get directions, and steel his resolve. There was danger in what he was planning: personal, psychological, and even political. But it needed to be done.

Happy that the Gold Flake tobacco everyone seemed to be smoking here had an aroma and smoothness that were foreign to him—downright foul if you were too close to it—Bishop walked down the paved main street, past open stalls selling foods and fabrics, to a two-story brick structure adjoining a hospital. He did not read or speak more than phrase-book Urdu, but he recognized the writing on the sign. SUKKUR SENIOR SCHOOL-HOUSE.

He had an appointment with the headmaster—a pleasant fellow in his sixties, who appreciated very much the iPod Bishop had brought him as a gift, loaded with the Sami Yusuf tunes he said he enjoyed. Bishop wondered if he would have to listen to that music.

Of course you will, he thought. Just as he had to listen to Miley Cyrus and Shane Harper for a year or so.

Together, he and the headmaster went to get Kamilah Fazari from her biology class. They stood outside the building, in the shade, waiting for the class to end. The teacher—a woman in a head scarf—brought the thin, tall girl over.

The twelve-year-old was well dressed, well mannered, and looked like her mother. Her expression wasn't neutral, as it was the first day Bishop had seen her, but she had the same poise, the same strong mouth, the same intense eyes, which were studying Bishop with a blend of interest and suspicion.

She had been crying fairly recently. Bishop recognized the look from his own reflection in the mirror. He knew that she had been informed by Akila Fazari that Yasmin Rassin was killed in an accident, but that was all she knew.

The headmaster explained—pausing to translate for Bishop—that this man was an acquaintance of her mother and wanted to take her to America to live and to study.

"Why would he do this?" she asked through the headmaster.

"Because your mother wanted you to have opportunities she never did," Bishop explained. When that had been translated, he added, "And because you might fulfill the promise and potential of one who was taken from me, just as your mother was taken from you," he said.

"A daughter?" she asked through the headmaster.

Bishop nodded.

"That is a big responsibility for a young girl," the headmaster told him, a trace of concern in his eyes.

Bishop nodded again. "Please tell her that I have no expectations and make no demands. All I have is the hope and a belief that we can set some kind of example for people who want to tear nations apart. But I want *you* to know—as a surrogate father to so many—that while I am prepared to give a great deal, I will never ask anything she is not prepared to give."

The headmaster smiled approvingly and explained to Kamilah. It was the first time that Bishop saw her smile. It was a radiant smile, untainted by the world outside. He imagined that once, long ago, her mother had smiled like that. He hoped so. He knew now that he was doing the right thing.

"As you can understand, Mr. Bishop, she is scared but appreciative. She would like to talk to her godmother about it," the headmaster said.

"I'll find lodgings in town and await her answer," Bishop said. "Please tell her that I would be honored if she and her godmother would join me for dinner." The headmaster hesitated. Bishop grinned. "And you, too, of course."

The headmaster translated.

Kamilah thanked him and told the headmaster to give him Akila's address. She asked him to come by at five. Bishop said he would be there.

When she left, the headmaster studied the American. "I think she will go with you," he said. "That girl has a very adventurous spirit."

"I'm not surprised," Bishop said.

"I know Akila wants the best for her, as well. You say you knew her mother?"

"I did, briefly."

"I only saw her once, for less time than I've seen you. I have often wondered, what was she like?"

"Complicated," Bishop said.

"She was successful in her work, I am told."

"She was," Bishop agreed, "but she kept all that to herself."

"Why?"

Bishop looked out at the sunbaked street, at the old cars and the occasional cow and sheep. "She had her reasons," he said. "But I can tell you she loved her daughter more than anything. And I think, in the end, that's a fitting epitaph for anyone."

The headmaster considered that as Bishop thanked him, shook his hand, and went off to find a place to spend the night.

And to buy two bus tickets to Islamabad.